‖‖‖‖‖‖‖‖‖‖‖‖‖‖‖‖‖‖‖

◁ T2-EYK-177

FICTION   BRAINERD

Griggs, Winnie.

Whatever it takes /

BR 34500006180516

FEB 1 3 2003

"Once ⎯ ⎯ ⎯ ⎯ that
wrenche⎯ ⎯ ⎯ ⎯ ⎯day

"Winnie Griggs has captured something special. You won't
want to pass up this wonderful story."

—The Write Lifestyle

"This book is a keeper! Ms. Griggs is a masterful storyteller!"
—Crazy for Words Book Reviews

WHAT MATTERS MOST

"A debut novel rarely comes together as perfectly as What
Matters Most. . . . The story is well written, absorbing and, oh,
so heartwarming. . . . This is a great start for an exceptional
writer."

—Romance Reviews Today

"A quiet tale of faith and fortitude, [this] is one to warm the
heart."

—Romantic Times

"Griggs creates likable characters in an engaging romantic
conflict that will keep readers wide awake turning the pages
and ignoring the lateness of the hour."

—Crescent Blues Book Reviews

"Ms. Griggs has given us a gentle read about strength,
devotion, forgiveness and love. As matters of the heart go, this
book is a must-read!"

—Old Book Barn Gazette

"What Matters Most is a heartwarming story. . . . I really
enjoyed this book!"

—The Romance Journal Reviews

CRITICS ARE RAVING ABOUT
WINNIE GRIGGS!

SOMETHING MORE

"Once again, Winnie Griggs has penned a story that touched my heart and warmed it at the same time."

—Romance Reviews To...

PLAYING THE PART

Clay played with a tendril of her hair. "I suppose, if you're certain you want to continue with our arrangement, I should begin acting my part in earnest."

Maddy's flesh tingled where his fingers brushed against her neck. "Yes." She cleared her throat. "I think the best way to proceed is—"

"Maddy," he interrupted, placing his arm along the top of the swing behind her. "I'm sure you have a very well thought out plan. But what do you say we try this my way first?"

"I don't think . . ." Maddy paused, distracted by his nearness.

"Good. You shouldn't think. To make folks believe this romance is genuine, it should appear spontaneous, impulsive." Clay's expression tendered a challenge as he casually moved his hand from the back of her swing to her shoulder.

Taking a deep breath, she lifted her gaze to meet his and hesitantly raised a hand to his face.

His skin was warm, the raspy stubble of his beard wonderfully rough against her sensitive fingertips. How would it feel against her own cheek? All the old longings she'd tried to suppress over the years came flooding back in full force.

"Much better," he said, his eyes darkening seductively. He turned his head, kissing her palm before she realized what he was about.

Other *Leisure* books by Winnie Griggs:
SOMETHING MORE
WHAT MATTERS MOST

WHATEVER
IT TAKES

WINNIE GRIGGS

LEISURE BOOKS   **L**   NEW YORK CITY

A LEISURE BOOK®

December 2002

Published by

Dorchester Publishing Co., Inc.
276 Fifth Avenue
New York, NY 10001

If you purchased this book without a cover you should be aware
that this book is stolen property. It was reported as "unsold and
destroyed" to the publisher and neither the author nor the
publisher has received any payment for this "stripped book."

Copyright © 2002 by Winnie Griggs

All rights reserved. No part of this book may be reproduced or
transmitted in any form or by any electronic or mechanical means,
including photocopying, recording or by any information storage
and retrieval system, without the written permission of the
publisher, except where permitted by law.

ISBN 0-8439-5138-9

The name "Leisure Books" and the stylized "L" with design are
trademarks of Dorchester Publishing Co., Inc.

Printed in the United States of America.

Visit us on the web at www.dorchesterpub.com.

To my parents, Carl and Shirley Duplessis, for raising me to believe that I can accomplish anything I set my mind to.

To my sisters—Joy, Tammy, Becca and Gina (a dear sister in spirit if not by birth)—for showing such amazing support of my writing endeavors, including the squeals and cheers that were just as enthusiastic for this third sale as for the first.

And last but by no means least, to my busy, macho brother Neil, who surprised the dickens out of me by reading my books as fast as I completed them and then prodded me to produce more.

You are all incredible and I love you more than I can say.

WHATEVER
IT TAKES

Chapter One

Pepper Cloud, Missouri
June 1894

"Don't fidget, dear."

Maddy Potter blew a stray lock of hair from her forehead and stood straighter on the low platform table. "Sorry." Normally she took guilty pleasure in serving as dressmaker's dummy for Miss Olive's flamboyant, somewhat scandalous, creations. After all, it was the only time she allowed herself to don anything other than her somber widow's weeds.

Today, however, she had too much on her mind to enjoy the sight of the rich colors, the feel of the velvet-trimmed taffeta, the heady sense of daring at the low-cut bodice and ankle-revealing hem. Mr. Kincaid, her soon-to-be-beau, was due to arrive tomorrow.

What sort of man would he be? One thing was for certain, he wouldn't be ordinary. How could he be, given he'd agreed to take part in her unorthodox scheme? But how did he *really* feel about this little charade? Was he searching

1

for a bit of adventure or merely desperate for money? Would he look sympathetically on her motives, or be disapproving?

More importantly, would the two of them be able to fool the Pepper Cloud Propriety Police?

"My, but we are distracted today, aren't we?"

Maddy smoothed the wrinkles from her brow, and smiled apologetically down at the seamstress's steel-gray bun. Few people looking at the primly demeanored fifty-year-old would believe she earned her living crafting gowns for the town's saloon girls. "I'm sorry, Miss Olive, did you say something?"

There was an understanding gleam in the look Miss Olive gave her. "I merely asked you to turn toward the door."

"I was thinking about Mr. Kincaid," Maddy volunteered as she made the requested turn. Miss Olive was the only person besides her friend Judith and Mr. Kincaid himself who knew about the scheme she'd concocted. Miss Olive had, in fact, helped her work out the particulars. As far as everyone else knew, Mr. Kincaid was a distant cousin of her deceased husband. He was supposedly coming here to go through some papers Winston had left behind.

Other than a non-committal "Hmmm," Miss Olive refrained from comment as she studied the dress with a critical eye. Her fingers, as lean and long as the rest of her, reached out to twitch the folds of the skirt more to her satisfaction. Then she straightened and gave Maddy a sympathetic look. "There's still time to back out, you know."

"No, that's not it." Maddy waved a hand, feeling the stiff black lace of the shoulder straps rasp against her skin. "This is still our best chance to hold on to Katie. I was just wondering what sort of man he'd be, is all."

"I suppose we'll know the answer to that soon enough."

Well, it seemed Miss Olive wasn't feeling the least bit of concern or stage fright over their upcoming production. But then, it wasn't Miss Olive who'd be playing the leading lady. Maddy sincerely hoped their three-act romance didn't turn into a farce.

The sight of a graceful black-and-white feline padding into the room diverted her attention. "Hello, Othello."

The cat ignored her and headed straight for the bolt of emerald green taffeta resting on the window seat. Miss Olive speared him with a less-than-fond glare. "Stay away from my fabrics, you arrogant beast."

Maddy hid a smile. Othello had a knack for stirring up mischief. The more innocent he looked, the closer you needed to watch him.

"My, my, Olive, you've outdone yourself this time."

At the husky drawl, Maddy turned back to the door to see Miss Adeline, Othello's aging but young-at-heart owner, striking a hand-raised-on-the-doorframe pose. She wore the Cleopatra wig today, and the smooth black locks spilled in a dramatic waterfall over her shoulder. An Egyptian-inspired gown, another of Miss Olive's creations, completed her ensemble.

Maddy spread the skirts of her own brightly colored gown. "It is a gem, isn't it? Ruby Jane will look gorgeous in it."

"She'll never set it off as well as you do." Miss Adeline flipped the hair over her shoulder, the coquettish gesture at odds with her age-lined face. "Olive, why don't you make something bright like this to replace Maddy's dreary black gowns? Something she can wear to greet that Mr. Kincaid tomorrow."

Maddy grinned as she had a sudden vision of herself wearing this flashy costume to greet her "guest." The poor man, especially if he was the proper gentleman she hoped Judith had found, would no doubt be scandalized. He probably already wondered what sort of woman would hire a man from hundreds of miles away to court her and then leave her at the altar.

Miss Olive eyed the dress's ruffled hem with a finger-to-her-cheek frown. "I'd like nothing better," she said without

3

looking up. "Though of course I'd do something a bit more understated. But there's no point in making a dress she won't wear."

"Then maybe we should make it harder for her to turn down the offer." Miss Adeline lifted her cat, stroking him absently. "Perhaps if Othello accidentally got into her wardrobe and unsheathed his claws on those frumpy gowns?"

Maddy shook her head. The former actress had been making similar outlandish plans almost from the day she and Miss Olive had moved into Barrows House seven years ago. "Miss Adeline, I'm a widow and it's only proper I dress like one." She owed Winston that, and so much more.

"Please, spare me. Winston has been dead since before Olive and I arrived on your doorstep. You've mourned long enough." She flashed Maddy a woman-to-woman look. "The problem is you've gotten comfortable with the role of widow and don't know how to be anything else anymore."

"But—"

"No buts." Miss Adeline wagged a finger. "You're still a young woman, but you won't be forever. There's going to be an eligible man spending time with us starting tomorrow. Might be just the opportunity you need to start stepping out again."

It appeared Miss Adeline's matchmaking instincts were out in full force. Good. But Maddy knew it wouldn't do for her to appear to give in too easily. So she set her lips in a firm line and shook her head.

"Be fair now, Adeline." Miss Olive's voice was muffled by her effort not to drop the pin she'd placed between her lips. "Maddy isn't exactly a recluse." She focused her pale blue eyes on Maddy. "Although I do agree, dear, that it's past time you put away your mourning."

Maddy twisted a lock of hair that had fallen free of her hairpins. "I know you both mean well, but I can't betray what I feel for Winston." Even Miss Olive, who knew her

4

better than anyone, had never understood the strength of her feelings in this matter. But then, how could she?

"Oh, pshaw!" Miss Adeline waved a hand with a dramatic flourish. "If Winston was a man worthy of all the loyalty you've shown him, then I'm sure he'd be the first to tell you to get on with your life."

When Maddy made no comment, Miss Adeline sighed and changed the subject. "I wonder what kind of man this Mr. Kincaid is?"

The topic of men was one the flamboyant thespian never seemed to tire of. Maddy decided to take advantage of the opening to lay some groundwork for her upcoming brush with cupid's arrow.

How much should she say? Her loyalty to Winston's memory was well known throughout the area. It was going to take a delicate bit of acting to make her abrupt turnaround believable.

"Actually, I'm looking forward to meeting him," she offered casually. "His letters were intriguing. Mr. Kincaid sounds like a well-educated, interesting man."

Miss Adeline's brow lifted. "Does he, now?"

Maddy nodded, resisting the urge to chew her lip. The speculative gleam in Miss Adeline's eye made her wonder if she'd overplayed her part.

"Letters, is it?" Miss Adeline mused. "Have you been holding out on us, Maddy dear?"

Maddy felt a small measure of her confidence return. Perhaps she could pull this off after all. If only she didn't have to keep secrets from her friend.

Seven-year-old Katie, the newest addition to their household, shot breathlessly into the room, providing a welcome distraction from the pinprick of Maddy's conscience. Seeing Katie reminded her what this bit of artifice was all about. And when it came to Katie, it was worth doing whatever it took.

The child skidded to a dramatic halt. "Aunt Maddy, come quick."

Maddy stepped down from the platform. But before she could question the youngster, the girl's expression changed to one of delighted appreciation.

"Aunt Maddy, you look be-yoo-ti-ful."

"Thank you, Buttercup." Maddy placed a hand on Katie's shoulder. "Now, what did you need me for?"

Katie wrinkled her nose. "Oh, yes. Miss Fanny's birdie is out of his cage again and she needs your help to put him back."

Miss Adeline lifted a hand from the cat's head long enough to wave it eloquently. "Fanny's always getting in a tizzy over something or other. That silly bird of hers just needs room to fly occasionally."

Maddy straightened, eyeing the much-too-innocent expression on her actress-friend's face. "Be that as it may, we'd best take care of this before Sweetie Pie finds an open window. Excuse me, Miss Olive. I promise to be careful with the dress."

Olive nodded. "Of course, dear. Just mind you don't let the pins prick you."

Not bothering to slip back into her shoes, Maddy tugged the bodice of the dress up a bit higher as she sailed from the room. The neckline was scandalously low and her arms were completely bare. What would her neighbors think if they could see her now—the proper widow Potter, barefoot and decked out in a barmaid's dress? Just one more reason for them to tsk over the goings on at Barrows House.

Reaching the bottom of the stairs, Maddy took a deep breath, then strode forward to push open the double doors to the library.

"Oh Maddy, at last!" Miss Fanny laid a plump hand on her ample bosom. "Mr. Wimberly thinks I'm overwrought, but Sweetie Pie is just being so naughty. I call and call, but he refuses to come to me. You must do something before he injures himself." Nearly a full head shorter than Maddy, the woman looked up at her with moisture-laden eyes.

Maddy touched the agitated woman's shoulder. "Of course I'll do something. And Mr. Wimberly is right." Maddy didn't bat an eyelash at this reference to Miss Fanny's deceased husband. "You must stop fretting." Her gaze scanned the room. "Just where is our feathered friend?"

Miss Fanny pointed a trembling finger toward the tall library stacks that lined the wall. "There, on top of the bookcase. Oh, what if he falls?"

"For goodness sake, Fanny, Sweetie Pie is a bird!" Miss Adeline trailed Maddy into the room and took a seat on one of a pair of wingback chairs.

"But—" Miss Fanny's defensive protest halted abruptly. "Adeline! How dare you bring that wicked feline in here while Sweetie Pie is out of his cage?"

Miss Adeline narrowed her eyes. "This is just as much Othello's home as it is Sweetie Pie's."

"Ladies, please." Maddy held up her hand. "We have to stay calm if we want to coax Sweetie Pie down. Now, Miss Fanny, bring me some birdseed, please."

With a last glare directed toward the smugly purring cat, Miss Fanny bustled across the room.

Maddy accepted the handful of seed, then flashed a re-assuring smile as Miss Fanny returned to wringing her hands. "Don't worry, we'll have Sweetie Pie back in his cage in no time."

Holding out the birdseed on her upraised palm, Maddy blew a soft, trilling whistle. The bird hopped forward, looking at her with tilted head.

"That's it, come get the nice seeds." She whistled another series of trills and held her hand higher. The bird sidestepped across the top of the bookcase, but made no move to come closer.

Oh well, she hadn't really thought it would work. She'd just have to do this the hard way.

"That wretched cat is making him nervous." Miss Fanny's bosom heaved with indignation.

Miss Adeline tossed her coal black tresses over her

Winnie Griggs

shoulder. "Othello is being a perfect gentleman. That silly bird of yours is just enjoying his taste of freedom."

Ignoring their bickering, Maddy guided the library ladder toward the stack where Sweetie Pie perched. When she had it positioned about a foot away from her quarry, she stepped up on the bottom rung.

Maddy held the handful of birdseed out ahead of her as she climbed. She stopped when she reached eye level with Sweetie Pie, and eased her hand to within a few inches of the bird. "Here you go, Sweetie Pie, some nice birdseed, just for you."

The bird took a hop closer, his gaze darting from her to the seed repeatedly.

"That's right," she crooned. "Come and get it." She blew a lock of hair off her forehead and tried again. "Good birdie, fine birdie," she crooned in a disgustingly syrupy tone. Making clicking noises with her tongue, she watched the bird reward her by at last taking the final hop onto her hand.

"Good boy, Sweetie Pie." Maddy continued to croon nonsense as she made her careful descent. Stepping onto the floor, she cupped a hand loosely over the bird and started toward the cage.

A loud, predatory *meow* from Othello disturbed the bird, and Maddy barely managed to hold on to it.

"Miss Adeline," she said without turning, "would you mind taking Othello out of the room for a few minutes please?"

"Well! Come, Othello. We won't stay where we're not wanted."

Maddy could imagine the dramatic flourish Miss Adeline made as she stood. She'd have to soothe her friend's feelings later. But she knew Miss Adeline wouldn't stay miffed for long.

When the bird was finally tucked back in his cage, Maddy straightened and let out a relieved sigh. "Now, Miss Fanny, please try to keep the latch securely fastened. We wouldn't want Sweetie Pie getting loose while Mr. Kincaid is here."

Miss Fanny bustled over to her side, peering anxiously into the cage. "I will, Maddy, and thank you, dear. Mr. Wimberly couldn't have done it better himself."

High praise indeed! Maddy smiled as she turned to Miss Olive. "Shall we finish with the fitting? I know Ruby Jane is coming by later today to pick this up."

But before the seamstress could reply, Katie tugged on Maddy's skirt. "Can I have a ride on the ladder? Please?"

Katie's eyes flashed with excitement at the prospect of her favorite game. It was a smile-maker Maddy had stumbled on almost by accident. One rainy afternoon two months ago, right after Katie had moved in with them, Maddy had recruited her to help shelve some books. Trying to make it fun for the child, Maddy had slid the ladder along the wall while Katie stood on it. The girl had been delighted. In fact, it had been the first time Maddy had seen her smile since her mother's death.

"All right, Buttercup." Maddy grabbed the ladder and rolled it to one end of the row of bookcases. "But I've only got a minute. After I help Miss Olive with the dress I still have a few other things I want to get done before Mr. Kincaid arrives."

Katie skipped across the room and scampered up the first three rungs of the ladder.

"Are you holding on tight?" At Katie's nod, Maddy placed a hand on either side of the ladder and took off at a run. Her efforts were rewarded with delighted squeals. When they reached the end, Maddy paused only long enough to turn around, then ran all the way back.

"All right," she said, grasping the girl under the arms and swinging her around, "down you go."

Grinning at Katie's giggles, Maddy absently flicked birdseed from the bodice of the sassy red dress. She paused when she caught the expression on Miss Fanny's face. Miss

Olive looked rather peculiar, too. Both of their gazes slid from hers to the doorway.

Still trying to catch her breath, Maddy turned and felt the gooseflesh prickle on her bare arms.

There in the doorway, cynically assessing her with a look that took in every inch of her inappropriately clad person, stood the most handsome man she'd ever seen in her life.

Chapter Two

Clay met the woman's shocked stare with a sardonic smile. He had no idea who she was, but that didn't stop him from admiring her obvious charms.

He'd entered the room expecting to find a reserved widow lady ensconced here. Instead the tall, blond-haired miss in the strumpet's dress had riveted his attention. The sight of her racing across the room, with her bare feet and trim ankles exposed, and her ample curves enticingly packaged, had caught him completely unawares.

Watching her standing there now, staring at him with wide green eyes and taking deep breaths that pushed at the limits of her bodice, didn't help his composure any. Damn, but she was an eyeful, and that tight-fitting, low-cut dress made sure everyone knew it.

Reluctantly, he tore his gaze from hers. He was here to perform a duty, to carry the Kincaid family banner on the field of honor, so to speak. It wouldn't do for him to insult his hostess by ignoring her.

With a quick glance, he took in the others in the room:

11

the aging, would-be-seductress who'd let him in; the broomstick of a woman with a pair of scissors skewering her silver, spinster-tight bun; the plump, befuddled-looking hand-wringer; and the curious, golden-haired urchin who peeked at him from behind the hoyden's gaudy skirts.

So where was the widow? He'd deliberately arrived a day early with the idea of catching her off guard. His family might owe Mrs. Potter a debt, one he fully intended to repay, but he knew next to nothing about her.

The information he'd received so far had been less than enlightening. Despite the fact that the packet charging him with this duty had contained letters from his mother, his brother and one of his sisters, all he really knew was that he was supposed to repay a family debt of honor to the widow Potter by pretending to court her for a few weeks. It would be interesting to hear the lady in question explain the "whys" of this little charade.

It was such an outrageous request, especially since he'd been emphatically assured the widow was not at all interested in marriage, only a temporary courtship. So outrageous, in fact, that he half suspected he was being manipulated by his matchmaking mother.

But he was willing to give everyone the benefit of the doubt, for the time being. After all, as long as he paid attention, he could outwit even as wily a woman as his mother.

The would-be Cleopatra reclaimed his attention as she patted his arm. "Maddy," she said with an arch smile. "Look. Mr. Kincaid is here a day early. Isn't that wonderful?"

She'd apparently been speaking to the provocatively clad miss. From the beauty's expression, it seemed she didn't share his escort's pleasure at his early arrival. Though why it should matter to her . . . Maddy? Surely this couldn't be—

Pasting a smile on her face that did nothing to fade the bright red in her cheeks, the woman in scarlet strode for-

12

ward with an outstretched hand. "Mr. Kincaid, welcome to Pepper Cloud. I'm Madeline Potter, your cousin Winston's widow."

It took every ounce of control Clay could muster to hide his surprise and instead bow politely over her hand. *This* was the widow Potter? His sister, Judith, the only one of his family who'd met the woman, had led him to expect he'd be dealing with a reserved, genteel lady who wore somber widow's weeds. In fact, the best description Judith could come up with was that she was "passable" in appearance.

Trust Judith to leave out important details.

He was becoming more curious about the widow Potter by the moment. At the very least, hearing her explanation for her current state of dress should prove interesting.

He released her hand and straightened. "I'm pleased to meet you, ma'am. I hope my early arrival won't present an inconvenience." Again he let his gaze travel over her dress.

She stiffened and he could almost hear the gritting of her teeth. "Not at all," she responded with a smile that didn't quite match the sincerity of her words. "Let me introduce you to the rest of my household."

Clay could think of several more intriguing matters to attend to, but for now he'd let her take the lead.

"I assume you've already met Miss Adeline Dupree." She indicated the woman who'd escorted him into the room.

At his acknowledgement, she moved on. He learned the prim broomstick was named Olive Simpson, the plump handwringer was Mrs. Fanny Wimberly, also a widow, and the child was named Katie Lynn Dooley.

Once the introductions were complete, Mrs. Potter gave him another of those false-polite smiles. "I hope you will forgive me for receiving you so . . ." she twitched her skirts, "informally. I was helping Miss Olive with some final touch-ups on a sewing project."

The gray haired spinster had created this? Was she the seamstress for a bawdy house?

He lifted a hand. "No need to apologize. Since I was arriving early I expected a certain amount of . . . informality."

Her lips compressed. "Nevertheless, if you'll excuse me, I'd like to change out of this dress so Miss Olive can finish it for her customer."

Clay waved expansively. "Of course. Please take as much time as you need." He was, after all, at her disposal for the moment. Besides, he could use a few moments to regroup also.

She gave a clipped nod. "Ladies, will you escort Mr. Kincaid to the parlor, and find him some refreshments, please?" Then, with a surprising show of dignity, considering how she was clad, Mrs. Potter made her exit.

Clay watched her walk away. Even with that poker-stiff backbone, her hips had a feminine sway to them that the dress accentuated seductively. If she wanted to present the image of a genteel widow-in-need, she was failing miserably.

Not that it mattered. He was here to render her a service, he reminded himself, and render it he would, no matter what she looked like, or how questionable her credentials might seem at first blush.

But there was nothing wrong with enjoying himself while he was at it.

Maddy marched up the stairs to her room. She wasn't sure if she was more upset with having Mr. Kincaid catch her wearing the barmaid's dress, or with Mr. Kincaid himself. How was she ever going to have him take her seriously after the disastrous first impression she'd just made?

Maddy stopped short of slamming the bedroom door behind her when she turned to find Miss Olive standing in the doorway.

"I thought you might need some help getting out of that dress," the seamstress explained.

Maddy flounced across the room as her friend closed the

door. She sat on the bed, but bounded up immediately. Oh, but this Mr. Kincaid, with his smoke-gray eyes and dimpled-chin charm, was entirely the wrong sort of man to play the part of her suitor.

"Did you see him?" she asked as she paced across the room.

"Oh, yes," Miss Olive answered, displaying none of the agitation Maddy felt. "And a very pleasant sight he is to look at too."

"Exactly!" Maddy sent Miss Olive a this-is-nothing-to-make-light-of look. "No one in Pepper Cloud would ever believe a man like *that* would seriously court a woman like *me*. He's too handsome, too smooth, too . . ."

"Too potent?"

The innocently uttered word stopped Maddy for a moment, but then she nodded. Yes, that was exactly the right word for what she sensed about this man. She threw up her hands. "How could Judith do this to me. She was supposed to find someone staid, someone *ordinary*."

Miss Olive shook her head. "I don't believe Mr. Kincaid could ever be called ordinary."

"What am I going to do?" Maddy frantically searched her mind for a way out. "Maybe we can still find someone else—"

"I'm afraid it's much too late for that." Miss Olive touched Maddy's arm. "Now stand still so I can remove these pins without scratching you."

Maddy ceased her pacing but not her fretting. "But—"

"I know you're upset," Miss Olive interrupted, "but take a deep breath and think this through. Mr. Kincaid walked here from the train depot, probably stopped and asked for directions along the way. Fanny and Adeline have met him. Too many people have seen him for you to substitute someone else now."

Maddy felt her shoulders slump. Miss Olive was right. Somehow, she'd have to find a way to salvage this, to work with Mr. Kincaid to make their charade believable. She had to keep reminding herself of what was at stake.

Then she caught sight of herself in the vanity mirror, and bit back a groan. Her reflection revealed her to be even more flashily immodest than she'd imagined. What in the world had he thought of her?

The seamstress unfastened the back of the dress. "There, I think you should be able to slip out of it now." Then as Maddy complied, "Don't take this so hard, dear. I'm sure Mr. Kincaid is a gentleman who'll do the right thing. Judith would have made sure of that." Then she gave Maddy a dry look. "Besides, there are worse things in this life than being courted by a handsome, smooth, *potent* man."

Maddy returned her friend's smile, feeling slightly foolish for her bout of panic. "You're right, of course. I guess part of the reason I'm so upset is that he caught me at such a disadvantage." How was she ever going to look Mr. Kincaid in the eye again? "Did you see the way he stared at me? Like I was some—"

"Beautiful woman?" Miss Olive finished for her. "Yes, I saw. It's just what any normal male would have done when unexpectedly coming upon a lovely young lady."

Maddy sincerely doubted *lady* was the word Mr. Kincaid would have used. Just remembering the look he'd given her did fluttery things to her insides.

She drew her shoulders back and crossed the room to her wardrobe. There was no point bemoaning what was past changing. She'd just have to brazen her way through the first few minutes of their next encounter and pretend there was nothing amiss. She hoped he'd take his cue from her and they could start over.

At least the Ladies' Society hadn't caught her dressed this way. *That* would have been a true disaster, she thought as she pulled one of her somber black gowns out of the wardrobe. There was no way she could have overcome their misguided objections to her adopting Katie if that had happened.

"Do you need any more help?" Miss Olive stood with

the barmaid's dress over one arm, watching Maddy with a sympathetic gleam in her eye.

Maddy shook her head, then impulsively walked over and gave her friend and confidant a peck on the cheek. "Thank you. For the help *and* the dose of common sense." She grimaced. "I just hope I handle my next encounter with Mr. Kincaid better than I did the first."

Miss Olive patted her arm. "You'll be fine. Now, I'll be right down the hall in the sewing room, and I'll leave the door open. If you need anything, just call out."

Maddy slipped on her dress as Miss Olive left the room. After buttoning it all the way to her chin, she grabbed her shoes and sat at the vanity to pull them on. Next she pulled the pins from her hair, shook it free, and relentlessly pulled it back into a tight, not-a-hair-out-of-place chignon.

The picture of Winston on her vanity table smiled at her, but there seemed to be a hint of gentle reproach in his expression today, as well. "Don't worry," she told the photograph, "I'll keep my promise. It doesn't matter how handsome or smooth-talking or *potent* Mr. Kincaid is, there's no danger of me letting down my guard. He and I will merely be doing a bit of playacting, nothing more."

She stood and studied her reflection in the mirror, feeling some of her confidence return. *There* was the proper widow Potter, reserved, poised, above reproach.

An image of the coolly assessing look Mr. Kincaid had raked her with flashed through her mind again, and some of her confidence ebbed.

Lifting her chin, Maddy reminded herself that he was just a man—a man, moreover, who was in her employ. But why in the world had such a man agreed to participate in her scheme? He didn't look like the sort who would take well to working for a woman. Then again, perhaps he hadn't had much choice. Maybe he needed the money.

Maddy descended the stairs at a sedate pace. She wouldn't let Mr. Kincaid rattle her. He'd caught her at a disadvantage with his early arrival, that was all. She'd just have to be sure she established herself as the one in charge when she faced him this time.

She tried to put aside her irritation at the man himself. It wasn't Mr. Kincaid's fault he was wrong for this role. Perhaps it was only her embarrassment that had made her defensive.

Or just maybe it had been the immediate sizzle of awareness she'd felt when she first turned to see him standing in the doorway, devouring her with his eyes. No man had ever looked at her like that before, as if she were a temptingly luscious piece of forbidden fruit. For just a second it had made her feel things she had no right feeling.

Of course, it had been the dress that had snagged his interest. Miss Olive's creations, at least the ones for her "special" clientele, were designed to make even the homeliest of women seem attractive, desirable. Now that she was more suitably attired, there would be no more inappropriate behavior from either of them.

With a bit of work and ingenuity, she could figure out some way to turn Mr. Kincaid into a believable suitor. There was too much at stake, a little girl's entire future, to give up without an all-out effort.

By the time Maddy reached the parlor, she had herself in hand once more. Which was just as well. From the vantage point of the doorway, it appeared as if Mr. Kincaid were holding court.

Miss Adeline sat beside him on the settee, coyly fluttering her eyelashes and patting his arm to punctuate her conversation. Miss Fanny was refilling his cup of tea with a blushing giggle at some comment he'd just made. Katie stood nearby, examining an expensive-looking pocket watch.

Well, she'd wanted him to be likable, someone for whom her friends would believe she could form an attachment. But the fact that they all seemed so taken with him jarred rather than pleased her. It almost felt like a betrayal.

Hadn't they seen the way he'd looked at her earlier?

They should be more aloof, more censorious.

Maddy called up what she hoped was a businesslike smile and stepped into the room. "Hello again. I apologize if I kept you waiting."

He stood, eyeing her changed appearance with a raised brow. "Not at all," he said smoothly. "It's given me the opportunity to get to know these very charming ladies better."

Miss Adeline stood as well. "Maddy, why don't you take my place here on the settee. I'm afraid I'll have to excuse myself from this pleasant company. It's time for Othello's mid-afternoon meal." She turned back to their handsome guest. "He has a delicate digestive system, you know, and gets quite out of sorts if his schedule is disrupted."

She offered her hand, and Mr. Kincaid took it, bringing it to his lips for a kiss that won him a dazzling smile.

"Such a charming man," Miss Adeline murmured. Then she turned to Miss Fanny with a pointed look. "Fanny dear, weren't you going to give Katie a cooking lesson this afternoon?"

It took a moment for comprehension to replace the befuddled expression on the plump woman's face, but then she rose to the occasion with a knowing smile. "Oh, yes, of course—the cooking lesson. You must excuse me, sir, but Katie and I had best get started if we're going to have things ready by supper time."

Even though she'd expected her friends to try their hands at a bit of matchmaking, it was all Maddy could do to keep from rolling her eyes at the heavy-handedness of their efforts.

Mr. Kincaid, however, appeared to see nothing amiss. "I quite understand, madam. And I look forward to renewing our acquaintance at my next visit."

Clay didn't miss the twinkle in the Egyptian-costumed matron's eye as she gave Mrs. Potter's arm a pat on her way out. It appeared the ladies were deliberately leaving the two of them alone.

It brought his earlier suspicions back to the fore again. For the past several years his mother and sisters had been relentlessly conspiring to end his bachelorhood. It was one reason that, although he cared deeply for his family, his visits home had grown fewer and shorter in duration. When the latest packet of letters had caught up with him in New Orleans a week ago, only the fact that Adam, his older brother, had written to him personally had convinced Clay that the outlandish request might be genuine.

But had his mother successfully recruited Adam to assist in her efforts to see her younger son "happily married?"

Mrs. Potter crossed the room and took a seat, though not the one next to him. Instead she chose a tapestry-cushioned chair that directly faced him. She did a creditable job of maintaining a composed, there's-nothing-amiss-here façade, but he detected a certain element of nervousness just below the surface.

What a transformation she'd made! Gone was the shoe-less, flustered wanton in the gaudily colorful dress. In her place sat a genteel, reserved widow who looked as if she'd rather throw herself on a sword than show a bit of ankle.

She might have fooled him into thinking she was the modest, proper matron he'd first expected if he hadn't seen her without her bombazine armor. But he *had* seen her earlier and had her measure now.

There was more than a touch of the hoyden in this woman. He didn't for one minute believe she hadn't en-joyed, even reveled in, wearing that revealing red dress. Before she noted his presence, she'd moved in it with ease, even a touch of joyful abandon. By contrast, the somber mantle of her widow's weeds set heavily on her, seemed to fit more like a uniform than a pleasant day dress. She might be used to her disguise, but it wasn't comfortable to her.

Knowing what creamy skin and luscious curves she hid

under that drab shell somehow made her seem more alluring in a woman-of-mystery kind of way.

The unconventional widow smoothed her skirts, then met his gaze. He was surprised by the hint of disapproval he read in her expression. Hell, she was the one with all the explaining to do. What did she have to disapprove of?

"Well, Mr. Kincaid," she began, "let's get to business." She tucked a non-existent tendril of hair behind her ear, reminding him of the wavy locks that had cascaded about her face earlier. "I'm sure you have several questions about this job I've hired you for."

Clay gave her credit for control and shrewdness. She was obviously nervous, yet she'd addressed him coolly and had opened with a remark that made it clear she was the one in charge.

It was time for him to clear up a few points with the widow cum barmaid. "Before we get to my questions, let's get one thing straight. You are not *hiring* me to do anything. As Judith's brother, I'm here to discharge the debt of honor the Kincaid family owes you for the service you rendered her, not to take your money."

Her brow creased. "You're Judith's brother?"

"I am."

She sat back and studied him severely, her nose wrinkling like a child's. "I never knew Judith's maiden name." She made it sound like that was his fault. "Since Judith's older brother is married, I assume you're the younger."

He inclined his head. "Clayton Kincaid, at your service."

"Mr. Kincaid, it was not my intent to seek such grandiose repayment for the small service I rendered your sister. I merely asked her to help me locate some trustworthy gentleman I could hire to play this part." She lifted a hand and let it drop back to her lap. "I assure you, neither you nor your family need feel in any way obligated to me for what was little more than a bit of neighborly assistance."

Was this woman truly so modest, or was it merely show? "On the contrary, from what I've been told, you rescued

21

Judith from a dire situation, one brought on primarily by her own impulsive behavior." His gut clenched again when he thought of what might have happened to his sister on that isolated roadside. Thank God Mrs. Potter had happened by, frightening away the bastard who intended to rob Judith and God only knew what else.

Remembering that, he unbent slightly. Regardless of whatever secrets she guarded, she *had* rescued his sister. For that, he would be forever in her debt. "My sister had high praises for both your generosity and your discretion."

Though this near catastrophe had happened over three years ago, neither he nor others in his family had known anything of it until Judith came to Adam with Mrs. Potter's letter.

Mrs. Potter shifted uncomfortably. "Your sister no doubt embellished the role I played."

He shrugged, unwilling to argue with her on that particular point. "Whether she did or not, the fact remains that you helped her when she needed it. Now I am here to do the same for you."

"I see," she said dryly. "Uphold the family honor at all costs."

She actually had the temerity to roll her eyes at him. Clay sat up straighter. "Now see here—"

Mrs. Potter held a hand up. "My apologies. What's done is done. Regardless of your motives, you're here and we must strive to make the best of it. However, I insist on paying you for this job."

Pay him? She obviously had no idea who she was dealing with. The Kincaids could no doubt buy all of Pepper Cloud, lock, stock and barrel, and have plenty of money to spare. "That won't be necessary. I have adequate resources to cover my expenses."

She drew herself up. "Mr. Kincaid, I'm sorry, but I insist. I will accept your help, but not your charity. If you won't let me pay you, then I'm afraid we have nothing further to discuss."

Clay returned her stare, noting the stubborn jut of her chin. This was ridiculous. She should be grateful he didn't want her money, not angry.

What would happen if he called her bluff, stood and walked away? Would she really abandon her scheme?

He had to remember that he was here to fulfill an obligation, not do battle with his sister's rescuer. He tried a conciliatory smile. "Why don't we approach this as a partnership? You pay for my travel costs, and I'll cover my day-to-day expenses."

After a considering pause, she gave a short nod. "Very well."

Clay barely had time to congratulate himself for that bit of diplomatic maneuvering before she sat up straighter.

"But understand this," she said firmly. "You can regard our arrangement as a partnership if you like, but don't forget that *I* am the senior partner. When it comes to how we carry out this courtship, I have the final say."

Clay frowned at the determination in her tone. Apparently the woman had aspirations of becoming a dictator. It had been his experience, with his mother and sisters especially, that setting a woman in charge of anything but domestic matters was just asking for trouble.

But he *was* here to help her. He just had to keep reminding himself of that fact. "Understood." Clay heard the lack of graciousness in his bitten-off response, and tried to compensate with a smile.

When it failed to have the usual result, namely charm a bemused smile from her in return, he leaned forward. "Mrs. Potter, I get the impression you don't approve of me."

A variety of emotions played across her face as she fought some inner battle. At last she gave a stiff nod. "My apologies if I've made you feel unwelcome. I realize it's not your fault you're not the sort of man I wanted. You can't help the way you look and act."

"The way I—" Clay bit off the rest of the sentence, irritated that he'd been about to parrot her comment. He didn't consider himself a vain man, but he'd never had any complaints from the ladies in regards to his appearance. In fact, quite the contrary. "Do you mind telling me just what you find wrong with the way I look and act?"

"Oh dear, I've insulted you. Actually, I don't suppose there *is* anything wrong, in the normal way of things. I'm sure any number of ladies would be quite pleased to have you court them."

"But not you?"

She shook her head. "I realize I'm just being vain, but I don't like the light it will paint me in when I finally do seem to accept your suit."

This had to be the strangest conversation he'd ever engaged in. "Would you care to explain that?"

She sighed, as if forced to humor a nuisance, and a slow-witted one at that. "When I buried my husband seven years ago, I vowed never to let another man take his place. There have been several fine men who have tried to test my resolve since then, but I've never wavered."

Clay wondered what sort of man would inspire that degree of loyalty from such a strong-willed woman. And what would it feel like to be the target of such devotion?

"Now *you* come along," she explained, "and in a matter of little more than a week, it will appear that you've swept me off my feet."

"But isn't that what you want?"

"Yes, but not like this." She grimaced. "If you'd been a plainly visaged, scholarly man, it would seem that I was drawn to you intellectually, that we were somehow kindred spirits who found each other." She waved a hand in exasperation. "As it is now, it will seem like I was simply taken in by a handsome face and a bit of smooth talking and empty flattery."

How had she managed to call him handsome and insult him all in the same sentence? Perhaps his suspicions had been misplaced after all. If she was party to some kind of matchmaking scheme, she was doing a devil of a job hiding it.

But before he could form an adequate response, she shrugged. "As I said, that's water under the bridge now. You're here and we'll make the best of it. It would help, though, if you'd try to downplay your appearance as much as possible. Perhaps comb your hair differently or muss your clothes a bit."

Was she serious? "Maybe I should try slouching and walking with a limp."

"That's the spirit." She wrinkled her nose again. "But I'm afraid we'll have to forgo the limp. Too many folks have seen you without one." Then she brightened. "Oh, I know. I have a pair of Winston's reading glasses around here somewhere. You can use those whenever the opportunity allows."

Clay bit off several choice responses. This woman could *not* be as artless as she pretended. She must be deliberately trying to ruffle his control. He refused to let her succeed.

Time to bring the focus back to the mock courtship. "Shall we move on to discussing the actual assignment?"

At her nod, he leaned back and laid an arm across the top of the settee. "The letter you sent Judith indicated you need someone to pretend to be your husband's cousin, and to appear smitten with you when we first meet. I am, in fact, to begin to court you almost immediately." He kept his tone businesslike, though the whole arrangement seemed farcical when spoken aloud.

She nodded. "Correct. Now, this is going to require a delicate bit of playacting to be convincing. Let me explain how we should proceed."

He spread his hands. "I await your instruction." But his sarcasm seemed lost on her.

"It's important that we spend as much time together as possible," she began. "That will lend a measure of plausibility to our whirlwind courtship."

His sisters always spoke of the subject of courtship with

breathless sighs and sublime phrases. It was jarring to hear Mrs. Potter speak of it so dispassionately. Then again, though he had trouble thinking of her that way, she was a widow, not a debutante.

"I will insist on going through Winston's papers with you, of course," she continued. "Also, it will seem perfectly natural for us to take occasional breaks from our work to stroll about in the fresh air or go for drives in the countryside. That will give us a chance to be seen in public together."

He noticed she fiddled with a button at her throat as she spoke. Perhaps she wasn't as composed as her words implied.

As if reading his thoughts, she dropped her hands back to her lap and lifted her chin. "After the second or third day, you will indeed strive to appear smitten with me. Nothing extravagant, mind you. Just some over-solicitousness in front of my household and neighbors to start with."

Her household? "Then the other ladies here aren't party to this plan of yours?"

She shook her head. "Only Miss Olive. I can't risk anyone giving us away. Not that Miss Fanny or Miss Adeline would deliberately betray any secrets," she hurriedly clarified. "But their reactions must appear genuine to the rest of the town."

So the dry-mannered seamstress was in on this little game, was she? Interesting. But it was time he got answers to his other questions. "Just who is it we're trying to convince?"

"Why, everyone." She waved a hand impatiently and returned to her explanation. "I will, of course, remain stand-offish at first."

He straightened. What was this? "Do you mean you want me to court you, but you plan to hold me at arm's length?"

"I said *at first*, sir. You will persist in your efforts despite my rebuffs, and eventually appear to win me over."

Good Lord, she planned to make him look like a love-sick milksop. No! He'd just have to find some way to satisfy the widow's demands and maintain his dignity at the same time.

She cleared her throat delicately. "Now, let's discuss the particulars of how you will go about courting me."

Enough was enough. "I believe you can leave that to me, madam. I'm not without experience in these matters." *Considerable* experience, as a matter of fact.

She lifted her chin, the censure in her expression more pronounced. "Mr. Kincaid, I don't know, nor am I interested in, what sort of *experience* you might have in these matters, but surely you will allow that *my* advice on how best to court *me* may carry some merit?" Her shoulders drew back. "And forgive me, sir, but please remember we agreed that I am in charge here."

Actually, he hadn't entirely agreed to any such thing. But now was not the time to bring that up.

She held his gaze. "First, let's talk about what you shouldn't do. Please don't employ spun-sugar flattery, don't write love poems, and by all means don't call me by ridiculous pet names. My friends and neighbors know that that sort of thing will only annoy me, and we *are* trying to be convincing." She paused, apparently waiting for his response.

Clay gave a short nod. If she chose to view that as acceptance of her terms, then that was her mistake.

She flashed a tight smile, then shifted in her seat. "What you should do, rather, is show deference and respect. Ask my opinion, pay close attention when I speak, be accepting of the ladies in my household. You should bring gifts occasionally, but not anything extravagant—things like a bouquet of fresh picked flowers, a book, maybe some stationary. Above all, you must be gentlemanly but persistent when I rebuff your initial overtures."

So, she expected him to carefully guard her dignity while throwing his to the wind. Well, she'd soon find that he had his own way of doing things. "Is that all?"

"There's no need for sarcasm, sir. Surely you had an idea what would be required when you agreed to come here?"

He hadn't, of course, though he couldn't very well say so. What he'd expected was one of two things. Either he'd find a mousy, plain-Jane lady-in-distress who'd look on with gratitude and admiration as he gallantly slew whatever dragons were bedeviling her. Or he'd find a scheming miss looking to be the beneficiary of his mother's latest match-making scheme.

He answered her with another curt nod, then changed the subject. "How will I know if we've been successful? You haven't yet told me *why* we're undertaking this elaborate deception."

She flinched at the word "deception," and he pounced on her reaction. "Does that word bother you?"

Her lips compressed. "It does seem rather harsh."

He couldn't resist the temptation to get a bit of verbal revenge for the swipes she'd administered to his pride. "But accurate. After all, the whole point of this little charade is to make your friends and neighbors believe a lie."

The glare she shot him almost masked the vulnerable flush of guilt in her cheeks. "It's a bit late for you to get an attack of conscience," she said haughtily. "But if it'll make this easier for you, we won't be lying to anyone in the strictest sense of the word. You *will* court me, you *will* eventually propose marriage, and I *will* accept your proposal. The fact that we won't ever marry is no one's business but our own. Ours won't be the first engagement ever broken off, and it won't be the last."

It seemed Mrs. Potter was practiced in twisting facts to fit her own needs. How far would he have to push before she admitted her duplicitousness? "Still, at the heart of this masquerade is your desire to deceive."

She surprised him with yet another show of assertiveness. "I don't deny that. But given what's at stake here, I'll do whatever it takes to make this work. If I have to bald-

28

face lie to the preacher himself, then make no mistake about it, I will."

She believed the ends justified the means, did she? Not surprising. "And just what *is* at stake?

Mrs. Potter took a deep breath and leveled him with an expression that dared him to make light of her concerns. "Katie's future."

Chapter Three

Her words set him back momentarily. "What has my court-ing you to do with the child's future?"

"I plan to adopt her." She said this as if she expected him to challenge her. "But there are those in the com-munity who think Barrows House isn't a fit place to raise a child."

A not entirely unreasonable attitude, as far as Clay could see. "But surely the fact that you're her aunt will—"

She interrupted him with a shake of her head. "I'm not really her aunt. Katie just calls me that for convenience sake." Mrs. Potter edged forward in her seat. "The adoption hearing is in four weeks. Some in the community have hinted they might speak against me. I want to make sure that doesn't happen."

He still couldn't find the connection. "And how will my courting you accomplish that?"

"Being engaged to a solid, above-reproach gentleman such as the one you are going to emulate will lend me an added air of respectability." She smiled, as if pleased with her own cleverness. "And if it appears that I am about to set up a new household, one that follows a more traditional family setting, there should be nothing left to object to."

This sounded about as sensible as something one of his sisters would dream up. "Mrs. Potter, that is a very flimsy bit of reasoning."

She raised her delicately pointed chin a notch. "Not at all. It should at the very least make folks think twice about the need to go to all the trouble of mounting a formal protest."

Did he really want to play a part in making that little girl a permanent member of this household? What sort of example would these unconventional women set for the child? How harmful would their influence on her life be? He owed Mrs. Potter a debt of honor, but he could not repay it at the expense of a little girl's future.

He'd have to keep a close watch on that matter over the next couple of weeks. If worse came to worse, a few private words with the adoption judge at the right time would be all it would take to ensure matters were handled properly.

Besides, he didn't see how this scheme of hers could work anyway. "Have it your way. I'm just here to play a part."

"I agree. Now, unless there is something else you feel we should discuss right now, I'll escort you to the hotel. I'm sure you'd like to get settled in and rest a bit before supper, and I have business to take care of in town." She shot him a stern, Sunday school–teacher look. "But before we step outside, please keep in mind we're going to be on display. Remember, we're supposed to act as if we like each other."

Affronted, Clay wondered if she was implying it would be a difficult part for her to play. He certainly wouldn't have any problem with it. Courting a woman who presented such diverse faces in such a short period of time would be interesting, to say the least.

31

He followed suit as she stood. "I'll try to keep that in mind."

The widow moved to the door, still issuing instructions. "It would speed things along if you'd take most of your meals here at Barrows House. I hope that's acceptable?"

Clay kept his tone even. "Of course." He'd thought flighty, emotional women like his sisters were difficult to please. It appeared bossy women were even worse.

With a tight smile of acknowledgement, she moved toward the staircase. "If you'll excuse me, I'll step upstairs and get my hat. I'll only be a moment or two."

He stood in the entryway, watching her climb the stairs. It was obvious Mrs. Potter believed he would meekly dance to her tune for the next several weeks. Well, she'd learn differently soon enough. Oh, he'd give her the courtship she wanted, and he'd make it extremely convincing. He owed her that much. He just planned to have much more of a say in how it was orchestrated than she realized.

A knock at the front door interrupted his musings. A few seconds later, Katie appeared from the nether regions of the house with a cheerful, "I'm coming."

She gave him an impish grin as she skipped by, then opened the door. "Hi, Ruby Jane," she said with a welcoming smile.

Ruby Jane proved to be a brassy redhead with ample curves and a saucy manner. Clay had seen the type before. Just not in any respectable home he'd visited.

The small-town Jezebel stepped inside, echoing the girl's grin. "Hi, Katie Lynn. I've come to see if Miss Olive ha—"

Her gaze fell on Clay and her mouth dropped open. Her surprise was quickly replaced by a slow, appreciative appraisal. With a flirtatious toss of her head, she gave him a bold, inviting smile and offered her hand. "Well snap my garters, but ain't you a handsome devil."

Clay's brow lifted. This was the kind of reception, at least in spirit, that he was more used to. But what was such a woman doing on *this* doorstep? If she was a regular visitor, no wonder the townsfolk were up in arms over Mrs. Potter's plans to adopt Katie.

His first impulse was to give this forward female a proper set-down for her impertinence.

The crisp rustle of bombazine from the top of the stairs, however, spurred the devil in him to do something entirely different.

Maddy watched Mr. Kincaid take Ruby Jane's hand and bow over it with a gallantly uttered, "Clayton Kincaid, at your service, ma'am."

The warmed-honey voice and appreciative smile he focused on Ruby Jane stirred an unexpected prickling of envy in Maddy. Were flashy girls like Ruby Jane the sort he admired? Not that she wanted such attention from Mr. Kincaid in particular, she told herself as she pushed away from the upstairs banister. It's just that any woman would be flattered to be so admired.

Ruby Jane seemed no exception. The normally jaded girl turned pink with pleasure, and visibly preened. "I'm Ruby Jane Hobbs, and it's most definitely a pleasure to make your acquaintance, Mr. Kincaid. I hope you're planning to stay in Pepper Cloud for a nice long visit."

He returned her smile. "I'll be here for three or four weeks. I already see much about this town to recommend it."

Maddy started down the stairs, determined to put a stop to this nonsense. How would she get anyone to believe he'd form an interest in her if he revealed his preference for someone like Ruby Jane? Was he going to flirt with every woman he met?

She pasted a smile on her face. "Ruby Jane, it's so nice to see you again. Have you and Mr. Kincaid introduced yourselves?"

Ruby Jane turned away from Mr. Kincaid with obvious effort. "Oh, hello Maddy. Yes, we've met." She slid her gaze back to the gentleman in question. A womanly smile, full of forbidden promise, played across her lips.

Maddy wondered if she could pull off a smile like that without looking like a complete fool.

Dismissing the idiotic thought, she stepped off the bottom tread and joined them. "Mr. Kincaid is a cousin of my late husband. He's here to go through some papers Winston left behind." She held Ruby Jane's gaze as she stepped closer to Mr. Kincaid. "Miss Olive is finished with your dress. I think you're going to be very pleased with the way it turned out."

The girl clasped her hands excitedly, latching on to the diversion as Maddy had hoped she would. "I can't wait to see it. Is it all right if I go on up?"

"Of course. She's expecting you."

Ruby Jane sashayed toward the stairs, then paused and turned back to Maddy. "Oh, I told Cassy and Lila you wanted them to join us for our Thursday afternoon, uhm, tea. Cassy said she will, but Lila's not so sure." Her gaze flickered back toward Mr. Kincaid. "Of course, she might feel a bit differently now."

Maddy resisted the urge to roll her eyes. "Tell her she's more than welcome to join us, anytime." Giving the strings of her reticule a tug before she looped them over her wrist, Maddy moved to the door.

Mr. Kincaid stepped forward to open it for her, and then followed her out onto the porch. "Thursday afternoon tea?" he remarked with a disbelieving lift of his brow.

"That's right." She didn't break stride or bother to elaborate. He'd no doubt picked up on Ruby Jane's telling pause, but she didn't owe him any sort of explanation. Besides, she and Ruby Jane *did* share a cup of tea at their weekly get-togethers.

A moment later, he took her arm, the touch sending a small tingle through her. "Mrs. Potter, if we intend to make folks around here believe we get along, don't you think you should stroll along beside me, not march ahead?"

Maddy felt her cheeks heat at his amused tone. He was turning her words back on her. For a few minutes she'd forgotten all about her plan. Nodding reluctant agreement, she slowed her steps and allowed him to draw her hand onto the crook of his arm.

"Much better." He patted her hand.

The exaggerated solicitousness in the gesture set Maddy's teeth on edge, but she kept smiling and refrained from comment.

"So," he continued, "the dress you were wearing earlier was constructed for Miss Hobbs?"

Was he picturing Ruby Jane in the flashy gown? Was he imagining how much better the saloon girl would look in it than she herself had? "Yes. Miss Olive earns spending money making gowns for Ruby Jane and her friends." She decided to turn the conversation to a more neutral topic. "What did you do with your baggage?"

"It's at the train station. I'll send someone for it after I check in at the hotel."

"Did you have any problems finding Barrows House?" Keep talking, she told herself. Don't think about how warm it feels where his skin touches yours.

"You've called it that before. Where does the name come from?"

She waved back the way they'd come. "Augustus Barrows, my great-grandfather, built it nearly sixty years ago. It's still called Barrows House, even though there hasn't been a Barrows living in it since my grandmother died."

"I see. And, no, I didn't have any problems finding it. Your directions were quite sufficient." His lips twitched. "It seems to be something of a landmark."

Maddy relaxed as she shared his smile. Barrows House was anything but unassuming. Located on the edge of town, her home was a sunflower-yellow, multi-gabled structure, and easily the largest home in Pepper Cloud. Square, substantial and three stories high, it was rescued from a box-like appearance by two notable features. The first was a spacious wrap-around porch, cozily furnished with a roomy swing and a number of comfortably worn chairs. The second was an overabundance of decorative fretwork. The fanciful curls and lattices adorned the house like elaborate frosting on a wedding cake.

"Good afternoon, Maddy."

Maddy paused, looking over the low picket fence to the woman who'd hailed her. The town's schoolteacher sat back on her knees, pruning shears in hand and her floppy bonnet pushed to the back of her head.

"Hello, Blanche. Your roses look lovelier every day." Blanche Crawford was a passionate gardener. One couldn't pay her a finer compliment than to praise her plants.

"Why, thank you, dear." The schoolteacher's gaze turned to Mr. Kincaid with obvious interest.

Maddy took her cue. "Allow me to introduce Mr. Clayton Kincaid. He's that cousin of Winston's I told you about. Mr. Kincaid, this is my neighbor and the town's schoolteacher, Miss Blanche Crawford."

Blanche fussed with her hair as she returned Mr. Kincaid's smile. "Welcome to Pepper Cloud, sir. I hope you enjoy your stay."

He gave a short, elegant bow. "Thank you, ma'am. I'm sure I will."

Maddy waved, and she and Mr. Kincaid moved on.

"Is she one of the people up in arms over your adoption plans?"

Maddy nodded at another of her neighbors but didn't stop this time. "You mean Blanche? No. At least, not overtly so."

"So, who is the real target of your little campaign?"

The Pepper Cloud Propriety Police. Maddy decided Mr. Kincaid probably wouldn't appreciate her irreverent nickname for the town's social arbiters. "Cybil Flaherty, Lavinia Thompson, and Vera Welborne—most of my fellow officers of the Pepper Cloud Ladies' Society." Maddy tried to keep her tone light. "They've made Katie's welfare their latest crusade."

"And you don't consider that an admirable cause?"

Was he questioning her judgment? "I'm afraid they have a different view than I do on what is best for Katie."

"Meaning they don't think she should be left with you?"

"Exactly." She fought the urge to defend herself. She did enough of that with Cybil and company. Instead, she gave him further instructions. "Lavinia Thompson's husband owns and operates the hotel. She'll undoubtedly be nearby when you register, so be prepared for prying questions. Lavinia's a terrible gossip."

"I'll be at my charming best."

Maddy frowned, irritated by his flippant attitude. "You don't plan to flirt with her, do you? She *is* a married woman."

"Mrs. Potter, you're going to have to trust me to handle this in my own way. I assure you I won't do anything inappropriate."

Why wasn't she reassured by his words?

They turned a corner, and the residences gave way to small shops and businesses. Maddy returned greetings as they strolled along the sidewalk, but otherwise pretended not to notice the attention the two of them attracted. Curiously, it was more difficult to ignore the warm feeling it gave her to be seen on the arm of a charming man.

A few moments later she felt a subtle stiffening in Mr. Kincaid as he glanced down the street. An expression she couldn't quite read flitted across his face.

Following his gaze, she spied Joey Brennan braced on the roof of Welborne's Mercantile. The strapping youth was pulling the slack out of a thick rope that stretched high across Main Street. Directly across the street, Harvey Thompson leaned over the third floor balcony of the Rosethorne Hotel, testing the security of the knot he'd made on the other end of the rope. They were stringing up a

bright yellow-and-blue banner proclaiming the upcoming
Founder's Day celebration.

Joey caught sight of Maddy and nodded over his shoulder
to the banner. "Hey, Mrs. Potter, does it look centered to
you?"

"It's perfect, Joey. Go ahead and tie it off."

From the corner of her eye, she noted that Mr. Kincaid's
flash of emotion, if it had been there at all, had been replaced by an urbane smile. A slight movement in his arm
drew her gaze to his hand. In a gesture she was certain he
was quite unaware of, his thumb worried at the heavy band
of a signet ring he wore on his third finger.

He paused and Maddy realized they'd reached the open
front doors of the Rosethorne. "Here we are," she announced unnecessarily. Then she caught sight of someone
exiting the bank next door. "Mayor Flaherty, a moment
please."

The tall, white-haired gentleman turned at her hail.
"Good day, Mrs. Potter," he greeted her as he approached.
"Is there something I can do for you?"

"As a matter of fact, yes. I was just headed over to your
office to have a word with you on an investment matter.
But first let me introduce you to someone." She turned to
her visitor. "This is Mr. Clayton Kincaid. He's a cousin of
Winston's from back East and will be visiting Pepper Cloud
for a few weeks."

As the mayor extended his hand in welcome, she executed the second half of the introductions. "Mr. Kincaid,
this is Pepper Cloud's mayor, Milton Flaherty."

"Welcome to Pepper Cloud, Mr. Kincaid." The mayor's
voice had taken on that overly hearty tone Maddy secretly
thought of as his mayoral voice. "I trust you'll enjoy your
stay here. We might be a small town, but I challenge you
to find a friendlier one on either side of the Mississippi."

"Thank you, I'm looking forward to my stay." Mr. Kincaid released the mayor's hand, then cut Maddy a bland

smile. "Mrs. Potter has already given me a taste of just how friendly your town can be."

Maddy chose to ignore the sardonic message his eyes sent her. "Well, Mr. Kincaid, I'll leave you to register and get settled in. Don't forget, Miss Fanny serves supper at seven."

Mr. Kincaid took his cue, and with a short bow of farewell, took his leave of them. Telling herself that his dimpled-chin smile had had no affect on her whatsoever, Maddy put her soon-to-be-suitor from her mind as she turned to the mayor.

"Now," she said, giving him an I'm-ready-to-hang-onto-your-every-word smile, "if you can spare me a few minutes . . ."

"Would you care for a roll, Mr. Kincaid?"

"Yes, thank you." Clay accepted the bread basket from Miss Olive. He took one of the warm, yeasty bread rolls, then offered the basket to Miss Adeline, seated on his other side.

Miss Adeline accepted with a slight nod of her head and a regally uttered "thank you." She had traded her black wig for a top-heavy, powdered affair suitable for Marie Antoinette, herself. Apparently, she also traded personalities along with her headgear. No longer mimicking a sultry Egyptian seductress, she was now the epitome of a cool European aristocrat. Her theatrical training, no doubt.

Lavinia Thompson had been all too eager to tell him about that, and more. Just as Mrs. Potter had predicted, the hotel proprietor's wife had pounced on him as soon as he'd registered. She'd tried getting his entire history from him, but a lifetime of dealing with social sycophants had made him adept at sidestepping such questions. When the topic turned to the ladies of Barrows House, though, he shamelessly let her chatter on.

She'd spoken in scandalized overtones of Miss Olive's and Miss Adeline's former careers with a traveling acting

39

troupe. Her manner had turned pitying when she mentioned poor, dear Fanny's insistence that she could still speak to her dead husband. And a motherly concern had crept in when she mentioned Katie, orphaned only a few months ago.

Clay glanced across the food-laden table and met Miss Fanny's expectant gaze. He finished chewing the bite of succulent roast beef he'd just popped into his mouth, and flashed her a smile. "My compliments, ma'am, on a delicious meal."

Miss Fanny's cheeks pinkened in pleasure. "Why, thank you. This particular recipe is one of Mr. Wimberly's favorites." She turned and murmured a few words to the empty chair beside her, then smiled as if she'd received a response. No one else batted an eyelash.

"I helped," Katie piped in from Miss Fanny's other side. The child, still small enough to require several large tomes be placed in her chair to provide height, apparently took her meals with the adults.

Clay saluted with his fork. "Then my compliments to you, as well."

Katie beamed proudly. "I helped with the dessert, too. It's something special—chocolate cake. Miss Adeline asked Miss Fanny to make it 'cause it's an aphro—aphro-tee-sic."

Mrs. Potter's strangled cough drew everyone's gaze to the head of the table.

Clay studied her red-faced struggles to compose herself with a barely controlled grin. Apparently the proper-widow side of her had trouble with such talk in mixed company.

But it did make him wonder just what other inappropriate conversations Katie was being exposed to.

His concern over assisting these women in gaining control of Katie's future rose. Lavinia Thompson had said they'd been unable to locate any relative of the child's after her mother's death. But how thoroughly had they searched? Perhaps he would set a few inquiries in motion himself. There was a discreet, reliable firm his family used to investigate sensitive matters. Checking out Katie's family tree would be a simple matter for Peterson's able staff.

Mrs. Potter finally regained her composure, though her color was still flatteringly high. After a quick, telling glance directed toward a bland-faced Miss Adeline, she turned to Clay, smiling politely, as if Katie's faux pas had never occurred. "Well, Mr. Kincaid, I must warn you that going through Winston's papers won't be an easy task. They're not arranged in any sort of organized manner. In fact, I'm afraid I packed his personal items together all higgledy-piggledy and stored them in a spare room after his death."

Clay, still concerned with the cavalier care Katie seemed to be receiving, gave Mrs. Potter his most tolerant smile. "That's understandable. One wouldn't expect a lady such as yourself to worry her pretty little head over something like her husband's papers."

Miss Fanny beamed. "Oh, Mr. Kincaid, you sound just like my Lester. He always said it was a man's place to shield his women from matters of business and politics."

"A very responsible attitude," Clay responded solemnly. He took a swallow from his glass, noting with satisfaction that Mrs. Potter's expression had stiffened.

"Really, Miss Fanny," she said, stabbing a carrot with her fork. "I'm not one of Mr. Kincaid's women." Then her cheeks reddened. "I mean, Mr. Kincaid has no need to feel any responsibility for me."

Clay aimed his most charming smile her way. "On the contrary, as Winston's cousin, I feel I have a responsibility to do what I can for you during the time I'm here. While I'm looking through Winston's papers, I'll be glad to organize his files and explain anything I come across that may have some significance to you."

Miss Adeline gave him an approving nod. "It's so nice to have a man around to take care of these tiresome business matters. Don't you agree, Maddy?"

Miss Olive cleared her throat. "Mr. Kincaid, would you mind passing me the bowl of potatoes, please?"

Clay obeyed her request, wondering if the prim spinster had deliberately forestalled Mrs. Potter's retort. If so, her innocent expression and politely uttered thanks gave nothing away.

"Just what is it you're looking for?" Miss Fanny gave him a child-like smile from across the table. She'd obviously noticed nothing amiss in the prior conversation.

Before Clay could respond, Mrs. Potter intervened. "Mr. Kincaid is here to look for a deed to some family property that he thinks may be among Winston's papers."

Miss Fanny nodded and then ducked her head toward the empty seat beside her. Looking up, she met Clay's gaze. "Mr. Wimberly just remarked that seven years is a long time to wait to lay claim to a piece of property."

"Yes, it most certainly is," Clay answered before Mrs. Potter could steal the conversational reins again. "But ownership just became an issue recently when my family decided to expand our farm operation."

"But if the property was Winston's, surely it is now Maddy's, not yours?" This time it was Miss Adeline who spoke up, and there was a surprising element of steel in her voice.

Clay turned to her, digging into the role he'd been assigned and making it his own. "I'm afraid not. This particular piece of land is entailed in such a manner that it always passes down to the closest male heir. Since Cousin Maddy wasn't aware this parcel existed until I contacted her, I hope she won't hold any hard feelings about it."

He was watching "Cousin Maddy" from the corner of his eye as he said this, so he caught the startled glance she shot him at the familiar address. She recovered quickly though, with only a hint of strain in her smile as she responded to his statement.

"Of *course* I won't harbor any ill will toward you. The property was meant to remain in the Potter family, so it is only fair that Winston's family reclaim it."

Miss Adeline, however, didn't seem entirely convinced.

She studied Clay as a queen would study a messenger bringing unhappy news. "But your name is Kincaid, sir, not Potter. Why should the property revert to you?"

It seemed Maddy Potter commanded a high degree of loyalty from her household. Or were they just a mercenary lot? "I'm afraid Grandfather had only one son, Winston's father. So now the estate must pass down through the female line, which makes my mother the heir."

"That's right," Mrs. Potter chimed in. "Thank you for your concern Miss Adeline, but Mr. Kincaid explained all of this to me in his letter. He's also provided documentation to satisfy me that his claim on the property is legitimate."

Miss Adeline gave a regal nod. "Forgive me if I sounded suspicious, sir. I was merely concerned for Maddy's sake. She tends to be overly trusting when dealing with others. And a windfall of that sort would not be ill-received right now."

Mrs. Potter quickly dismissed her friend's concern. "Nonsense, Miss Adeline. We've gotten along all these years without it and we're perfectly capable of continuing to do so in the future."

But it would be easy for the widow to cavalierly wave away her claim to an asset she knew to be fictitious. Were the ladies of Barrows House experiencing some financial difficulties? Again, the specter of this being an elaborate rouse to cover a matchmaking scheme reared its head.

Pushing her chair back from the table, Miss Fanny stood. "It appears everyone has finished their meal. Katie, why don't you help me serve the dessert?"

The two Barrows House chefs moved to the sideboard where an elegant silver cake plate held a position of honor. Lifting the cover with a flourish, Miss Fanny revealed a dark chocolate confection topped by a jewel-like crown of cherries. As she cut thick slabs of the cake, Katie proudly distributed them to the diners.

Once everyone was served, and the pair resumed their

seats, Miss Adeline dug in with relish. "Uhmm-uhmm, Fanny, you've outdone yourself. This cake is sinfully delicious."

Clay watched Mrs. Potter's fork hover over her slice without actually digging in. From the peculiar expression on her face, he guessed she was remembering Katie's mangled aphrodisiac reference. The widow looked as if she thought the dessert might suddenly spring to life and attack her.

With a challenging grin, he caught her gaze and tackled his own slice with gusto.

Her cheeks suffused with a dull ruddy color, but she lifted her chin gamely and speared a bite of cake. Their gazes locked as they both chewed the rich, moist, chocolate dessert. Suddenly, it was a contest of wills, and Clay would be damned if he'd glance away first. He swallowed with exaggerated relish, then took another bite without breaking eye contact.

Clay felt supremely confident of his ability to best his "partner" at this, at least. But the longer he stared into her expressive blue-green eyes, the less he saw of her "genteel widow" guise, and the more he remembered the hoyden he'd first encountered.

The aphrodisiac reference no longer seemed quite so amusing.

Peripherally, he noticed a tiny crumb clinging to the corner of her mouth. Fascinated, he watched it quiver and tremble with each movement of her jaw, but it clung there tenaciously, refusing to abandon her lusciously full lips. Then her tongue darted out to capture it, drawing it into her mouth with unconscious sensuality.

Or *was* it unconscious?

Who was the real Mrs. Potter—the prim and proper widow, or the free-spirited, slightly naughty hoyden?

Chapter Four

Katie let out a squeal, blessedly ending their standoff.

Clay gave himself a mental shake, feeling as if he'd been released from a spell. For just a moment, those siren's eyes and rich full lips had made him forget the widow's weeds and prickly character of the woman who bore them.

Glad no one else had noticed his lapse, he followed suit with the others and turned in the direction Katie pointed.

Othello stalked across the polished maple sideboard, his eyes firmly fixed on the chocolate cake. Clay, glad of the excuse to push away from the table, marched to the sideboard and plopped the lid back on the cake plate, neatly cutting off a furry-pawed swipe.

Othello yowled, regarding Clay with narrow-eyed dislike. Then the cat jumped to the floor and, with tail-high hauteur, minced his way to his mistress's side.

Miss Adeline regally ignored the censorious looks leveled at her pet. As she reached down to scratch the feline's ears, she aimed a mild frown across the table. "Fanny, dear, you really must learn to keep the food covered when it's not on the table. It's not right to tease poor Othello with things he can't have."

Miss Fanny stiffened and Clay could see an indignant retort forming on her tongue. But before she could say anything, Mrs. Potter intervened. "I believe it's time we adjourn to the parlor. Miss Fanny, why don't you escort our guest. It's my turn to clear the table."

Miss Olive pushed her chair back. "Nonsense, dear. You took care of it last night. That makes it my turn and I'm sure Katie will keep me company. Now, run along with the others. I'll join you in just a bit."

As they moved toward the parlor, Clay found himself beside Miss Fanny.

"I'm sorry we don't have spirits to offer you, Mr. Kincaid. Mr. Wimberly did so enjoy his brandy and cigar after dinner."

Clay stood aside, allowing the ladies to precede him into the parlor. He gave them his most winning smile. "Don't let it worry you, ma'am. Pleasant company such as this is all the after-dinner stimulation I need."

Miss Fanny beamed in response. Even Miss Adeline's lady-of-the-manor expression warmed, as if to say she was not above dallying with the common folk.

Mrs. Potter, however, sailed past him without so much as a sideways glance. He'd never met a woman so immune to his charm before. Not that he wanted her to fawn over him. But you'd think she'd at least pretend to view him with some measure of warmth, considering the roles they were supposed to be playing.

The ladies took their seats, Miss Fanny and Maddy Potter on the settee, Miss Adeline on one of a pair of delicately carved chairs across from them. Clay commandeered a sturdy looking armchair that placed him at the head of the table, so to speak, as he faced the space between the settee and the chairs.

"So, Mr. Kincaid." Miss Adeline stroked the cat stretched out on her lap. "How is it that a handsome, charming man such as yourself is still unattached? Do you harbor an aversion to married life?"

Why did women always see his single status as an ill to be cured? But a warning look from "Cousin Maddy" reminded him he'd promised to play a part. Very well, but he'd do this his way.

"Not at all," he replied, leaning toward Miss Adeline earnestly. "In fact, I don't believe a man is truly complete without a family of his own." Which was absolutely true, as far as it went. He spread his hands, allowing a bit of melancholy to shadow his tone. "Unfortunately, I've yet to meet a woman whose character meshes with mine in the proper manner." Also very true.

"Perhaps the fault is not with the ladies of your acquaintance, but with your expectations," his hostess offered dryly. "If you are seeking perfection then you are doomed to disappointment."

Clay thought sourly that that sounded very much like something his mother would say. If Mrs. Potter wanted to conduct their courtship with verbal sparring, however, he was quite willing to follow her lead.

"Not at all." He kept his expression carefully earnest. "I'm well aware that every person has flaws. In fact, I consider myself a prime example."

Clay rubbed his chin, striking a thoughtful pose. "It's hard to put into words just what I'm looking for. Naturally, she must be demure and ladylike. No man wants to shackle himself to a bossy or brash woman." He watched his would-be fiancée from the corner of his eye, taking devilish pleasure in her frown. "And it goes without saying that she must be honest—I can't abide liars or cheats."

He shrugged. "Beyond that, I'm looking for intelligence and humor, and someone who shares interests and opinions similar to mine."

"Now, don't you give up," Miss Fanny offered with a motherly tsk. "I think you're on the right track, and Mr.

47

Wimberly agrees. Those are all fine qualities and I'm sure you'll find her someday."

Mrs. Potter, her eyes flashing, appeared less sympathetic. "So, your idea of the ideal woman is a meek, mannerly mouse, who is so spiritless she takes on your thoughts and goals as her own?" She gave him a pitying smile. "What an orderly, peaceful, *bland* future you plan for yourself."

Clay straightened in his seat. "That's not—"

"Hello, doesn't everyone look comfortable." Miss Olive breezed into the room, Katie at her heels. "Katie and I decided to let the dishes soak for a bit." She took a seat on the chair beside Miss Adeline.

Katie plopped on the settee between the other two ladies and turned to Miss Fanny. "Are you gonna play the piano for us tonight?"

Miss Fanny's cheeks pinkened and she fluttered her hands. "Oh Katie, I don't think Mr. Kincaid wants to hear—"

"Of course he does, dear," Miss Olive interrupted. "We all do."

"Miss Fanny used to teach piano," Mrs. Potter added. "And she was an accompanist for the church choir for more years than I can count."

Clay stood. "Well then, no question about it, you must play for us. Please, allow me to escort you to the piano."

Miss Fanny placed a hand to her bosom. She looked from Clay to the others in the room, then back to Clay. "Well, if you're really sure. . . ." She rose and Clay tucked her hand securely in the crook of his arm. Once he'd settled her on the piano bench, he moved to stand beside the fireplace, leaning comfortably against the low mantel.

As the music started, Katie shifted, leaning back against her "Aunt Maddy." The widow's arm slipped around the child's shoulder, giving her a light squeeze and settling her more comfortably against her side. A few minutes later she began to fiddle with the child's hair, stroking and finger combing the golden tresses. Mrs. Potter had a soft glow about her, seeming both tender and vulnerable as she mothered the little girl. The sweet domestic picture she and Katie made was at odds with his earlier impression that the child was not being cared for properly.

How long had it been since he'd spent an evening like this with his own family, teased his sisters about their latest beaux, watched his mother preside over a family gathering? Perhaps, when this little family obligation was satisfied, he'd take a trip to the Kincaid estate in Virginia for a few weeks before he returned to his office in New Orleans.

Miss Fanny proved to be an excellent pianist, playing snippets of music that moved effortlessly from quiet to exuberant pieces, from classical to modern tunes. She obviously enjoyed performing, and entertained them for nearly thirty minutes. When she'd finished, Katie was yawning and struggling to keep her eyes open.

Clay stepped forward and offered a hand to help Miss Fanny rise. Then he sketched a short bow. "That was truly delightful, ma'am."

He turned to include the others in his gaze. "My thanks for the meal and the pleasant company, ladies, but it's been a long day and I find I'm ready to retire. So I'll make my farewells and look forward to seeing you all again tomorrow. Shall we plan for ten o'clock?"

His hostess gently disengaged from Katie and stood. "That sounds fine, Mr. Kincaid. I'll see you to the door."

He held up a hand. "It would give me great pleasure, ma'am, if you'd address me by my given name. After all, we are cousins, of sorts."

She seemed momentarily nonplussed by his suggestion, but recovered quickly. "Of course." She leaned down, touching Katie's shoulder. "Why don't you let Miss Fanny take you upstairs to get ready for bed, Buttercup. I'll be up in a little while to tuck you in."

As Clay escorted the widow out onto the front porch, he felt a soft breeze tease the hair at his collar. It was dark now, but the moon was full, and the street lamps cast warm pools of light at regular intervals.

"Mr. Kincaid—"

He shook an admonishing finger. "First names, remember?"

Her lips pursed.

"I was sure you'd be pleased," he continued, as if she'd commended him. "After all, we need to dispense with all these cumbersome formalities as soon as possible if we're to begin enacting this little courting ritual you're orchestrating."

She gave a grudging nod, then frowned. "I feel I must caution you, sir. If you thought your little speech at supper about taking care of business matters was what I meant when I told you to be solicitous, you are mistaken."

Clay spread his hands. "My apologies. I'm sure I'll do better as I get more comfortable with the role." He took her hand and gave it a squeeze, feeling her pulse jump in response. "Now, you'd best wipe that stern look off your face. Remember, we're always on display. And I do believe the parlor curtains just moved."

Her eyes shifted, but to her credit she didn't turn around. Instead she returned his smile with an almost-genuine one of her own. "Then we'd best appear to be friends, had we not?"

"My thoughts exactly." He lifted her hand to his lips for what he intended to be a courtly farewell salute. As soon as his lips touched her flesh, however, a spark of awareness ignited, sharpening his senses.

The chirping of crickets played counterpoint to the deep-throated croak of a frog in the otherwise still night. He caught a faint whiff of the scent she wore, a combination of rose and lavender. The sweet smell of honeysuckle wafted by on the breeze, almost overpowering her more subtle perfume. Despite what he'd said earlier, the night shadows gave the illusion of privacy.

Clay gave himself a mental shake, irritated by the direction his thoughts had taken. What was wrong with him? He barely knew this woman, had some questions about her motives, and she'd made him party to a scheme he had strong reservations about. And she'd made it abundantly clear, more than once, that she didn't altogether approve of him, either.

No, he couldn't be attracted to her—it was just reaction to the setting and the long day he'd endured.

He had himself back under control now, though. She wanted to put on a performance for her friends and neighbors, did she? Perhaps it was time to let her see that he intended to add some of his own lines to her script.

Clay allowed his lips to linger on her hand while his finger stroked the underside of her delicate wrist. Her pulse jumped again. He straightened slowly, retaining his hold on her hand as he offered her his most seductive smile.

He felt a smug satisfaction when a light shiver fluttered her shoulders and her eyes widened with a startled, doe-like intensity. Apparently she wasn't as immune to the Kincaid charm as she'd like to have him believe.

Her lips parted slightly, drawing his gaze with the sultry promise of a siren's song. If he kissed those full, lush lips, would they live up to their promise of rose-petal softness and warmed-honey sweetness?

His head had already lowered toward hers when he suddenly came to his senses. For the second time.

Blast! What was wrong with him?

He leaned back, forcing himself to give her a lazy grin. "That's probably enough of a show for the first night, don't you think?"

As if he'd dashed cold water in her face, her head snapped up and her expression lost its soft, unfocused quality. She looked as if she wanted to slap his face.

Was it because he'd gone too far?

Or because he hadn't gone far enough?

"Yes, quite enough," she agreed with a short nod. "Good night, *Cousin Clayton*. I'll see you in the morning."

He gave her a farewell salute and set off down the front walk, whistling a jaunty tune.

But jaunty was the last thing he was feeling.

Seems it would be more difficult to remain distant while he played Romeo to her Juliet than he'd first imagined.

Maddy leaned against the closed front door for a moment, Mr. Kincaid's—no, Cousin Clayton's carefree whistle taunting her even as it faded.

She gripped her hands to quiet the shaking. Thank goodness that particular reaction had waited until he walked away.

Of course it had all been an act, and a very good one, too. It was her own fault she'd let herself believe, just for a moment, that he felt some genuine attraction. He'd only been doing what she'd instructed him to do. How could she have forgotten—

A noise from the parlor brought her head up, reminding her she wasn't alone. Time to pull herself back together. She pushed away from the door and moved to the stairway, determinedly ignoring the roiling of her stomach. It was time to tuck Katie in for the night. Consistency and order were important to a child.

They were important to her, too. Not that she couldn't deal with the occasional break in routine or spontaneous display, she assured herself. After all, look at the household she maintained. She was rather proud of the fact that the ladies of Barrows House were considered eccentrics by the small community of Pepper Cloud. It was just that today had been rather more full of surprises than a body could rightly be expected to absorb in so short a space of time.

She used the handrail for support as she trudged up the stairs. Why had Clayton come a day early? Why couldn't he have been the kind of man she'd described in her letter? And why had he made her remember that she could never, ever let herself love another man?

Well, she had Clayton Kincaid's measure now. He obviously wasn't accustomed to taking orders, and seemed to be in the habit of using his charm to get his way. It wasn't realistic to think she could change him in the short time available, so she'd just have to figure out how to use his arrogant manner to suit her purpose.

Not an easy charge, but not impossible. After all, she only had to make it through four weeks of what he'd called their "courting ritual" and then she could settle back into the comfortable, familiar life with the family she'd built for herself.

She put aside her fear that Clayton I'll-do-it-my-way-thank-you-very-much Kincaid would somehow change her world forever as she reached the door to Katie's room. The tucking-in routine was too precious to taint with cloudy emotions.

She stepped inside the girl's room to find her still awake. "Hello, Buttercup. Sorry to take so long."

"That's okay." Katie squirmed her way to a half-sitting, half-reclining position. "Is Mr. Kincaid gone?"

Maddy sat on the edge of the bed. "Uh-huh. But he'll be back in the morning."

"He's nice, isn't he? And pretty, too."

Maddy grinned, picturing how the very manly Mr. Kincaid would react to *that* description. "Yes, I suppose he *is* rather good-looking. But men prefer to be called handsome rather than pretty."

Katie placed her arms on top of the covers. "Well then, he's a very handsome man." She grinned excitedly. "He let me play with his pocket watch. It has a bird design on the outside of it. But it's nothing like Sweetie Pie. He called it an eagle."

"Is that right?" Maddy tried to sound suitably impressed.

"Yes ma'am. I bet he'd let you play with it, too, if you asked him."

"Perhaps." Maddy refrained from further comment. Instead she changed the subject. "Now, have you said your prayers?"

Katie nodded, allowing Maddy to help her slide back down under the covers. "Miss Olive listened to me. But I told her I wanted you to sing my lullaby 'cause your singing makes me feel all warm and snuggly inside."

Maddy felt her throat tighten at this unexpected tribute. The love and trust shining up at her from the child's eyes both humbled and uplifted her.

She gave Katie's shoulder a gentle squeeze and spoke past the lump in her throat. "I'm glad you did, because singing to you makes me feel all warm and snuggly inside, too." She reached over to turn down the lamp, then gave the little girl a bracing smile. "Now, close your eyes."

As she sang the soft strains of Katie's favorite lullaby, she mulled over the miracle of a child's love. Amazing and wondrous what having Katie in her life just these few short months had done for her. She couldn't have loved the child more if she'd been her own flesh and blood.

Her plan to adopt Katie had to succeed, regardless of Mr. Kincaid's shortcomings.

The alternative was too bleak to contemplate.

"All of Winston's things are stored in here." Maddy stopped in front of the door at the end of the second-floor hallway. Ridiculous for her heart to be beating so quickly, for her hands to be so clammy.

Concentrate on something else, she told herself. Like remembering to address Mr. Kincaid as Cousin Clayton.

Her unlikely suitor stepped past her to open the door. He swept his arm out in a broad gesture. "After you."

Realizing he'd noted her hesitation, Maddy forced a serene smile and sailed past him, stepping into the room for the first time in seven years. She looked around and slowly relaxed. Why had she been so apprehensive? There weren't any ghosts to confront her here, no misty shade of Winston to stare at her with gentle accusation in his eyes.

The only thing here besides the mismatched and frayed pieces of furniture was a daunting number of packing containers in every size, shape and composition imaginable.

A low, incredulous whistle sounded from behind her. She turned to see Mr. Kincaid studying the contents of the room, an eyebrow quirked in disbelief. "Good heavens, you weren't exaggerating about the job ahead of us, were you?"

Maddy spread her hands. "I tried to warn you."

The boxes were everywhere—in orderly rows along the floorboards, on the tops of the furniture, even under the scarred wooden desk. There were trunks, crates, cartons and hatboxes. At least there weren't layers of dust covering everything. Though Maddy had avoided this room, the other ladies had seen that it was periodically cleaned and aired along with the rest of Barrows House.

"Are these arranged in any kind of order?" His tone indicated he didn't hold out much hope.

She grinned and shook her head. "I'm afraid not." She sobered as her gaze scanned the contents of the room. "Winston was the type who never threw anything out. When he died, I just packed everything away until I could tackle sorting through it. After a while, it just didn't seem important."

Then she turned back to him with a reassuring smile. "But don't worry, we're only pretending to look for that fictitious document, remember? We don't have to expend much effort in the attempt, we just need to make sure it appears we're diligently searching."

His expression had already lost that dazed quality. "We're going to be stuck in here for the greater part of the next four weeks," he said, shrugging out of his coat, "so we might as well put the time to good use." He draped his coat over the back of a chair and rolled up his sleeves, exposing well muscled arms dusted with fine hairs. "There's no telling what documents might be buried in the midst of all this flotsam."

He crossed the room like a captain on deck of his ship. "This desk will make a good work bench. We can clear it off and move it out to the middle of the room. Then we'll start tackling the boxes one at a time." He lifted the first of four crates from the desk and set it on the floor.

As he reached for the next one, Maddy couldn't help but admire the ease with which he handled the task. When he hefted the container, his shirt stretched tightly across his back and arms, displaying an impressive masculine physique.

She shook off those inappropriate thoughts and bustled over to help him, but he waved her away. "I'll take care of this. You find some writing materials so we can catalog any important papers we might uncover."

By the time Maddy returned, he had not only moved the desk, he'd rearranged some of the boxes, clearing the area in front of one wall.

He nodded approvingly when he saw she'd brought the requested items. "Good. Now, here's how I suggest we tackle this. We'll go through one box at a time and sort the contents into separate piles." He gestured broadly. "One pile will be for business documents that you need to keep, such as investment certificates or property deeds. Another will be for items you want to keep for purely sentimental reasons, such as pictures or other mementos. Then the last, which will undoubtedly be the largest, will be for items that should be discarded entirely."

He bent down to lift a lopsided hatbox onto the top of the desk. There was a virile energy to his movements, a masculine grace that took her by surprise. He obviously wasn't a stranger to physical labor.

"Anything that doesn't go into the discard pile," he instructed, "should be cataloged and filed in some logical manner so you can readily locate it when you need to." He paused with his hand on the lid of the box. "Any questions?"

If she'd had any doubts about him liking to be in control, they were put to rest now. Oddly enough, it didn't bother her as much as it would have normally.

"Only why you feel the need to work at this so hard."

Not that the thought of the work bothered her. She was quite proud of how little impact being among Winston's things was having on her. Was it because Mr. Kincaid's presence provided such an interesting distraction? Still, the busier she could keep herself while she was here, the better.

He shrugged. "There's no better way to make this search appear real than to approach it as if it were."

She supposed that made sense.

He opened the hatbox, revealing a messy collection of papers and ledgers. Taking a deep breath, Maddy prepared to help him sort through the jumble.

Clay rolled his shoulders as he leafed through a handful of faded receipts. They'd been working steadily for an hour and a half now. He had to give the devil his due; though his "partner" clearly had doubts as to the value of what they were doing, she'd attacked the task with efficiency and vigor. Seems she wasn't afraid of hard work.

Surprisingly, once they'd forgotten they were acting out roles, they'd worked well together. And over the course of the morning they'd moved from the stiffly polite "Cousin Clayton" and "Cousin Maddy" appellations, to just plain Clay and Maddy.

He held the papers up in one hand. "These are about five years worth of receipts for rental payments on a property at three twenty-four Main Street."

Maddy looked up from the notes she'd been making. "That was Winston's law office. I think we can safely throw those away."

One thing he'd discovered about Maddy Potter this morning, given the fact that she'd been in strict mourning for seven years, she was surprisingly without false sentimentality. The vast majority of the items they'd sorted through had gone into the discard pile with barely a second look from her.

Clay cast another glance at her classicly lovely profile, then turned back to dig through the ancient portmanteau.

It was the third receptacle they'd tackled this morning. The dented case overflowed with a hodgepodge of what looked like personal, mostly discardable, items.

The papers shifted and he caught sight of a book that looked more interesting than the ledgers they'd already unearthed. He grabbed hold and pulled out a large, leather-bound Bible.

She accepted it from him. "Winston's family Bible. He was an only son." Her expression closed, turned unreadable. "There's no one to pass it on to." She stood and carried the Bible across the room toward the box where they were packing the small pile of personal items she planned to keep.

Clay, at a loss for something to say, turned back to the portmanteau. He lifted a small ledger and then froze. There, looking up at him, was an unframed photograph of Maddy and a distinguished-looking gentleman. They were posed quite formally, standing side by side, with shoulders back and eyes facing the camera.

But this Maddy was younger than the Maddy of today, and not just in years. The light-colored dress and loosely styled hair softened her appearance. And even in the stilted pose, the girl in the picture exuded a kind of shy, youthful enthusiasm for life. What had happened in the ensuing years to replace that open optimism with the guarded control she exhibited now?

He noticed the Maddy in the picture held a beribboned nosegay of flowers, and realized that this must be her wedding picture. Which made the man in the photograph Winston.

He studied the image more closely, curious in spite of himself. He was surprised to note that Winston appeared to be much older than Maddy, a dozen years at least. He was of medium height and build, with light-colored hair and a trim mustache. His clothes seemed well-made and he wore spectacles, which gave him a studious, no-nonsense look. Not a handsome man, exactly but—

"What are you looking at?"

Clay started at the nearness of her voice. She'd crossed back to his side without him noticing. Before he could answer, she looked past him and spied the picture.

Her breath caught audibly. Instead of her expression closing off as it had before, a keen flash of some painful emotion drained the color from her face, caused her fists to clench with white-knuckled intensity.

He touched her arm, feeling the need to offer comfort. "Maddy, are you all right?"

She straightened and offered him a caricature of a smile. "Yes. . . . Of course. Forgive me, I'd just forgotten about that picture. Winston had it taken on our wedding day." She stared back down at the photograph. "He had someone come in special from St. Louis just to take it. He liked to do generous, unexpected things like that."

She turned back to him. "I think we've done enough for one morning," she said briskly. "Why don't we go down and see if Miss Fanny's ready to serve lunch."

Clay reluctantly moved his hand from her arm. She probably needed a few minutes to herself. "You go on ahead. I'll bundle up some of this unwanted stuff we've weeded out and carry it down to put with the trash. It'll give us more room to spread out our work."

After only a second's hesitation, she nodded and left the room.

Clay began to toss unwanted items into one of the emptied crates. Being able to read people was a skill he prided himself on. He didn't have a single doubt that the reaction she'd just had to that photograph was genuine. It seemed her drawn-out mourning period hadn't stemmed from an exaggerated sense of duty or even an eccentric conceit. She obviously still had deep feelings for her former husband.

What manner of man could inspire such raw emotion after an absence of seven years?

What would it be like to have someone love him so devotedly?

He looked at the picture again, and frowned. This image of Winston matched perfectly the description Maddy had sent Judith of the kind of man she preferred to play the part of her suitor. Had that been deliberate or coincidental? Was this truly the kind of man she was drawn to?

For the first time in his life, Clay knew what it felt like to lack confidence in his ability to attract a woman.

Chapter Five

"That was another excellent meal, Miss Fanny." Clay pushed away from the table and stood, as did the ladies.

He watched Maddy wipe Katie's chin with the corner of her napkin. She'd recovered her composure by the time he followed her down the stairs earlier. Over lunch, she'd chatted amicably, even engaged in some mild verbal sparring with him, as if nothing had happened. But he sensed she still felt unsettled.

She met his gaze, and her chin tilted up as if she dared him to mention her earlier weakness. "Shall we resume our search?"

Before he could respond, Miss Olive chimed in with a prim tsk. "You two young people spent all morning in that stuffy room digging through musty boxes. Why don't you get out for a spell, enjoy the fresh air. Go for a walk, or better yet, a buggy ride. Maddy, you can show Mr. Kincaid some of the local landmarks."

Maddy tucked a strand of hair behind her ear. "Of course. That is, if Mr. Kincaid is agreeable."

Remembering that Miss Olive was a party to this charade, and that his being seen about town with Maddy was part of his "job," Clay spread his hands. "I am. I'm feeling replete and lazy after that excellent meal. A bit of outdoor activity sounds like just the thing to revive me. Do you ladies have a horse and buggy?"

Maddy nodded. "Yes, we board them at the livery. It's just a short walk past the hotel." She frowned apologetically. "But I'm afraid we'll have to content ourselves with just a stroll today. The Ladies' Society meets here on Tuesdays. We convene in just a little over an hour. I must be back in time to help prepare."

Clay made a short bow. "Then a stroll it'll be."

"Don't worry about hurrying back," Miss Olive offered. "Fanny's preparing the refreshments, and Adeline and I can take care of straightening the parlor."

"Not that the old biddies deserve—"

"Miss Adeline." Maddy's I'll-brook-no-arguments tone squelched the uncomplimentary mumblings of the colorful diva.

"Well they don't." Miss Adeline gifted them all with her haughtiest stare, flipped a long, blond braid over her shoulder, and flounced out of the room carrying the bowl of leftover stew.

"Can I come?" Katie's wistful plea drowned out Maddy's sigh.

Maddy ruffled the child's hair. "Of course. You can help me show Mr. Kincaid around town."

Maddy had seemed just a bit too eager to agree to the girl's request. Was she afraid of what turn the conversation might take if they were alone together?

A few minutes later, they closed the front gate behind them. Clay tucked Maddy's hand on his arm as Katie skipped ahead on the sidewalk.

"So," he said, "the Ladies' Society meets at your house. Isn't that a bit like inviting marauding pirates to board your ship?"

Maddy laughed. He decided she should do that more often. It added a sparkle to her eyes, gave her a younger, softer look.

"That's a rather extreme way of looking at it," she said. "It's a holdover from my grandmother's day. Barrows House has the roomiest parlor of any house in Pepper Cloud and she always enjoyed hosting these things. It's become a deeply entrenched tradition now. Besides, I prefer to think of it as keeping a close watch on the opposition."

Then she sobered. "Actually, Cybil, Lavinia and Vera aren't *bad* people. They do a lot of good work for the community. And they truly think they're doing the right thing for Katie. I just happen to believe I know better."

Her chin thrust out as she spoke, like an Amazon ready to do battle. Did she realize he wasn't entirely on her side in this?

Then she cut him a quick, slightly sheepish glance and lightened her tone. "I think of them as the Propriety Police. Those three have been trying to redeem me since Winston died." She waved a hand. "You'd think by now they'd have given up."

Or that she would have learned to behave more conventionally. But Clay refrained from comment. Besides, he was beginning to enjoy the unconventional aspects of the residents of Barrows House.

"Aunt Maddy."

Katie's excited call drew both their gazes. She was several yards ahead of them, visiting across a picket fence with a girl about her age.

As soon as Katie saw she had their attention, she launched into an animated bit of pleading. "Anna says I can have one of Daisy's new puppies if it's all right with you. Is it? Please?"

Maddy didn't answer Katie directly. Instead, she turned to the other child.

"Hello Anna. I'd like you to meet Mr. Clayton Kincaid. Clay, this is Anna Welborne."

Clay caught the slight emphasis Maddy put on the child's last name, and realized it was the same as one she'd mentioned yesterday. Was this the daughter of one of her Propriety Police?

"Hello Mr. Kincaid," the girl replied, studying him with the open curiosity of a child.

He returned the child's greeting, then Maddy picked up the conversational thread again. "Anna, are you sure you want to give up one of your puppies?"

Anna toyed with the end of her frizzy brown braid. "Yes, ma'am. Daisy had five, and Momma says I can only keep one. They won't be ready to wean for another couple of days, though."

Maddy turned back to Katie with a doubtful look. "A puppy is a big responsibility. It would require a lot of time and attention. He would have to be fed, and played with, and trained, and cleaned up after. And this means every day, even when you have something else you'd rather be doing."

So she intended to teach the child responsibility. That was a point in her favor.

Katie's head bobbed eagerly. "I promise to take real good care of him, Aunt Maddy, you'll see. And I won't let him bother Othello or Sweetie Pie, either."

"Who's Othello and Sweetie Pie?"

Katie turned back to her friend. "Othello is a cat, and Sweetie Pie's a bird."

Anna's eyes grew rounder. "A bird? You have a pet bird at your house?"

"Uh-huh. It's Miss Fanny's. Want to come over and see him?"

Anna bit her lip and then shook her head. "I can't. Momma won't let me go to Barrows House."

Clay felt Maddy stiffen beside him. And well she might. This was obviously one reason why her Propriety Police frowned on her as a guardian for Katie. Maddy might have good intentions and actually care for the child, but her disregard for conventions could hurt the little girl in ways Maddy might never anticipate.

Fortunately, Katie didn't seem to see anything out of the ordinary in the strictures imposed on her friend. She merely shrugged and turned back to Maddy.

"Please, can I have the puppy?"

Maddy nodded. "Very well. But remember, taking care of him will be your responsibility."

Katie's face lit up with excitement. "Oh, thank you, Aunt Maddy. I promise I'll take real good care of him."

Anna moved toward the gate. "Do you want to come up to the house and pick yours out now?"

"Oh, yes!" Katie turned back to Maddy and Clay. "If it's okay?"

Maddy waved a hand. "You go on with Anna. Mr. Kincaid and I will stop back by here to get you when we finish our walk."

Pausing only long enough to grin her thanks, Katie joined Anna, and the two girls raced around to the back of the house.

As he and Maddy resumed their stroll, Clay did a bit of probing. "So, how did Katie come to be in your care in the first place?"

"Katie's family lived on a small farm they leased from me. Six months ago, her father died from a fall. Hester, Katie's mother, was increasing at the time. The Dooley's didn't have any close neighbors or relatives. So, when it came close to time for the baby to arrive, I invited Hester and Katie to stay at Barrows House for a while. Unfortunately, neither Hester nor the baby survived the childbirth. That was in March. Katie's been with us ever since."

It was amazing how generously this woman opened her home to others in need. And now she wanted to add Katie to her already large adopted family. But was that truly in the child's best interest? "And you're sure there are no other relatives?"

Maddy shook her head. "None that I know of. After

Hester died, the Ladies' Society took care of seeing that the livestock was sold off and put the house to rights. We looked through the family Bible and the few papers we came across, but there wasn't anything to help us find Katie's kin, if any even exist."

Clay hoped the investigator he'd hired would have better luck.

"Thank you for that report, Blanche. It sounds as if this year's student pageant will be another uplifting event."

Maddy tried not to fidget as Cybil Flaherty, president of the Pepper Cloud Ladies' Society, quizzed each of the committee chairwomen on preparations for the upcoming Founders' Day Festival. As secretary, Maddy had responsibility for taking the minutes of the meeting, but she was having trouble concentrating today. Much as she tried to focus on the discussion, her thoughts kept drifting to other topics.

Like little Anna Welborne's artless comment about not being able to come to Barrows House.

The community's narrow-minded disapproval of her household had never really bothered Maddy very much before. She and her ladies were happy, and the town's raised brows and whispered *tsks* were easily ignored. Truth be known, she'd secretly felt a bit of rebellious pride at the colorful reputation they enjoyed.

It had never occurred to her that it would have a more adverse affect on Katie. Until now. She'd grown to love the child dearly. And adopting Katie was probably the only chance she'd ever get to have a child of her own, something she yearned for with an ache that grew keener with each passing year.

But had she let her own desires blind her to what was best for Katie? Were the Propriety Police in the right this time?

". . . your cake walk committee is to be commended for their efforts in pulling this together."

Maddy sat up straighter, chagrined to realize she'd missed the last report. Luckily, she could make an accurate enough guess to summarize it for the minutes, but she'd better start paying closer attention.

"Vera," Cybil prompted, "how are the arrangements for the picnic basket auction going?"

Vera Welborne patted her hair, a self-satisfied smile on her face. "I'm pleased to report that so far thirty-one ladies have signed up to provide baskets. That includes all nineteen ladies of this society, with one exception."

Vera politely refrained from turning in Maddy's direction, but nevertheless Maddy felt an uncomfortable heat climb in her cheeks. Her cooking skills had always been indifferent at best, but the basket she'd prepared last year had been an absolute disaster. Poor Calvin Miller, the unfortunate gentleman who'd placed the winning bid on her basket, had done his best to swallow down the overcooked chicken and rock hard biscuits. The suspiciously salty tasting cherry pie he'd apologetically passed on altogether. His valiant efforts might have spared her a large measure of public embarrassment, if he hadn't gotten sick right in the middle of the town square.

Looking around now, she found herself the center of attention. There seemed as many pitying, superior expressions in the room as there were sympathetic ones. Maddy carefully kept her expression blank and refrained from comment. She refused to display any emotion that would provide additional fodder for the gossip mill.

It was a relief when Cybil reclaimed everyone's attention by asking Vera to move on to her report on the raffle committee.

As Vera sang the praises of the treadle sewing machine her husband had donated for the raffle prize, Maddy doodled in the margin of her report and let her thoughts drift once again. Clay hadn't seemed to approve of her adoption efforts. Of course, he didn't really know anything about her or Katie, so she shouldn't let his censure bother her. But somehow, it did.

It had been chivalrous of him not to comment on her reaction to the picture he'd uncovered. He must think her a silly goose to let a mere photograph rattle her so thoroughly. It had just been so unexpected. Seeing herself as she was that day, so determined and sure she was ready to face whatever the world had to offer, had brought home to her how much she had changed, how much she had lost. She hadn't been the girl in that picture since the day Winston died.

But she was ready now. She was ready to face whatever other surprises they unearthed amongst Winston's things with unruffled composure.

She wondered how Clay was faring upstairs.

Clay closed the dusty ledger and placed it with the things he'd decided could be safely discarded.

As he reached into the trunk for yet another dog-eared sheaf of papers, Katie stepped into the room. She stopped a few feet from where he sat and clasped her hands behind her back. The pose provided an unencumbered display of the dusty smudges on her pinafore. She swung her shoulders rhythmically from side to side, reminding him of the way his sister Meredith used to approach him when she wasn't sure if she should interrupt.

Clay smiled a welcome as he placed the papers on the table. "Hello, Katie."

She returned his smile. "Hello, Mr. Kincaid. Can I help?"

At least Katie's manners didn't seem to be suffering from her exposure to this household. "Well now, you could open one of those windows over there to let in a bit of fresh air. And then you could sit over here and keep me company."

With a quick nod, Katie skipped across the room and opened both windows. A soft breeze ruffled the stacks of paper, but not enough to overset them.

Once she'd accomplished her first task, Katie pulled a stool up to the table and propped her chin on one hand. "Did you have a puppy when you were a little boy?"

Clay smiled as he remembered. "Yes, a Labrador retriever named Pacer. He and I covered a lot of territory together."

"Anna calls my puppy Tiny, but I think that's a silly name 'cause he won't always be so small." She swung her crossed ankles back and forth. "I think I'm going to call him Skipper when he's all mine."

Clay nodded solemnly. "Sounds like a fine name."

Katie gave a quick nod, as if his agreement had settled the matter. Then she changed the subject with a blandly innocent expression. "Anna has a new swing in her back yard. She let me take a turn on it."

Clay wasn't fooled by Katie's pose of nonchalance. The tone she'd used was very reminiscent of Judith's when she was about to ask for something outlandish. "That was nice of her," he responded non-committally.

Katie traced circles on the table, watching Clay from the corner of her eye. "That big old oak tree behind the house would be just right for hanging a swing from, don't you think?"

Clay paused, then went back to sorting papers. So that's what this was leading up to. "Perhaps. But it seems to me you already have a swing on the front porch."

The child made a sound suspiciously akin to a snort. "That's only an old porch swing. It can't go real high like Anna's can." She straightened, her expression hopeful. "I already looked in the shed out back, and there's plenty of rope and a board that 'pears to be just the right size."

That explained the smudges on her clothes.

As if she'd heard his thoughts, Katie twitched her skirt. "I caught my dress on a nail," she said solemnly.

He'd already noted the triangular rip just below the tie at her waist. "Did the nail scratch you?" When she reassured him it hadn't he returned to his task, hoping she'd turn to another topic.

"Anyway," Katie said as she propped her elbows back on the table, "all I need now is somebody to hang the rope for me." She wrinkled her nose. "I'd do it myself, but Aunt Maddy doesn't like me to climb things."

Clay shifted in his seat, trying to forestall her inevitable request. He had a hard time turning down little girls' pleas for help—a weakness his sisters had learned early on. "Your Aunt Maddy might not like for you to swing 'real high.' Have you asked her?"

"Not yet. But I will, just as soon as the meeting is over." She hopped off of the stool. "Miss Fanny wanted me to let you know she has cookies and lemonade in the kitchen if you want some. It's supposed to be for Aunt Maddy's meeting, but Miss Fanny made extras."

"That sounds good." Clay stood and rolled down his sleeves as he hid a grin. The little imp had made sure she got in her pitch for the swing before she delivered her message. Was she looking for allies before she approached Maddy?

Katie kept up a steady stream of chatter about how wonderful it would be to have a backyard swing and the virtues of her new puppy all the way to the kitchen.

Clay discovered the kitchen was a large, sunny room, with lots of cupboards and counters. A rustic wooden table, solidly built and large enough to seat ten, dominated the center of the room.

Miss Fanny stood at the stove, stirring the contents of a pot. From the taste-tempting aroma, it was likely she had a cobbler in the oven, as well.

Across the room at the sink, Miss Adeline, still sporting thick blond braids, washed dishes.

Miss Olive, arranging items on a tea cart under Othello's greedily watchful eyes, noticed them first. "Oh, there you are. Katie, Miss Adeline will serve your lemonade and cookies if you're ready for them."

She turned to Clay, sparing a less-than-fond warning glance toward the feline. "Mr. Kincaid, I'm ready to bring the refreshments in to the Ladies' Society meeting. Would you mind lending me a hand with that tray of cookies? It won't fit on the cart with the rest."

Clay eyed the cart, noting that the items could have easily been rearranged to make room for the tray. Obviously Miss Olive wished him to accompany her on this delivery. He supposed she and Maddy thought parading him in front of the Pepper Cloud Ladies' Society was all part of the job they'd hired him for.

He groaned inwardly. This was likely a small-town version of the gatherings his mother held in her own parlor. A group of well-dressed matrons, full of self-importance and misplaced good intentions. They would greet an eligible bachelor in their midst the way a replete cat would greet a mouse.

"Of course." He picked up the tray and allowed her to precede him from the room. "If you don't mind my prying," he asked as they stepped into the hall, "why aren't the three of you in the meeting with Maddy?"

Miss Olive maneuvered the cart around a corner. "For the simple reason that we're not members." She glanced at him, her expression more prim than usual. "By our own choice, you understand. It's better for Maddy if we stay out of it."

"Is that what Maddy thinks?"

"Of course not. Maddy treats us like members of her family, and expects the community to do so as well." She shrugged. "But not everyone else does, and we just didn't want to put her in the position of having to stand up for us yet again."

They reached the parlor and Clay steeled himself as he stepped forward to open the door. He hoped he'd been mistaken about what he'd find inside, but felt supremely confident he could more than hold his own, regardless.

Maddy stood as soon as they entered. "Miss Olive, let me help you with that."

"Why thank you, Maddy dear." Miss Olive stepped past

Clay as she pushed the cart farther into the room. "But as you can see, Mr. Kincaid is already lending a hand."

As Clay followed the seamstress into the room, he noticed Othello, who'd stalked them all the way from the kitchen, halt at the threshold, stopping just short of entering the parlor. Smart cat.

Conversation faded into silence as Clay found himself the focus of over a dozen speculative, assessing glances. With a mental sigh he sketched an elegant bow, stepping into his assigned role. "Ladies, I trust you'll forgive this clumsy male intrusion into your delightfully feminine gathering."

The hotel owner's wife gave him an arch smile. "Why Mr. Kincaid, don't be silly. You're not intruding, and I'm sure there's nothing at all clumsy about you."

Clay flashed the plump, petite woman a smile as he allowed Maddy to take the tray from him. "Mrs. Thompson, a pleasure to see you again."

"Mr. Kincaid," someone else chimed in, "I do hope you're enjoying your visit to Pepper Cloud."

Clay identified this speaker as Maddy's neighbor, and nodded acknowledgement. "Miss Crawford, yes, thank you. I noticed on my walk earlier that your roses were in full bloom. The yellows seem to be doing especially well."

The schoolteacher pinkened in pleasure, as if he'd complimented her on her own looks.

Maddy helped Miss Olive serve the refreshments. She paused in front of a tall, handsome woman with reddish gold hair. From the looks of her, Clay would guess she'd been the town belle in her day.

"Maddy dear," the woman said as she reached for a tea cake, "do please introduce the rest of us to your guest."

The woman's gaze remained fixed on Clay as she nibbled delicately, eyeing him as if he himself were a particularly delectable treat. Clay had seen that look before. It was an expression worn by mommas with eligible daughters who'd just decided he was perfect son-in-law material.

"Of course." Maddy straightened, and waved a hand toward Clay. "Ladies, this is Mr. Clayton Kincaid. He's a cousin of Winston's and will be visiting here for a few weeks."

"Mr. Kincaid," Maddy turned to Clay and indicated the red-haired nibbler, "this is Cybil Flaherty. You met her husband, Mayor Flaherty, yesterday. Cybil is the president of the Pepper Cloud Ladies' Society."

So, this was Maddy's prime nemesis. She definitely had an I-know-I'm-someone-to-be-reckoned-with air about her. He gave her a short bow along with a smile he'd used to great effect with self-important matrons in the past. "Mrs. Flaherty, it's a pleasure to meet one of this town's most prominent citizens."

Cybil preened. "Why, thank you, sir. It's always a pleasure to meet a gentleman with such charming manners. Maddy tells us you come from back East. We must seem a rather provincial lot by comparison."

"Not at all. My hometown of Grisham, Virginia, is itself a small town. I find myself quite taken with Pepper Cloud and its citizenry."

"And what is it you do in Grisham?"

"My family owns some prime farmland there that my older brother manages." He gave a self-deprecating shrug. "I'm afraid I don't have much talent for agriculture so I manage the family's modest investment interests out of an office located in New Orleans."

"How very nice." Smiling as if she scented interesting quarry, Cybil turned to a young lady seated farther back in the room. "Sue Ellen, come here a moment, please."

Clay watched a reserved-looking girl of no more than nineteen years meekly rise and come forward as requested. Her strawberry blond hair and patrician nose announced her relationship before Cybil introduced her.

Mrs. Flaherty took the girl's hand. "This is my daughter, Sue Ellen. Sue Ellen, tell Mr. Kincaid hello."

Clay felt a measure of sympathy as the girl's cheeks

73

heated with embarrassment. But she gamely stepped forward. "It's a pleasure to meet you, sir. I do hope you enjoy your stay in Pepper Cloud."

Clay took her proffered hand and bowed before releasing it. "Thank you, Miss Flaherty, I'm sure I will." He gave her a warm, reassuring smile, hoping to put her more at ease. This time the color in her cheeks was accompanied by a sparkle of pleasure in her eyes.

Sue Ellen's mother lifted a hand, reclaiming his attention. "I do hope you'll still be here for the Founders' Day Festival. The Ladies' Society is planning several enjoyable activities, and most of the proceeds will be going to charity." She gave him an arch look, then glanced meaningfully at her daughter. "And there will be a dance that evening to cap off the festivities."

Maddy stepped forward, relieving him of the need to answer. "Now Cybil," she chided, "you've monopolized Mr. Kincaid long enough. Let me introduce him to some of the other ladies here."

Nodding his head in farewell, Clay allowed Maddy to draw him away. He took the opportunity to take her arm in a proprietory manner he was sure was duly noted by most of the ladies present. Maddy's step barely faltered as she proceded to escort him across the room.

Maddy stayed by his side, leading him around to each cluster of women and making the introductions.

Clay'd spoken to about half the ladies present when he noticed Katie slip into the room. His lips twitched when he got a clear view of her. She held a half-eaten honey-cake, and from the sticky appearance of her chin and fingers, it wasn't her first.

The urchin sidled up to Miss Olive, obviously trying to remain as unobtrusive as possible. What was the child up to?

Miss Olive finally took notice of Katie's presence. "Oh, hello, dear. Did you need something?"

Her question drew a few glances her way, and Clay noticed Mrs. Flaherty study the child closely.

"Yes ma'am." Katie's stage whisper projected easily to most occupants in the room. "Ruby Jane and Lila are in the kitchen. They came for Lila's fitting."

A few gasps went up at the mention of the saloon girls' names, then conversation slowed to a halt.

For a couple of heartbeats it was almost quiet enough to hear the brows lift.

Chapter Six

Maddy hoped her expression didn't betray her exasperation. Honestly, sometimes Miss Adeline and Miss Fanny acted as if they didn't have the sense God gave a goose between them. They should have known better than to send Katie in here on such an errand.

Katie seemed to suddenly realize everyone was watching her. She caught her lower lip between her teeth as her gaze sought Maddy's.

Maddy immediately crossed the room, summoning a reassuring smile. She had to take control of the situation before someone hurt the child's feelings. "Thank you for delivering the message, Buttercup."

As soon as she was in touching distance, the child clutched at Maddy's skirts with one sticky hand. Maddy stroked Katie's hair briefly, then picked up an empty tray from a nearby table. "Would you do me a favor and take this back to the kitchen, please. Tell Miss Fanny I said you could have an extra cookie, and tell Miss Olive's visitors that she'll be ready for them in just a few minutes."

With a quick nod, Katie clutched the tray to her chest and disappeared into the hall.

Maddy turned back to the room, mentally daring anyone to comment. Amid a general shifting in seats, several furtive glances were directed toward Cybil Flaherty. Undoubtedly, the Propriety Police contingent awaited a signal from their captain before they would react.

It didn't take long.

"Well, Maddy," the mayor's wife began, "this is just what I was afraid of. If you want to have saloon girls traipsing in and out of your home, I suppose that's your own business. Though your poor grandmother, God bless her soul, would be downright mortified to see such carryings-on in Barrows House."

Cybil drew her shoulders back. "But to expose a tender young girl such as Katie to their influence is simply irresponsible." She flashed a condescending smile. "Not that anyone thinks you don't care about the child. It's—"

"I should say not."

Startled, Maddy realized Clay had spoken up in her defense.

He sauntered across the room, pausing at her side. "Why, just in the short time that I've been here, I can see Cousin Maddy and Katie share a genuine affection for each other. I'm sure a woman as discerning as you are, Mrs. Flaherty, must see it as well?"

Maddy had an almost overwhelming urge to hug him. It was a novel feeling to have someone outside her household rise so quickly to her defense. Then she recollected herself. He was just doing what she had hired him to do.

Cybil blinked. "Why . . . uhm . . . of course." She straightened her spine, recovering her composure. "We all know Maddy has a generous, loving spirit. It's why we are all so fond of her."

Maddy resisted the urge to grind her teeth.

Cybil's lips turned in a regretful moue. "Unfortunately, it tends to be somewhat *too* encompassing." She turned to

Maddy with a motherly smile. "No offense, dear, but as I've told you before, you must learn to draw the line between your charitable instincts and standards of propriety. It is so important to shelter your home life from unsavory elements."

There was a loud clatter as Miss Olive set a tray down on the cart with a bit more force than necessary. But when Maddy turned, her friend wore her customary unflappable expression.

"It appears everyone has been served," Miss Olive said calmly. "I'll take these back to the kitchen and see to my visitors." She turned and pushed the cart into the hall.

Once Miss Olive left, the conversation, thankfully, turned to other topics. At one point, Maddy noted Cybil, one hand firmly clamped to her daughter's arm, had Clay cornered in animated conversation. It was no secret that Cybil had ambitious plans for Sue Ellen's future. Freddie Clemmons, the banker's son and Pepper Cloud's most eligible bachelor, had lately been the target of Cybil's matchmaking efforts. Was she thinking of changing her focus to Clay? Maddy sincerely hoped not. Her simple plan had become way too complicated as it was.

Finally, the ladies began taking their leave. As Maddy said her farewells at the door, she overheard Clay in discussion with a group standing nearby. Vera Welborne made a reference to the sorry state of Katie's clothes, and Clay responded with a laughing reference to the consequences of bright, inquisitive children in general, and his younger sisters in particular.

Surprised by the reference, Maddy glanced in his direction. There'd been a wealth of affection beneath the exasperation in his tone. She'd wager he'd been a very protective older brother.

"By the way, Mrs. Welborne," he said as they approached Maddy, "I believe I met your daughter this morning. A polite child named Anna, with brown braids and your lovely brown eyes. She was offering one of her puppies to

Katie. You must be very proud of her generous nature."

Vera's considerable bosom swelled with pride. "Yes, Mr. Welborne and I are quite proud of our Anna. She's an exceptional child, if you'll forgive a bit of motherly boasting."

Maddy watched Vera's cheeks pinken under the influence of Clay's flattering smile. "Of course," he said warmly. Then, as the group moved toward the door, "In fact, you sound just like Cousin Maddy when she's singing Katie's praises. But with bright children like Anna and Katie, I believe you ladies can be forgiven such modest bragging."

Maddy had to admit, there were times when the man's smooth-talking charm could be useful.

When the last of her guests had exited, Maddy closed the front door and breathed a sigh of relief. Then she sensed Clay's presence behind her and felt suddenly self-conscious.

He'd seen the condescending way Cybil and some of the others treated her. Yes, he'd spoke up for her, but had it been because he believed in her, or because of the role he was playing?

Turning, she flashed a quick smile and allowed her gaze to slide away from his as she moved back to the parlor. "Thank you for coming to my defense so quickly." She began gathering up cups and saucers, straining her senses for some hint of his thoughts.

"You're welcome." He rescued a cup from the piano stool and added it to her tray. She felt a tingle of awareness as his hand brushed hers. Her gaze flew to his, but if he'd felt anything, he gave no sign.

"It is, after all, why I'm here," he added.

The disappointment that shot through her effectively cooled the warmth she'd been feeling. So, her earlier suspicion as to his motives had proved correct. Ridiculous to feel so bothered by this. Hadn't she been the one to insist that they keep things strictly business between them?

Not that she would be averse to a simple friendship. But

any warmer relationship between them would be inappropriate, even dangerous.

It was definitely time for a change of subject. Maddy carefully wiped a non-existent spill with a napkin. "I suppose your joining us in the parlor was Miss Olive's idea."

Clay placed the last of the dishes on the tray and took it from her with a cheerful smile. "She suggested it. I must admit, I'd thought she was acting at your direction."

Maddy was able to summon up a dry smile of her own. "Miss Olive isn't afraid to take the initiative when an idea strikes her." She moved with him into the hall, determined to show no sign of her earlier weakness. "Overall, I must admit, this turned out rather well. Most of the ladies seemed to take a shine to you."

She cast him a sideways look, unable to resist watching for his reaction. "In fact, I found myself on the receiving end of several rather envious glances as they took their leave." She was honest enough to admit, at least to herself, that she had enjoyed the feeling it gave her.

He raised a brow, an I-told-you-so expression on his face. "So, do I take it you think you're getting your money's worth?"

His smug tone irritated her. Did women always fall under his spell with no more effort on his part than quirking his lips into that devilishly charming smile? Someone should take him down a notch or two.

"For now," she said primly. "But I suggest you work on looking at me more like a besotted suitor and less like an older brother. And it would be better if you'd drop the word 'cousin' when you address me. That hardly conjures up romantic images."

Clay's back stiffened, and the teasing glint left his eyes. Good! *This* emotion she could handle.

Clay strolled along the sidewalk, trying to sort through his impressions of the last few days. He'd decided to go for a walk shortly after depositing the tray in the kitchen. The ladies of Barrows House had made it clear they had business to take care of that didn't include him, and he wasn't ready to return to the paper-cluttered second-floor room.

He returned greetings and even paused to chat when he encountered a familiar face or two. His thoughts, however, kept returning to the events of the afternoon.

To Maddy, to be more specific. She had to be the bossiest, least amenable woman he'd ever crossed paths with. Even when he gave her *what* she wanted, she fussed because he hadn't done it the *way* she wanted. He just couldn't seem to win the woman over.

God knew he had lots of experience with female contrariness—his three sisters qualified as some of the world's most contrary. He'd given up trying to decipher their volatile mood shifts long ago.

Clay kicked a pebble. He thought he'd handled himself quite well at the Ladies' Society meeting. He'd had them practically eating out of his hand. And Maddy had seemed cautiously approving as well. So what had made her turn so stiff-necked all of a sudden?

Of course, by the time they'd reached the kitchen with the tray of dishes, she'd reverted back to her old, I've-got-everything-under-control self, as if her little snit had never occurred.

Women!

Still, he couldn't help but admire the way she'd acted so quickly and competently to take Katie out of the line of fire. And she'd looked absolutely magnificent when she'd turned to face that room full of ladies, knowing what would happen next. Truth be known, he'd ranged himself beside her before he'd even remembered that she had hired him to do just that.

Maddy hadn't underestimated her situation. In his opinion, Mrs. Flaherty *would* take Katie away from her if she could. He'd met women like the mayor's wife before. That social-arbiter, self-righteous do-gooder type always made for a formidable foe in the social arena. But he was confident he could win her over. His particular brand of charm and flattery worked wonders with such women. And where she led, the others would follow.

Problem was, he found himself feeling some sympathy for Mrs. Flaherty's goal, if not her motives or methods. While it was obvious Maddy and Katie shared a genuine affection for one another, he still wasn't convinced Barrows House provided the proper setting for raising a child.

Clay was more certain than ever that he'd done the right thing in sending that telegraph to Peterson this morning. With a bit of luck, the investigator would meet with swift success in finding some member of Katie's family. It would be difficult enough for Maddy to give up the child when the time came—it might make it somewhat easier on her if she knew Katie would be cared for by blood relations.

Clay stopped in his tracks, chagrined to realize he was standing back at the front gate to Barrows House. He hadn't intended to return until supper time.

Still wavering over whether to turn around or go forward, Clay caught site of Katie, dejectedly dragging a stick behind her as she appeared from behind the house.

The child brightened considerably when she caught sight of Clay. "Mr. Kincaid, could you help me, please?"

The decision taken out of his hands, Clay opened the gate and strode forward. "Sure thing, Katie. What do you need?"

She took his hand and began to lead him back the way she'd come. "My ball is stuck up in the tree and I can't get it down. Would you try? Please?"

Clay frowned, remembering the size of the oak that dominated the back yard. He'd hate to dash that you'll-fix-it-for-me smile from Katie's face, but—

"See." Katie's question interrupted his thoughts.

To Clay's relief, it looked like something he could handle quite easily. "Uh-huh. If you'll fetch a broom or mop, I think I can knock it loose in two shakes of a lamb's tail."

Katie giggled at his words, then skipped off to the house to find the required tool.

As he waited for her, Clay noticed a long stick on the ground that just might serve his purpose. Moving toward it, he heard voices coming from an open window.

". . . hadn't realized it would cost so much. Forget I even suggested such a thing."

That was Miss Adeline's voice. They must be discussing the "business" they'd mentioned earlier.

"Yes, it's a lot of more than we'd figured on, but I'm determined to do this," Maddy responded.

He picked up the stick and started to move away again, not ready to stoop to eavesdropping. But a question posed by Miss Fanny caught his attention.

"But Maddy, where in the world would you ever find so much money?"

"I have a plan, one I've already set into motion. If things work out the way I hope they will, we won't have to come up with all the money ourselves."

Clay frowned as Maddy's words triggered an alarm bell in his head. Did these plans she'd mentioned have anything to do with him? Qualms over eavesdropping pushed aside, he took another step closer to the house.

"What kind of plans?" Miss Adeline asked, voicing his own question.

"I'm afraid I can't go into detail on that right now."

"Maddy, you aren't contemplating anything illegal are you?" Miss Adeline didn't sound so much scandalized as amused.

Maddy laughed. "Unorthodox and perhaps a bit underhanded, but neither illegal nor immoral, I assure you. Let's just say it'll require my taking on a partner. Now, if everyone is in agreement—"

Katie's reappearance, broom in hand, put an end to Clay's eavesdropping. But as he dislodged the ball and accepted the little girl's delighted thanks, he had to work to keep the frown from his face.

83

The widow's less than lover-like attitude and genuine affection for Katie had lulled him into thinking he might be wrong about there being a matchmaking scheme afoot. Now he wasn't so sure.

Unorthodox and underhanded she'd said. Well if this whole courtship charade was an elaborate ploy to get him to the altar, then it sure fit that description. The financial angle fit as well, since anyone who married into his family would have access to more money than she could ever spend.

As Katie skipped away to play with her ball, he raked a hand through his hair. He was fairly certain Maddy's desire to adopt Katie was genuine, but was she out to snag a rich husband, as well? After all, having a husband would make her petition to adopt all the stronger.

If that was her plan, he aimed to disappoint her. He'd escaped that net many times before. While Maddy Potter was certainly clever, she would soon find herself outmatched if she tried to pit her wits against his.

Now that he was forewarned, though, he could take control of the game and make sure it progressed by his rules.

Maddy tucked the blanket under Katie's chin as she finished the lullaby. It had been a long, rather stressful day, but now Mr. Kincaid's introduction to the community was behind her, and things were bound to go smoother in the days to come.

"There now," she said, stroking the child's hair. "Comfy?"

Katie gave a sleepy nod. "Yes ma'am."

Maddy placed a goodnight kiss on the little girl's brow, but before she could rise, Katie slipped a hand out from the covers and touched her arm.

"Aunt Maddy?"

"Yes, sweetheart?"

"When Skipper is my dog for real and comes to live with us, do you think he can sleep in here with me?"

Maddy hid a smile. "I suppose, if you keep him clean, and he doesn't keep everyone awake, we might work something out on that score."

"Thank you."

"You're welcome." She patted the child through the coverlet. "Now, time to shut your eyes and go to sleep."

"Yes ma'am."

But Maddy had barely made it to her feet before Katie's eyes popped open again. "Aunt Maddy, can we hang a swing like Anna's from that big oak tree out back?"

Katie obviously didn't want to settle down tonight. Maddy adjusted her covers. "We'll talk about that in the morning."

Katie snuggled beneath the blanket. "Okay." Then, for the third time, she halted Maddy's exit. "Aunt Maddy?"

Maddy resisted the urge to sigh. "Yes, dear?"

"Why do you suppose Anna's mother won't let her come here to play? Is it because I don't have a mommy of my own?"

A fist squeezed painfully around Maddy's heart. Had Katie been fretting over that all day?

She sat back down on the edge of the bed. "Oh no, darling, it isn't that at all. In fact, it has nothing to do with you."

Katie looked somewhat reassured. "Then why?"

How could she explain adult prejudices to a child? But she didn't want to lie or make believe they didn't exist either. "I'm afraid Anna's mother, and some of the other people in town, don't approve of the way we do things at Barrows House."

"Like what?"

"Oh, little things, really." Maddy wondered how much to say. She didn't want to influence Katie to look askance at the other ladies in the household. But on the other hand, it was very important Katie understood she had no reason to blame herself.

Maddy decided to trust in Katie's loyalty. "Like the way

85

Miss Fanny talks to her husband when no one can see him," she explained diffidently, "or the way Miss Adeline dresses sometimes. So you see, it has nothing to do with you."

Katie stuck out her chin. "But it makes Miss Fanny happy to talk to her husband, and I like Miss Adeline's costumes."

Maddy breathed a silent sigh of relief. Her instincts had been right. "I know, sweetie, I do, too. But other folks just don't understand. It makes them uncomfortable when people act differently from everyone else."

"That's silly. And Anna thinks our house sounds like a fun place. She told me so." The child's nose wrinkled, as if she were trying to puzzle something out. "Anna's mother was here today. If she doesn't like us, why doesn't she stay home and let Anna come?"

"Oh Katie, I didn't say Mrs. Welborne doesn't like us. She's just extra careful about Anna, is all. That doesn't mean you and Anna can't still be friends. And we'll continue to invite her over whenever we can. Someday her mother might just say yes."

Katie seemed ready to settle down at last. "That would be nice," she said between yawns. "Good night."

Maddy kissed her forehead. "Goodnight Buttercup. Sweet dreams."

But as she slipped out of the room, Maddy's mind was riddled with worries over what the future might hold for Katie if she became a permanent part of Barrows House. Would the overflow of love the child would surely experience from the members of the household be enough to override the slights she would receive?

Maddy knew her own dreams would not be so sweet this night.

"Mr. Kincaid, I think we should go over the rules of this courting arrangement one more time."

Clay hid a grin as he noted the suppressed outrage in

Maddy's tone. She hadn't even waited until the buggy reached the outskirts of town to voice her grievance. Not that she'd forgotten their "audience" scattered along the sidewalks and storefronts. Her words had been pitched so that only he could hear them, and she'd carefully maintained a polite smile on her face.

He flicked the reins lightly. "Must we?"

The quick look she shot him could have frozen a pond over, even in this early afternoon heat. "Apparently so."

The buildings were growing sparser now and Maddy seemed to decide the smile was no longer necessary. She tilted her chin up as she folded her hands primly in her lap. "I specifically instructed you to handle this courtship in a gentlemanly fashion. Not to manhandle me like some libertine."

My, my but she *was* in a huff, wasn't she? "All I did was help you into the buggy like you asked."

"What I requested, sir, was that you lend me the support of your arm while I climbed in. I did *not* ask you to bodily lift me into the conveyance."

And hold you a little too close for a little too long. Clay sure had enjoyed the moment, even if she hadn't. Not that he was entirely convinced she hadn't. She was complaining just a bit too forcefully.

He caught her gaze and raised a brow. "Yesterday you told me I treated you too much like a relation, and now you're saying I'm treating you too much like a lover. Which way do you want it, Maddy?"

Her cheeks pinkened as she shifted in her seat. "I just think there's room for a middle ground."

He shrugged. "You're the one who imposed the deadline of four weeks. If we're going to make everyone start to see wedding bells in our future, we need to show signs that we're feeling some stirring of attraction for each other."

"Yes, well . . ." Her words trailed off as she picked at a bit of lint on her skirt. Then she straightened her spine, wobbling a bit as they hit a rut. "In the future, let's discuss these notions of yours before we act on them, shall we?"

He grinned. "I'll try. But I'm afraid I tend to act impulsively, at times. I just can't seem to help myself."

She narrowed her eyes, as if trying to decide whether to chide him or not. Apparently she decided to let it pass. "When you come to the fork in the road," she said, changing the subject, "bear to the left."

He nodded. "So, where are you taking me?"

"Dragon's Teeth."

"Sounds gruesome."

"It's named after a rock formation. Two boulders shaped like large yellow fangs. But that's not the best part." She leaned back, finally seeming to relax. "I won't tell you more, though. It has greater impact if your first view comes as a surprise."

The road forked, and Clay obediently took the narrower left branch. They were definitely out of the town proper now. The buildings dwindled to scattered homesteads and farmhouses. The fresh air and sunshine, even though hot and a bit dusty, were welcome after a morning cooped up inside sorting through papers.

Feeling a trifle guilty for his deliberate, and admittedly enjoyable, attempt to raise her ire, Clay tried for a safer topic. "Miss Fanny mentioned you like to sketch. She says you're quite good at it."

Surprisingly, she didn't display false modesty, nor did she preen. Instead she shrugged. "It's something I like to do when I want to escape."

As if realizing how that had sounded, she straightened. "I mean, when I need time to myself, to just think through a problem or let my mind focus on something uncomplicated." She wrinkled her nose. "Oh dear, I'm not explaining myself very well, am I?"

He smiled. "Actually, I understand exactly what you're trying to say. It's something that's yours alone, something that provides a sense of rightness and peace to your life for a small measure of time."

88

She indicated he was to turn onto an even narrower road that branched off to their left. This track, barely more than a wide, grassy path, didn't seem to get much use. But it offered a welcome relief from the dust and heat of the main road.

Maddy tilted her head, studying him intently. "And what provides that sense of peace for you?"

He kept forgetting how adept the widow Potter was at turning the tables on him. "Horses," he answered. "I have a small breeding farm I escape to whenever I can."

"You own a breeding farm?"

He shrugged and gave her a rueful grin. "I'm afraid right now it's costing me more in expenses than it's earning in revenue. My family thinks it's a waste of time and money. But I hope to make a go of it someday." All of which was entirely true.

He changed the subject. "This doesn't seem to be much more than an overgrown trail. Are you sure we're going the right way?"

She nodded. "Uh-huh. It's out of the way so folks don't come up here much. And most who do come by horseback instead of carriage. But trust me, it's worth the effort."

Clay tried not to think about the fact that this would make an ideal lover's tryst. Instead, he watched the horse lean into the harness and realized they'd been traveling at a gentle but steady uphill slope since they'd turned on this track. The trees slowly began to thin, yielding ground to brush and boulders.

"There they are," she announced suddenly, pointing ahead and to his right.

He recognized them immediately, twin boulders, one upright, the other listing slightly. Yellowish in color, they appeared tall enough to top him by a good half foot. Slender, curved and tapered to a point on top, they looked remarkably like a monstrous set of serpent fangs.

"Impressive." He slowed the buggy to a halt and looked around, searching for some sign of whatever else it was she'd wanted him to see. But, except for the namesake rock formations, the place seemed remarkably *un*remarkable. Just a wild jumble of brambles and trees and rocks. Even the road, such as it was, dwindled into nothing more than a rough footpath a few feet away.

Maddy, however, still wore that I-can't-wait-to-show-you-this expression on her face. She hopped down from the buggy without his assistance, and gestured impatiently. "Come on. We'll go the rest of the way by foot. It's just a little farther."

As Clay took Maddy's elbow to help her negotiate over the uneven ground, he noticed a subtle change in her. Gone was the prim and proper widow Potter. Her cheeks were flushed from the heat and activity, and wisps of hair had escaped the confines of her pins to curl softly around her face. But it was more than that. There was an almost girlish energy and enthusiasm about her, as if she'd left her problems behind on the main road and for the moment had no cares to weigh her down.

So intrigued was he with observing this new side of Maddy, he didn't realize they'd reached her target destination until she halted. "Well," she said, sweeping her arm out expansively, "what do you think? Isn't it magnificent?"

Clay tore his gaze away from the becoming woman and focused on the area in front of him.

His stomach clenched and the smile froze on his face.

Chapter Seven

Maddy inhaled deeply as she drank in the breathtaking vista. This was, without reservation, her favorite place. They stood on the edge of a small, grassy clearing that also served as the crown of a sheer cliff face. About a hundred and thirty feet below them, though you couldn't see it from here, a tributary of the Mississippi meandered through the countryside. From their position, they had an unobstructed view of miles and miles of checkerboard farmland and thickly wooded hills. She felt as if she stood at the top of the world.

She lifted her chin, letting the soft breeze caress her face. "Isn't it magnificent?" she repeated.

A bit-off exclamation drew her head sharply around. "What is it?"

Clay stood beside her, white-faced and clutching his wrist, blood dripping from his hand.

"Oh my goodness, what happened?" Maddy gently took his wrist, surprised to feel his hand tremble slightly. She carefully examined the two puncture wounds on his palm, wincing in sympathy.

Clay gestured to a nearby bush with his free hand, then raked his fingers through his hair. "I got a bit careless."

Maddy grimaced when she saw the wickedly pointed, spike-like thorns. "I'm sorry. I should have warned you about tangling with those."

"No need to apologize, it's not your fault. Anyone with eyes in his head could tell that bush is trouble. I just wasn't paying attention." He flashed a lopsided grin. "I guess it was the view."

His tone was strained, his whole bearing stiff, as if he exerted a rigid control. Those thorns must have pierced deeper than she'd first thought.

He eased his hand out of her grasp and began toying with his ring. "Don't want to get blood on your dress," he explained with a half-smile.

She waved away his concern. "Don't be silly, the dress will wash." She pulled a cotton handkerchief from her skirt pocket. "This will do for a makeshift bandage. Don't worry, it's clean." She took his wrist again and began wrapping the cloth around his hand. "I'd feel better if we got you on back to Barrows House so I can tend it properly. We need to make sure there's not a bit of thorn broken off inside."

"Yes ma'am." Clay nodded meekly and held still while she tied the handkerchief.

Meek? Such a strange reaction—especially from him.

"There." She eyed her handiwork critically. "I hope it's not too tight, but I wanted to make sure it stopped the bleeding."

"It's fine," he assured her. They started back toward the buggy but hadn't gone far when he touched her arm lightly. "Thank you for your help—and for the sacrifice of your handkerchief. Sorry to distress you with such an indelicate task."

Maddy stepped around a small pile of stones. Was it this contrition she'd sensed in him earlier? "Don't worry about my sensibilities. I've dealt with worse." She remembered briefly the last three months of her grandmother's life when the woman had rarely left her bed. Then she dismissed her memories as she cast a quick sideways look toward Clay and caught his thoughtful glance. Did her remark make her seem less feminine in his eyes?

Once they were seated in the buggy, Maddy reached for the reins. No point in pretending she was a stranger to flouting conventions. "I'd better drive."

Clay grabbed the reins first. "That won't be necessary."

"But—"

"My hand's not hurt that badly," he assured her. "And besides, I really only need one hand for this job."

Maddy, singularly unimpressed by his stoicism, shook her head in disgust. "You, sir, are the epitome of mule-headed stubbornness. I do believe you would choke to death on your own pride before you'd accept a simple offer of assistance."

His lips twitched as he set the carriage in motion. "Don't women consider that sort of attitude heroic?"

"Not if they've got a lick of sense." She tossed her head, determined not to let him see how affected she was by his playful teasing, by his close masculine presence. "I'll take a man who has the self-confidence to accept help when he needs it over a strutting bantam rooster any day."

He laughed outright at that, a sound that thrummed through her with a warm tingle. "I won't ask which category you place me in. I have a feeling I wouldn't care for the answer."

They reached the end of their narrow track and Maddy watched as he effortlessly slowed the buggy and maneuvered them back onto the road. "How did you injure yourself anyway?" she asked, trying to drag her thoughts to a safer topic. "It looks almost as if you grabbed onto the bush."

He grimaced. "I did. Stumbled and tried to catch myself." Then he cast her a quick, sideways look. "I'm sorry I spoiled your outing."

She waved a hand. "That's all right. I hadn't planned to

stay long anyway. I'm just sorry you hurt your hand before you could take in much of the view."

"I saw enough. You were right—it was absolutely breathtaking."

Maddy's pencil glided across the paper in smooth, sure strokes. Seated in profile on the roomy window seat in her attic studio, she had her feet propped in front of her, with her knees steepled to form a make-shift easel.

Not that her perch provided any natural lighting save that of the soft glow from the nearly full moon. But it was all right, she wasn't sketching anything in particular. Lamplight was all she really needed for her random doodles. As she'd told Clay earlier, sketching helped relax her, and for some reason she felt too restless to settle down tonight.

The image of Katie's face began to take shape on her pad. Not the sweet, angelic countenance she'd kissed goodnight earlier, however, but rather a comical, cross-eyed, grimacing imp.

Maddy smiled, remembering the scene she'd witnessed this morning. Hearing Katie's giggles coming from the parlor, she'd peeked inside just in time to see the little girl pull at the corners of her mouth and stick out her tongue. To Maddy's surprise, Clay had responded by putting his thumb on the end of his nose and waggling his fingers, sending Katie off into peels of laughter all over again. The two seemed engaged in a face-making contest, of all things.

Maddy had quietly backed away, leaving them to their fun. But the sight of Clay sacrificing his dignity to entertain Katie had warmed her to him more effectively than his easy charm or rugged good looks ever could have.

Maddy continued to embellish and doodle, putting in bits of background, as she tried to redirect her thoughts.

She would *not* allow herself to get emotionally attached to the man. It was too dangerous, and besides, she didn't deserve such a relationship. But she had to admit, his rakish charm was seductively potent.

Her mind balked at pursuing that train of thought. So, like the coward she was, she began to mentally tick off the other reasons anything more than a friendship with Clay was impossible.

He was her business partner in this effort and such feelings were entirely inappropriate under the circumstances. Not to mention the fact that he'd made it quite clear he was in this strictly to repay some imagined debt of honor. And she dare not forget the vow she'd made to herself at Winston's graveside.

Still. . . .

With a sigh, Maddy stood. It was late and she really should try to get some sleep.

She descended the stairs and stepped into the second floor hallway to discover she wasn't the only one still awake. Miss Olive, a gown draped over one arm, stepped out of the sewing room and closed the door behind her.

The seamstress offered a sympathetic smile when she caught sight of Maddy. "Having trouble sleeping, dear?"

Maddy returned her smile. "A little. The past few days have been a bit hectic." She raised the pad with her sketch of Katie. "Drawing my favorite subject always helps to settle me down, though."

Miss Olive slid the dress off her arm and held it up. "Actually, I'm glad you're still up. I can give this to you now rather than wait until morning."

Maddy eyed the altered garment uncertainly. No longer an unrelieved black, the dress now sported dove-gray cuffs and collar, each edged in delicate white lace. The jet buttons were gone as well, replaced by shiny silver ones.

"Lovely work, as usual," she said slowly, uncertain how best to voice her objections, "but I don't really think—"

Miss Olive held up a hand. "Before you say no, think about this for just a minute. If you are serious about convincing folks you're beginning to fall for Mr. Kincaid, you have to start acting like a woman who's ready to let go of the past."

Maddy caught her lower lip between her teeth. What Miss Olive said made sense.

She took the gown and held it up in front of her. It wasn't an extravagant change, after all, just a few touches here and there. And it looked so much more feminine now, less austere.

Miss Olive nodded approvingly, as if the matter had been settled. "There now, you can wear this one in the morning. I'll work on your other dresses and should have a couple more ready by tomorrow evening."

Knowing she was letting herself be persuaded too easily, Maddy made a token effort to put her foot down. "Nothing extravagant or frivolous, mind you."

"Of course not." Miss Olive patted Maddy's arm and turned toward her bedroom. Then she paused and took a good look at the sketch pad Maddy still held. "Interesting study of your favorite subject, dear."

Maddy, still studying the dress, heard a hint of dry humor in her friend's voice. Miss Olive must have seen Katie's silly-faced expression. "Thank you," she said, fingering the newly added lace trim. "I know it's not portrait quality, but it suited my mood tonight."

"On the contrary, I think it is a singularly revealing bit of work. Good night dear."

Something in Miss Olive's tone set off a silent alarm in Maddy's head. She draped the dress over her arm and looked at her pad.

And groaned as the heat climbed in her cheeks.

There, beside the picture of Katie, was a sparingly drawn, wonderfully lifelike, flatteringly handsome picture of Clay.

"Why Mr. Kincaid, I do declare, it is just so nice to have a big strong man such as yourself around the house for a change." Miss Adeline tilted her head to one side, causing her chestnut ringlets to bounce playfully.

"It's my pleasure to be of what help I can, ma'am." Clay lifted the framed picture, hanging it on the nail he'd just driven into the wall. "How's this?"

Miss Adeline, today a southern belle from the tip of her beribboned curls to the toes of her pink slippers, closed her lace fan and touched it to her cheek. "Just a dab more to the left, I think." Then, when he complied, she clapped her hands. "Oh you darlin' man, that is just absolutely perfect."

She graced him with a wide-eyed, adoring look, as if he'd performed the labors of Hercules. "I am just ever so grateful to you, sir. I declare, I don't know how we poor women managed before you came along."

"Now Miss Adeline," Clay said with a deliberately roguish lift of his brow, "surely you wouldn't have me believe that a houseful of lovely charmers such as yourself don't have any number of strapping young men at your beck and call." He paused briefly then added with a mock-innocent smile. "To help with mundane chores, of course."

Miss Adeline rapped his arm with her fan. "Land's sake, how you do go on, sir." Then she gave him a coquettish simper. "But I always did prefer scoundrels to so-called gentlemen."

Clay bowed as he rolled down his sleeves. "I'll take that as a compliment, ma'am. Now, if you're through with my humble services, I have a question for Maddy about some of the papers I came across this afternoon."

He watched the tell-tale hint of consternation flit across her face before she covered it with another of her flirtatious smiles. So he'd been right. Ever since Maddy had excused herself this afternoon because of a prior commitment, Miss Adeline had been fluttering around him. She'd regaled him with stories of her past successes on the stage, flirted outrageously, and found numerous odd jobs that required a "man's touch."

At first he hadn't thought much more than that it was part and parcel of the former leading lady's obvious need to be the center of attention. But he'd begun to suspect over the last half hour or so, that she was deliberately trying to keep him occupied.

And he'd just now realized what Maddy's "prior commitment" was. Today was Thursday, the day Ruby Jane had said she'd be coming over for afternoon tea, along with a couple of her cronies. He was suddenly more than a little curious as to why Maddy would invite barmaids into her parlor.

As he moved purposefully toward the stairs, Miss Adeline managed to step oh so casually into his path. "I'm afraid Maddy is entertaining guests at the moment," she said, running her fingertips down his upper arm. "It would be rude of us to barge in uninvited." She slipped her hand into the crook of his arm. "Why don't we step out into the garden for a stroll while we wait? The flowers are lovely right now, and you can talk to Maddy about all that dry paperwork business later."

That tore it—there was more going on here than a simple afternoon tea party. What were they trying to hide from him? A vividly detailed memory of Maddy in that saucy, revealing, cherry red dress convinced him he needed to find out.

He patted Miss Adeline's hand. "My dear lady, I doubt there is a blossom to be found that could match your flamboyant brand of beauty."

She preened at the compliment, fluffing her hair as she allowed him to escort her down the stairs.

"And a stroll in the garden sounds delightful," he continued as they stepped onto the ground floor. "Just as soon as I have a quick word with Maddy." He gently disengaged his arm from her grasp and turned to the parlor.

Miss Adeline stamped her satin-shod foot, reclaiming his attention. "Mr. Kincaid, you are behaving in a most ungentlemanly manner."

Clay couldn't quite suppress the slight twitch of his lips.

"But my dear lady, didn't you just say you prefer scoundrels?"

Her eyes narrowed in irritation and her lips pursed to deliver what would undoubtedly prove to be an acerbic comment. Miss Olive's appearance, however, forestalled her from voicing it.

"Mr. Kincaid, there you are." Miss Olive seemed oblivious to her friend's agitation.

Clay cynically wondered what signal Miss Adeline had used to summon reinforcements. "Were you looking for me, ma'am?"

"Yes. Joey Brennan is here to fix one of our upstairs shutters, and he needs someone to hold the ladder steady for him. I was hoping you would be willing to lend a hand."

The muted sound of feminine laughter drew Clay's gaze back toward the closed parlor door. "Of course, I'll be glad to help, just as soon as—"

"I would appreciate it if you'd come along right now," she interrupted. "Joey is young enough to think he's invulnerable. He's not likely to see the wisdom of waiting for you."

Miss Olive's severe tone would have put a general addressing recalcitrant troops to shame. Clay acknowledged his defeat with a short bow. At least she hadn't asked him to climb the blasted ladder himself. "Of course. Please, lead the way."

Five minutes later, Clay found himself holding the ladder steady under Miss Olive's watchful eyes. Joey stood nearly ten feet above him, blithely working on removing the offending shutter as if he were perfectly at home on such a lofty perch.

Katie, her dress more than a trifle muddy, wandered around from the back of the house. "Watcha' doing?" she asked, peering up with interest.

Joey paused long enough to wipe his brow with his sleeve. "Hello, half-pint. I'm taking this shutter down so I can replace the damaged slats. After that," he said giving the child a knowing grin, "Mrs. Potter asked me to hang a swing from the big oak around back."

Katie clapped her hands excitedly. "A swing! Can I help? I'm a good climber."

Miss Olive eyed the little girl's bedraggled appearance with disapproval. "I think not. Heavens, child, how did you manage to get so wet and dirty?"

Katie held her skirt out and peered down at it as if just now noticing its condition. Then she looked up at Miss Olive with a touch of pride. "I was gardening. I saved the seeds from my apple and planted 'em in the kitchen garden just like I saw Miss Fanny do with the beans." Her smile turned wistful. "Now we can have an apple tree just like the one that grew outside momma's kitchen window."

Miss Olive's expression softened. "Well now, that was very thoughtful of you, dear. But we need to get you cleaned up. Come along inside and I'll fetch you some wash water and clean clothes."

Katie's lip turned down. "But I want to help with the swing."

"I've got to get this shutter fixed first," Joey called down. "You've got plenty of time to change." He put a hand to his heart. "And I promise not to let anyone sit on it before you test it out for me. Okay?"

Katie gave him a toothy smile. "Okay." Then she offered her hand to Miss Olive. "I'm ready."

Miss Olive took her hand, then turned back to Clay. "I trust you'll make sure the ladder is held steady until Joey is finished."

She wasn't even trying to be subtle any more. For a moment Clay was tempted to say no, just to see what she'd do. But he couldn't quite bring himself to be disrespectful. "You have my word, ma'am."

Her expression relaxed and she gave him an approving smile. And was that just a hint of amused sympathy in her gaze as well?

Once the woman and child were out of earshot, Joey

paused. "You know," he said, "I don't really need anyone to hold the ladder for me. Beats me what has Miss Olive so all-fired worried about this all of a sudden. I've been climbing ladders like this one on my own for years, and I ain't had an accident yet."

Clay shook his head. "Don't bother trying to figure it out. And whether either of us wants me standing here or not, I gave her my word." And the crafty old seamstress knew he wouldn't renege on his word.

The sound of the front gate opening caught Clay's attention. His first reaction was irritation that Maddy's guests were leaving before he'd learned what they were up to. But a moment later, Cybil Flaherty's daughter, fetchingly attired in a light green dress, approached them from the front walk.

"Hello, Joey. I thought I recognized you dilly-dallying up on that ladder."

A broad smile lit Joey's rather plain face. "Hello, Sue Ellen. You're looking mighty pretty today."

"Thank you." She turned to Clay and offered her hand, though he could tell her attention was still focused on the young man hovering above them. "Hello Mr. Kincaid. How are you today?"

Clay gave her hand a light squeeze. "I'm doing just fine, thank you." Unless you count the fact that his curiosity was driving him crazy. "Are you just out enjoying this beautiful day, or is there something we can do for you?"

Sue Ellen removed the cloth from the basket she carried. "Father asked me to deliver this to Maddy," she said, taking out an envelope. "And Mother asked me to bring this jar of fresh blackberry jam to you. Sort of a welcome-to-Pepper Cloud gift."

"Why thank you Miss Flaherty," Clay said, taking the proffered gift, "and please thank your mother for me, too. This is very thoughtful of the two of you."

Joey looked down with a mock-frown. "What, nothing

101

for me? Now that just ain't fair, Sue Ellen. You know how much I dote on your blackberry jam."

Sue Ellen gave him a sassy toss of her head. "Joey Brennan, you dote on anything with a bit of sugar in it. Besides, how could I bring you something if I didn't know you'd be here?"

Joey gave Clay's parcel a wistful look. "You're in for a real treat, Mr. Kincaid. Sue Ellen makes the best jam a body could ask for. Why, she took three blue ribbons at the county fair last fall."

Then he met Clay's gaze with a challenging one of his own. "But don't let a taste of that jam give you any ideas. I aim to place the winning bid on her basket at the Founder's Day Festival."

Sue Ellen's cheeks pinkened becomingly. "Oh, Joey, Mr. Kincaid's not interested in such nonsense." Then she squared her shoulders. "Besides, what makes you think you'll even know which basket is mine? It's all supposed to be a secret, remember?"

Joey gave Sue Ellen a cocky grin. "Don't you worry, I have a feeling that I'll recognize your basket when the time comes."

Clay's lips quirked up in a smile as he listened to their banter. He wondered if Mrs. Flaherty knew her daughter was sweet for the handyman. One thing for sure, the Ladies' Society president wouldn't take kindly to the notion.

"Since this is going to be my first Founders' Day Festival," he interjected, "you'll have to tell me how this basket bidding thing works."

"It's one of the ways we raise money for charity," Sue Ellen explained. "The morning of the festival, many of the ladies in town will fix up picnic baskets with homemade delicacies and drop them off at the schoolhouse, *anonymously*." She speared Joey with a don't-you-contradict-me look. "Then just before lunch, the menfolk gather round and bid on the baskets."

"The best part," Joey added, "is that the lady who prepared the lunch shares the meal with the lucky fellow who ends up with her basket." The young man met Sue Ellen's gaze with a look that was part possessive, part hopeful. "There's always a long line of fellas trying to guess which one is Sue Ellen's so they can get their bid in. And not just because she's such a good cook."

"Oh, Joey, go on with you now." Sue Ellen twisted a strawberry blond lock around her finger.

Clay did his best to ignore the not so subtle flirtation going on. "I suppose Maddy prepares one of these baskets, too?" he commented idly. Maddy would, of course, expect him to bid aggressively for her basket.

But rather than a quick affirmative, Joey and Sue Ellen exchanged uneasy glances. Then, as if to say *you tell him*, Joey suddenly turned his full attention back to the shutter. The saucily adoring smile Sue Ellen had graced the handyman with earlier turned to an accusing glare before she turned back to face Clay.

"I believe Maddy has decided not to do a basket this year," she said, not quite meeting Clay's gaze. "But I'm sure she has plans to help raise funds in other ways."

Hmmm, there was something here Sue Ellen was carefully not saying. Should he try to probe for answers?

Clay decided to let the matter drop for now. He'd just realized Sue Ellen had handed him the perfect opportunity to go back in the house without breaking his word to Miss Olive.

"Sue Ellen, I wonder if I could ask you to do me a favor." He flashed her his most charming smile. "If you would hold this ladder steady for a few minutes, I'd like to set this jar down somewhere inside. Wouldn't want to run the risk of dropping it and spoiling my treat." He pointed to the letter she still held. "And I'll be glad to deliver that to Maddy for you while I'm at it."

Sue Ellen's apparent hesitation was belied by the glance she directed to the top of the ladder. "Why, I suppose that would be all right. If Joey trusts me to hold the ladder for him, that is."

Joey thrust out his chest. "Sue Ellen, I'd trust you with my life."

Clay resisted the urge to roll his eyes. "That's settled then." He stepped back as Sue Ellen took his place at the foot of the ladder. "I'll be right back so you don't have to stand out here too long."

"No hurry," Sue Ellen assured him. Her gaze never wavered from Joey's.

Clay headed for the front door, inordinately pleased with himself. Luck was definitely on his side, despite the obstructive scheming of the ladies of Barrows House. He was free to investigate the goings-on in the parlor with a clear conscience that he had not broken his word to Miss Olive. And he *would* get in to the parlor this time, no matter who had been set to guard the door.

But he was careful to enter the house quietly and reconnoiter the entryway. No need to go out of his way to announce his presence.

To his relief, the only occupant of the front hall was Othello. Closing the door behind him, Clay silently laughed at himself. How had he come to this, employing stealth to avoid the devious machinations of a trio of little old ladies?

Othello, as if reading his thoughts, stared at him with a disdainful twitch of his whiskers.

"You're right," he told the cat as he straightened his shoulders. "It's time to quit tiptoeing around."

The feline's only response was a singularly unimpressed sneeze. Then Othello's ears perked up and his head swung around toward the parlor. Clay caught the sound as well, the faint tinkle of dishes rattling.

As if stalking prey, Othello approached the parlor with graceful purpose. To Clay's surprise, all it took was a nudge from the cat's nose to open the door wide enough for him to slip inside.

Now he could make out intriguing snatches of conversation. Following the cat, he had his hand on the door when he heard a chagrined "Oh!" uttered from the head of the stairs.

But Miss Olive was too late. Clay had already pushed open the door and pulled up short on the threshold. He wasn't sure exactly what it was he'd expected, but it definitely wasn't this.

Maddy and her three guests sat around a square wooden table. Despite his earlier suspicions, there wasn't a hint of flashy dress or inappropriately exposed flesh to be seen amongst them.

They were all appropriately attired for an afternoon visit. Dainty porcelain saucers and tea cups sat near each lady's right hand. But this was no ordinary tea party.

"Ante up, ladies," Maddy announced. "The game is five-card stud."

Chapter Eight

The brassy blond seated to Maddy's right noticed Clay's presence first. Her lips curved up into a provocative smile. "Why hello there, handsome. Care to join us for a hand or two?"

Maddy started guiltily, sending one of the cards she was dealing sailing completely off the table.

Clay kept his expression carefully free of amusement as he saw her fight to regain her composure. He couldn't wait to hear what sort of inventive explanation she came up with for this unconventional little scene. It reminded him of the time he'd caught the twins peeking between the bushes at the boys' swimming hole.

"Mr. Kincaid." Her tone and bearing were admirably haughty as she turned to acknowledge his presence, but she couldn't hide the tell-tale flush of guilt that warmed her cheeks. "Is there some emergency that caused you to come barging in here without so much as a knock at the door?"

Nice tactic, but it wouldn't work. He wasn't about to let

her put him on the defensive. "The door was open," he said with a shrug. Holding out the envelope, he sauntered closer to the table. "The mayor sent these papers to you by way of his daughter."

What *was* going on here anyway? Miss Adeline and Miss Olive had been helping Maddy keep this from him. He hid a smile as he envisioned this being the Barrows House version of a gaming hall. He wouldn't put anything past these unconventional women.

Miss Olive stepped into the room behind him and he could feel her gaze boring into his back. But she didn't say anything, and he didn't turn to face her.

The well-endowed brunette seated across from Maddy eyed him as if he were a tasty comfit. "Maddy," she drawled, "aren't you going to introduce us to this handsome devil."

Maddy's lips pursed as if she'd rather not. But she was trapped by her own good manners. With an abrupt movement, she waved a hand in Clay's direction. "Ladies, this *gentleman* is Mr. Clayton Kincaid, a cousin of my late husband's." Her chin jutted out defiantly as she faced him.

"Mr. Kincaid," she continued, "I believe you've already met Ruby Jane Hobbs." She paused while Clay exchanged greetings with Ruby Jane, then moved on to the pouty-lipped blond on her left. "This is Lila Jenkins."

Clay bowed slightly and nodded. "Miss Jenkins."

"You don't need to be so formal, sugar," the less-than-shy girl said with a wink. "Just call me Lila."

He returned her smile. "My pleasure, Lila." That earned him a sharp glance from Maddy. Not jealous, was she?

Maddy quickly moved on to the last of the introductions. "And this is Cassandra Webb."

Another bow. "Pleased to meet you."

The apple-cheeked brunette gave him a practiced smile. "The pleasure is all mine, sweet cakes." She traced the contour of her lower lip with a scarlet-tipped nail. "And you can call me Cassy. Why don't you pull up a chair and join us?"

107

Clay was tempted, just to see what Maddy would do. But before he could form a response, Katie materialized beside him. "Can I play, too?"

Suddenly, he was no longer amused. What only a moment ago had seemed a harmlessly eccentric pastime, now took on a less innocent tone. Unconventional was one thing, but did Maddy have any idea how inappropriate her current activities were with a child in the house? How could she possibly expect anyone to support her adoption efforts if she continued to 'act so irresponsibly?

Her reaction, surprisingly, was to send *him* an accusing glare. What had brought that on? None of this was his doing.

Her expression softened as she turned to Katie. "Sorry, Buttercup, this game is for adults only. And besides, it's about time for us to wrap things up for today."

She stood and turned with a gracious smile to the three other women seated at the table. "Ladies, thank you for a delightful afternoon. Cassy, it appears you're the winner today."

Clay had noticed the pile of assorted buttons beside each tea cup. At least they hadn't been playing for actual money. Unless those represented stakes the way poker chips did.

But there was no movement to exchange the buttons for cash.

Cassy rose slowly. "From where I'm sitting, Maddy girl, it looks to me like *you're* the winner."

Maddy ignored Cassy's comment as she pushed her chair up to the table. "Same time next Thursday?"

Ruby Jane and Lila stood. None of them seemed in much of a hurry to take their leave.

"Of course, Maddy." Ruby Jane patted her hair and watched Clay from the corner of her eye. "I wouldn't dream of missing one of our Thursday afternoon get-togethers."

"You can count me in," Lila agreed, her gaze resting openly on Clay as she moistened her lips. "If I'd have

108

known what yummy treats you serve here at Barrows House, I'd have started coming with Ruby Jane weeks ago."

As they drifted toward the hall, Cassy tapped Clay on the arm. "Me too. And perhaps next time, sugar, we can talk you into joining us."

"You don't have to wait that long, darlin'," Lila chimed in. "Any time you're ready for a game, just step on over to the Silver Buckle and look me up."

Clay tipped his head non-committally and stepped aside for them to pass. Normally, their blatant flirtatiousness would have amused him, but not in front of Katie.

He tried to curb his impatience as Maddy escorted her guests to the front hall and said her farewells.

Once the door had closed behind the visitors, she turned and gave him a quelling look. He opened his mouth, but she forestalled him with a raised hand and a frostily uttered, "One moment, please."

She marched past him and back into the parlor. As soon as she saw Katie, industriously playing tiddlywinks with some of the buttons, her manner softened. She ruffled the girl's hair, then bent to retrieve a large tin canister from beneath the table. "Help me pack up these buttons, will you Buttercup?"

Clay watched them silently, unwilling to speak his mind in front of Katie.

The job seemed to take forever. In fact, Clay was certain Maddy insisted they search out the buttons that had fallen and rolled across the floor just to drag things out. Did she want to delay their confrontation because she was embarrassed to face him, or because she just wanted to make him stew a bit longer? Well, he could be patient.

When they were finally done, Maddy handed the box to Katie. "Take these up to Miss Olive's sewing room, please. And then I believe Miss Fanny has some fresh-baked cookies waiting for you in the kitchen."

"Yes ma'am!" Katie skipped out of the room, obviously eager to get to the promised treats.

At last, Maddy turned to face Clay squarely. Her brow lifted haughtily. "I believe you had something to say to me."

Her cool manner irritated the fire out of him. "Are you going to stand there and tell me, given that you have a child under your care, you see nothing wrong with what went on in here today?"

She clasped her hands in front of her, her expression controlled. "And just what do you think went on in here today?"

"Come on, Maddy, we both know this was no genteel social gathering. You were entertaining three women of questionable morals in your home, and doing it by turning your parlor into a gaming hall."

Her hands fisted against her hips. "Oh, is *that* what I was doing?"

Surely she wasn't trying to deny it? He'd given her credit for more integrity than that.

"And I must say," Maddy continued, "that's a very judgmental attitude for someone who barely knows these women."

Clay kept his tone even, refusing to let her ruffle his control. "They all but propositioned me right here in your parlor. In front of Katie, I might add."

Her cheeks did pinken at that. "Mr. Kincaid, I'll thank you to remember who you're speaking to." Then she tossed her head. "Besides, who I choose to entertain in *my* home, and how I choose to do it, is no concern of yours."

"On the contrary," he said, enunciating each word with utmost precision, "you made it my business when you made me party to your adoption scheme. Do you really think this is the kind of home life Katie should be exposed to?"

A sharp emotion of some sort flitted across her face, but it was swiftly replaced by her now-familiar glare. "Ruby Jane has been coming over on Thursday afternoons for over a month now, and this is the first time Katie has stepped inside this room while she was visiting. Unlike you, Katie knows not to open a closed door without knocking first." She stepped forward and jabbed a finger to his chest. "If you'll recall, Mr. Quick-to-judge-others Kincaid, it was *you* who carelessly left the door open and allowed Katie in, not me."

"Now wait just one minute, you're not blaming this little fiasco on me, are you?"

She tossed her head again, her eyes flashing angrily. "As my grandmother used to say, if the shoe fits. . . ." Nose pointed toward the ceiling, Maddy scooped up the letter, turned on her heel, and sailed past him without another word. He followed her out of the room in time to see her march majestically up the stairs.

Of all the brassy, short-sighted, won't-admit-when-she's-wrong females. He'd only been trying to give her some much needed advice. There was absolutely no justification for her trying to turn this back on him, except her own feelings of guilt.

He was *not* judgmental.

Clay decided he needed fresh air and something physical to do. Maybe he'd rent a horse from the stables and find someplace where he could put the animal through its paces.

He had his hand on the knob of the front door, when Miss Olive halted him.

"Mr. Kincaid, join me in the library, please."

"I don't really think now is—" He paused, wincing at the sound of a door slamming from somewhere on the second floor.

"Now is the perfect time." She swept a hand out toward the library.

Clay had had his fill of being ordered around by a group of eccentric spinsters and matrons. He set his jaw, ready to stand up to her. But her implacable expression brooked no arguments.

Clay raked a hand through his hair. Smothering an oath, he marched past the gray-haired harridan and into the library.

111

Miss Olive followed, closing the door behind her. She calmly took a seat in one of the padded wingback chairs, then eyed him with a raised brow. "Do stop fidgeting, Mr. Kincaid, and I'll thank you not to glare at me. We're not enemies, you know."

Clay, realizing he'd been pacing, took a seat across from her. "My apologies, ma'am. I wasn't aware I was scowling at you. Now, was there something you wanted to discuss with me?"

She studied him for a moment. He returned her stare, refusing to look away, refusing to soften or back down any further than he already had. Devil take it, he was in the right here. For all her good intentions, Maddy showed a distinct lack of concern over the example she was providing Katie. She just didn't know how to accept advice gracefully.

He was more glad than ever that he'd sent that telegram to Peterson. It would be wise to have another option for the child if things continued on their current course.

Finally, Miss Olive folded her hands in her lap and sat back. "Mr. Kincaid, I'm very disappointed in you."

Disappointed in him? "Look, if you're referring to my promise to make sure your handyman's ladder was well-anchored, I assure you, I didn't break my word. Sue Ellen Flaherty came along and was more than happy to take my place."

Miss Olive frowned reprovingly. "Please, young man, we both know that you merely lived up to the letter of your promise, not the spirit." She narrowed her eyes. "But that's not what I was referring to. You attacked and misjudged Maddy."

Clay straightened. "Attacked? I've never attacked a woman in my life. I merely tried to point out—"

"You accused her of not taking her responsibilities for Katie seriously. That's not only attacking the very heart of who she is, but it couldn't be further from the truth."

Clay spread his hands. "Miss Olive, no one is arguing

112

that Maddy is anything but a generous, well-intentioned, soft-hearted woman. Problem is, she may be just a tad too soft-hearted for her, and Katie's, own good."

Miss Olive showed no sign of unbending, so he tried again. "If you think about this dispassionately, you must see that she didn't use much common sense." He shifted in his seat. "Look, I'm not one of Maddy's so-called 'Propriety Police.' I don't look down my nose at anyone merely because they act unconventionally." His lips quirked wryly. "In fact, I find myself looking forward a little more keenly each morning to my visits here."

He leaned forward. "But Maddy doesn't seem to understand the responsibility that goes along with caring for a child."

Miss Olive eyed him sternly. "You think not? Maddy always leaves strict instructions that neither Katie nor anyone else is to be let near the parlor during her Thursday afternoon gatherings."

"Yet Katie found a way in after all." Clay steadfastly ignored the twinge of guilt as he remembered Maddy pointing out the part he'd played in that.

The seamstress compressed her lips. "I'm afraid I must take the blame for that. I underestimated my charge's curiosity and resourcefulness."

They both knew it wasn't Katie she referred to. Clay resisted the urge to defend his actions once more. Better he keep to the point. "Surely whatever shallow enjoyment Maddy gets from these 'gatherings' isn't worth exposing a young child to such influences."

Miss Olive seemed unimpressed by his arguments. "Mr. Kincaid, just exactly what do you think you know about what went on in our parlor this afternoon?"

Clay gestured impatiently. "What do you mean—they were gambling. What more is there to know?"

"Did you ask Maddy?"

He didn't like the look she was giving him, as if he'd failed some crucial test. Shifting slightly in his seat, he waved a hand. "No, but she didn't offer any explanations, either."

"Of course, she didn't. She has her pride. You know how that is, don't you?"

Clay decided not to grace that with an answer.

"Let *me* give you the explanation," she continued. "Ruby Jane and her friends drop by here whenever they need to place an order for a new dress, or when I need to fit them on a work in progress. Maddy, as is her way, always has a friendly word for them when they do. She found out a couple of months ago that Ruby Jane has a secret yearning to learn how to read. In fact, she did a bit of probing and was appalled to realize that none of the girls had had any schooling."

Her expression softened. "Being Maddy, she decided to do something to rectify the situation. But she took care to do it in such a way as to maintain their pride. So she told Ruby Jane she had a burning desire to learn how to play cards, and that she'd exchange card lessons for reading and writing lessons."

She smiled. "Ruby Jane jumped at it, though it's taken a bit of prodding to get Lila and Cassy to join in."

Her smile disappeared as she gave him another of those stern, mother superior looks. "That, Mr. Kincaid, is what goes on behind those parlor doors on Thursday afternoons. Serious lessons in reading and writing for three girls no one else seems to care a fig about."

Clay found himself trying to absorb the unpalatable thought that he might have misjudged the situation after all. He resisted the urge to lean back as Miss Olive leaned forward.

She narrowed her eyes. "Too bad she has to follow up this worthwhile activity with such a scandalous pastime as a bit of gambling. And for such high stakes, too." Her tone turned conspiratorial. "Why, do you know, if one of those girls comes out the winner, she gets a whole nickel discount on the next dress she orders from me? And if Maddy

114

wins, well, she has the audacity to require each of the girls to write out her name twenty times before the next meeting." She shook her head with an exaggerated tsk. "Absolutely disgraceful."

He was glad Miss Olive didn't employ sarcasm often. It was much too effective a weapon in her hands.

She shook her head and placed a hand on her chest. "Such a poor example she's setting for Katie. I can see why you're concerned. Much better that the child learn to turn her back on such riff-raff, and reserve her charitable impulses for those more worthy." She sat back and met his gaze squarely. "Of course, I am a bit worried that there are some whose definition of worthy might exclude former actresses and widow women who take comfort in speaking to their deceased husbands."

Clay held up his hands ready to admit defeat. "All right, madam, you've made your point."

She cocked her head to one side. "Have I, now?"

"Yes, yes, I get it." He stood and paced across the room. "Perhaps I was a bit hasty in my assessment of the situation." He glanced over at her prim, raised-brow expression and hastily amended his statement. "All right, in this particular instance, I was definitely too quick to judge."

Clay raked a hand through his hair as he looked up toward the second floor. He could still see Maddy march up that graceful flight of stairs, her stiff-backed demeanor eloquently communicating her anger. "I suppose I owe her an apology."

Miss Olive's smile hinted that she might just forgive him, after all. "I believe I'd wait until supper tonight," she advised. "Maddy would likely be more inclined to listen to what you have to say after she's had a chance to, shall we say, recover her composure."

Which, Clay knew, was a polite way of saying he ought to wait until Maddy had cooled down enough not to want his head served up on a platter.

He decided to wait.

Chapter Nine

Clay cleared his throat. "Nice evening."

"Uhmm."

He frowned at Maddy's less-than-enthusiastic reply. She'd given him non-committal responses all through supper—when she'd bothered to respond at all.

He was more than ready to apologize and get this whole thing behind them. That's why he'd invited her to sit out on the porch swing with him rather than join the others in the parlor this evening. After all, he was man enough to admit he'd been wrong. He just hoped she was woman enough to accept his apology graciously.

Glancing again at her frosty profile, he had his doubts.

Clay cleared his throat again. Best get this over with, dragging it out wouldn't make it any less painful. "I had a little talk with Miss Olive after you went upstairs this afternoon."

"Oh?"

She wasn't going to help him out at all. But then, he supposed he shouldn't begrudge her her pound of flesh.

"Yes," he answered, doggedly pressing on. "She explained to me about the reading lessons." He shifted slightly and then squared his shoulders. "It appears I owe you an apology. I should have gotten the whole story before I leapt to any conclusions."

"Yes, you should have."

There was no visible thawing in her manner. In fact, if anything, the look she turned on him seemed more withering than it had earlier.

"In the future," she said, enunciating carefully, "please keep in mind that you have no right to sit in judgment of my actions, whether you have the whole story or not."

Clay's jaw tightened. Of all the high and mighty, stiff-necked, ice-queen attitudes—he'd just swallowed his pride and apologized to her, and her only response was to *lecture* him? No woman, other than his mother, had taken that tone to him since he'd left the nursery. He was willing to admit he'd been wrong, but there were limits to how much crow he'd eat over it.

"I'll try to keep that in mind," he said with what he considered admirable restraint, "if you'll remember that I'm supposed to be courting you. That means anything that reflects on your character reflects on me and my standards as well. From where I'm sitting, it seems I have *every* right to challenge your actions and expect explanations for your more unorthodox behaviors."

Her eyes narrowed. "Keep in mind, sir, that we are only pretending here. You're not truly my beau, so you have no real rights in this matter."

Enough was enough. Time she admitted he wasn't the only one who had stepped over the line today. "But I'm a very real party to your adoption scheme, and I do consider Katie's welfare my business, whether you like it or not."

Despite Maddy's still simmering indignation, she knew in her heart that he had been doing his best to apologize. And she supposed their activities had looked pretty shady to someone walking in cold this afternoon. Besides, at the time he'd seemed more amused, albeit at her expense, than outraged, until Katie slipped in behind him.

She nodded with grudging acceptance. "I don't suppose I can fault you for being concerned about Katie. Apology accepted." Not that she was ready to let him off the hook completely. "But just what makes you such an authority on the kind of home life a child needs?"

A sudden thought made her draw in her breath sharply. "You don't have children of your own, do you?"

"Of course not."

She decided not to analyze why that news filled her with such relief.

"But," he continued, "I do have four sisters, three of them younger than me. Not quite the same as being a parent, I'll allow you that, but it does give me some modest perspective on the matter."

Maddy leaned back against the swing. She could feel Clay's gaze on her, but she kept her own eyes focused on the honeysuckle-laden trellis at the other end of the porch. Her irritation eased as her imagination toyed with what he'd just said.

He had four sisters, did he? He obviously cared a great deal about them. She could tell from his voice. And she'd bet her next meal that they adored him, as well. Which probably explained a large part of his arrogance—they'd no doubt petted and looked up to him when they were growing up. And for all his arrogance, he'd make a wonderful brother—charming, protective, indulgent.

Unbidden, the thought came to her that those same qualities would undoubtedly make him a wonderful lover, as well. But not for her.

Never for her.

Sighing, she slid him a sideways glance. "You don't think I'd make a very good mother for Katie, do you?" She kept her tone casual. Her pride wouldn't allow her to reveal how important his answer was. She'd been having more and more doubts herself lately about her suitability for the role.

He eyed her closely, as if weighing his words. "I don't doubt that you love her."

His tone was infinitely kind. Which made what he *hadn't* said all the more damning. "But you don't believe that's enough."

He spread his hands, his lips quirking in a wry smile. "Why ask me? I'm just your hired beau, remember?"

She sat up straighter. He was right. This was a decision she had to make for herself. Besides, Katie had nowhere else to go, and Maddy refused to consider turning her over to strangers, or worse yet, an orphanage. "Let's talk about something else, shall we?"

He tilted his head. "Like what?"

She ignored the sympathy in his expression and took a deep breath. "Like, given how you feel about my 'adoption scheme,' whether you will follow through on our arrangement."

He sat back, a flicker of surprise and something akin to guilt crossing his face. The next few seconds seemed to stretch interminably long. Even the swing stilled as she waited for his answer.

Finally, he set the swing in motion again. "I don't make a habit of reneging on bargains I've made," he said firmly.

Disappointment stabbed through her at his lack of enthusiasm. "That's not good enough. If you stay on, I need your word that you'll put your best effort into what you call our little charade. A begrudging, half-hearted effort is worse than none at all." She had to be sure of him, had to hear him say the words.

His lips tightened, as if he wasn't used to having his commitment questioned. "You have my word on it." Then, before she could say anything, he raised a hand. "However, you should understand that I'll continue to speak my mind, at least when we're in private."

She thought about that a moment. "Fair enough." She'd rather know what he was thinking than have to guess, anyway.

119

He leaned back again. "So, what now?"

"What do you mean?"

"I've been in Pepper Cloud a little over three days. I believe, according to your schedule, we were supposed to show signs of being 'smitten' by this time."

"True." She suppressed a sudden urge to fidget in her seat. There was something about the way he was looking at her. . . .

He touched her collar, and she jumped. His lips turned up in a knowing smile. "Making a change in your wardrobe was a nice touch."

She shifted, not quite sure whether she wanted to move away or move closer. "It was Miss Olive's idea." Surely the slight tremor in her voice was barely noticeable?

"Smart lady." He brushed away a June bug that had landed on her shoulder, then rested his hand lightly on her back. "Sends a subtle message that you're making changes in your life." He captured her gaze with a warmly intense one of his own. "Not to mention how much younger and softer it makes you look."

She swallowed, suddenly finding it difficult to form a coherent sentence.

He twined a tendril of her hair around his finger. "I suppose, if you're certain you want to continue with our arrangement, I should begin playing my part in earnest."

Maddy's skin tingled where his finger had brushed against her neck. "Yes." She cleared her throat and tried to regain her businesslike perspective. "I think the best way to proceed is—"

"Maddy," he interrupted, placing an arm behind her shoulder along the top of the swing. "I'm sure you have a very well-thought-out plan. But what do you say we try this my way first?"

"I don't think . . ." Maddy paused, distracted by the nearness of his arm. He wasn't actually hugging her, but . . .

"Good. You shouldn't think. To make folks believe this

romance is genuine, it should appear spontaneous, impulsive." Clay's expression tendered a challenge as he oh so casually moved his hand from the back of the swing to her shoulder.

Maggie stiffened at the unaccustomed familiarity of the gesture. What was wrong with her? She felt like a green girl just out of the schoolroom instead of a widow woman in her mid-twenties. She had to do better than this.

"Easy," he said as if calming a skittish horse. "We're putting on a show, remember?"

If that reminder was supposed to make her feel better, it fell miserably short of the mark. The warmth of his fingers as they subtly massaged her shoulder, however, made her uncomfortable in an entirely different way.

"Right now," he continued, lifting his thumb to stroke the lobe of her ear, "there are at least two people on the front porch across the street watching us, and I'm certain I saw your parlor curtain twitch a time or two."

Her earlobe seemed unaccountably sensitive to his touch. Heat skittered across the back of her neck. Her nerve endings fluttered in reaction.

"Well," he murmured, his free hand tucking a strand of hair behind her ear, "are you going to play your part, or have you changed your mind?"

She was grateful for the counterpoint his less-than-romantic words made to his actions. It kept her from making a complete fool of herself. It would be so easy to let herself enjoy this, to revel in his touch, in his tender smiles. . . .

This is all just an act, she told herself. And he was right, she had an obligation to do her part. Taking a deep breath, she lifted her gaze to meet his, and hesitantly raised a hand to his face.

His skin was so warm. The raspy stubble of his beard wonderfully rough against her sensitive fingertips. How would it feel against her own cheek? All those old longings she'd tried to suppress over the years came flooding back full force.

"Much better," he said, his eyes darkening seductively. He turned his head, kissing her palm before she realized what he was about.

As if burned, she yanked her hand away.

"You're thinking instead of feeling again," he chided.

"One of us has to." She resisted the urge to bring the hand he'd kissed up to her face.

"But what about our audience?"

She had no trouble keeping her gaze downcast as if in embarrassed confusion. "What our audience will see, is me pulling back after an attempted intimacy on your part. That will appear perfectly natural. The fact that I allowed you the intimacy in the first place, and am still sitting here beside you, will be enough to set the tongues to wagging, believe me."

It was his turn to sigh. He shook his head "Definitely thinking too much." Giving her a crooked smile, he stood and took her hands to raise her up as well. "I suppose I should be going." Before she knew what he was about, he gave her a quick peck on the cheek.

Maddy remained on the porch after he'd gone, unwilling to retreat inside just yet. She'd like to think she was outraged by that kiss she could still feel branded on her cheek, but truth to tell, it had left her yearning for something more. What would those warm, firm lips feel like on her own?

Clay was treating this like an amusing game. Why couldn't she do the same? Of course, it might help if he'd quit constantly rewriting the script.

She rubbed her hand against her skirt. It too still tingled from his kiss. She could still feel the rugged texture of his cheek, the warm velvet caress of his lips. If his mere touch could affect her so strongly, how would she make it through all that came with a supposed engagement with her control intact?

* * *

Clay had trouble falling asleep that night. He stared at the shadowy ceiling, wrestling with his conscience over the promise he'd given Maddy.

Why couldn't she have been satisfied to merely accept his help? Why did she demand he put his heart and soul into the effort? Her questions, demands really, had backed him into a corner, and he didn't like the feeling.

Her ultimatum had forced him to evaluate his stance, and suddenly he'd realized it didn't seem such a black-and-white issue any more.

Maddy might be outlandish and scheming, but she had her own unique code of honor. Poker games, barmaids and impossible charades were all grist for her mill. But she was generous to those in need and her loyalties ran deep. She held firm to her convictions, even under pressure. And, of course, he'd never doubted she truly cared for Katie.

A child could do worse than live with such a passionately caring woman who loved her.

A man could do worse, as well.

He'd watched Maddy sitting there, waiting for his answer, and he'd glimpsed the same don't-tread-on-me determination he'd seen when she'd stood up to Cybil Flaherty in her parlor. And he hadn't been able to deal her the blow she'd obviously been braced for.

So he'd given her his promise.

What bothered him even more, though, was the fact that his feelings on the issue of Maddy adopting Katie weren't the only ones undergoing a change.

Of course, the tug of attraction he felt for the unpredictable Mrs. Potter was no more than a healthy male's reaction to a pretty woman. He still wasn't sure Maddy hadn't conspired with his mother to force him into a marriage he didn't want. But even if she had, he was way too clever to let himself be tricked into such a relationship.

Of course he was.

With an oath, Clay rolled over, punched his pillow into

a more accommodating shape, and tried to will himself to sleep.

Maddy blew a strand of hair out of her eyes, feeling not only frustrated but more than a little ridiculous. Perched ten feet above the ground on Joey's ladder, she'd been trying for the past five minutes to disengage the back of her skirt from a very unchivalrous tree branch's clutches.

She tried contorting her body to reach the snag one more time and nearly lost her balance in the process. Much as she hated to, it looked like she'd have to call for help.

But could she get the attention of one of the ladies inside Barrows House without alerting the neighbors to her plight? She'd really rather not provide another tidbit for the Pepper Cloud gossip brigade. Well, no help for it.

Maddy had already opened her mouth to form the words when she caught the familiar creak of the front gate opening. An answer to her prayers! At this time of morning it was either Clay arriving a few minutes early, or one of Miss Olive's customers. At this point, either one would do just fine.

"Yoo-hoo," she called, as nonchalantly as she was able.

"Maddy?"

It was Clay. Curiously, she felt relieved. He'd likely give her a good ribbing over this, but at least she could count on his discretion. "Yes, I'm out back."

She could tell by the sound of his boots on the brick walkway that he was already headed her way. "Would you mind giving me a hand with something?"

"I'll be right there."

She gripped the ladder a bit tighter, hoping to steady her nerves as she watched for him to appear around the corner of the house. When he did, he looked around, a puzzled frown on his face. "Maddy, where—"

Catching sight of her, he froze, practically in mid-stride. "What the devil—"

Maddy waved self-consciously. "Hello. I guess this must

look rather comical from where you're standing. I was just trying to adjust the height of this swing Joey hung for Katie yesterday, and managed to get my dress tangled." She realized she was talking way too fast, and paused to take a deep breath.

When he made no attempt to come to her aid, she tried a self-deprecating smile and some gentle prodding. "I'd appreciate some help before I ruin a perfectly good dress, or fall down and break a perfectly good neck."

Her little attempt at humor didn't succeed in raising so much as an answering smile from him. He just stood there, staring up at her without saying a word.

"Mr. Kincaid," she began stiffly. Then something about his appearance caught her attention. His face had paled and he stared at her as if facing his worst nightmare. Something was wrong. Was he ill?

"Never mind," she said brightly, her mind churning to find a way to help him save face. "I've changed my mind. Don't you dare come up here. I'm determined not to let an ornery old tree get the better of me."

She heard the ominous sound of ripping as she gave her skirt a ruthless yank. "This dress is old and a bit worn anyway." But she still remained caught. Would she have to sacrifice her modesty to get out of this fix?

The back door thumping open kept her from having to make that choice.

"Aunt Maddy, whatcha doing up there?" Katie skipped over to the ladder, peering up curiously. Then she wrinkled her nose. "Oooh, you're caught. I'll help."

Before Maddy could say yea or nay, Katie had scampered up, nimble as the squirrels that nested in the tree's branches. Within a matter of seconds, she had freed Maddy's dress and was on her way down again.

Maddy followed, though her pace was more sedate. By the time she stepped off the bottom rung, Katie was chattering to Clay, oblivious to any undercurrents.

"See my swing, Mr. Kincaid? Joey hung it for me yesterday. This one can go even higher than Anna's. Want to see?"

Maddy stopped the little girl with a touch on the arm. "Just a minute, Buttercup. Let me move this ladder out of the way so you don't hurt yourself."

Clay, his face now a dark, ruddy color, stepped past her without meeting her gaze. "Here, let me get that for you."

Maddy watched him grab hold of the ladder as if he wanted to snap it in half. Carting it away from the tree, he placed it next to the house, careful to lay it lengthwise behind the hydrangea bushes.

He turned back to them, straightening his cuffs, and smiled at Katie. "Now, let's see this swing in action."

Maddy moved to stand beside Clay and watched him as he studiously avoided eye contact with her. He had his expression back under control now, but in her mind she could still see the startled starkness of it when he'd first spied her. And she knew he was very aware of her gaze on him. The tension between them was almost palpable.

Glimpsing the way he twisted the ring on his finger, she remembered the two other occasions when she'd seen him do likewise. A sudden inkling of what was at the heart of his problem began to dawn on her.

After a few minutes of praising Katie's prowess on the swing, he finally turned to face her. "My apologies for not coming to your aid earlier."

Studying Clay's stiff back and even stiffer smile, Maddy felt at a loss as to how to make him more comfortable. "No harm done," she said lightly.

He raised a brow. "That rip in your skirt says differently. And based on the purple trim it's sporting, it appears to be one of your new ones."

Maddy resisted the urge to twist her head around to survey the damage. Instead she shrugged. "Not new, refurbished. I'm sure this is nothing a needle and thread can't fix."

"I suppose I owe you an explanation," he said, shoving his hands into his pockets.

Her fingers itched to brush the hair, as well as the worry lines, from his brow. She settled for a light touch to his sleeve instead. "You don't owe me anything."

He flashed her a crooked smile. "That tears it, now I'll have to tell you."

Maddy felt goose bumps prickle her skin as he took her hand and placed it on his arm.

"Come on, let's go for a walk."

Clay escorted Maddy out the front gate. They turned away from town, heading instead toward the open countryside.

She held her peace, walking composedly beside him as if this were nothing more than a casual stroll, and for that he was grateful. For once in his life, he was uncomfortably at a loss for words. The glib phrases he needed were like rainbows, frustratingly out of reach. This was one subject he'd avoided speaking of his entire life.

He'd become resourceful at a very early age in devising ways to cover up his shameful secret. His father had known, and his older brother had guessed. But it had never, ever been spoken of. As far as he knew, no one else had any idea what a craven coward he really was.

Not far past Barrows House, a small stream cut through the road. Rather than take the bridge across, they turned onto the path that paralleled the bank.

Deciding he'd been silent way too long, Clay raked a hand through his hair. He stooped to pick up a pebble, then flung it into the stream.

But before he could say anything, she gave his arm a gentle squeeze. "You know, you really *don't* owe me any sort of explanation. Sometimes there are things in a person's life that are too personal or too painful to share with others. If—"

"I'm afraid of heights."

Clay groaned inwardly at the oafish way he'd blurted the

words out. Where was his much-touted eloquence, his so-called easy grace and charm? But he'd been desperate to get the thing said before Maddy's attempt to be understanding weakened his resolve altogether.

How was she reacting to the damning words? He cut a sideways glance her way and was surprised by her unruffled appearance.

With a shrug she offered, "I'm afraid of snakes and spiders." She gave a delicate shudder, as if just the thought of the creatures distressed her.

What kind of response was that? "That's hardly the same sort of thing," he protested through clenched teeth.

She raised a challenging brow. "And why not?"

"Well, for one thing, you're a woman, and women are expected to have delicate sensibilities."

Her back stiffened at that. "I hardly think my being a woman is a reason to dismiss my fears so lightly. Regardless of how inconsequential or foolish an individual's personal terrors may be when viewed by others, to that individual they are very real."

Clay couldn't let himself off the hook so easily. "Be that as it may, I doubt your so-called fear would keep you from helping someone in need."

She waved a hand dismissively. "If you're talking about my little difficulty up on the ladder, I wasn't in any real danger. I'm sure if I *had* been, you would have attempted to do what you could to assist me."

"In that you are mistaken," he said harshly. He knew himself for the coward he was, and he refused to hide behind excuses and platitudes.

She laid her free hand on his arm. "I don't believe—"

"Don't ever put your life in my hands," he interrupted with a clenched jaw, "if it involves faith in my ability to overcome my gutless fear."

He could tell by the sympathy in her eyes and the thrust of her chin that Maddy still didn't believe him. This discussion would be much easier to get through if she wasn't trying so hard to smooth it over for him.

God, he'd have to tell her the full extent of his shame to make her understand.

Well, so be it. He pointed to a large, exposed tree root. "Why don't you sit there and let me tell you a little story."

She eyed him cautiously, then nodded, and with his help, sat where he'd pointed. As she adjusted her skirts, he leaned back against the tree trunk, reluctantly replaying that long ago scene in his mind. It was as vivid as if it had happened yesterday.

"The family who owned the property next to ours had a son my age," he began. "Brian and I practically grew up together and were as close as brothers. Then, right after my twentieth birthday, I spent a year abroad. When I returned home, things had changed. Brian had changed. Where he'd always had a deep love of the land, he was now spending more of his time in the city and less on the family estate. And he'd gotten engaged to a predatory young woman who was more enamored of his money and position than of Brian, himself. Brian, however, fancied himself deeply in love with her."

He raked a hand through his hair, remembering the heated confrontation the two of them had had when Clay tried to convince his friend just how blind his love had made him. "Unfortunately, over the next few months, Brian made several disastrous investments. Overnight, he lost his money and was on the verge of losing most of his properties—land and holdings that had been in his family for generations. Of course, his fiancée showed her true colors and immediately broke off the engagement."

He tore a twig from a low hanging branch. "When I got wind of how dire his situation was, I went to his home to offer what help I could." The twig snapped in his hand and he flung it away. "I found him standing on the ledge of a third-floor window, contemplating the flagstones below."

"No!"

129

Her cry had a bitten-off sound to it. Her eyes closed momentarily, as if to block out some unpleasant sight, then flew open to meet his gaze again.

It seemed he'd finally succeeded in shocking the unflappable Maddy Potter. And she still hadn't heard the worst of it.

"Oh, yes," he continued, forcing the words, forcing open old wounds. "I tried to talk to him, offered my support and the money he needed to get back on his feet. But he only smiled and shook his head." Clay stared straight ahead, seeing Brian's face again, feeling that same self-loathing at his inability to help his friend. "For a full ten minutes I stood at that window, coaxing, arguing, demanding—but it wasn't enough."

Those had been the longest, most hellish ten minutes of his life. His hands fisted in self-directed anger. "Ten minutes! Plenty of time to step out on that ledge and take him by the arm, to pull him back inside to safety. But I couldn't do it."

Clay shoved away from the tree and paced a few steps toward the stream. Keeping his back to her, he stoically finished his story.

"So he jumped."

He gave a bitter laugh. "Brian thanked me for leaving the decision in his hands, then just stepped off the ledge." His hand reached out reflexively, and he covered the movement by raking it through his hair. Though *tearing* his hair out would be more what he deserved.

"Even then, I couldn't make the effort to lean out and try to grab for him." He was acutely conscious of her sitting deathly quiet behind him. Now that she knew the depth of his cowardice, what was she thinking? He'd never felt so dirty, so exposed, in his life. If she wouldn't say it, he would. "Because of me a fine, decent man is dead."

"No. *Not* because of you."

Clay swung around, surprised by the vehemence in Maddy's tone.

130

"Suicide is a terrible, heartbreaking business." She twisted her hands in the fabric of her skirt. "It leaves behind a legacy of painful conjectures and self-accusations."

Then she met his gaze and tilted her chin up once more. "But you are not responsible for your friend's death," she said with unexpected conviction. "You had nothing to do with his reason for wanting to end his life."

"But I should have—"

"I say again, you did not *do* anything, either deliberately or unintentionally, to goad him into such tragic action. His fiancée's coldness and his own foolish actions led to his desperation." The hand she used to tuck a lock of hair behind her ear trembled ever so slightly. "Perhaps you could have stopped him if you'd been able to step out on that ledge, but then again, it's more likely that you'd have only spurred him to quicker action."

That thought brought precious little consolation. "But at least then I would have known I'd done everything I could. The fact remains, I did nothing to stop him, though I had ample opportunity."

He locked gazes with her. "So you see, ma'am, you were quite wrong in your earlier conviction that I would set my fears aside in cases of extreme emergency. I've proven myself unable to overcome my paralyzing cowardice, even when a life hangs in the balance."

Maddy made as if to stand and he stepped forward to help her rise.

She'd obviously been deeply affected by his confession. Her face was pale, her hands were trembling, and she couldn't, or wouldn't, meet his gaze. What emotion was she feeling? Shock? Disappointment? Revulsion?

Maddy dusted her skirts with a sharp, no-nonsense movement. "I still believe you're being too hard on yourself. Your friend was in control of his own fate."

Was it so difficult for her to admit she'd been wrong about him? How could he not seem less of a man to her now than before?

131

She finally met his gaze, and he was surprised by the sympathy and understanding he saw there. They were standing so close he could see the pulse beating in her throat, could feel the air stir at her soft sigh. "Clay," she said, touching his arm lightly, "it wasn't your fault."

It was the hint of moisture in her eyes that undid him. With a smothered oath, he pulled her close and bent to taste her lips. He'd intended for it to be a short, tender acknowledgement of his appreciation of her as a woman, but when she placed her hands on his shoulders and leaned closer, his good intentions were forgotten.

His lips claimed hers with a hungry, elemental urgency that she seemed to return. It was only when he sought to deepen it, to taste her fully, that he felt her stiffen.

Lifting his head slightly, he stared into her eyes and saw a maelstrom of conflicting emotions warring there—desire, need, denial, regret. "Maddy?"

She gently stepped out of his embrace with a tight smile. "It's time I returned to the house."

It was hard to tell how much she'd been affected by the kiss. Her rigid control and coolly self-possessed matron guise were back in full force. He, on the other hand, felt like he'd just been poleaxed. Who would have imagined a kiss could have such an impact on him? He tried to believe it was just that it had come on the heels of that emotionally charged confession he'd made, but he had a feeling he was only lying to himself.

Clay offered her his arm, and felt a measure of relief that she readily placed her hand there. Whether she'd allowed him the kiss out of a misguided show of sympathy or because she'd desired it as much as he had, at least she wouldn't treat him like a criminal or leper after learning his disgraceful secret. He only wished he could read her mind and find out how she truly viewed him now.

Then again, perhaps it was best that he not know.

He gave a short bow. "As always, I'm at your service."

132

Chapter Ten

Maddy prayed he wouldn't feel the slight tremble that she couldn't quite control. She *would not* let him see how much his kiss had affected her.

Goodness gracious, what had she been thinking? She *hadn't* been thinking, that was the problem. Why was it her good sense seemed to fly out the window so often when Clay was around, leaving her wayward emotions free rein to take over? But she'd only wanted to offer a measure of comfort to him.

No, that wasn't entirely true. She'd felt the need to comfort him, yes, but she'd wanted that kiss, too, for her own sake. How long had it been since she'd felt so thoroughly desired. And it had helped her forget for a moment how much his story had affected her.

Dear God, suicide! If only she'd had a little warning, hadn't been caught so off guard. The shock had almost choked the breath from her.

He remained silent, obviously wrapped up in his own thoughts. Were they of his confession or of that sweet, painfully revealing kiss? If they were going to have any sort of conversation at all, it was up to her to get it started.

"So, tell me a bit about your family." There, that was a nice safe topic, and one that would require him to do most of the talking.

"My family?" Clay seemed to shake off his preoccupation with difficulty. Then, assuming an I'll-humor-you-for-now expression, he nodded. "All right. Let's see, I've mentioned before that I have four sisters. I also have a brother. Adam is older than me by six years, and is the sober, responsible member of the family." He flashed her a self-mocking smile that set her pulse fluttering again. "We're nothing alike."

"Meredith is next. She's unapologetically bookish and the only one of my sisters to escape the giddy-coquette transformation when she hit adolescence."

Some of Maddy's tension eased as she listened to him. She liked the way his expression softened and warmed when he spoke of his family.

He held a low-hanging branch out of her way. "Meredith is now quite happy with her role as a university dean's wife and mother of three."

His expression changed from warm approval to an amused smile. "Next is Judith. If Meredith and Adam are the family's calm center, Judith is its flamboyance. She's flighty and melodramatic—a lot like Miss Adeline, come to think of it. On the other hand, she is also unaffectedly charming and she genuinely loves people. Surprisingly enough, Judith, whose husband is a congressman, is the perfect politician's wife."

His words conjured up Maddy's own memories of the brave but badly shaken girl she'd rescued that fateful day. "I can see that. For all her femininity, I sensed a core of steel in your sister."

Clay looked surprised. "I'd forgotten you'd already met her. Perceptive of you to see that on such short acquaintance."

He eyed her a moment longer, then continued with his

descriptions. "Then there are the twins, Colleen and Bridget." He rolled his eyes in brotherly exasperation. "They've just turned twenty and are minxes of the first order. If there's mischief to be found, they'll uncover it. The two of them will likely turn my brother's hair gray before they find men who are brave enough to take them off his hands."

He wasn't fooling her. Maddy could hear the affection in his tone beneath the exasperation. "They sound wonderful. I've always thought it would be such fun to have brothers and sisters."

He gave her a wry smile. "Spoken like an only child."

That was her—an only, lonely child. Orphaned at age two and taken in by her grandmother, Maddy had often looked with envy at the conventional, close-knit families her friends had. She'd spent hours dreaming of the large, boisterous family she'd have when she married and set up her own household.

Winston's death had put an end to *that* dream, as well.

She determinedly shook off her melancholy as they stepped off the footpath and back onto the road. "Is that everyone?" She wanted to keep the conversation going as long as possible.

"Everyone except Mother, the glue that holds us all together." He cast her a sideways glance. "You haven't met her, have you?"

Why was he staring at her so strangely? "Why, no. I—"

The sound of a carriage approaching from behind them intruded, and they moved to the side of the road. Clay solicitously kept himself between her and the carriage, but he couldn't block the dust it kicked up.

Was that Sue Ellen riding with Joey Brennan? Maddy decided she must have been wrong as she pulled a handkerchief from her skirt pocket and sneezed twice. Cybil had her eye on handsome young Freddie Clemmons as a suitable match for Sue Ellen. And Cybil usually got her way.

Naturally, *Clay's* nose didn't so much as twitch. The man could remain cool and unruffled in a hailstorm.

Maddy kept a firm grip on his arm to keep from stumbling on the uneven terrain. Not that she minded the physical contact. As she sneezed a third time, though, her handkerchief fluttered away on an errant breeze.

With an exaggeratedly gallant bow, Clay released her arm. "Allow me."

Maddy watched as he stalked the fluttering scrap of cloth. It finally snagged on a bush and he had to jump a shallow ditch to retrieve it. The man was graceful, she had to give him that. It was a pure pleasure to watch him move.

Clay turned to retrace his steps, flourishing the handkerchief like an enemy's captured flag. With a grin at his theatrics, Maddy moved to join him.

Suddenly, her foot slid on a bit of loose rock and with a sharp cry, she stumbled to one knee.

For a moment, all Maddy could focus on was a nauseating spiral of pain. She'd stopped her fall with her hands, and the force of the impact jarred her arms all the way to her shoulders. She could feel stinging abrasions on both her palms and her knee. But worst of all was the terrible throbbing of her ankle.

Strong, gentle hands took her shoulders, easing the weight from her arms still braced against the ground. "Easy now. Let's have a look at you."

Clay's voice, warm with concern, provided a soothing counterpoint to the churning of her head and stomach. He eased her into a sitting position, then examined her hands, gently flexing her wrists.

"We'll need to tend to the scrapes, but nothing appears to be broken. Where else does it hurt?"

His touch felt so tender, the concern in his eyes so comforting, that Maddy's cheeks heated in reaction to her own thoughts—thoughts of how nice another one of those kisses would be right now.

"I think I scraped my knee," she hedged, hating the timorous sound of her voice. "I may need your help getting up."

Her ankle ached, but not unbearably so. They weren't far from Barrows House. If she could just get upright, perhaps she could hobble her way home. Then she'd allow herself the luxury of a few hours on the sofa in the parlor to recuperate. She might even let her ladies fuss over her.

But Clay looked uncertain. "I don't know if your getting up just yet is such a good idea. Your face is white as a sheet, and that's quite a grip you have on my hand, especially given the scrapes on your palm. You might be hurt worse than you think."

Maddy released his hand as if it were a hot poker, and lifted her chin. "That's ridiculous. Don't you think I'd know if I was badly hurt? Now, are you going to behave like a gentleman and help me, or are you going to make me scramble up on my own?"

"Have it your way," he said stiffly. She also thought she heard him mutter *stubborn woman* under his breath as he stood and held out a hand to her. But she could have been mistaken.

Trying to maintain an air of dignity, Maddy took his hand, along with a deep breath. Doing her best to place all her weight on her uninjured foot, she slowly rose.

There, that hadn't been so bad. It hurt like the devil, but if she set her mind to it . . .

Maddy shifted, placing a bit of weight on her injured foot. "Oh!" White hot pain wrested the sharp cry from her, and only Clay's firm hold kept her from collapsing entirely.

"I knew it! Blast it Maddy, why won't you just admit you're hurt. What is it, your knee?"

She winced at the vehemence of his tone. There was no need for him to get in such a snit.

Then she noticed his worried expression and felt shame-faced remorse for her churlishness, along with a warmer, softer feeling. "No, it's my ankle," she confessed when she could speak again. "I must have turned it when I slipped."

137

"Put your hand on my shoulder," he commanded in a voice that brooked no arguments. "I'm going to have a look at it."

Maddy did as she was told, and he stooped down to unlace and remove her shoe. His touch was feather light as he examined her ankle, but she still had to grit her teeth to keep from crying out.

At last he stood. "Sorry if I hurt you." He took her arm again with a worried smile. "There doesn't seem to be anything broken, but your ankle is badly swollen. I think we'd better get you home and call in a doctor to have a look at it."

Maddy nodded. "Of course. If you'll lend me a bit of support, I think I can hobble that far."

Would he put his arm around her? The thought of leaning so closely against him for the short trek to Barrows House set her pulse fluttering.

What was wrong with her? She wasn't some giddy schoolgirl, she was a twenty-four-year-old widow woman.

He handed her the shoe. "I'll do better than that."

His I've-got-the-devil-in-me tone gave her a mere heartbeat of warning before he scooped her up in his arms and settled her snugly against his chest.

"Mr. Kincaid!" How dare he handle her so familiarly! Had that kiss given him the idea that she'd allow such liberties? "Put me down this instant." Surely it was indignation that had set her heart racing and her flesh tingling.

But Clay shook his head. "Sorry, but your role as senior partner doesn't extend to this." He set off at a purposeful pace. "Just relax like a good little girl and let me get you home where the ladies can tend to you."

Like a good little girl? With a huff, she leaned back stiffly. Then she caught the twinkle in his eye. He'd been deliberately teasing her.

"You're right," she said, appreciating the humor of the situation and feeling slightly sheepish for her behavior. "I *was* acting like a twit. Thank you for your help."

138

"You're welcome." He met her gaze with a sideways look. "I'm just glad to discover you *can* fall prey to occasional fits of twit-like behavior."

Then he hefted her, settling her more snugly against his chest. "Now, this will be more comfortable for both of us if you'll put your arm around my neck and relax. I promise not to bite, and I'll have you home in a minute"

She obeyed his very sensible request that she hold on, but comfortable wasn't exactly the feeling it engendered. Acutely aware of him—his warm breath on her hair, his spicy masculine scent, the feel of his arms holding her securely, the strong, steady rhythm of his heartbeat—made her too tingly, too edgy, to feel truly comfortable. It was like that delicious kiss all over again. There was a strange tension thrumming inside her, a tug of war between the part of her that wanted to snuggle down, lean her head on his shoulder, and revel in his closeness, and the part of her that was afraid of those yearnings and what they could do to her and him both if she gave in.

But oh, this closeness fed a need inside her she hadn't even realized was there. Surely it wouldn't hurt to indulge herself in a bit of harmless—

Maddy clenched her jaw, silently berating herself for even contemplating such a thing. This was the first serious temptation she'd been faced with since she'd made her vow at Winston's graveside. It was humbling to discover just how weak-willed she'd become.

She must have made some sound or movement because he looked down in concern. "Sorry if I jarred you. We're almost there."

The rumble of his chest against her as he spoke sent answering tremors through her. If he wanted to think her reactions were due to her injury, then that was all right with her. But truth to tell, she hadn't thought about her ankle for several minutes now. "I'm fine," she said, trying to summon up a reassuring smile. "I'm just sorry to be so much trouble."

His lips twitched. "Trouble? On the contrary, I've never considered holding a pretty lady to be anything but a pleasure."

He thought she was pretty? Maddy contemplated that thought for the remaining few minutes it took them to reach her front gate. The way he carried her made her feel dainty and fragile and . . . cherished.

"Maddy?" Blanche had just stepped out of her own front gate. "Is everything all right?"

"Oh, hello Blanche." Seeing her neighbor's surprised, assessing gaze, Maddy felt cheek-warmingly conscious of her arm around Clay's neck and how snugly he held her to his chest. "I'm afraid I turned my ankle."

Blanche's hand flew to her bosom. "Oh my goodness. Is there anything I can do to help?"

"No, I—"

"As a matter of fact," Clay interrupted, giving Maddy a light squeeze, "if you're headed downtown anyway, would you stop by the doctor's office and ask him to step over here? The sooner he has a look at Maddy's injury the better I'll feel." Clay shifted Maddy in his arms, holding her closer and more possessively.

Blanche's eyes widened. "Of course," she assured them. "I'll head there right now." She gave them another long, speculative look, then turned and walked away at a brisk pace.

She can't wait to spread this juicy bit of news, Maddy thought sourly. Thanks goodness she hadn't seen the earlier kiss.

"That ought to start the gossips buzzing," Clay commented, echoing her thoughts but in a much more cheerful tone.

Of course. She had to keep reminding herself that she *wanted* the townsfolk to see her and Clay as a couple.

Clay maneuvered the gate open without visible effort. It had barely creaked closed behind them when the front door opened.

"Now doesn't this look cozy." Miss Adeline, lilac ribbons threaded through her flaming red locks, watched their progress with an arch smile.

"Maddy had a little accident," Clay explained as he climbed up the front steps. "She's hurt her ankle."

Miss Adeline stepped aside to open the door and let them pass. "Oh dear. But I'm glad to see she doesn't seem to be in much pain."

"It's just a trifle tender," Maddy said, trying to swallow the prickle of irritation she felt at the way they were speaking over her. She'd twisted her ankle—she hadn't been knocked unconscious. "I'm sure I'll be fine in just a little bit."

"Oh my goodness, Maddy." Miss Fanny came bustling down the hall, wiping her hands on her apron. "Are you all right?"

"I was just telling Miss Adeline, I'm fine. I—"

"Maddy?" Miss Olive started down from the second floor, a worried frown on her face.

With a sigh, Maddy tried to explain the situation one more time. "Don't worry, there's nothing seriously wrong. I just turned my ankle, and Clay is chivalrously making sure I stay off my feet until the doctor can take a look."

She turned back to her knight errant. "Speaking of which, I'm sure you're ready to put me down. The sofa in the parlor will do nicely, if you don't mind."

To her surprise, he moved toward the staircase instead. "Where are you going?" she asked. Surely he wasn't thinking about—

"Why, up to your room, of course. Your bed is the best place for you right now." He caught Miss Olive's gaze. "If you'll be so kind as to lead the way, ma'am."

Miss Olive, who'd made it about half way down, nodded. "Of course. But shouldn't we send someone for the doctor?"

Clay shook his head. "We saw Miss Crawford on our way in and she graciously agreed to send him right over."

"Good."

"But—"

"Hush now, dear, and do as Mr. Kincaid says."

Maddy felt her mouth drop open at Miss Olive's gentle reprimand. Didn't her opinion count with *anyone* in this household anymore?

Miss Olive looked past Clay's shoulder. "Fanny, why don't you fix Maddy a nice, soothing tisane. Adeline, let Katie know what's happened so she doesn't wonder when she sees the doctor arrive." With another deferential smile toward Clay, the seamstress turned to retrace her steps.

Good grief, did he truly mean to carry her up those stairs? "Really, this isn't necessary. If you'll—"

"I told you," he interrupted, "you're not in charge today. You might as well just lean back and hold your peace, because I'm not putting you down until I can set you on your own bed."

Well! There was no need for him to take that tone. She'd only been trying to spare him. She'd never been exactly sylph-like, and the stairway was rather steep. But if he wanted to be stubborn, then so be it.

As he started up the stairs, however, she was surprised at how effortlessly he managed the climb. Her weight didn't seem to be an undue burden on him. In fact, the only signs he gave that he was under any kind of strain was the bunching of the muscles in his arm and the quickened pace of his breathing.

As he reached the top of the stairs, he flashed her a cocky smile, as if he knew exactly what she'd been thinking.

Clay stepped into Maddy's bedroom and took a moment to look around while Miss Olive turned down the bed. The first thing he noted was that Maddy carried none of her somber widow guise into her inner sanctum. The curtains and bedspread were sunshine yellow sprinkled with tiny blue flowers. There was a rag rug on the floor beside her bed, woven of brightly patterned calico cloths. Children's artwork, no doubt of Katie's making, dotted the walls. A low chest at one end of the room was decorated with a scattering of miniatures, books and colorful bric-a-brac. On her vanity was a vase of fresh picked flowers and a prominently displayed picture of Winston.

That last brought an annoyed frown to Clay's face as he crossed the room to her bedside.

"Here we go," he said, setting her down with her legs stretched out on the bed in front of her. "And I expect you to stay right here until the doctor has a look."

"I don't appear to have much choice," she groused.

"Glad to see you've finally accepted that," he replied cheerfully. He flexed his arms, still savoring the memory of the arousingly feminine burden he'd carried.

Holding her close enough to inhale her flowers-and-Maddy scent, embracing the soft curves his eyes had feasted on during their first meeting, watching her try so hard not to let him know how affected she was by their closeness, had been both a treat and a trial. Even now, seeing the way she all but glared at him from her bed held a definite smile-tugging, kissable appeal.

Which was a totally unacceptable turn of events.

Clay felt a sudden urgency to distance himself from the occupant of that bed. "I'll leave Miss Olive to settle you in," he said with a slight bow. He moved toward the door. "I'll be down the hall, sorting through more of those papers. Please let me know when the doctor arrives."

A few minutes later, Clay was staring sightlessly at a handful of ten year old billing receipts.

Was he mad? How could he be attracted to a woman like Maddy? He'd grown up in a house full of flighty, mischief-prone, constantly clamoring-for-attention women. He'd long ago promised himself that when he married, it would be to a different kind of lady—a lady who was sweet, biddable, and above all, had a concerned-for-her-man's-comfort outlook on marriage.

Maddy in no way fit that description. If anything, she

was more exasperating than his sisters had ever been. Not to mention two very strong factors that would preclude her ever feeling any strong attraction to him.

One, she was still deeply in love with her deceased husband.

And two, she now knew his shameful secret.

Then again, she'd participated in that kiss quite willingly. And he hadn't been oblivious to her reaction as he carried her a few minutes ago. Maddy most definitely showed signs of a heightened awareness and sensitivity to his presence lately.

Perhaps he was looking at this all wrong. So, he was attracted to her. He'd been attracted to women before. In this case it was quite likely more a product of the unusual circumstances of their arrangement than a prelude to any lasting relationship.

Why not just settle in and enjoy the next few weeks? After all, he'd been given carte blanche to flirt outrageously with a lovely, spirited woman, without any strings attached or danger of permanent entanglements. Wasn't that every man's dream?

He'd worry about any less visible, more personal, repercussions later.

"Mr. Kincaid, a moment please."

Clay paused, offering Vera Welborne a friendly smile. This was the fourth interruption he'd met with on his morning stroll down Pepper Cloud's main street. Not that he minded. In fact, he'd taken steps to make certain he attracted just such attention.

"How do you do, ma'am? It's a lovely day, isn't it?"

"A bit warm, but yes, quite nice." Mrs. Welborne's gaze darted to the roses he carried, as if irresistibly drawn there. Then she looked back up with polite concern. "I understand Maddy met with an unfortunate accident yesterday. I do hope it was nothing serious."

"She turned her ankle, I'm afraid. Luckily, I was there

to help her." Clay shook his head. "I admire Maddy's pride and her air of being able to handle any crisis, but beneath it all she's just as fragile, just as vulnerable, as any member of the fairer sex."

He eyed his doily-wrapped bouquet uncertainly. "I got these to cheer her up. Mrs. Thompson generously allowed me to pick them from her bush outside the hotel. Do you think Maddy will like them?"

Mrs. Welborne gave him a knowing smile. "Oh, I'm quite sure she will."

Clay let out a relieved breath. "Good. The doctor assures me she'll be good as new in just a couple of days. That is, if we can persuade her to stay off of her feet for that long." He gave her a just-between-us look. "And I aim to do my part to see that she does."

"Is that so?" He could almost see the wheels of possibility turning in her mind.

"Yes, ma'am. In fact, if you'll excuse me, I'm headed that way now. I know those three dear ladies she lives with would do anything in their power to help Maddy, but none of them is her match when she sets her mind to something."

"Of course. And please tell Maddy I hope she's feeling better soon."

"Thank you, ma'am, I'll be sure to pass that on." Clay gave her a short bow and resumed his walk.

If Maddy wanted the town to start speculating that she was no longer the determined-to-stay-unattached widow, she should be pleased with the way things were shaping up. Blanche Crawford had obviously done a thorough job of spreading the word about how he'd carried Maddy into Barrows House yesterday. And he, himself, had made it known to more than one person how concerned he was that Maddy receive the finest care possible during her recuperation.

A few minutes later, Miss Olive greeted him at the door

of Barrows House. "Why, what lovely flowers. Are those for Maddy?"

"Yes, ma'am. And how is our patient doing today?"

"The swelling's gone down quite a bit. Doc Perkins has already been by and says she's mending nicely. He even went so far as to tell her she could try hobbling about her room a bit with a cane this afternoon if she felt up to it."

Miss Olive paused and her lips twitched. "Of course, if it's her temperament you're concerned with, she's feeling restless and crotchety, I'm afraid. Maddy isn't the best of patients."

Nothing surprising there. "I thought I might offer to carry her down to the parlor for a change of scenery."

She gave him an approving smile. "That's very thoughtful of you. But don't expect to be greeted with open arms."

He grinned. "The thought never crossed my mind."

"All right then, get along with you." Miss Olive gestured toward the stairs, then gave him another of those dry smiles. "Maddy's got too good a heart to take her frustration out on old ladies and little girls. It'll do her good to have someone she can really take aim at and pick a quarrel with."

Clay raised a brow. "Thanks for the warning."

As he headed up the stairs, though, he was grinning in anticipation. Sparring with Maddy was quickly becoming one of his favorite pastimes.

His grin faded, however, when he discovered Maddy was not in her room.

Where could she have gone off to?

Chapter Eleven

Clay stepped back into the hall, trying to decide where to look first. There was no telling what sort of darned fool notion she'd have acted on.

Had she decided to go into the room where Winston's papers were stored? She hadn't shown much interest in their task up until now, but perhaps boredom had engendered a change of attitude.

Clay had his hand on the knob, when a sound from farther down the hall caught his ear. The door at the far end was open. He hadn't paid much attention to it on previous visits, vaguely assuming it concealed a closet of some sort. But now he could see it opened onto a set of stairs leading up, presumably to the attic. Surely Maddy wouldn't—

Of course she would.

He marched down the hall, his earlier good humor toward her stubborn behavior forgotten. As soon as he reached the foot of the stairs, his suspicions were confirmed. She stood about five steps from the top, with a cane in one hand and the banister white-knuckle gripped in the other.

"Just where the devil do you think you're going?"

He regretted his stormily uttered question when she started and wobbled unsteadily. He took the stairs two at a time, but she had herself back under control before he reached her side.

"Not that it's any of your concern," she said, glaring at him over her shoulder, "but I'm going up to my studio." Then, as he took her arm, "My *private* studio. No one comes up here but me."

"Well now, that's just too bad." He handed her the flowers, then lifted her in his arms despite her protest. "You decide whether we go up or down, but you're not going any farther without my carrying you."

"Mr. Kincaid," she said frostily, "I assure you, your chivalrous attempt to spare me is quite unnecessary. Dr. Perkins himself has released me to move about on my own, as long as I use this cane."

Clay eyed the wooden stick warily, not completely convinced she wouldn't use it as a club. He doubted she even realized what it was he'd handed her. "It won't wash Maddy. I've already spoken to Miss Olive. The doctor said you could try using the cane in your room this afternoon, not climb stairs this morning."

He frowned at the mutinous tilt to her chin. "Good grief woman, if you're not worried about your neck, at least give some thought to the other members of your household. Do you want one of the ladies, or Katie for that matter, to find you crumbled in a heap at the foot of the stairs?"

He could tell by the stricken look that crossed her features that he'd gotten through to her. Not that she'd admit as much.

"I was doing just fine without your help," she insisted. "I wasn't in any danger of falling."

"That's a matter of opinion." He hefted her, in the process pulling her a bit closer against him. She felt just as good, as right, cradled in his arms as he remembered. "Now, what shall it be, up to your 'private' studio, or back down to your room?"

He watched her silently fume, knowing it was aimed at both him and at her own helplessness. His anger eased a bit, a measure of sympathy taking its place. He'd probably feel something of the same if their positions were reversed. Besides, holding her so close had him feeling something far different than anger.

"Upstairs," she said at last through clenched teeth.

Clay nodded and climbed the few remaining steps to the third floor. Ready for a distraction and curious as to what sort of retreat she'd created for herself, he looked around with interest.

The surprisingly bright, spacious loft seemed an ideal art studio. A sturdy table and bench were situated on one end of the room. The table was home to neatly organized paint jars, inks, pencils and brushes. Sketch pads shared shelf space with journals and periodicals. A large easel was set up across the room, positioned to make the best use of the light from the numerous windows that lined the wall. Next to it, a stool and elbow-height table stood, ready to accommodate the artist when the muse called.

He paused in the center of the room. "Where shall I set you down?"

"On the window seat, please."

He obliged, taking care not to jar her injured ankle. As he straightened, he saw she'd finally taken notice of the flowers he'd given her. His lips twitched as he watched her struggle to school her features into a polite smile.

"The roses are lovely," she said in a conciliatory tone.

"Uhm." No point making this easy on her when it was so much fun to watch her squirm.

"It was very kind of you to bring them." She shifted her weight and worried at her bottom lip with her teeth.

He shrugged.

Maddy sighed. "How long are you going to let me wallow in my guilty conscience?"

Clay couldn't suppress a slight twitch of his lips. "I'd think another few minutes would do it."

"Oh, do you?" She tossed her head. "Well, I think I've done quite enough already." She waved a hand dismissively. "Now, if you don't mind, I have some sketching to do."

"No, I don't mind."

Maddy glared at him a moment, then apparently decided it would be best to ignore him all together. She gingerly swung her legs over the edge of the window seat and placed the tip of her cane on the floor as if ready to stand. The woman just didn't know how to stay off her feet.

"Where do you think you're going now?"

"I can't do much sketching without my sketchbook and pencils."

"Just point out whatever it is you need and I'll bring it to you."

After he'd handed her the requested items, she settled back and flipped the pad open. He caught a glimpse of a half-finished drawing of Katie on her swing before she angled it away from him.

Pencil poised, she glanced up at him with a haughty lift to her brow. "Isn't there something else you need to be doing?"

"Nothing that can't wait. I'm dancing attendance on the object of my affections, remember?"

Her lips thinned, but she apparently decided not to grace his remark with a response.

Clay waved his hand in a sweeping gesture. "Do you mind if I look around a bit?"

Maddy hesitated for the space of two heartbeats, then nodded stiffly. "Of course." She pointedly turned her attention back to the sketchbook on her lap.

The first thing he noticed was that Maddy sketched more than she painted. While there were a half dozen canvases scattered around the studio in addition to her work in progress on the easel, these were overwhelmingly outnumbered by her line drawings. Pages torn from her sketch pad were everywhere, on tables, tacked to the walls, stuffed in overflowing journals. Sparingly etched pieces shared space with intricately detailed works, whimsical renderings with more sober studies.

The only common denominator was the subject matter: people. There was not a landscape or still life to be seen.

He focused on the paintings first, and one in particular caught his eye.

At first glance, it seemed a quite simple study of the three older residents of Barrows House. They were seated in the parlor, just as he'd seen them on numerous occasions.

Examining the picture a bit closer, however, revealed the artist not only knew the women intimately, but felt a great deal of affection for them as well.

Miss Olive had been captured industriously plying a needle and thread on some mundane mending task. While she sat out of the limelight at the edge of the portrait, the sensitive rendering of her pose and expression made it obvious she presided over the room.

Miss Fanny stood in front of a window, peering into the bird cage and cooing to her pet. The artist had managed to imbue her with both motherliness and childlike innocence.

Miss Adeline dominated the center of the canvas. She was seated on the sofa, one arm outstretched along the top, the other caressing the head of her cat. She wore a tall white wig and an elaborate gown of ice blue. Beneath the coquettish expression one sensed a zest for life that was infectious.

It took a rare talent to be able to convey such nuances of personality and emotion. Clay glanced back over his shoulder and caught Maddy watching him, though she quickly turned back to her sketchbook.

151

His lips curved up in a smile. Was she self-conscious about showing her work? "You've been much too modest," he said. "You have an amazing talent for portraiture."

She met his gaze, her face pinkening with pleasure. "Thank you. That one you're looking at is one of my favorite pieces."

"I can see why. You've captured not only their appearances but their personalities, as well."

He moved on to study the picture on the easel. It was a portrait of Katie, about three-quarters complete. A second easel, to one side and slightly behind the first, held a dozen or so sketches of Katie in various poses. There was Katie at play, Katie asleep, Katie frowning in concentration as she tied her shoes. He particularly liked the one depicting the little girl stifling a giggle at some bit of silliness.

As far as Clay could see, Maddy hadn't used any of the sketches to model the picture on the easel. It was an entirely different pose. Katie stood on the front porch near the honeysuckle trellis, her hand outstretched with one finger extended. A brilliant purple and gold butterfly hovered just inches away, seemingly on the point of perching on that childishly pudgy finger. Katie's whole being radiated a heart-tugging image of breath-held wonder and delight.

But slowly, as Clay studied the picture, he found himself focusing on the other presence portrayed there. Behind the child, at the very edge of the picture, stood a woman. She was barely there, with only her skirt and part of one arm visible. Somehow, with just that tiny bit to work with, Maddy had managed to reveal volumes.

The woman's hand rested on Katie's shoulder, both protecting and encouraging. The folds of her skirt caressed and supported the child whose upward-reaching stance had her leaning back slightly. Through these and other subtle shadings of pose and gesture, the viewer was given a poignant vision of a mother's care and yearning. The faceless woman in the portrait was the very essence of motherly love.

152

Did Maddy know how much of herself she'd revealed?

Still pondering this personal glimpse of the artist, Clay lifted his gaze from the easel and slowly scanned the sketches scattered about the room. There didn't seem to be any sort of order to them. Age-yellowed pages shared wall space with crisp new images. Household members and neighbors captured in lighthearted poses overlapped more poignant renderings.

Clay was familiar with many of the faces, though there were several he didn't recognize. One in particular, an older woman, featured prominently in quite a few of the earlier drawings.

Clay turned to Maddy. "Is this your grandmother?" he asked, pointing.

She looked up and nodded. "Yes. She was a handsome woman, don't you think? I'm not sure my sketches do her justice."

Since she didn't seem to expect a response, and he had none to offer, Clay returned to studying the sketches. He had glanced over about half of those easily visible before he found one of Winston. The pose was idealized, with the subject standing, elbow propped on the back of a chair, and smiling benignly at someone just out of sight of the artist. One could almost see the fellow's halo, Clay thought sourly. He scanned the area for other sketches of Maddy's husband, looking for some that would exhibit her knack for getting below the surface and revealing personality, but he only found three more and they had been done in a similar vein.

Strange? He would have expected her to have quite a few more of the man she so obviously still felt strongly about. Had she put them away because the reminders of her loss were painful? Or did she keep them in her bedroom where they would be in easy reach?

Not liking the direction of his thoughts, Clay abandoned his perusal of her work and turned back to Maddy. "I think I'll go downstairs for a bit. Can I have your word that you won't try to navigate those stairs on your own?"

She glanced up from her sketch pad with a theatrically fierce frown. "Only if I have your word that you won't forget to fetch me for lunch."

Clay swept an arm out as he gave a mock-gallant bow. "May lightning strike me down if I should act so unchivalrously to my lady love."

The words, for all that they were uttered in a spirit of tomfoolery, sliced through Maddy like a blade. She managed to hold her smile as he took his leave. But as soon as he disappeared down the stairs, she lowered her sketch pad and slumped back against the window seat wall.

Lady love.

She wanted those words to be true with an intensity that stunned her. This was an absolute disaster.

For the past seven years she'd known there was no place for romantic entanglements in her life. She'd come to terms with that, accepted it as her lot, and had even convinced herself she was happy with the life she had.

But somehow, Clayton Kincaid had slipped past her defenses, invaded her eccentrically ordered world, and made a mockery of all her firmly held convictions about her own happiness.

Goodness, she'd even allowed him to come up here to her studio, her refuge. No one outside of the members of her household had ever been up here. And even her own ladies, respecting her desire for privacy, rarely intruded.

Maddy looked around. She didn't just sketch to record images. She captured feelings, emotions, her own as well as those of her subjects. Every picture she drew contained a bit of herself in it. The sketches and paintings she kept in this room, especially.

Watching Clay inspect them so closely had been like watching him read pages of her diary. It left her feeling exposed, vulnerable. What had he thought of the display? He'd seemed impressed, but had he seen past the surface, or had her work merely been "nice little sketches" to him? Did he know how edgy watching him, waiting for his reactions, had made her feel?

She'd noticed the way he'd paused in front of one of the few sketches of Winston, then let his gaze scan the walls. Was he wondering why there were so few?

Well, that was one secret she'd never reveal—not to him or anyone else.

Maddy gingerly swung her legs over the side of the window seat and grasped the cane. She limped her way to a set of bookcases across the room and pulled out a sketch pad. It was one that had remained closed and put away for nearly as long as those ledgers of Winston's in the room below.

Moving paint pots and pencils aside, Maddy lay the book on her worktable and opened it up. Winston, somber and aloof, stared past her. Turning the page, she uncovered another Winston, seated at his desk, looking up with resigned patience, as if to a child. The next one was of him listening attentively to her grandmother as she lay on her sickbed.

Maddy started turning the pages more rapidly. There was one with him facing away, his hands clasped behind his back, his shoulders tense as if under some sort of strain. Another, a half-finished picture showed his nostrils dilated in fastidious distaste. The next one met her gaze with an accusing, brooding stare.

Maddy slammed the book shut.

She'd needed this reminder. She would be, could be, no one's *Lady Love*. The price was just too high.

Clay found the ladies in the parlor. Miss Fanny stood by the birdcage in a pose eerily reminiscent of the one he'd seen in the portrait upstairs. Miss Olive sat on the sofa, employing her needle with practiced expertise. If that was another of Maddy's dresses, it appeared she'd be wearing much more than just a hint of color soon.

155

Miss Adeline stood nearby, polishing the piano with sweeping strokes. She wore a black wig today, possibly the same one he'd first seen her in. But it was styled in a loose bun on top of her head and secured with a pair of ivory sticks. And rather than Egyptian-themed attire, she wore a gown with a more Oriental flavor.

The geisha-like piano polisher was the first to notice him standing in the doorway. Looking up, she favored him with a demurely coy smile and a bow that lacked any hint of subservience. "Do come in and join us, Mr. Kincaid."

The other two ladies offered him smiles of welcome.

"And how did you find our invalid faring this morning?" Miss Olive paused from her task long enough to peer up at him. "You seem to have come out relatively unscathed."

Clay, standing with his back to the mantel, gave her a dry smile. "No easy task, if I do say so myself." He shook his head. "She was trying to climb the attic stairs when I found her. I'm afraid she was *not* pleased when I insisted on carrying her up the rest of the way."

Miss Adeline straightened, a look of disbelief on her face. "She let you into her studio?"

Clay nodded, then spread his hands. "But not happily. I gave her the choice of going anywhere she wanted, just as long as she didn't walk there. She chose to continue on to the attic."

Miss Fanny took a seat on the sofa. "But Maddy never lets *anyone* into her studio."

A flash of pleasure warmed Clay at that bit of news. So, he'd been allowed to see a part of her world she held private from most others, had he? Did that mean she was beginning to trust him?

"I didn't give her much choice," he said with deliberate nonchalance. "The only way she could get to the top of those stairs was if I carried her." Even so, she *could* have turned away if she really hadn't wanted him to see her studio.

"Still . . ." Miss Adeline, apparently sharing his thought,

156

gave the piano a last flick with her cloth. She exchanged meaningful looks with the other two ladies as she minced across the room, taking a chair opposite the sofa.

"I must admit, I was quite unprepared to learn how talented she is. I'd venture to say some of her work is museum quality."

"She let you see her sketches?" Miss Fanny examined him as if he'd suddenly sprouted wings.

"Why, yes. At least she didn't object when I asked to look at them."

Again the ladies exchanged glances. Miss Olive peered up at him with a speculative gleam in her eyes. But she said only, "Yes, our Maddy is quite the talented artist. We're very proud of her."

"That child was born drawing," Miss Fanny offered. "Even as a little girl, no scrap of paper was safe from her pencil, including sheets of piano music."

Clay shifted, wondering how to introduce the topic he was most interested in—Maddy's marriage to Winston. Perhaps if he approached it obliquely. . . .

"I was wondering how well you ladies knew my cousin Winston," he tried. "I never met him personally, and I was curious as to what sort of man he was."

Miss Olive's gaze narrowed, as if she were weighing his motives for asking such a question. Surely she didn't suspect he had any personal interest in the subject? He was merely adding a nice touch of verisimilitude to his role.

Miss Adeline waved a hand apologetically. "I'm afraid he died before Olive and I arrived in Pepper Cloud. Fanny knew him, though."

Miss Fanny nodded. "That I did. Your cousin was a fine man, well-respected in these parts." She glanced to her left and then back to Clay. "Mr. Wimberly said to tell you that he never met a man with a finer head for business and finance than Winston Potter had."

"That's good to hear. He was a solicitor, wasn't he?"

Again Miss Fanny nodded. "Yes. He also gave investment and financial advice to a few clients, such as Maddy's grandmother."

"So, I suppose he visited here regularly?"

"Oh, yes." She sat up straighter. "I gave Maddy piano lessons when she was still in pigtails, so I was here quite often, myself."

Clay smiled at the sudden image of a much younger Maddy in pigtails and pinafores, industriously practicing her scales.

"But they weren't just business associates," Miss Fanny continued. "Your cousin and Edith, Maddy's grandmother, were personal friends, as well. They shared a common interest in literature and the arts. He even made a point to escort her to St. Louis on several occasions to visit the theater and exhibits."

She folded her hands and settled more comfortably, as if for a cozy chat. "I think Edith, for all that she was a sharp-witted woman, was a bit flattered by his attention. Winston was such a dapper fellow, you see, with his sophistication and polish. Not to mention the fact that he had a rather stand-offish manner that some women just can't seem to resist trying to break through."

"And Maddy liked him, as well, of course." The words were out before Clay could stop them. Fool! Of course she'd liked the man. She'd more than *liked* him, she'd married him and mourned his passing for years.

Miss Fanny waved a hand absently. "Well, I suppose so. But Maddy was only ten or eleven when Winston took on her grandmother's financial affairs."

"So Winston was a good deal older than Maddy?" They were finally getting to the part that interested him.

"Oh my, yes. Fifteen years or so, I'd imagine." Miss Fanny wrinkled her brow. "But didn't you know how old your cousin was?"

Clay shifted. "I hadn't given it much thought, I'm afraid."

Miss Fanny nodded in understanding. "Their engagement came as a surprise to everyone, and ended quite a few matchmaking schemes." She gave him what, for Miss Fanny, passed as an arch smile. "He was quite sought-after, you know. For years he was considered the most eligible bachelor in these parts."

"A status I'm sure Mr. Kincaid is quite familiar with," Miss Adeline drawled.

Clay winked at her, then turned back to Miss Fanny. "So my cousin saved himself for Maddy, did he?"

Miss Fanny shifted uncomfortably. "I'm afraid it wasn't quite like that. It was all Edith's doing, you see."

"What do you mean?"

Miss Fanny sighed. "Edith found out she was dying. Maddy was only seventeen at the time and had never been on her own. Edith wanted to make sure Maddy would be taken care of once she was gone."

Seventeen—so young. "So it was an arranged marriage?"

His matronly informant nodded. "Yes. Not that either Maddy or Winston objected," she hastened to assure him. "Winston seemed finally ready to settle down, and Maddy was so worried about her grandmother she was willing to do anything to give her extra peace of mind."

So, it hadn't been a love match after all. Though that had obviously changed later.

Miss Fanny sighed again. "It's just as well Edith died before she learned her well-intentioned planning had been wasted."

Clay straightened. "Wasted?"

Miss Fanny's round face quivered in distress. "Why, yes. Winston died in a tragic accident just three weeks after they were married. He fell into Fenny Pond and drowned."

All of Clay's perceptions about Maddy's marriage suddenly turned on their axis, reconfiguring themselves into something else entirely.

"Edith slipped into a coma that same day," Miss Fanny continued, "so she never knew. Poor Maddy, it was such a frightful shock to her. Edith passed on two days later."

Her words barely registered with Clay.

Maddy had been married to Winston for only three weeks?

In an arranged marriage?

At age *seventeen?*

Even if theirs had been the most blissful, albeit brief, of unions, such a relationship seemed an unlikely basis for seven years of determined mourning and adamant widowhood. Something wasn't quite as it seemed here.

And if there was one thing he couldn't let be, it was an unanswered question.

"I'm sorry, Mr. Kincaid."

Clay pulled his thoughts back to the occupants of the room as Miss Fanny addressed him. "Sorry?"

She nodded. "You wanted to know about your cousin, and I seem to have gotten off the track a bit."

"Nonsense, ma'am. You were quite helpful." He caught a you're-not-fooling-me look from Miss Olive, before continuing smoothly. "I have a much clearer picture of Winston now than I had before."

Though he also had a lot more questions now than he'd had before. The scarcity of Winston's pictures in Maddy's studio was more puzzling than ever. Were some of the answers buried in the contents of that storage room?

He pushed away from the mantel and straightened. "Now, if you ladies will excuse me, I'd best check on Maddy. Wouldn't want her to try to navigate those stairs on her own."

Not when it would spoil his chances of carrying her down in his arms.

Chapter Twelve

Maddy wadded up the piece of paper she'd been drawing on and dropped it to the floor. None of her efforts pleased her this morning.

Unwilling to explore the reasons too deeply, she glanced out the window, hoping for a distraction, and found one. Katie was gliding with leg-pumping vigor on her new swing.

Maddy opened the window and stuck her head and shoulders out. "Hello, Buttercup."

Katie stopped pumping her legs momentarily as she looked up with a proud grin. "Aunt Maddy, look how high I can go."

"My goodness, you're practically flying."

"Just like Sweetie Pie," Katie agreed gleefully, her legs working with renewed vigor.

Alerted by the creak of a floorboard, Maddy glanced over her shoulder to see Clay had returned. Her smile of greeting, however, faltered as she took in his rigidly furious demeanor.

"What the devil do you think you're doing!"

How dare he speak to her in that tone of voice. "Not that it's any of your concern, but I'm talking to Katie." She leaned back toward the window, making a sweeping motion with her arm as she pointed to the child below.

His involuntary flinch at her gesture brought memories of his confession yesterday flooding back. Of course! Her position at the window would provoke a stomach-clinching response from someone with a fear of heights. Not to mention the fact that it would likely have reminded him of his friend's suicide, as well.

Maddy twisted around to pull the window closed, then turned back to him, an apology on her lips.

But his mouth quirked up in a humorless smile as he raised a hand to halt her words. "Please don't say it. We both know I'm the one who needs to apologize. I shouldn't have snapped at you that way."

Maddy mentally chastised herself for her insensitivity. How could she have so completely forgotten the pride-wounding story he'd told her yesterday? "No apology needed. I should have remembered—" She bit her lip, realizing too late she'd only made the situation more awkward.

"Remembered my gutless reaction to heights, you mean?"

Maddy mentally winced at the bitterness of his tone. Good heavens, he *truly* felt his fear somehow made him less of a man.

Instinctively, she knew he expected but would not welcome a show of sympathy from her. So she merely shrugged her shoulders. "Exactly."

Ignoring the flicker of surprise on his face, she gingerly swung her legs down to the floor and picked up her cane. "Now, if you'll be so kind as to assist me, I'd like to go down to the library."

Without a word, Clay crossed the distance between them and extended his arm.

He let her hobble as far as the head of the stairs before

he halted their progress. "I'll carry you from here."

"That's not necessary. My foot's barely bothering me at all anymore. And it's much easier going down than up." The fact that she actually yearned to feel his arms around her again was another good reason to avoid it at all costs.

"Nevertheless, I think it best you don't try to navigate stairs just yet."

"Mr. Kincaid, really, there's no need—"

"If you're concerned about my fear—"

It was her turn to interrupt. "Nonsense. That has nothing to do with this. I've seen you climb stairs before, remember?"

He raised a disbelieving brow. "Well then, what is the problem?"

She glared at him. Trapped! She couldn't tell him the real reason she didn't want him to carry her. How could she possibly admit that she was becoming too sensitized to his touch, that having him hold her in his arms made her long for other intimacies, for things she couldn't have. And if she continued to refuse his offer without explanation, he'd believe she really did worry that his fear of heights would endanger her.

Maddy nodded in capitulation. "Oh very well, have it your way."

Clay effortlessly lifted her and started down the stairs. Maddy held herself as stiffly aloof as possible, but the warm tingle of contact, the caressing softness of his breath on her hair made it very difficult.

And somewhere inside of her, a small piece of her heart bled for his wounded pride. How awful it must be for someone as proud as Clay to be burdened with such a vulnerability?

Up until that confession, Clayton Kincaid had seemed the most smoothly arrogant, self-assured man she'd ever met. In fact, his charm and confidence had given him a bit of a knight in shining armor quality. A quality she deemed romantically admirable but woefully impractical for anything but slaying dragons.

To be honest, this glimpse of a rusty chink in his otherwise blindingly polished armor made him more appealing to her than before. Not that she'd give him any indication she felt that way.

For one thing, he'd never believe her. Instead, he'd likely see such an admission as condescending and get all huffy and insulted.

And for another, there was no way she'd ever admit to anyone but herself that she had other than business-partner-like feelings for him.

As they stepped out into the second-floor hallway, rather than putting her down as she'd assumed he would, he merely hefted her more closely to his chest and continued on. Surely it was only her imagination that sensed a certain warm possessiveness in his manner?

"You can put me down now." For some reason it came out more as a question than a command.

He met her gaze, his expression cryptic. "No need. It's only a short walk to the next flight of stairs."

Maddy settled back against his chest, happily resigned to the fact that she had no choice but to accept his help. Not satisfied with this one crumb of guilty pleasure, however, she couldn't quite suppress the wistful desire that he would take some enjoyment from holding her, as well.

Sweet heaven above, but holding her felt so *good!* Wrapping his arms around those softly rounded curves and inhaling her enticingly feminine scent would lure a monk from his vows—and he'd never aspired to the celibate life.

It was both better and worse now that she'd relaxed. Having her all but snuggle against his chest, one hand around his neck, the other placed softly near his heart, warmed him and brought out all his protective, possessive urges. Knowing he couldn't do anything about the "possessing" feelings made him want to howl in frustration.

He was under no illusions that she would welcome another show of affection from him. Her reluctance to let him hold her in the first place was proof enough of that. And how could he blame her? He might do for a pretend-suitor, as long as no one else uncovered his shameful secret. But no woman worth her salt would want to spend her life with a man who possessed such a gaping hole in his claim to manhood.

In a way, it was just as well he'd been forced to confess his failing to Maddy. He was starting to feel things for her he had no right to feel. Now that she knew about his fear of heights, she would be sure to keep their relationship on the proper businesslike footing they'd agreed to in the beginning.

Yes, it *was* best that it had come out before he made a fool of himself. But that thought brought him no pleasure whatsoever.

Cybil pounded her gavel on the polished rosewood block strategically placed on the table in front of her. "This meeting of the Pepper Cloud Ladies' Society is hereby adjourned."

Maddy glanced up at the clock on the mantel, made a last notation in the minutes, and set her notebook down.

As if on cue, there was a perfunctory knock on the door, and it opened to admit Miss Olive with the tea cart.

"Here, let me help you with that." Maddy rose, grateful for the excuse to move about the room. After enduring four days of restricted activity she'd had her fill of sitting still.

Not that it had truly taken a full four days for her foot to heal. In fact, truth be known, she'd felt recovered enough to do away with the cane the day after her and Clay's little tête-à-tête in the attic. But Miss Olive had had other ideas.

Maddy's injury provided a wonderful excuse for Clay to publicly pay her extra-special attention, the seamstress was

Winnie Griggs

quick to point out to both of them. It would play into their plans perfectly, she noted, and it would be a shame for them not to take advantage of such an opportunity.

But after three more days of Maddy hobbling about, trying to appear helpless, even Miss Olive admitted it was time to put the cane away.

Lavinia Thompson accepted the cup of tea Maddy handed her. "Have you made a decision about whether or not you will be preparing a picnic basket for the auction yet, Maddy?"

Maddy kept her smile firmly in place despite her irritation. She thought she had already delivered a firm no on that subject.

"It *is* for charity, after all," Lavinia continued before Maddy could respond. "And no one will know which basket is yours until the bidding is over." The smile she gave Maddy was full of thinly veiled pity. "In fact, I'll be glad to deliver yours to the auction tent so that your identity will be protected up until the moment the basket is claimed."

"Why that's an excellent idea," Cybil chimed in. "And Maddy, you could even take steps to warn off Mr. Kincaid if you don't want to be embarrassed in front of him."

That did it. She would *not* let them continue to hold last year's fiasco over her head. She might not be the best cook in the county, but by heavens, she could put together a passable picnic lunch. "Of course I'll fix a basket for the auction," she said, handing Cybil her cup of tea. "And Lavinia, thanks so much for your offer, but I'm sure you'll have your hands full with all the other things you have to do. I'll take care of delivering my basket myself."

Cybil plopped a sugar cube into her cup. "That's the spirit, Maddy. And we'll all do our part to make sure your basket brings a respectable sum." She stirred her tea delicately. "Of course, it goes without saying that Sue Ellen's will bring the top dollar again this year."

166

Sue Ellen's mortified gasp punctuated her mother's boasting. "Mother, please!"

"Now, now, Sue Ellen," Cybil chided, "there's no need for false modesty. You're among friends here. Everyone knows what a great cook you are." She turned back to Maddy. "Why even Mr. Kincaid complemented Sue Ellen on how delicious her blackberry jam was."

Maddy felt a twinge of sympathy for Sue Ellen. It couldn't be easy to be Cybil's daughter, but somehow, even given all her mother's constant boasting and pushing, Sue Ellen remained surprisingly unspoiled and actually quite nice. In Maddy's book, that took a great deal of inner strength and character.

"You're absolutely right, Cybil," Maddy agreed. "Sue Ellen *is* a wonderful cook. I'm sure the competition for her basket will be as fierce this year as it was last."

Not that Maddy believed for one minute that the *only* reason the fellows vied for the right to share Sue Ellen's basket was her skill as a cook. The fact that she was pretty, sweet-tempered and came from such a prominent family made her one of the most sought-after girls in Pepper Cloud. But so far the town belle didn't seem to be in any hurry to select a favorite from her bevy of beaus.

Maddy moved on to serve tea to another of the ladies present, but Cybil wasn't quite through with her.

"I'm so glad to see you're finally able to get along without that cane, dear," she said placing her spoon on her saucer. "I was beginning to wonder if your injury was perhaps a bit more serious than Dr. Perkins had thought."

Handing Blanche her cup allowed Maddy to delay answering long enough to form a polite response. "Thank you for your concern. I'm afraid between Clay and the ladies here at Barrows House I was spoiled shamelessly. Why, it was all I could do to convince them that I was able to get about on my own this morning."

Cybil nodded benevolently as she raised her cup. "I'm

glad your *cousin* is taking such a familial interest in your well-being."

Maddy resisted the urge to roll her eyes as she caught the slight emphasis Cybil put on the word cousin. It wouldn't surprise her a bit if the Ladies' Society president had matrimonial designs on Clay in regards to Sue Ellen.

How would Cybil and the rest of these ladies react if they knew she felt something much warmer than "cousinly affection" toward Clay? Or did they already suspect as much?

"I hope you don't think it impertinent of me to say so, Maddy," Blanche spared a smile for Maddy as she moved toward the pastry cart, "but I'm so glad you've finally decided to relax your mourning attire." She made her selection and waved the fluffy pink confection toward Maddy. "That shade of blue you're wearing today is particularly becoming on you."

Maddy turned back to Blanche with a pleased smile. The "little touches" Miss Olive kept adding to her wardrobe, while still quite tasteful and understated, had grown bolder with each passing day. The dress she wore today, with its royal blue bodice, was the most colorful to date.

"Why thank you. And *of course* I don't mind receiving such a nice compliment." She fanned out her skirt with her free hand. "Miss Olive does such fine needlework, don't you think?"

Blanche cut a nervous glance from Miss Olive to Cybil before she answered. "Why, yes, it's just lovely."

"I do wonder, Maddy," Lavinia said with a coy smile, "if perhaps this sudden desire to spruce up your wardrobe wouldn't have anything to do with a certain charming, well-to-do gentleman who's been spending quite a bit of time with you recently."

"Nonsense, Lavinia," Cybil interjected before Maddy could respond. "Mr. Kincaid is a relation of Maddy's husband. It's perfectly understandable that he would be solicitous toward her since Maddy has no close male relatives of her own. But Maddy is a sensible woman. I don't believe she would be foolish enough to interpret his attention as motivated by anything but duty, *would* you dear?"

Maddy held her irritation in check as she felt all eyes on her. "Actually," she said with what she considered to be admirable aplomb, "the changes I'm making have more to do with having Katie in my life. Raising a child helps one to look forward rather than back."

Then, spurred by a devilish impulse, she gave the room at large a just-between-us-ladies grin. "But I must say, having a handsome gentleman take such approving notice is an unlooked-for bonus."

She received several smiles of agreement. But Cybil's smile didn't quite reach her eyes. "I'm pleased to see Katie's presence has had such a positive influence on you, Maddy. I hope the same can be said for the impact you're having on Katie's life."

Cybil paused as she took a sip from her cup. Then she met Maddy's gaze with a challenging lift of her brow. "I hear you recruited two new young women for your Thursday afternoon tea party last week."

Maddy mentally counted to ten. She would *not* let Cybil get a rise out of her. Then a conversational lifeline came from an unexpected source.

"Speaking of Katie," Vera asked, "how is she enjoying her new puppy?"

Maddy turned to Anna's mother with a silent sigh of relief. "She is absolutely delighted with Skipper. The two have been inseparable since she brought him home yesterday. It was so sweet of Anna to offer Katie one of her puppies. Be sure to thank her for us again."

Vera preened slightly. "Of course, dear. But as I told Mr. Kincaid when he brought Katie by yesterday, Anna is always happy to share with her friends."

Maddy, realizing Clay had been responsible for this softening in Vera's attitude, had a sudden inspiration. "Clay is planning to give Katie croquet lessons tomorrow afternoon.

Perhaps Anna could join them." She offered what she hoped passed for a guileless smile. "You'd be welcome to come as well, of course."

There was the barest of hesitations before Vera returned Maddy's smile. "That sounds delightful. I'm sure Anna would be happy to share Katie's croquet lesson."

Maddy felt a quiet surge of triumph at this minor victory. She had won Vera over to her side. No, she told herself, ready to give the devil his due, Clay had won Vera over to her side.

Now all she had to do was thank him by telling him that his role of suitor had just been expanded to include that of croquet instructor.

Clay sat on the back steps, watching Katie play with her new puppy. He'd set himself the task of ensuring the little girl stayed clear of the parlor this afternoon. He wanted to make sure she wasn't exposed to the same censure she'd encountered at the last Tuesday afternoon gathering.

He wished he could protect Maddy, as well. He didn't like to think of her having to face down any spiteful or catty comments on her own.

Not that she couldn't take care of herself. But he'd grown used to giving her his shoulder to lean on these past few days, literally. And, much as he hated to admit it, it had felt darn good. He'd been almost disappointed to find she'd put her cane away this morning and was back to her old, independent, I-can-face-the-world-on-my-own self.

A spate of giggles from Katie caught his attention and made him smile. Watching her right now, he had to admit that the child was not only happy here at Barrows House, she seemed to be thriving. Had he been wrong about the effect living here would have on a child? Would Maddy be able to overcome the town's prejudice against the eccentricities of her household enough to give Katie some semblance of a normal childhood? Would she even make the effort, or would her stubborn pride and independence get in the way?

He pulled out the letter he'd gotten from Peterson this morning. The investigator hadn't found any relatives of Katie yet, but he reported uncovering some very promising leads. It was quite likely that before the adoption hearing, Clay would have information on another candidate for the little girl's guardian, one who perhaps had a stronger claim on the child. But he found it hard to believe it would be someone who would love and want Katie with a fierceness anywhere close to what Maddy felt.

What should he do with Peterson's information? He was no longer sure *what* was in the child's best interest. And he was very much afraid his growing attraction to Maddy was clouding his judgment.

The door opened behind him and he looked over his shoulder to see the lady in question stepping out on the porch. He stood, guiltily stuffing Peterson's letter back into his pocket.

Luckily, Katie immediately claimed her attention. "Aunt Maddy, look what Skipper can do." The little girl waved a rag in front of her pet's nose. The clumsily energetic puppy latched onto the cloth with his teeth and began a vigorous tug of war effort with Katie.

Maddy reacted as if it were the most amazing trick she'd ever seen. "Oh my, what a clever puppy, Katie," she said, clapping her hands. "Skipper must surely have been the pick of Daisy's litter."

Then Maddy turned her attention to Clay. "Mind if I join you?" she asked, waving toward the steps.

Something about her tone alerted Clay that she had more than casual conversation on her mind. "Of course." He took her hand to help her be seated, then tucked it securely to his side as he sat beside her. He was pleased when she didn't protest. "I take it your guests have departed."

She nodded. "Just left."

Had something occurred in the meeting to upset her? But she seemed more thoughtful than worried. "How did it go?"

Maddy kept her attention focused on Katie. "Actually, it went rather well. I think Vera Welborne is beginning to regard my adopting Katie more favorably." She finally turned to meet his gaze. "And I have you to thank for it."

Clay was completely caught off guard by the warmth of her expression. "I don't think—"

But she interrupted his protest. "No, it's true. Whatever ground I've gained this past week has been entirely due to your efforts." She gripped the lip of the stair with her free hand. "If things don't go the way I'd like them to at the adoption hearing in a few weeks, it won't be your fault."

Peterson's report suddenly weighed heavy in his pocket. Like the way his conscience troubled his thoughts. She was making it more and more difficult for him to contemplate doing anything to separate her and Katie.

Then Maddy laid her hand on his arm. "I want you to know that I appreciate all you've done, especially given how you feel about my plans. You're a man of your word, and I apologize for ever doubting that."

Her touch, warm and soft, ignited something inside him, something that heightened his awareness of her. Did Maddy have any idea how attracted he was to her? If it wasn't for Katie's presence, he'd be quite tempted to give in to the urge to lean over and kiss her absolutely senseless. As it was, he felt mesmerized by her expressive shamrock-green eyes, unable to look away, unable even to blink. The accelerated pace of her breathing was a seductive melody, playing counterpoint to the thrum of his own pulse.

A sudden exclamation from Katie intruded. Maddy started, as if coming out of a trance. Her cheeks pinkened, and she pulled her hand away as if she'd been burned. She turned to face Katie and Skipper again, but a quick glance in their direction told Clay there was nothing amiss.

"Well, anyway," Maddy began, tucking a non-existent

stray lock behind her ear, "I just wanted to say thank you."

"You're welcome, of course," Clay answered, amused by her uncharacteristically ruffled air. "But I'm not so sure you should be thanking me just yet."

She merely smiled, as if humoring him. Then she wrapped her arms around her knees and schooled her features into an oh-so-casual expression.

Clay immediately went on the alert. She was definitely up to something.

"Do you play croquet?"

"Croquet?" *Now* she'd surprised him.

"Yes, croquet." She chewed her lower lip. "It's a lawn game you play with mallets and balls."

"I *know* what croquet is. But I haven't held a mallet since I got out of short pants."

Her brow cleared. "But you are familiar with the game?" At his nod, she tilted her chin toward the girl and puppy. "It's good to see Katie having so much fun."

"Yes, it is." Clay couldn't quite see where this conversation was leading yet, but it was always interesting to watch the way Maddy's mind functioned. "Every child should have a pet."

"Uhm-hmm. But pets can't take the place of human playmates."

"True."

"There's a croquet set around here that Grandmother bought as a present for my eighth birthday. I thought Katie might enjoy learning the game."

So she'd circled around to that again. What was her sudden obsession with croquet?

Her gaze slid to meet his. "Do you think you could teach her?"

"Me? I'm afraid croquet isn't really my game. Like I said, I haven't played since I was in short pants. To be honest, even then, my brother and I found other, more interesting things to do with the mallets than hit balls through hoops." Clay smiled, remembering the mock sword fights and cavalry charges of his childhood. He shook his head. "No, Katie'd probably be better off if you taught her."

"Well, the thing is," she said with a nervous smile, "I told Vera that you'd be teaching Katie the game tomorrow, and invited her to bring Anna over."

So, that was it. He drew his brows down and frowned. No point in making it easy on her.

"And she said yes," Maddy said with a bright smile. "Isn't that wonderful?"

Clay resisted the urge to give in to her cajoling. "Maddy."

She reacted to the warning in his voice by tilting her chin up. "Strictly speaking, it won't have been a lie if you go ahead and teach them tomorrow."

There was that whatever-it-takes attitude again. He held his frown a moment longer.

Her chin came down. "I know I should have asked first," she said, hugging her knees tighter. "But for the first time, Katie will have a friend come over to Barrows House to play with her. Do you have any idea how much that will mean to her?"

Clay dropped his stern demeanor and gave her arm a squeeze. "Actually, I think your plan was inspired." He grimaced. "But if you want me to teach two little girls how to play croquet, you're going to have to give me a refresher first."

Her breath came out in a relieved sigh. "Fair enough," she said. "Katie has a piano lesson with Miss Fanny this afternoon—we'll do it then."

She flashed him a dewy-eyed smile that took his breath away. "Thank you."

"You're welcome." Clay, feeling a bit lightheaded by the effort it took not to gather her in his arms, leaned back against the porch rail.

It was time to lighten the mood a bit. "Croquet!" he said, rolling his eyes in disgust. "Why couldn't you have promised fishing lessons or even horseshoes?"

174

As she laughed at his grousing, Clay felt a quiet sense of satisfaction. Croquet might not be a "manly" pastime, but he would be helping Maddy help Katie.

And after all, having Maddy give him private lessons on the finer points of wielding a mallet seemed laced with all sorts of interesting possibilities.

Clay stepped into the quiet lane behind the Rosethorne. The sun had gone down hours ago, but it was a clear night and the moon and stars provided plenty of light.

He turned right, for no particular reason other than he'd turned left on his last nocturnal walk. There wasn't much to do in Pepper Cloud after dark, and he'd never been one to retire early. Since appearances required he avoid the sort of places that employed Ruby Jane and company, and he didn't relish staring at the walls of his room, he'd begun taking evening strolls.

He smiled, remembering the afternoon's croquet lesson. After reminding him of the rules, Maddy had asked him to demonstrate his skills. She hadn't been at all happy with the way he gripped the mallet and had repeatedly tried to correct his hand placement. Having her purposely touch his hands and arms in such a manner, not to mention accidentally brushing up against him in other places, left him in no hurry to show signs of improvement.

It had made for an entertaining, and quite stimulating, afternoon.

The hooting of an owl caught Clay's attention, making him aware that he'd walked a bit farther than he'd intended. Hearing another sound, he also realized he wasn't alone. There, nearly hidden in the moonlit shadow of a knurled oak, a couple were entwined in a passionate embrace. His body hardened as his mind immediately turned to thoughts of sharing such an embrace with Maddy.

Before Clay could execute a quiet retreat, a startled gasp told him he'd been spotted.

The male half of the silhouette, who Clay now recognized as Joey Brennan, stepped forward, shielding his partner from view. "Oh, hello Mr. Kincaid." The youth ran one hand through his hair as he jammed the other in his pocket. "Just out for a stroll, are you?"

Clay hid a smile at Joey's nearly successful attempt at nonchalance. He'd formed a loose friendship with the lad over the past few days and had a pretty good idea who was hiding in the shadows behind him. "That's right," he agreed, discreetly maintaining his distance. "Nice night for it."

"Uh, yeah," Joey looked around as if just noticing his surroundings, "it sure is."

Clay felt his lips twitch as an urgently whispered "Jo-ey" hissed across the pathway from the old oak.

"But nice as it is," he said, "I think I'm ready to call it a night." He gave Joey a mock salute and turned back toward town.

"Mr. Kincaid."

At the hail, Clay paused and turned back around. "Yes?"

Joey rubbed the back of his neck. "There, uh, there's no need to tell anyone you saw me and . . . you saw me out here tonight."

Clay gave him a reassuring smile. "No need at all." Then he turned and headed back to the hotel, whistling a jaunty tune. But not before he caught a glimpse of strawberry blond hair glistening in the moonlight behind Joey's shoulder.

Young love—impetuous, daring, thrilling.

He jammed his hands in his pockets. It was unfair that Maddy had never had an opportunity to enjoy that heady you-and-me-against-the-world exhilaration. She would have blossomed, would have found such joy in the experience.

What would it have been like to court a seventeen-year-old Maddy, to sneak kisses from her beneath the stars and listen to her dreams of a happily ever after?

What would it be like to truly court her now?

Chapter Thirteen

"Look out, Skipper!" Katie's expression contorted into a melodramatic, eye-squinching grimace as her puppy's game of chase-the-croquet-balls placed him in the path of her latest hit.

Maddy half rose from her seat on the veranda, then eased back down as the dog scampered out of harm's way. She had to settle down, quiet this nervous buzzing in her stomach. It was just so important, for Katie's sake, that this afternoon tea go well. She turned to find Vera watching her indulgently.

"Don't worry," Anna's mother offered, "puppies are much hardier than they appear."

Maddy smiled. "I never had one of my own—Grandmother was allergic to them. But Katie would be devastated if anything happened to Skipper. She's already formed such a strong attachment to him."

Vera nodded. "I know what you mean. Anna was like that from the moment she set eyes on Daisy." She turned back to the girls to watch Anna take her turn.

Maddy followed suit in time to see the little girl whack her mallet against the ball with more enthusiasm than accuracy. Clay's praise for her attempt wrung a smile from both mother and daughter. He was a surprisingly good teacher. And both girls were taking full advantage of the attention he was giving them.

He'd make some child a wonderful father someday.

The door behind the ladies opened and Miss Fanny stepped onto the veranda carrying a tray containing a water-beaded pitcher and several glasses. "I thought you might care for some lemonade," she said, setting the tray on the table between Maddy and Vera.

"Why, thank you." Maddy lifted the pitcher. "Something cool to drink will be a welcome treat." She poured a glass and handed it to Vera. "Would you mind taking this to Miss Adeline?" she asked Miss Fanny as she poured a second glass. "I'm sure she would enjoy a bit of refreshment, as well."

Miss Adeline, wearing garden gloves and wielding a variety of hand tools and a flower basket, had been working among the rose bushes a discreet distance away from the veranda. Decorously attired in a gingham gown and a wide-brimmed straw bonnet, she was the picture of homespun industriousness.

Maddy felt a quiet glow of affection for all three of her ladies. Without her saying a word, they'd understood how important it was to have this visit go smoothly.

As Miss Fanny bustled away with the glass of lemonade, Clay gave a melodramatic groan that echoed across the lawn, closely followed by the music of little-girl giggles. Apparently his latest attempt had shot wide of the mark.

"I must admit," Vera commented approvingly, "Mr. Kincaid is demonstrating admirable patience with the girls. Most men would think such a chore tiresome."

"Clay seems to enjoy spending time with Katie." Maddy didn't have to fake the pleased smile that went with that observation. "And children do seem to enjoy his company, as well."

Vera leaned back and slid a finger along her cheek. "He'll make an excellent father some day," she said, echoing Maddy's earlier thought. She speared Maddy with a considering look. "Add that to the fact that he's handsome, charming and well-to-do, and it seems the woman who lands him for a husband will be lucky, indeed."

A blush heated Maddy's cheeks. Then, reminding herself that she was *supposed* to appear love-struck, Maddy threw herself into the role of a smitten-but-not-ready-to-admit-it damsel. She slid her gaze away from Vera's and ducked her head to take a sip from her glass. Glancing toward Clay as if she couldn't help herself, she allowed a light stammer to creep into her reply. "Oh, I agree, absolutely." She sighed. "I imagine any lady Clay turned his affections toward would feel truly honored." Funny how she didn't really have to do much pretending to sound convincing.

Vera's lips curved in a knowing smile. "My thoughts exactly." She leaned forward conspiratorially. "Cybil has moved her sights from Freddie Clemmons to Mr. Kincaid as a husband for Sue Ellen, but just between you and me, I think she's going to be disappointed."

"Oh?" Maddy tried for a tone of merely causal interest, knowing Vera would see through that quite easily.

"Yes indeed." Vera's expression had the self-important smugness of one with a juicy insight to share. "Not only is Sue Ellen *not* exhibiting signs of being smitten with Mr. Kincaid, but Mr. Kincaid himself seems to have focused his own interest elsewhere."

"Do you think so?" The hopeful inflection in her tone was feigned, she told herself. She wasn't naïve enough to take any of this conversation seriously.

"Oh, most assuredly." Anna's mother turned back to watch the game in progress. "It's plain to see Katie's settled in quite happily here. Why, the only thing the child lacks right now is a father." She cast Maddy a sideways look. "I imagine if you were married there's not a soul in Pepper Cloud who would think twice about the propriety of your adopting the child."

Maddy wasn't quite sure how to respond to that. Thankfully, a gleeful shout from Anna provided a distraction.

"I did it! It went right through. Look Katie, I won."

Katie applauded her friend, apparently not at all put out by her own lack of victory.

Clay congratulated both girls on their game as he placed his mallet and ball back in the game rack. He moved to join the ladies on the porch, effectively forcing them to change the topic of discussion.

"Mr. Kincaid," Vera greeted him, "I was just telling Maddy how good it is of you to take such an interest in the children."

Clay smiled with a combination of modesty and cocky self-confidence that was lethally attractive. "Not at all, Mrs. Welborne. The girls' exuberant approach to the game is a pure delight. I'm sure I enjoyed the time every bit as much as they did."

He waved toward the lemonade. "Do you ladies mind if I help myself?"

Maddy reached for the pitcher. "Here, allow me."

A moment later, when she handed him the glass, she "accidentally" brushed her hand against his. Drawing her hand back, she assumed a flustered air and willed herself to blush, an action helped significantly by the warm look Clay favored her with.

"Thank you, Maddy." Clay's words sounded as intimate as a caress. He locked his gaze to hers as he took a long drink from the glass.

When he finally broke eye contact, Maddy let out a deep sigh, unaware until then that she'd been holding her breath. It seemed she was throwing herself into her role a little too well. Glancing Vera's way, Maddy wasn't at all surprised to see a knowing smile play at the corners of her guest's lips.

Vera turned to Clay. "That burgundy color is rather becoming on Maddy, don't you agree?"

Good heavens, had Vera decided to play matchmaker? And was she referring to the color of the trim on Maddy's gown or to the blush on her face?

Clay's slow, appreciative perusal brought additional heat to Maddy's cheeks. "Most definitely, ma'am," he agreed.

Vera turned back to Maddy. "I do hope, dear, that this relaxation in your mourning means you'll be participating in the dance at this year's Founders' Day Festival?"

Caught off guard by the question, Maddy didn't have to fake the stammer in her reply. "Well, uhm, I don't—"

"Mr. Kincaid," Vera interrupted, "you must help me convince Maddy that it's time for her to start enjoying herself again. She's much too young to put herself on the shelf the way she has these past seven years."

Clay gave the would-be cupid a wink. "You can count on me ma'am. I aim to claim a dance from her myself on Saturday."

"Well then," Vera said with a smug smile, "that's settled."

Maddy's back stiffened. They were talking about her as if she weren't even there. And how dare Vera assume that just because Clay said he'd convince her to do something it would happen.

But, remembering a scant second later that she *wanted* Vera to believe she was besotted, Maddy resisted the urge to toss her head. Instead, she forced herself to give Clay a lash-lowered smile. The glint in his eye as he smiled back revealed that he knew just what she was feeling. When had he learned to read her so well?

"Well then," Vera said as she got to her feet, "it's time for me to get on home and see to supper." Then, as Maddy rose, "Thank you for the invitation, Maddy. I enjoyed the visit and our little chat. We'll have to do this again sometime soon."

Maddy moved with Vera toward the girls. "I enjoyed it as well."

"It's time to go, Anna," Vera told her daughter. "Help Katie pick up the game." Then she turned back to Maddy. "I hope you'll give our little talk some thought over the next few days."

Maddy nodded. Her plan seemed to be working even better than she'd anticipated. Vera was now primed to believe it was all *her* idea.

But as she watched the girls do Vera's bidding, the primary emotion she felt was not that of satisfaction. Rather it was a tingly anticipation as she thought of the upcoming festival and the dance Clay promised to claim.

Clay rolled down his sleeves and buttoned his cuffs. His lips curved in amusement as he watched Maddy say farewell to her guest. He wasn't sure how the resourceful Mrs. Potter had pulled it off, but if he'd read the previous conversation properly, it seemed she had Vera Welborne ready to assume the role of Cupid. That could prove to be a very interesting turn of events.

He put the croquet set away in the tool shed. That done, he wandered around to the front of the house in time to see Maddy close the front gate behind the Welbornes. Katie called a final good-bye to her friend, then raced back around the corner of the house with Skipper.

That left him alone with Maddy.

He fell into step beside her as they strolled toward the front porch. "I take it the visit was a success?" he said.

"Yes." Maddy shook her head as if she couldn't quite credit what had happened. "I actually believe Vera is going to turn into a strong ally now."

Clay leaned against a support post as Maddy took a seat in the porch swing.

"I'd like to discuss the Founders' Day Festival, with you," she announced abruptly.

He folded his arms across his chest, wondering what was

coming. Did she have additional plans for their "court-ship"? "All right."

She toyed with the chain holding up the swing. "Naturally, we'll spend the day together."

Surely the redoubtable Maddy Potter wasn't feeling self-conscious? "Naturally."

"For the most part we can just stroll about the festival, visiting some of the booths and watching the programs and competitions being staged during the day. But there is at least one activity you need to take an active part in."

He raised a brow. "If you mean the dance, I fully intend—"

"That too, of course," she interrupted. "But that's not what I was referring to." She took a deep breath. "There's a traditional method the Ladies' Society uses to raise money for charity. It has to do with who you'll share your lunch with."

Clay remembered the uneasy glances Sue Ellen and Joey had exchanged over this topic. His interest piqued, he nodded. "The picnic basket auction."

Maddy stiffened. "What have you heard?"

He shrugged. "Only that the town's ladies prepare picnic luncheons that are auctioned off to the gentlemen, along with the pleasure of their company." He grinned. "Don't worry, I'll make sure I end up with yours, no matter how high the bidding goes."

Maddy shifted in her seat. "I don't believe that will be a problem."

Before he could figure out what she meant by that cryptic comment, she squared her shoulders and determinedly met his gaze.

"I'm not a very good cook. In fact," she said, clasping her hands together in her lap, "I'm rather dreadful. And the whole town knows it."

So that was the problem. His I-can-handle-anything Maddy had to admit to a failing. "Oh come now, I'm sure it's not as bad as all that."

But his attempt at reassurance only served to turn her expression more glum. "Last year, Calvin Miller was unlucky enough to place the winning bid on my basket. Less than thirty minutes after he ate, he was very miserably, very publicly, indisposed."

Good heavens, she must have been mortified. As it was, she looked as if she'd just confessed to a crime. But he knew better than to offer sympathy. So instead he nodded soberly. "I'll consider myself forewarned."

Maddy eyed him suspiciously, but he didn't bat an eye, though it was hard not to grin indulgently.

"Well," she said finally, "I only thought it fair that you should know. You shouldn't have much competition for my basket if folks recognize it." She worried at her bottom lip with her teeth. "I promise that, even if it isn't the most delicious meal you've ever eaten, it won't make you sick."

Clay moved to sit beside her. "I'm not worried." Then he gave her a deliberately cocky smile. "We Kincaids are a hardy lot."

He was pleased to see the hangdog slump of her shoulders disappear and some of her former confidence reassert itself.

"I could have guessed as much," she said with a touch of asperity. But Clay detected a spark of gratitude in her expression, as well.

He casually placed an arm along the back of the swing behind her. "So, tell me about this dance. I take it from Mrs. Welborne's comment that you don't normally participate."

Maddy nodded. "I usually help out with the refreshments or with watching the babies and younger children."

"But not this year." It was a statement, not a question. He wasn't about to let her play wallflower while he was around to do something about it.

She fidgeted with her hair. "No, not this year."

"Good." With only a little over a week left of his time in Pepper Cloud, Clay had every intention of claiming several dances from Maddy. He couldn't pass up such a prime opportunity to hold her in his arms with no questions asked.

He refused to think about the fact that memories of such times would soon be all he had left of Maddy, all she seemed willing to give him.

Much more pleasant to picture her twirling gracefully about the dance floor, face flushed with pleasure and animation. Just like the first time he'd seen her romping across the study.

But this time he'd make sure she'd be looking at him, not Katie.

Maddy blew a stray hair out of her eye and wiped her brow with the back of a flour-dusted hand. She'd barricaded herself inside the kitchen right after the household's earlier-than-normal breakfast, almost two hours ago. Leaving strict orders not to be disturbed, Maddy had been working to put together her basket for today's auction ever since.

Sending up a silent prayer, she opened the oven and pulled out the pan of biscuits. This was the third batch she'd attempted and there just wouldn't be time to try again. Clay would be by in less than an hour to escort her to the festival, and she still had to clean up and get ready.

The kitchen door opened a crack. "Maddy, are you sure you wouldn't like me to help just a little bit?"

Maddy took a deep breath as she silently counted to ten. "No thank you, Miss Fanny," she said as pleasantly as she could manage.

The color looks good, she thought hopefully, a perfect golden brown. "It's really sweet of you to want to lend a hand." She set the pan down on the counter. "But you know· the rules of the auction as well as I do." Maddy picked up one of the biscuits, tossing it from hand to hand to help it cool.

"I'm sure there are others who bend the rules a bit," Miss Fanny said from the other side of the door. "Most folks turn a blind eye to it. Adeline let me help with *hers* last night."

That statement got Maddy's attention. "Miss Adeline's preparing a basket this year? When did she decide that?"

Fanny stuck her head inside the room, apparently taking Maddy's question as a softening of her resolve. "Just yesterday. Said she was going to enjoy spicing up the festival a bit." As if conjured by mention of his mistress's name, Othello took advantage of the open door to slip into the room.

Maddy smothered a groan. Heaven only knew what mischief the flamboyant leading lady was up to this time. She just prayed it wouldn't stir up another scandal.

Right now, though, she had a more immediate concern to see to. The biscuit had cooled enough for her to stop juggling it. This one seemed lighter than those from the last batch. While Othello watched her with a hopeful expression, Maddy broke it open, inhaling as the steam rose. Yes! It was cooked all the way through. "Come on in," she said feeling just a trifle smug, "Try one of my biscuits, if you like."

Miss Fanny was through the door and into the kitchen almost before Maddy finished speaking. Her eyes grew rounder as she surveyed her heretofore neat-as-a-pin kitchen.

Maddy looked around, feeling some of her smugness change to sheepishness. At least a half dozen dirty mixing bowls and twice as many spoons were piled up next to the sink. Egg shells and a sticky-looking wire whisk lay nearby. On the stovetop, a pan held the sorry-looking results of her first two efforts, one batch of rock hard lumps, and one batch of crunchy-on-the-outside-gooey-in-the-center blobs. And over everything lay a fine dusting of flour.

Maddy gave her friend an apologetic grimace. "I'm afraid I've laid waste to your kitchen. But don't worry, I promise to set everything back to rights."

Miss Fanny shook her head, her customary motherly

smile returning. "No need to apologize dear. Now, let's try one of those delicious-smelling biscuits you have there."

Maddy handed her a piece of the one she'd just torn open, and took a cautious nibble of the other half herself.

Miss Fanny's face lit up as she chewed. "Why Maddy, this is wonderful. I couldn't have done better myself."

Maddy, swallowing her own bite, knew her friend was exaggerating. It was satisfactory, but nothing more. Still, she decided as she gave Othello the last bite, she was pleased. The biscuits had been the trickiest part of the meal she'd planned. With that obstacle successfully overcome, she wouldn't have to worry about anyone getting sick on her cooking this year.

"Thank you. Now, I'll just wrap these in a cloth, pack them away, and my basket is ready."

Miss Fanny eyed the food hamper, her fingers obviously itching to lift the cover. "What else do you have inside there?"

Maddy closed the lid with a thump. "Sorry, that's going to be my little secret for the time being." She pushed the recalcitrant lock of hair from her forehead again and then moved to the sink. "I'll get this mess all cleared away before I clean up and change clothes."

But Miss Fanny bustled over, making shooing motions with her hands. "Don't be silly. You've got a handsome gent coming over to escort you to the town's biggest, most festive event of the year. You should be spending your time getting gussied up, not cleaning a kitchen."

"But—"

"I won't hear of it." Even with a frown on her face and hands on her hips, Miss Fanny managed to look like an elderly cherub. "This kitchen is my domain, no one else can set things to order the way I like it anyway. Now you just run along and leave me to it."

Then she gave Maddy a conspiratorial smile. "Besides, Olive made a special dress for you to wear today, and she's growing impatient for you to see it."

187

Maddy untied the strings of her apron, guiltily eager to see the "special dress" and to get "gussied up" for Clay. "Well, if you're sure."

"I wouldn't say it if I wasn't sure, now, would I?"

Impulsively, Maddy leaned over and kissed Miss Fanny's cheek. "Thank you. I promise to help with your chores next week."

Miss Fanny blushed. "And don't think I won't hold you to that. Now, scat. Clay will be here any time now."

"Yes, ma'am!" Maddy headed for the door, then turned back to wag a finger at her friend. "And don't you be slipping any of those pies you baked last night into that hamper."

The guilty expression on Miss Fanny's face gave her away.

"Promise me," Maddy demanded.

Miss Fanny threw up her hands. "Oh, very well. I promise."

With a last shake of her head, Maddy exited the kitchen.

Clay smiled at Katie as she opened the door to admit him. "Hello, Little Bit, are you and your aunt Maddy ready to go to the festival?"

"Aunt Maddy's still getting dressed," Katie announced as he stepped inside, "but I'm ready." She spread the skirts of her ruffled pinafore, setting Skipper to dancing at her ankles. "Do you like the new dress Miss Olive made me?"

Clay tilted his head, studying her from head to toe as she preened for him. "Very nice. The blue is mighty pretty on you and I like the matching hair ribbon." Not that he thought the neat, sweet-little-angel appearance would last long. He predicted by lunch the hair ribbon would be bedraggled or missing altogether, and the immaculate dress would be sporting a smudge or two. There was a dab of snips and snails and puppy dog tails mixed in with Katie's sugar and spice.

"Thank you," she said, tilting her chin in what she probably thought was a dignified manner. Then she grinned. "But wait 'til you see Aunt Maddy's dress. It's even prettier."

"Is that so?"

Katie nodded vigorously. "Uh-huh. It's bee-yoo-ti-ful." She took his hand and tugged him toward the staircase. "Come on, I'll show you."

"Show him what?"

At the question, Clay looked up to see Maddy standing at the top of the stairs, and felt his pulse speed up. Oh yes, Katie was definitely right. It was a bee-yoo-ti-ful sight, and he didn't mean just the dress.

The vibrant dusky rose fabric, highlighted with a softer pink at the cuffs and sash, was a perfect complement for her coloring. He noted approvingly that there was not a speck of black to be seen anywhere on the garment.

Before she could move, Clay started up the stairs, his eyes drinking in the changes in her. As he neared, he noticed the ivory lace, delicate as an angel's wings, edging the neckline. And unlike the throat-encasing armor of her other gowns, this dress actually did have a neckline. Modestly cut for daywear, it showcased the graceful column of her throat, revealing soft creamy skin his fingers and lips itched to explore. Even her hair was styled differently today, looser, less severe.

This was the softer, more feminine Maddy he'd only had glimpses of before. The Maddy he hoped to see more of in the days to come.

As he reached the top of the stairs and offered her his arm, he noticed one other thing. She was nervous and trying very hard not to show it.

"I'm going to be the envy of every man at the festival today," he said, placing a hand over hers on his arm.

She rolled her eyes at him. "Don't be absurd."

But as they started down toward the waiting Katie, Clay could feel her relax. Had she worried about his reaction to her appearance? A tender warmth stole over him at the thought.

"Is it time to go yet?" Katie asked. Skipper punctuated her question with yips as the girl's excitement communicated itself to her pet.

Maddy nodded. "Yes, just as soon as you put Skipper in his pen."

Some of Katie's enthusiasm waned. "Can't he come with us, please? I'll take real good care of him."

But Maddy held firm. "We've already discussed this, Buttercup. Skipper's not accustomed to crowds and he's still just a baby. He really will be better off staying here today."

"Yes ma'am."

Clay repressed a smile. It seemed Miss Adeline wasn't the only actress in Barrows House. The dejected slump to Katie's shoulders would have done a condemned man proud.

"Come along, Little Bit," he said, placing a hand on her back. "I'll help you make Skipper comfortable." Then, to turn her thoughts to a more pleasant topic, "How's Ferdinand this morning?"

Katie's expression flashed into pleased animation. "Great! I did another practice with him this morning, just like you showed me, and he jumped at least this much farther than he did yesterday." Katie spread her fingers apart about four inches, and puffed her chest out proudly. "He's gonna be the best frog there, I just know it."

Clay commended her and Ferdinand, then looked up to meet Maddy's gaze. She regarded him with a rather dreamy expression on her face. Now what had he done to bring that on? Whatever it was, he wanted to do it again. "We'll be right back," he told her. "This shouldn't take more than a minute or two."

"Take your time," she said with a wave of her hand. "I need to check on Miss Fanny and fetch my hamper. Just look for me in the kitchen whenever you're ready to go."

Maddy watched them until they'd disappeared down the

hall, then turned toward the kitchen. Seeing the two of them together did funny things to her insides. Clay and Katie had grown close this past week, ever since he'd accompanied the little girl to Anna's house to fetch Skipper and bring him home.

He'd spent several hours with Katie that first day, teaching her what she needed to know about grooming and caring for a puppy. The next day, he'd shown up at Barrows House with Joey Brennan in tow. The two of them had consulted Katie, then gathered up materials and tools and set to building a nice, roomy pen for the dog, perfectly situated to get a fair measure of both shade and sunshine.

Then, when the little girl had wistfully mentioned that at last year's festival, her father had promised she could place an entry in the frog-jumping contest, Clay had declared there was no reason she couldn't do just that. He'd helped her capture a frog, practice with it, and even built her a small wire-and-stick cage to carry it in.

Somewhere along the way, he'd started calling her by that nonsensical nickname. Little Bit. And Katie loved it.

Yes indeed, Clay would definitely make a wonderful father some day. Maddy felt a tightening in her chest. If only things could be different, if only she didn't have to pay a lifetime of penance to the ghosts of her past.

If only . . .

Maddy pasted on a smile and pushed open the kitchen door.

Chapter Fourteen

"Anna told me they're going to have monkeys!"

Hearing the excited awe in Katie's tone, Maddy smiled down at the child skipping along between her and Clay. This year, at the suggestion of the Ladies' Society, the town council had invited a traveling circus to set up in Pepper Cloud during the festival. The news had fired Katie's imagination from the moment she'd heard it.

Maddy made a "how impressive" noise as she ruffled Katie's hair. She was determined to take today as it came, to make the most of this day of pretend-courtship with Clay. Surely it wouldn't hurt to make believe, just for this one day, that it was real, to accept his attentions and perhaps flirt a bit herself.

Of course there was always the danger that she wouldn't be able to walk that tightrope between making everyone else believe she was in love with Clay and making him believe she wasn't.

As Maddy absently shifted the food hamper to her other arm, Clay raised a brow.

"Are you sure you wouldn't like me to carry that?" he asked over Katie's head.

"No, thank you." Maddy smiled to soften her refusal. "We wouldn't want anyone to think you had a look at my basket." And, if they were being literal about it, he hadn't. All baskets were delivered to the auction covered, birdcage fashion. But there was no doubt in her mind Clay would know exactly which basket was hers as soon as he saw it—she'd made sure of that.

Katie added a one-legged hop to her skip. "And there's a tiger and a hyena, too."

"Careful, Little Bit," Clay cautioned as Katie twirled around. "You don't want to make poor Ferdinand sick, do you?"

Katie lifted the carrier and peered inside. "Sorry Ferdinand." Then she lowered her arm with exaggerated care and turned back to Maddy with a frown. "What's a hyena?"

"Well . . ." At a loss for words, Maddy sent a *help me* look Clay's way.

"It looks sort of like a dog," Clay explained, coming to her rescue, "but it makes a strange sound when it barks, almost like a laugh."

Katie giggled. "A laughing dog. I can't wait to see it." She resumed her skipping. "Can we go there first?"

Maddy sent a silent thank you Clay's way before answering Katie's question. "First," she said, "I need to drop off my hamper at the schoolhouse. Then we need to get Ferdinand signed up for the frog-jumping contest. After that we can walk over to the circus tents if that's what you and Mr. Kincaid prefer."

"Good morning, folks." Joey Brennan, who'd just stepped out of the mercantile, matched his step to theirs. "Fine day for a festival, isn't it?"

Maddy offered him a smile of greeting. "Hello. Yes, it's a picture-perfect day, all right."

Joey cocked his head, studying Maddy with an appreciative gleam in his eyes. "The day isn't the only thing picture perfect this morning, Miz Potter. You sure are looking mighty fine in that pretty pink dress."

Maddy smoothed her skirt self-consciously. "Why, thank you, Joey."

"What about me?" Katie demanded. "Don't you think my new dress is pretty, too?"

Joey did a double take, as if he hadn't noticed the child until she spoke up. "Why, Miss Dooley," he said, placing a hand over his heart, "you are nigh 'bout as pretty as a bluebird in a spring garden." He made a sweeping bow and crooked his arm toward her. "Please allow me the honor of escorting you to the festival grounds."

Katie giggled at his antics. Then, preening a bit and lifting her chin, she took his arm. The little girl managed to maintain a sedate pace for all of a minute before she began skipping ahead again.

As the steeple of the Methodist Church came into sight, the flow of traffic, both pedestrian and carriage, increased, and Maddy called Katie back to her side. The grounds of the church as well as the adjacent schoolhouse were where most of the booths and activities were to be found on festival day.

Activities that required a bit more room, such as the relay race and the rifle-shooting competition, took place in Mr. Benson's pasture on the other side of the school. It was also where the circus had set up when it arrived in town yesterday.

As they rounded the corner past the livery, Katie grabbed Maddy's hand. "Aunt Maddy, look!" she said, pointing with Ferdinand's cage.

Up ahead, surrounded by a crowd of wide-eyed children and equally impressed adults, a gaudily dressed performer juggled four bright red balls, expertly shifting from one intricate pattern into another.

With a wave, Joey parted company with them, headed for the rifle-shooting competition. A few minutes later, Maddy moved on as well, leaving Clay and Katie watching the juggler while she proceeded on to the schoolhouse.

Vera, who'd been talking to Cybil and Sue Ellen, looked up when Maddy walked in. "Maddy, hello!" Vera waved her over. "Bring your basket and set it with the others."

As Maddy complied, Vera gave her an approving smile. "My, but don't you look festive today. That dress is quite flattering on you."

Before Maddy could get out more than a *thank you*, Cybil raised a brow. "I see you've decided to put your mourning aside altogether."

Maddy set her basket down alongside several others, feeling a sudden stab of guilt at Cybil's words. Was she being disloyal to Winston? "No . . . I mean yes . . . that is—" Realizing she was stammering, Maddy halted her flow of words.

Cybil gave her a you-poor-thing smile. "No need to get flustered, dear. You've been so loyal to Winston's memory these past years, I'm sure no one will fault you for it." The words were uttered in a tone that said just the opposite.

But Maddy had herself back under control now. "Thank you Cybil. Those are my feelings as well." Then she turned back to Vera. "It looks like you've done an outstanding job of organizing the auction."

Vera graced her with a beaming smile. "How sweet of you to say so. But I do believe this is the easiest of the jobs at the festival."

"I must say," Cybil interjected, "I admire your composure, Maddy. There aren't many women who'd have the courage to participate again after what happened last year."

Maddy frowned, more puzzled than stung. Cybil was normally so much subtler with her digs. Did she feel threatened by something?

"Really, mother." Sue Ellen linked her arm supportively through Maddy's. "I'm sure no one believes Calvin's getting sick last year had *anything* to do with Maddy's basket. Why, he said himself that he'd been feeling a bit sick all morning."

Maddy gave Sue Ellen's arm a grateful squeeze for her unexpected support. Sue Ellen was a sweet girl, but it wasn't often she stood up to her mother in such a public manner.

Cybil also seemed surprised at her daughter's show of backbone, but she recovered quickly. "I quite agree, Sue Ellen. I was only admiring Maddy's good sense in ignoring the idle gossip that surrounded the incident."

Another group of ladies, hampers in tow, entered the schoolhouse, putting an end to the uncomfortable conversation.

Sue Ellen disengaged her arm from Maddy's, but as Maddy turned to make her exit, she discovered Cybil at her side.

"And where is that charming cousin of yours this morning?" the mayor's wife inquired. "I do hope he plans to attend today's festivities."

Maddy wasn't fooled by Cybil's casual tone. "As a matter of fact, Clay escorted Katie and me here this morning. I left them watching one of the circus performers a few moments ago."

Cybil *tsked.* "Maddy dear, I would never presume to tell you how to deal with your cousin."

Which Maddy knew meant she intended to do just that.

"However, I know you are not accustomed to dealing with menfolk. While I'm sure Mr. Kincaid is much too polite to say so, men, as a rule, don't like to be left alone to deal with children, especially little girls. Most men look upon such responsibilities as a woman's duty."

Maddy's annoyance added an extra dose of relish to her assumed role of Juliet to Clay's Romeo. Knowing Clay would spend the day paying court to her and that that would drive Cybil to distraction was guiltily satisfying.

"You're right about my lack of experience in the ways of gentlemen," she admitted demurely, "and I appreciate your lending me the benefit of your vaster knowledge." She allowed a dreamy sigh to escape her lips. "But as you've no doubt noticed, Mr. Kincaid is not *most men.*"

Maddy opened her eyes wider as she turned an isn't-he-wonderful smile on Cybil "He and Katie deal quite nicely together, and in fact greatly enjoy each other's company." Prompted by a mischievous impulse, she added, "It's almost as if they were father and daughter."

Cybil's expression was almost comical in its pompous displeasure. "Now, Maddy—"

But Maddy didn't let her finish. "Oh, look, there they are now. Katie, Clay," she called, waving to get their attention.

Katie sat perched atop Clay's shoulder, a vantage that allowed her an excellent view of the juggler, despite the press of the small crowd. At Maddy's hail, Clay turned and set the excited child down on the ground.

"Aunt Maddy," Katie called, racing up to take her hand, "can we go see the monkeys now?"

"Of course, Buttercup." Maddy wiped a smudge from Katie's cheek with her thumb.

"Hello, Mr. Kincaid." Cybil graced Clay with a just-the-person-I've-been-looking-for smile.

Clay inclined his head in greeting. "Hello ma'am, Miss Sue Ellen. Are you ladies enjoying the festivities?"

Cybil's smile grew a little more fixed as she noted the familiar way Clay tucked Maddy's hand on his arm. Maddy almost felt sorry for her.

Almost.

"Why yes," the matron answered. "We bumped into Maddy in the schoolhouse. Sue Ellen is placing a basket in the auction as well, you know."

"Is that so?" Clay turned to Sue Ellen. "I'm sure whoever wins your basket will consider himself a very lucky fellow."

Sue Ellen returned his easy smile with one of her own. But before she could comment, her mother spoke up again.

"You have the right of it there," she said proudly. "Sue Ellen's baskets have been the most sought after the past two years, and there's no reason to think it'll be any different this year."

Clay greeted this bit of maternal boasting with a perplexed frown. "But I understood the identity of the preparer remained a secret until the baskets were claimed at the end of the auction."

"That's true," Cybil answered. "But somehow the lads all seem to find out which one is my Sue Ellen's." She shook her head as if to indicate she had no idea how they managed it.

A second later, Cybil touched her daughter's arm. "By the way, Mr. Kincaid, isn't that a fetching ribbon Sue Ellen is wearing in her hair today?"

Oh for heaven's sake, it seemed Cybil had dropped all pretense at subtlety. Sue Ellen's basket would no doubt be sporting a ribbon that matched her hair bow exactly.

But if Clay was aware of the ploy, he didn't give any sign. He merely smiled and offered a smoothly worded compliment on Sue Ellen's appearance in general.

Katie, who'd stood quietly until now, reached for Maddy's hand again. "I think the monkeys are over there by that big tent," she said helpfully.

"My, Katie, but don't you look nice today." Cybil's voice had that cloying, condescending tone some adults used when speaking to children.

Katie released Maddy's hand and fanned out her skirt on one side. "Thank you. Miss Olive made me a new dress."

"Very nice." Cybil waved toward the small cage in Katie's other hand. "What is that you're holding there, a prize Mr. Kincaid won for you at one of the games?"

"Oh no," Katie answered, lifting the cage up to Cybil's face for her viewing pleasure. "It's my frog, Ferdinand. I'm going to enter him in the frog-jumping contest."

Cybil recoiled as if bitten. "A frog!" She drew herself up, favoring Maddy with a disapproving frown. "Isn't that a competition more suited to little boys than young ladies?"

Maddy placed a hand on Katie's shoulder. "I don't be-

lieve there are any restrictions against girls participating if
they wish to."

"I'm sure it never occurred to anyone that there would
be a need to have such restrictions." Cybil gave a delicate
shudder. "Thank goodness my Sue Ellen never took an interest in handling such nasty creatures."

Katie's chin came up at that. "Ferdinand is *not* a nasty
creature."

Clay placed a hand on Katie's other shoulder. "Of course
he's not. I don't think that's what Mrs. Flaherty meant,
was it ma'am?"

Maddy, aware of the united family front they displayed,
hid a smile as she watched Cybil search for a proper response to Clay's question.

"Of course not," the matron said, patting her hair in a
flustered manner. "I only meant—"

"Cybil!" Lavinia Thompson hailed breathlessly, "There
you are."

Cybil turned with obvious relief as her friend bustled up
to join them. "Yes?"

"There's trouble at the cake walk." Lavinia took a deep
breath, wringing her hands. "Cletus Walker won the last
round, but dropped his cake. And now he's demanding we
give him another one."

Cybil drew her shoulders back. "Oh he is, is he?" She
turned to Maddy and Clay. "If you'll excuse me, it seems
I'm needed elsewhere." With that, she marched off in the
direction Lavinia had come from, her friend following in
her wake.

"I wouldn't want to be Cletus Walker right now," Clay
said, the mock-fear in his tone belied by the twitch of his
lips.

As Sue Ellen watched her mother's retreating form,
Maddy could swear she heard the girl utter a sigh of relief.
"Well," Cybil's daughter said, "If you'll excuse me, I'll run
along, too. Perhaps we'll meet up again at the auction."

The girl gave Clay a look Maddy couldn't quite interpret. Was she hoping he would bid on her basket? Had Vera been wrong about Sue Ellen's lack of interest in Clay?

That thought left Maddy feeling less certain of her plans than she had been earlier.

"Can we leave now?"

Clay looked down at Katie to see, not the excited merriment the child had viewed the monkeys with or the respectful awe she'd viewed the tiger with, but rather a wrinkled-nose and curled-lip distaste. He felt some sympathy for her reaction—hyenas had never been his favorite animals, either.

"Sure, Buttercup." Maddy placed a hand on Katie's back and led her away from the animal cages. From the expression on her face, it seemed she hadn't thought much of the raucous hyenas, either.

Clay offered an arm to each of them. "Shall we see what else the circus has to offer?"

They strolled through the field, letting Katie steer them in whatever direction took her fancy.

"Oooh, look!" The little girl darted ahead to join the crowd standing in front of a magician. She watched, enthralled, as the would-be-Merlin amazed the gathering with a set of metal rings that seemed solid one moment and able to pass through each other the next.

Seeing Katie hop and shuffle to peer around the crowd, Clay swooped her up and lifted her so that their heads were at the same level. "How's this?"

She placed an arm around his neck and graced him with a beaming smile. "Just right."

"Like you," he said, tapping the tip of her nose with his index finger.

A collective *ooooh* from the spectators drew Katie's attention back to the show. Clay however, had more interest in watching his two companions. Maddy seemed as fascinated as Katie. Had she never visited a circus before? Had she ever been very far from Pepper Cloud?

If they enjoyed this small troupe with its paltry offerings, what would they think of a truly grand circus? He could show them one that boasted a big top, elephants, wild-animal trainers, trick riders, and the dozens of other acts that had fascinated him as a boy. It would be fun to watch their faces light up with awe and excitement. And he could also show them. . . .

Stopping in mid-thought, Clay's smile faded. Foolish of him to forget that when he left Pepper Cloud it would be alone. As appealing as the charade had become, this ready-made family was not really his to claim. At the moment, though, he couldn't imagine one that would be more perfect for him.

He was going to miss them. Not that he'd admit that to anyone but himself. Then again, how would Maddy feel if they turned this mock-courtship into the real thing?

Was *he* ready for that?

He probably should take this slow. After all, such a commitment was a big step. There was nothing that said he couldn't keep in touch, make return visits from time to time. Give things a chance to develop naturally. How would Maddy feel about such an arrangement? Would she welcome him, or consider it an intrusion?

He shifted Katie against his shoulder, squeezing a light hug from her in the process. And it wasn't as if he'd be coming back just to see Maddy. It would be nice to watch Little Bit grow up.

Assuming Maddy *did* adopt her.

In Peterson's last missive, he'd reported success in locating a blood relation of Katie's—a cousin of her mother's. The man was married and had several children of his own. Peterson was in the process now of doing some discreet research into the family's background. Before Clay would even alert these kin to Katie's existence, he wanted to be absolutely sure they were the right kind of people to care for her.

He already knew, though, that they would never love

the child as much as Maddy did. Would she forgive him for digging into Katie's background this way? Or would she see it as intruding where he had no right? Surely, as much as she loved Little Bit, she would want to know if the child had living relatives to call her own.

Wouldn't she?

Another *ooooh* burst from the crowd, accompanied by enthusiastic applause. The magician bowed, indicating his performance was at an end. In pairs and clusters, mostly family groupings, the audience began to disperse.

"That was amazing," Maddy said as Clay set Katie down.

"It was magic," Katie amended, her eyes still wide with awe. Then something else caught her attention. "A clown! Look, he has a doggie." And away she ran.

Maddy took Clay's arm, giving him an I'm-having-a-wonderful-time smile, and the two followed their charge at a more sedate pace.

Yes, he was definitely going to miss this.

At Katie's insistence, they watched the clown put the performing terrier through his paces, not once but twice. When they finally convinced Katie it was time to move on, she let out a heartfelt sigh. Then she gave a little hop skip, and said with utter conviction, "I'm going to teach Skipper how to do tricks like that."

Maddy stroked Katie's hair. "Not all dogs can be trained to perform on command the way that one did," she warned gently.

"But Skipper can do it," Katie insisted. "He's a very smart dog."

"Of course he is," Maddy agreed. "But he's still just a puppy. And teaching a dog to do tricks takes a lot of time and a lot of work."

"I don't mind." Then Katie turned to Clay. "And Mr. Kincaid will help me, won't you Mr. Kincaid?"

Clay felt a tightening in his chest as he looked into that trusting face. How could he tell her he wouldn't be around to help?

Thankfully, as he struggled to come up with an answer, Katie was distracted by a group of children who swooped her into their midst like a group of chattering blackbirds.

His relief was tempered by the sight of Maddy watching him with a half-smile. "She's rather hard to say no to, isn't she?" he commented, fighting a ridiculous urge to scuff his shoe in the dirt.

Her lips quirked knowingly. "Most little girls are."

Just like one woman he knew, Clay thought.

Katie raced back up to them. "The tightrope walker is going to start in just a few minutes," she announced breathlessly. "Can we go watch, please?"

Clay forced himself to maintain a relaxed pose as a familiar tension tightened his chest for just a heartbeat. But something of his reaction must have communicated itself to Maddy.

Her smile flattened and the *yes* that had been on the tip of her tongue was swallowed before it could escape. She sent him a sideways, uncertain glance, before avoiding his gaze altogether. "I don't know, Buttercup. There's still other things to see right here, and it'll be time to head over to the frog-jumping contest before too much longer."

Katie's shoulders drooped.

Clay swore silently and willed his hands not to clench. Sympathy and mollycoddling were not what he wanted from Maddy. And he sure as hell didn't want her tiptoeing around his feelings at the expense of Katie's fun.

Did Maddy really think he was so craven that he couldn't even watch a circus performer risk his fool neck on a high wire? Arial acts weren't his favorite circus attraction, but he'd sat through them before and he could again without a qualm.

As long as no one expected *him* to climb up there, he reflected bitterly.

"Nonsense!" The startled expressions on Maddy and Katie's faces told him he'd said that a bit more forcefully than he'd intended. "The frog-jumping event isn't for an hour yet," he added in a milder tone. "We have plenty of time to look around here, watch the tightrope walker, and still get to the contest area on time."

Katie perked up immediately.

Maddy's reaction was more subdued. What did she really think when she remembered his shameful secret? And how could she look at him and not think of it?

Setting his jaw, Clay decided he would do his best to make sure that, for this day, at least, she *would* see something entirely different when she looked at him.

The schoolroom was crowded with as many observers as participants. Maddy counted thirty-three baskets lined in a single row on the four tables stretched across the front of the room. More than half of them sported distinctive ribbons or cloths that matched the gown or hair bow of a lady in the audience. The remainder were unmarked, indicating either the preparer wished to remain anonymous until the end, or had revealed some subtle tag only to a favored bidder.

Her own basket, fifth one on the right, didn't boast a ribbon, and the cloth that covered it was plain gingham. It was, however, far from anonymous. Anyone viewing the image of Barrows House painted boldly across the wicker front would know without a doubt who had prepared *that* basket.

She could tell the exact moment Clay caught sight of it. His lips quirked up and he met her gaze with an admiring smile. At just about the same moment, Vera and Cybil moved to the front of the room.

"Ladies and gentlemen," Cybil began, "welcome to the Tenth Annual Pepper Cloud Ladies' Society Founders' Day Charity Auction. As you know, the proceeds from this auction will go into the local widows and orphans fund, so you gentlemen plan to dig deep in your pockets. Now, I'll turn the floor over to this year's committee chairwoman, Vera Welborne."

Vera stepped forward to a smattering of applause. "Thank you, Cybil. I believe we're ready to get started, so will all ladies responsible for a basket, please step forward."

Clay gave Maddy an I'm-ready-if-you-are smile as she disengaged her arm from his. Taking a deep breath, she joined the ranks of the ladies lining up at the front of the room. Turning to face the crowd, she felt more than a trifle self-conscious, wondering how many of the observers were remembering the fiasco she'd created with last year's basket.

Deciding to ignore what she couldn't change, Maddy looked for and found Katie. The little girl stood whispering in Anna's ear under the watchful eyes of Miss Olive and Miss Fanny. Katie, proudly sporting the second-place ribbon she'd won at the frog-jumping contest, met her gaze and gave her a cheerful wave.

Then Miss Adeline, attired in a flowery organza gown and a riotously curled chestnut wig, sashayed to the front of the room, her furled parasol held in her outstretched hand like an elegant walking stick. There was no doubt this time that the ripple of whispers and raised brows were all directed toward someone other than Maddy. And Miss Adeline was enjoying every minute of it.

Maddy wondered again what had prompted Miss Adeline to participate in this year's auction. Was it just another theatrical bid for attention? Or had she some thought of taking a bit of the unwanted attention off of Maddy?

When Miss Adeline had finally taken her place with the others, Vera pounded her gavel. "All right gentlemen, take a last look at the ladies whose baskets and company you'll be bidding on." Then, with another bang of her gavel, "Ladies, take your places at the back of the room. Bidders, step forward, please."

There were several minutes of shuffling and rearranging as folks sorted themselves into the proper groups. The ladies who had brought baskets ranged along the back of the room, the lads and gentlemen planning to bid on the baskets gathered in the center and the observers crowded along both sides.

When things settled down once more, Vera moved to the first basket on the right. Maddy wasn't at all surprised to note it sported a large bow that matched the one in Sue Ellen's hair. She approved of Vera's strategy—auction off the most sought-after basket first. That way, those who didn't end up with it were freed up to bid on other baskets.

As expected, there was fierce competition to get a bid in on that first basket. The bidding started at fifty cents and moved quickly up to three dollars. At that point most of the bidders dropped out. By the time it reached four dollars there were just two left in the running. If Cybil was disappointed that one of those two was not Clay, she hid her feelings well. The fact that Freddie Clemmons *was* one of the remaining bidders probably helped.

It was Sue Ellen's reaction that puzzled Maddy most. It was the air of suppressed excitement, the subtle hint of amusement, as if the girl were privy to some secret she was hugging close to herself.

Apparently tired of the dickering, Freddie placed a bid of six dollars, a full dollar higher than the last bid offered. All eyes turned to Sam Goodwin, his competitor. After a moment of visible indecision, Sam shook his head and clapped Freddie on the back as a gesture of congratulations. There was light applause as Vera brought down the gavel. Freddie, chest puffed out, strutted to take his place behind the first basket, his grin focused on Sue Ellen with the cockiness of a victor ready to claim his prize.

In response, Sue Ellen tossed her head, giving him a saucy smile. The audience watched this by-play with grins and nudges. This was the sort of theatrics they were here for.

Catching sight of Miss Adeline standing just past Sue Ellen, Maddy felt her own lips twitch. Her friend stood with both hands resting on the handle of her parasol, watching the goings on with obvious relish. What was she up to? That smug confidence boded mischief for someone.

The next basket, easily identified as belonging to Dulcie Mason, a pert, freckle-faced brunette who was the darling of the church choir, saw energetic bidding as well. This time Sam Goodwin prevailed and he took his place next to Freddie behind the tables. As the bidding began on the next basket, Maddy idly scanned the tables, trying to identify which entry was Miss Adeline's. As the next few baskets sold, she slowly looked down the length of all four tables but didn't spot any that matched Miss Adeline's flamboyance. She was making a second visual pass through when she spotted the most likely candidate, about two thirds of the way down the line. She'd overlooked it the first time because of its modest appearance. The only decoration it sported was an understated eyelet bow on the basket's handle, but that bow was a perfect match for the trim on Miss Adeline's parasol.

Vera's gavel came down again, and Maddy's stomach clenched as she realized her own basket was up next. She tried to maintain an unruffled appearance, but her smile felt fixed and unnatural.

"All right, gentlemen," Vera began, "what am I bid for this very artistically decorated basket?"

A quickly shushed snicker was followed by a moment of almost complete silence.

Then, in a gracefully lazy movement Clay raised a hand and said in a voice that carried easily throughout the room, "I bid twenty dollars."

Maddy's gasp was drowned out by the dozens of others that shot through the room. What in the world had he done?

Vera slammed her gavel down. "Sold!" she exclaimed with enthusiastic approval.

Excited applause burst out at Vera's declaration, quickly followed by the buzz of whispers. As Clay made his way through the gauntlet of back-thumpers to reach the front of the room, Maddy found herself on the receiving end of

Winnie Griggs

a sea of pointed looks. Sue Ellen congratulated her with a quick hug and Miss Adeline smiled on approvingly. Maddy steadfastly refused to look Cybil's way. She wouldn't let a sourpuss expression mar her moment.

As Clay took his place behind her basket, Maddy looked across the crowd to meet his gaze. He wore a cock-of-the-walk grin, letting all who watched know he was quite pleased with the commotion he'd caused. It was all Maddy could do not to roll her eyes at his little-boy bravado.

Aware of the avid watchers surrounding them, Maddy managed what she hoped was a shyly pleased smile. What in the world had possessed Clay to bid such an outlandish amount? It was such an extravagant waste of money when he could have had her basket for so much less.

But she had to admit, this was a spectacular way to focus the town's attention on their "courtship."

"That was my Aunt Maddy's basket." Katie's proud boast, directed toward her friend, carried clearly across the room. "I bet she gets the *first*-place ribbon."

There were several good natured chuckles for the girl's misunderstanding. Maddy noted, however, that Cybil was not among the amused.

But before the matron could set the little girl straight, as she appeared on the brink of doing, Vera's gavel came down, signaling time for the next basket to go up for bid.

Now that Maddy's own basket had sold, she was able to relax and enjoy the fun.

Ten minutes later, it was time to bid on the basket Maddy had mentally tagged as Miss Adeline's. Joey Brennan placed the first bid. Three other bids were placed before the gavel came down. Not a bad showing for a basket whose owner was anonymous. And she was glad Joey had placed the winning bid. He was a good sort who wouldn't react rudely when he discovered with whom he'd be sharing lunch. And since Miss Fanny had "helped" with the preparation, the lad would have a good meal for his money.

When the gavel rang down on the final bid of the day,

the less lucky men who'd remained basketless, stepped aside to join the audience. Vera stared across the now empty space to the waiting ladies and announced, "Ladies, time to 'fess up and identify your baskets."

Maddy was two-thirds of the way across the room before she realized something was amiss. It was the shocked expression on Freddie's face that alerted her. She'd thought the buzz of sound from the onlookers was just the normal whispers that came with discovering who'd prepared each of the baskets. But turning to see what had Freddie tugging on his collar, Maddy stopped dead in her tracks.

Miss Adeline, looking very much like a cat with cream on her lips, was headed straight for that first basket.

Where was Sue Ellen?

Chapter Fifteen

Maddy, with dawning suspicion, turned to her left. Sure enough, Sue Ellen was making a beeline for the basket Joey guarded. And Joey didn't look at all surprised to see who had prepared his basket. If anything, he looked a trifle smug.

So, the two had conspired on this little surprise. It must be serious if Sue Ellen was willing to take this step with her mother looking on. Joey and Sue Ellen, who would have thought it?

Of course, she had to give the girl credit: Sue Ellen sure had picked the perfect moment to show her cards. There wasn't much Cybil could do with the whole town looking on. Especially since this was all in the name of charity. But Maddy didn't have to seek her out in the crowd to know Cybil would *not* be pleased.

Maddy resumed walking toward her place at the front of the room. Miss Adeline must have been in on the scheming of this little sleight of hand. That surprised Maddy, not because she thought Miss Adeline would have been hard to convince. This attention-garnering display of mischief was just the sort of thing Miss Adeline thrived on. But Maddy just hadn't known that either Joey or Sue Ellen was that well-acquainted with Miss Adeline.

Seeing Sam Goodwin clap Freddie on the back in an it-couldn't-happen-to-a-better-man way, a grin splitting his face, Maddy hid her own smile. But when she caught the snickers from some of the watchers, her grin faded.

What would Freddie do? It was obvious he'd been duped. Would he take his disappointment out on Miss Adeline, rebuff her in front of all these people? But to Maddy's relief, Freddie pulled himself together quickly, and after a glower directed at Sam, stepped around the table and offered his arm to Miss Adeline with a creditable smile of welcome. "Miss Adeline, ma'am, what an unlooked for honor."

Miss Adeline took his arm with a graceful nod and a knowing look. She said something to him that Maddy didn't quite catch, but it made Freddie laugh and pat the hand she'd placed on his arm.

Maddy relaxed—her friend would be all right.

Then Clay stepped around the table to her side. "Shall we?" he asked. Plucking the painted basket from the table as she placed her hand on his arm, he said, "And this time, I get to carry the basket."

The two had turned toward the door when Maddy caught sight of Cybil, storm clouds gathered around her, bearing down on Joey and Sue Ellen. She slowed to a stop.

"Uhm, Clay, do you mind if we invite Joey and Sue Ellen to share our picnic blanket?"

Clay followed her gaze and gave her arm a squeeze. "Excellent idea." He redirected their steps toward the newly unmasked lovebirds. They reached the couple just a few seconds behind Cybil. Joey stepped in front of Sue Ellen, as if to protect her from attack.

But before Cybil could say anything, Clay stepped forward. "Mrs. Flaherty," he said, taking her hand and bowing over it. "I just had to take a moment to offer my congratulations. Your Ladies' Society raised quite a bit of money for charity today."

Cybil preened a bit under Clay's admiring smile. "Why thank you, Mr. Kincaid. But of course, even though I am the president, it's not *my* Ladies' Society. The other ladies involved deserve some of the credit, as well."

"What a generous sentiment." Clay casually turned from Cybil to Joey. "And it seems you deserve some congratulations, as well." He released Cybil's hand and took Joey's to pump it vigorously. "Lady Luck is obviously on your side today. That's quite a coup you pulled off, taking a chance on a virtually anonymous basket and walking away with such a prize."

Maddy noticed Cybil stiffen again, but a hint of uncertainty had crept into her expression. Was she trying to decide if Clay's version of what happened was accurate, or had she merely realized how much attention they were getting? Those standing nearby were making no bones about their eavesdropping.

"Sue Ellen," Maddy said, hooking her arm through the girl's, "Clay and I were wondering if you and Joey would mind sharing our picnic blanket."

Before Sue Ellen could answer, Cybil pounced on the suggestion. "What an excellent idea. You can share baskets, as well." She cut her gaze toward Clay. "I'm sure Mr. Kincaid will appreciate getting another taste of Sue Ellen's preserves, as well as her other delicious fare."

There was a youthful snigger from behind Maddy. "Might be healthier for the gent, too."

Maddy did her best to pretend she hadn't heard.

Clay offered her an adoring smile. "I wouldn't dream of poaching from Joey's prize." He hefted the basket he held. "Especially not when I have Maddy's succulent wares to tempt me."

The warmth in his expression looked genuine, and Maddy found her skin tingle with a feeling of being appreciated.

Then Clay turned to Sue Ellen and Joey. "But the pleasure of your company would be most welcome."

The young couple looked at each other uncertainly. But Clay adroitly took the decision out of their hands. He clapped Joey on the back. "That's settled then." With a nod toward Cybil and a politely uttered, "If you'll excuse us, ma'am," he indicated the ladies were to precede him.

Maddy, her arm still linked through Sue Ellen's, began to shepherd Cybil's daughter toward the door, leaving Joey with no choice but to follow behind with Clay.

Once they exited the schoolhouse, Clay and Joey moved up to take their places on either side of the ladies. They strolled around the corner, behind the schoolhouse where the plank tables were set up for lunch. Maddy noted Miss Adeline and Freddie were already seated there.

Clay set a course for the tree line several yards farther along, where already several couples had claimed choice patches of shade. As they passed the tables, Maddy could hear Miss Adeline regaling her partner, as well as the nearby listeners, with a story from her glory days in the theater. She'd have them all eating out of the palm of her hand before it was over.

Well, the men at any rate.

Maddy was glad this new business venture they were working on with Mayor Flaherty had come together so nicely. It would give the former leading lady an outlet for her unique talents and at the same time satisfy a lot of her hunger for the limelight.

It took nearly five minutes and considerable discussion for Clay and Joey to select the perfect spot, one that had just the right mix of shade and sunlight, privacy and openness. Once that was accomplished, the blankets were quickly spread, and the four of them paired off, taking their places on either side of the blanket. Maddy nibbled at her lower lip as she watched Sue Ellen pull out one delicious-looking dish after another from her hamper. There was fresh baked bread, thick slabs of ham, fluffy mashed potatoes, carrots that smelled as if they'd been baked in maple syrup, golden corn on the cob, richly sparkling preserves, and a jar of what looked like apple cider. To cap it off, Sue Ellen lifted out a peach cobbler that smelled downright heavenly.

Taking a deep breath, Maddy raised up on her knees and reached into her own hamper. What would Clay think of the very different fare she had provided? Especially since he'd paid so dearly for it.

Clay stretched out his legs. "Stop being so coy, woman. I'm hungry."

She met his gaze as she set out the dinnerware, and was gratified to see a hint of understanding behind the teasing expression. He was right, of course. The sooner she got this over with, the better.

She pulled out the cloth-covered biscuits. Unwrapping them, Maddy was pleased to note they still looked fluffy and golden. It wouldn't have surprised her to find they'd changed into black lumps since she'd left the house this morning.

Taking courage from that paltry accomplishment, she quickly set out the rest of her items. There was a large wedge of cheese, a half dozen boiled eggs, two apples, neatly cored and sliced, blackberries she'd picked herself just yesterday, and a generous-sized jar of lemonade. Spartan fare, but all perfectly edible and filling.

Setting the last item out, she looked up to find not only Clay, but Joey and Sue Ellen studying her offering, as well. Wanting to break the awkward silence, Maddy spread her hands apologetically. "I'm afraid you're not exactly getting your money's worth, Clay. Perhaps Sue Ellen and Joey will take pity on you and share their meal."

Sue Ellen spoke up at once. "Of course, we'd be glad—"

Clay interrupted, reaching for one of Maddy's biscuits, brushing her arm as he did so. "Nonsense. This is exactly the sort of meal I was hoping for." He took a bite. "Uhm, uhm this is good eating."

214

Now that was carrying politeness a bit too far, even for a smooth talker like Clay. But then Maddy caught the knowing smiles Joey and Sue Ellen were sending their way. Did they think Clay was being gallant because he was so besotted with her?

Joey held out a plate for Sue Ellen to serve, sending Clay a broad smile. "Sue Ellen and I sure are beholden to you. Don't think we could have pulled this off without your help. If there's anything we can do to return the favor," he cast a meaningful glance Maddy's way, "you be sure to let us know."

What was this? Maddy paused in the act of pouring lemonade into the glass Clay held, and looked up to find him watching her. His oh-so-innocent expression failed to mask the devilment dancing in his eyes. Of course—Clay was the link between Joey and Miss Adeline. She should have figured that out on her own.

"Glad I could help," Clay drawled, keeping his gaze locked to Maddy's. "I'll let you know if I need to take you up on that offer."

Maddy finished pouring Clay's lemonade, giving him a men-are-such-little-boys shake of her head as he lifted the drink to his lips. But she had to bite her tongue to keep from laughing as he flashed her an unrepentant wink over the rim of his glass. She couldn't remember the last time she'd felt so alive, so *young*.

She had barely finished serving her and Clay's plates before the parade started. It seemed half the town had decided to take a "casual stroll" past their patch of shade. Out to see if the four of them would provide any additional fodder for gossip, Maddy supposed.

Sue Ellen and Joey seemed almost unaware they were the focus of so much interest. They were too involved in each other to pay much attention to anything else.

And if Clay was bothered by this excess of open curiosity, he didn't show it. He appeared perfectly at ease, sitting there with his sleeves rolled up and the light wind ruffling his hair. He had one leg angled under the cocked knee of the other and his movements as he spoke and ate were fluid, relaxed and drew Maddy's gaze like a feast would a starving man's.

Clay was at his charming best this afternoon. He ate the austere meal with relish and complimented her lavishly on the fare as he did so. He "accidentally" touched her arm or hand time and again as he reached for second helpings, causing thrills of awareness to course through her each time he made contact. He even wiped crumbs from the corner of her mouth with his napkin, meeting her gaze with a warmth that kindled a responsive heat in her cheeks, as well as other parts of her body.

It was so easy for Maddy to respond in kind. Being the focus of Clay's attentive flirtation and the townspeople's envious curiosity left her feeling dream-come-true happy and a bit giddy. It was as if the attention, and more importantly the feelings behind it, filled a hole inside her that a few weeks ago she would have refused to acknowledge even existed.

Everything was going better than she could have imagined. Her and Clay's appearance together at the festival especially with her I'm-done-with-mourning change in wardrobe, had solicited the level of notice she'd hoped for The auction, too, had turned out better than she had anticipated. If anyone had doubted her and Clay's relationship was gossip-worthy, his twenty-dollar bid on her basket should have convinced them otherwise. From now on their relationship would be viewed as anything but "cousinly."

Joey laughed at some comment Clay tossed his way drawing Maddy's attention to the couple seated across from her. Joey and Sue Ellen were so obviously in love—how had she failed to see it before now? It was there in the way they looked at each other, in the way their heads tilted together as they whispered, in the glow that seemed to surround them.

What did the passersby see when they looked at her and Clay? Was there some outward sign of the tingly warmth she felt?

"A penny for your thoughts."

Maddy looked up to find Clay watching her with a half smile tugging at his lips, tugging at her heart. Flustered, she hedged. "You wouldn't get your money's worth."

His smile broadened. "Why don't you let me be the judge of that?"

She wasn't about to step into *that* trap. "A woman should never divulge all her secrets," she said with a toss of her head. "It makes her too predictable."

Clay held a blackberry up to her mouth. "Maddy, my dear, you are many things, but no man in his right mind would describe you as predictable."

Maddy accepted the juicy offering, feeling a tiny jolt of excitement when his fingers brushed her lips. She'd never realized being teased could be so satisfying, could give one such a sense of belonging. A leaf drifted down from the tree and landed on the cuff of Clay's pants. She reached out to pluck it off, feeling a connection to him as she did so.

Clay brushed her outstretched hand with his fingertips. The contact was light and brief, lasting a mere heartbeat of time, but Maddy felt it all the way to her soul. Was this what love felt like?

Before that unbidden thought could settle in, could shock her with its implications, a glint of reflected sunlight winked at her from her finger. Her wedding band, the one remaining physical link to the vow she'd made to Winston, flashed at her like a warning beacon.

The sight doused Maddy's dreamy happiness with the suddenness of a bucket of ice water. What was wrong with her? These thoughts of love were not only hopeless, but dangerous, as well. It would be cheating Clay to let him believe there could ever be more. Assuming he wanted more.

She had no business looking for reciprocated feelings. Not when she wouldn't, *couldn't* act on them. She didn't have the right.

Glancing back toward Joey and Sue Ellen, jealousy stabbed through her with an intensity that was almost physical. Why couldn't she have that kind of genuine, the-heck-with-the-consequences, I'll-slay-dragons-for-you passion?

"Maddy?" Clay watched her with a brow-furrowed question on his face. "What's wrong?"

She forced a smile back to her lips. "Nothing to worry about." Realizing she still held the leaf, Maddy let it flutter to the ground beside her. Dropping her gaze from his, she lifted herself up on her knees. "Just a little touch of a headache. I'll be fine." She reached for a plate. "What do you say we pack this up? It'll be time for the pie-judging contest in a little bit and Miss Fanny has an entry. I'd like to be there to cheer her on."

Clay didn't look entirely convinced, but to her relief, he let the subject drop. He helped her store everything back in the hamper, continuing in the flirtatious banter he'd employed earlier. But to Maddy, the exchanges were now bittersweet.

The whole idea of pulling the wool over everyone's eyes no longer held any appeal to her. She wanted too badly for his interest in her to be real.

Clay was so perceptive. Could she successfully walk the line between hiding her true feelings from him and convincing the townspeople she was in love with him? How could she get through the rest of the day, the rest of the week, without giving herself away?

More importantly, how could she do it without destroying what was left of her heart?

*   *   *

Clay's feet moved in time to the lively strains of the fiddles. He'd danced in marble-tiled European ballrooms and on sawdust-covered saloon floors, and lots of places in between, but he'd never enjoyed himself as much as tonight on this wooden platform under the stars. His pretty, cheeks-flushed-with-enjoyment partner, attired in a dress Miss Olive had no doubt created for the occasion, had had to be coaxed onto the dance floor. But he wouldn't take no for an answer, and after the first few steps she'd thrown herself into the dance with an exuberance that more than made up for what she lacked in skill.

She looked up at him now, as if seeking approval, and he met her gaze with a wink. Then he released one of her hands and twirled her around under his arm in a move that brought a wide-eyed look of surprised pleasure to her face. The happy, trusting smile she flashed his way wrapped a warm tendril around his heart.

From the periphery of his vision, Clay could see approving glances aimed their way from all around the dance floor. Even Miss Olive seemed to look charitably on him, for once.

A light pressure on his left foot brought his gaze back down to the pretty girl in his arms.

She wrinkled her nose in a guilty grimace. "I'm sorry."

He brushed a recalcitrant wisp from her forehead. "Oh no, you're not getting off that easily." Placing his hands on her waist, Clay lifted her effortlessly. She reflexively grabbed his shoulders, and as the fiddlers played the final notes of the chorus, he swung her around in a broad circle that brought her nearly parallel to the floor. A giggly squeal rewarded him as he set her feet back on the ground.

Clay made a deep bow. "My thanks for the dance, Little Bit."

Katie spread her skirts in a creditable curtsey. "You're very welcome." Then she giggled again. "That was fun!"

"Indeed it was." Clay smiled as she turned and skipped off the dance floor toward Anna.

The two girls had their heads together immediately, giggling and whispering as they cast glances in his direction.

"I think you've made a conquest."

Clay turned to find Maddy had slipped up behind him. "Jealous?"

She raised a brow. "Asking me to divulge secrets again?"

He shrugged. "You can't blame a fella for trying." Behind them, the fiddles started up again. It was another fast-paced reel. Clay offered her his arm. "All this dancing's made me thirsty. Care to join me for a glass of punch?"

He could tell by the flicker of surprise in her eyes that she'd expected him to ask her to dance. They'd danced the first dance together, an exhilarating, fast-paced number punctuated by a caller who led them through a rousing round. By the time the music ended, Maddy had been flushed, breathless, and slightly disheveled. It had been all Clay could do to keep from kissing her senseless. When the second dance started, however, Joey claimed her for his partner and Clay escorted Sue Ellen onto the dance floor, much to her mother's apparent delight. When that set finished, rather than returning to Maddy, Clay had claimed Miss Adeline's hand, then moved on to Miss Fanny, Miss Olive, and finally Katie.

It pleased him no end that Maddy had finally approached him before he could seek her out again.

Maddy placed her hand in the crook of his arm. "That was a good thing you did, dancing with Katie. You've built a happy memory she'll carry with her for years to come."

Clay rubbed the back of his neck as they stepped off the dance floor and onto the trampled grass of the schoolyard. "Thanks, but you're making too much of this. It was only a dance."

She gave his arm a light squeeze. "Not to Katie," she said.

The warm approval in her eyes added a softness to her demeanor that had been missing since Lord-knows-what stiffened her spine at the picnic this afternoon. It surprised him just how much he'd missed that warmth.

They strolled in comfortable silence to the punch table, where Lavinia Thompson ladled them both up a glass. Maddy took a sip, then pinned him with an accusing gaze. "I noticed you bullied Miss Olive into dancing with you when she resisted your invitation."

He frowned. "Bullied? I only—"

"No excuses." She wagged a finger at him. "And I don't want to hear how you were only doing your duty. If that had been the case, you would have given up after the first *no thank you.* You must have spent a good five minutes cajoling and teasing her until you got her to say yes."

He hadn't realized she'd seen that. "It's my opinion," he said, titling his chin in a deliberately pompous manner, "that every woman loves to take a spin on the dance floor, especially with an excellent partner such as myself, whether she'll admit it or not."

Her lips twitched at his bit of verbal chest thumping, just as he'd expected. "Is that so?"

"Of course." Miss Olive had actually turned out to be a graceful dancer, very light on her feet and fluid in her movements. "Besides, I can't resist a challenge, especially one presented by a stubborn woman."

"You, Mr. Kincaid, are something of a fraud."

"Quite possibly." He liked the way she was looking at him, as if she saw through his disguise and liked him anyway.

The fiddles stopped and couples drifted toward the refreshment table. Clay took Maddy's elbow and escorted her away from the press as one of the fiddlers announced the next set. It was what Clay had been waiting for. He plucked the glass from her hands and set it down with his. "Let's try this number, shall we?"

With a nod, she allowed him to escort her back onto the dance floor. But when the soft strains of a waltz floated through the night her expression closed off again, just as it had earlier today. He'd give a pretty penny to know exactly what was going on in that lovely head of hers.

He placed his hand on her waist, and after only a second's hesitation, she reciprocated. "Relax," he whispered. "Remember our audience."

Her gaze shot guiltily to his. After a moment she nodded and they moved into the stately steps of the dance. Her warm smile and graceful movements were probably enough to fool the onlookers into thinking she was enjoying herself, but Clay could feel the tension thrumming through her. How could he put her at ease?

"Katie's a good dancer for a seven-year-old. Did you teach her?"

This time Maddy's smile reached her eyes. "Not by myself. Whenever we have a rainy afternoon, we push back the furniture in the parlor and dance or perform little skits for each other. Everyone participates."

"Now, that must be something to see. Here's hoping it rains soon."

She gave him a challenging grin. "Watch what you wish for. As I said, everyone participates. Miss Adeline is always bemoaning the lack of leading-man material in our household. You might find yourself playing Romeo to her Juliet."

Miss Adeline was not the one he wanted to play Romeo to. Lord, but Maddy felt good in his arms. The tension he'd felt in her earlier had eased now. It was all he could do not to pull her up against his chest, to bury his face in her meadow-scented hair, to taste her lusciously full lips. He could no longer deny that Maddy had gotten under his skin in a way no woman ever had before.

Holding her gaze captive, Clay drew her slightly closer. He commanded his hand to remain at her waist, to resist the urge to slide up and caress the softness of her breast. He wanted her, desired her with an urgency that was painful to hold in check.

When her breath caught and her eyes darkened with evidence of her own awareness, he nearly groaned aloud. When she moistened her lip with the tip of her tongue, he felt the jolt through his entire being. This was both paradise and hell. Like the hapless moths that circled the lanterns overhead, he was enthralled by the beauty and heat of her fire, helpless to resist, even knowing that to cross the final barrier between them would be a fatal mistake. No matter how much he might want to cross that line between pretense and reality, she didn't want anything from him but this sham courtship.

When the music ended he released her reluctantly. Was that regret in her eyes, as well? Or only wishful thinking on his part? Without speaking, he escorted her from the dance floor.

Miss Olive met them as they stepped onto the ground. "There you two are. Maddy, I just wanted to let you know that Fanny, Adeline and I are going to take Katie home and turn in for the night."

"Perhaps I should—"

"Nonsense," Miss Olive interrupted. "Between the three of us, we're perfectly capable of getting Katie tucked in proper. You young folks stay and enjoy yourselves. We won't bother to wait up." As if it was all settled, she turned to Clay. "It goes without saying that I expect you to see Maddy gets safely back to Barrows House tonight."

Clay bowed. "You can rely on me, ma'am."

She gave him a dry smile. "I'm sure I can." Then she patted Maddy's arm. "Good night, dear. Enjoy yourself."

"Just a minute." Maddy turned to Clay. "If you'll excuse me, I want to say goodnight to Katie before she leaves."

Clay nodded. Apparently she'd needed to put a bit of distance between them, as well.

He watched her walk away with Miss Olive. The wind had picked up, plucking mischievous fingers at her skirt and hair. He could feel a touch of dampness in the air. It would probably rain soon. He wasn't sure if he'd be relieved or disappointed to have the night's activities cut short.

Giving in to the wind's goading, a few recalcitrant curls on the back of her neck sprang free from the pins that

223

secured them. Fascinated, he watched them bounce and dance, beckoning him like a siren. He had a sudden longing to see the rest of it unbound, to watch her hair tumble down her back and across her shoulders, to comb his fingers through it while she lay beside him.

With a growl that earned him worried frowns from a nearby couple, he turned away. This was ridiculous, absurd. He, Clayton Randall Kincaid, the most sought-after bachelor in his home county and several others besides, was acting like a callow youth in the throes of his first bout of puppy love. What kind of spell had the exasperating widow Potter cast on him?

Restless, he paced across the lantern-dotted schoolyard, weaving around children playing tag and couples strolling arm in arm. If he didn't regain his control soon, he was going to make an absolute ass of himself.

Maddy felt some of the same physical attraction that he did, he was sure of it. But she'd also made it clear that wasn't enough for her, and that she had no intentions of acting on desires she might be feeling in regard to him.

Did knowing his secret make it easier for her to push him away? She'd seemed sympathetic rather than censorious, but sympathy didn't equate to respect. You could feel sympathy for a crippled polecat, but that didn't mean you'd invite the critter into your home.

Clay raked his hand through his hair. Was the memory of his unmanly fear of heights what kept surfacing to stiffen her back whenever she seemed on the point of surrendering?

"Mr. Kincaid?"

He looked up to see a shadowy form disengage from one of the schoolyard swings. As she stepped out of the gloom and into the moonlight, he smiled in recognition. "Hello, Sue Ellen."

"Is something wrong?" she asked with a concerned frown.

"No, of course not. I was just trying to get a breath of

air away from the crowd at the dance floor." He quickly turned the subject away from himself. "What about you? What are you doing out here, and where's Joey?"

She wrinkled her nose as they began to stroll away from the playground. "Daddy asked him to help fix a broken gate over by the circus area. I don't see why it had to be taken care of tonight. I think mother put him up to it, just to separate us."

Clay smiled sympathetically. "Be fair now, you haven't given her much time to get used to the idea."

Sue Ellen's chin jutted out and there was a distinctly militant gleam to her eyes. "Well, she'd better get used to it quick. No matter how she feels, she's not going to be able to keep me and Joey apart much longer."

Clay believed her. Cybil Flaherty was going to be surprised to find her meek mouse of a daughter had turned into a tigress.

"Sue Ellen, there you are!"

Clay looked up to find their walk had taken them back to the schoolhouse. Sue Ellen's mother stood on the steps, eyeing her daughter like a general surveying troops. He hid a smile as he heard Sue Ellen smother a groan under her breath.

But old habits die hard, and the girl stepped forward dutifully. "Yes, Mother, did you need me for something?"

"Three of the hymnals the children used for the chorale this afternoon were left in the schoolhouse. Would you be a dear and put them and the gavel we used at the auction back in the church storeroom where they belong? I don't want anything to happen to them."

"Of course, Mother." Sue Ellen started up the steps, then paused when her mother touched her arm.

"Oh, and Mr. Kincaid," Cybil said, turning to Clay, "could I impose on you to accompany her. That storeroom door tends to stick in damp weather and can be quite difficult to force open."

Clay bowed. "Of course." He didn't miss the smug, come-into-my-parlor smile she flashed as he passed her on the steps.

"I'm sorry," Sue Ellen said once they were inside. "Mother can be quite stubborn and single-minded at times."

Clay grinned. "Don't worry about me. Besides, I don't consider escorting a pretty girl to be much of a hardship." He helped her gather up the books and gavel, then turned to see Maddy standing across the room talking to Blanche and Vera.

He drank in the sight of her, feeling like it had been days since he'd seen her last rather than minutes.

A sound drew Clay's focus back to Sue Ellen. Her gaze had followed his and a slow smile spread across her face. "I think it's time to repay that favor." Her expression put him in mind of a bear who'd just spied a honey comb.

Exactly what was she up to?

Chapter Sixteen

"Now, Sue Ellen," Clay cautioned, but she was already half way across the room and he had no choice but to follow.

"Hello Maddy," Sue Ellen hailed as soon as she drew near to the women.

Maddy returned the greeting, but the moment she caught sight of Clay he felt the change in her, the subtle sense of awareness that sizzled across the space between them. He couldn't tell if she was pleased or not to see him, but he was quite sure she was anything but indifferent.

"Mother asked me to take some things back to the church and Mr. Kincaid has kindly offered to accompany me." Sue Ellen linked her arm through Maddy's. "Why don't you come with us? I wanted to talk to you about your dress. Do you think I could hire Miss Olive to make one for me?" Sue Ellen gave Maddy little opportunity to demur. She kept up a steady stream of chatter as she made a bee-line to the side door of the schoolhouse.

Clay hid a grin at her maneuvering as he trailed behind the two of them. She was obviously trying to do a bit of matchmaking, and he was quite happy to let her. But just as he stepped forward to open the door for them, Sue Ellen stumbled and let out a yelp.

"What is it?" Clay reached out to help Maddy steady the girl.

"My ankle," Sue Ellen gasped. "I must have stepped on it wrong."

"Perhaps I should fetch Dr. Perkins?" Maddy offered.

"I don't think it's serious," Sue Ellen said as she limped to a chair with Clay's assistance. "I'm sure I'll be all right in just a minute."

Maddy hovered nearby as Clay helped the injured girl ease down into the chair. "Do you want me to find your mother?"

"No!" Sue Ellen took a deep breath, then gave Maddy a weak smile. "But there *is* something you can do."

"Of course," Maddy responded, "just name it."

Sue Ellen chewed on her lip. "I hate to ask this, especially since I'm sure I saw a few raindrops falling a second ago, but would you and Mr. Kincaid mind going on without me to put these things away? I think I need to stay off my feet for a little while."

The little fraud. Clay felt his lips twitch as he quit worrying about the extent of her injuries. Far be it from him to interfere with her plans, especially since they so closely paralleled his own desires.

He kept his expression impassive as Maddy's gaze slid quickly to his and away again. What was she thinking? Did she realize Sue Ellen was playing games? Or was she worried about being alone with him?

"We'd be glad to," she said at last, taking the gavel from Sue Ellen. "But are you sure I can't fetch you anything first?"

Sue Ellen shook her head. "I'll be fine after I sit here a minute. Are you sure you don't mind the rain?"

Maddy waved a hand. "It's nothing more than a sprinkle. Besides, I like the rain."

Whatever It Takes

"Thank you, Maddy." Sue Ellen slipped the shawl from her shoulders. "Here, take this. It's not much protection, but at least it'll keep your hair dry."

"Oh, I don't think—"

"I insist." Then she gave Maddy the most angelically beseeching look Clay had ever seen. "Please? Promise me you'll keep this over your head. I feel terrible already for dumping my responsibility on you. I'd only feel worse if I thought you were going to suffer from this damp weather because of it."

"Oh, all right." Maddy accepted the shawl with obvious reluctance. "But I think you're being overly cautious."

As Maddy arranged the shawl across her shoulders, Clay eyed Sue Ellen's much-too-innocent expression with head-shaking admiration. In one fell swoop, Sue Ellen had arranged for him and Maddy to have some time alone together, provided an unwitting Maddy with a disguise that would keep Cybil unaware of the switch, and left herself free to slip out and find Joey if she so choose. Not a bad bit of handiwork for such an innocent-seeming miss.

Sue Ellen met his gaze, and he could tell from the mischief dancing in her eyes that she was quite pleased with herself.

Did Joey have any idea what he was letting himself in for?

Taking Maddy by the shoulder and turning her toward the door, Clay shot Sue Ellen a tip-of-the-head salute. Sue Ellen's grinning response reminded him of the way his younger sisters looked when they thought they were getting away with a particularly spectacular bit of mischief.

Maddy moved toward the door, feeling ambivalent about her upcoming walk with Clay. Should she pretend the emotional heat that had crackled between them on the dance floor had never happened? Would *he* make reference to it? Did she want him to?

As she reached the door, Sue Ellen called out her name.

229

"You promised," the girl reminded her as she pantomimed lifting something over her head.

With a sigh, Maddy placed the shawl over her head. Really, Sue Ellen was being unnecessarily cautious. There hadn't been enough of a drizzle to even settle the dust.

Then Clay placed a solicitous hand at the small of her back and all thoughts of Sue Ellen were replaced by heightened consciousness of the man beside her and a futile effort to keep her pulse from racing.

"I hope Sue Ellen's foot isn't seriously injured," she said as they stepped outside.

Clay's lips twitched. "Oh, I have a feeling she'll be up and moving about in no time at all."

Clouds had gathered overhead, blocking out the light from the moon and all but the occasional twinkle of a star. Once they left the main festival area, they also left behind most of the artificial light. The occasional street lamp provided enough illumination for them to avoid obstacles, but little more. The twilight shadows created a sense of isolation, of intimacy, that heightened rather than muffled her awareness of the man at her side.

The wind had picked up again, setting leaves and dust skipping around them like children on a playground. She kept one arm at her side, clamping down her skirt that seemed eager to skip and play with the dirt devils, as well.

The church, one of the most substantial buildings in Pepper Cloud, was constructed of gray stone and boasted six beautiful, arched stained-glass windows, three on each side. The heavy wooden doors, which were never locked, opened easily on well-oiled hinges. They stepped inside to almost total darkness.

"There's a lamp there just to your left," Maddy instructed Clay.

She removed Sue Ellen's shawl as he retrieved the lamp and lit the wick. Then, leaving the door open to supplement their meager light, Maddy led Clay down the center aisle. An unwanted memory of walking this same path on her wedding day intruded, sending a shiver down her spine.

"Cold?" Clay inquired solicitously. He rubbed her forearm where goose bumps had formed.

"Just a rigor," she answered, smiling brightly for his benefit. His touch had magically transferred those skittering, dancing dirt devils from the churchyard to inside her stomach. "There's a storm approaching," she added, trying to explain away her edginess. A storm that was charging the very air between them.

She could feel his gaze on her, feel the questions hanging between them. Surely he sensed it, too? But he said nothing, gave no sign, no response beyond a non-committal *hmmm*.

Stepping past the pews, Maddy indicated they should turn left. The tension inside her was building, making her skin prickle and her heart beat irregularly. Could he sense her distress? If so, what did he make of it?

"I've never been in here when it was so dark and empty before," she said by way of explanation. "It's a bit unnerving."

Clay handed her the lamp and placed an arm around her shoulders. "Is this better?"

Oh yes. Not that it did anything to steady her heartbeat, but the warmth of his touch was oh-so-marvelous. In fact Maddy was rather disappointed when they reached the storeroom a moment later and he stepped away from her.

Clay gave the doorknob an authoritative tug. It swung open with only token resistance. He took the lamp from her again, then let her precede him into the small room.

"You can put the books there with the others," Maddy said, pointing to a shelf just inside the door. She quickly crossed the eight feet or so of floor space to the far wall. The faster they finished this little chore and returned to the safety of the crowded festival, the better off she'd be.

Wouldn't she?

Setting the gavel down in its appointed place, she turned and drew in a sharp breath. With the quiet stealth of a jungle cat, Clay had slipped up behind her. They now stood face to face, so close the linen of his shirt almost brushed the lace of her bodice.

His eyes, they were so dark, so . . . so *intense*. If she didn't look away soon, they would scorch her. But heaven help her, she yearned for that fire. This delicious, passion-induced heat was something she'd never experienced before, had only dreamed could blaze between men and women. This is what her marriage had cheated her of.

Lifting a hand, he moved a strand of hair from her temple, tucking it behind her ear. Unsatisfied by that almost non-existent contact, Maddy nuzzled her cheek into his palm.

"Maddy." His voice was heavy, thick. It thrummed through her from head to toe, setting the dirt devils dancing inside her again.

He lifted his other hand, gently cupping her face as if it were fragile porcelain, stroking her cheeks with the pads of his thumbs. "So soft," he murmured, "so delicate." Then one thumb slipped down to trace her lip. "So desirable."

The dirt devils shot up in a startled leap.

Craving additional contact, she lifted her hand to his cheek. She caressed his jawline, reveling in the raspy, masculine feel against her sensitized skin. As he had once before, he turned his head and kissed her palm, his gaze never leaving hers.

The dirt devils' dance turned to a whirling frenzy.

Was he going to kiss her, kiss her the way he had before, the way she wanted to be kissed, no, *needed* to be kissed? There was an ache inside her that couldn't be soothed any other way. Surely, it wasn't selfish of her to want to know what it felt like to be kissed thoroughly.

To be kissed with passion and desire.

To be kissed by a man she was in love with.

Please, she silently begged, *I won't pull away this time.* Just one perfect kiss. A memory she could tuck away in her heart.

As if he'd heard her, Clay made a sound low in his throat, a sound that was somehow both triumphant and needy. He lowered his head to hers and she hungrily lifted her face.

His lips touched hers in an achingly tender claiming that ignited a fire deep inside her. Her arms slipped around his neck, and her body, as if jealously mimicking her lips, pressed closer to his.

His lips moved from hers, but never left her face. He trailed feathery kisses along her jaw and cheek until he reached her ear. Then he nipped and teased and laved her lobe, sending sensations through her that caused her to squirm and clutch at him. She was barely aware of his hands at her nape, removing hairpins, releasing bound tresses, until it all came tumbling free.

With a growl of pleasure, he buried his hands in her hair and returned to her mouth, kissing her with more urgency this time. She was startled when his tongue darted out to trace her lips. When he sought to part her own lips, she did so shyly, hesitantly. But as his tongue teased at hers, coaxing it to dance with his, she grew bolder.

This was heady, intoxicating! She'd never dreamed a kiss could be filled with so much exhilaration, so much pure sensation.

He abandoned her mouth once more, this time to trail hot kisses down her chin and onto the column of her throat. Feeling blissfully wanton, she threw her head back to give him freer access.

Oh, this felt so wonderful, so unimaginably *right*.

Maddy's world narrowed to this moment, to this time. The only sounds left in the world were those of their breathing and Clay's murmured endearments, the only sensations remaining were the feel of his lips and hands caressing her and the waves of desire shimmering through her.

Dimly, she was aware that his fingers moved to the buttons of her bodice, then his hands were on her skin, warm

233

and firm and oh, so magical. The sensation of the rough pads of his fingers on her sensitized body, massaging, teasing, paying homage, sent waves of pleasure rippling through her.

Boldly, she reached to unfasten his shirt, wanting to feel his skin under her own hands, wanting to remove any barriers separating them. This was how it was meant to be between a man and a woman, this was the unnamed something she'd yearned for since she'd first set eyes on Clayton Kincaid.

Surely nothing could surpass this heady, intoxicating feeling of building passion, of cascading sensation.

Then his head dipped to her breast and she realized just how wrong she'd been.

A loud creak and thud shattered the idyll as the door closed behind them. As if doused by a bucket of cold water, Maddy stiffened and jerked away from Clay.

Dear Lord, what had she done? One kiss, she'd told herself. But this had been so much more. So much more beautiful. So much more glorious.

So much more devastating.

"Maddy?" Clay stared at her, his expression dazed, his brows drawn in puzzled concern. "What is it?"

"The door," she answered inadequately, her fingers fumbling with her buttons. She couldn't explain her distress to him. He'd never understand, not unless she went into the whole sordid story.

He rubbed her upper arms in a gesture she was sure he meant to be comforting. Comfort eluded her, however. On the contrary, his touch ignited a hunger so fierce it frightened her.

"Don't worry," he assured her. "It was only the wind, we're still alone." He flashed her a teasing smile as he raised a hand to brush the hair from her face. "The storm must have picked up while we weren't paying attention."

Maddy stepped away from him, unable to meet his gaze, afraid of what he would see in her eyes. She needed some distance, some time to regain her composure. Otherwise she might just throw herself back into his arms again.

"Maddy?" That concerned furrow lined his brow again.

She gave him a smile that felt as brittle as her control. "We should leave, before we get trapped by the storm." She marched to the door, feeling both relief and loss as she put distance between them.

Clay tried to rein in his still-reeling senses. That had, without a doubt, been the most incredible, arousing bit of love play he'd ever experienced. He'd always suspected her proper widow façade hid a passionate nature, but he'd had no idea just *how* passionate.

He watched her cross the room and frowned. What was this sudden preoccupation she had with the closed door? Surely, she wasn't concerned with the proprieties all of a sudden.

What had happened to turn her from a woman who was so full of heat and ardor, to one who was so stiff and brittle? Had he moved too fast? It wasn't as if she were some untried virgin—she was a widow for goodness sake.

Was she scared of her own passion? Or was she embarrassed that she'd shown how she really felt about him?

One thing for sure, after that kiss, that passionate abandon, there was no way he'd believe she didn't feel *something* for him. Question was, what did he intend to do about it?

He winced as she grabbed the knob and turned it with what seemed an unflattering eagerness to escape. But when she pushed, nothing happened. The door didn't budge.

Rattling the doorknob, she pushed harder, her motions taking on a frantic edge.

Clay crossed the room. "Easy," he said, placing his hand over hers. What in the devil had her so on edge?

Maddy stepped aside, making room for him to take her place. "We're trapped in here." She said it as if she couldn't conceive of a worse fate.

"Nonsense." Clay put his shoulder to the door, then

frowned when his efforts were no more successful than hers had been.

"I told you," she said, finger-combing her hair away from her temples, "It's stuck tight."

"Don't worry," he assured her, "I'm not giving up yet."

"You don't understand." It was the tone she used with small children. "This isn't the first time it's happened. Reverend Posey was trapped in here for two hours once before someone finally realized what happened and helped him out."

Clay rolled his cuffs up. "No offense, but Reverend Posey is older than my grandfather and twice as frail. Give me credit for possessing a bit more brute strength."

Five minutes later, winded and bruised, he was feeling somewhat less certain of his ability to set them free. He turned to find Maddy sitting on the floor, her chin propped glumly on her knees. At least she had the grace to refrain from voicing the *I told you so* that colored her expression.

Clay rolled his shoulders. "I don't understand how the door could have swollen so tight in such a short space of time." Then he had another thought. "When Reverend Posey got trapped in here, how did they get him out?"

She lifted her chin off her knees and waved a hand. "They pulled the pins from the hinges."

Well, why hadn't she said so in the first place? Clay swung around, then stopped short. Of course. The hinge pins were on the other side of the door.

Ready to admit at least temporary defeat, Clay plopped down next to Maddy. "Well, I guess like Reverend Posey, we wait for someone to rescue us." He could think of worse fates then to be trapped here with her for a bit longer. Even if her ardor had cooled. There was nothing to say he couldn't try to restoke the fires.

"We may be here a while," she said, refusing to be consoled. "You heard Miss Olive—they won't be waiting up for me. And I don't imagine anyone will send out alarms if you don't return to your hotel room any time soon."

"Cybil Flaherty knows where we are. She might—"

"Cybil thinks Sue Ellen accompanied you. When she sees Sue Ellen, she'll assume the errand has been taken care of. And I have a feeling Sue Ellen will think we are in no hurry to be interrupted."

She had a point. They might be here for quite some time.

"We could try yelling for help," she continued, "but I don't think it would do much good. The walls are pretty solid, and there's no one nearby to hear. Besides, it sounds like the storm is picking up."

At least she no longer sounded panicked. Instead, there was a resigned, almost fatalistic air about her.

He offered her his most reassuring smile. "But we *will* be missed eventually." He leaned back and stretched his legs out. "I suppose there's nothing for it but to just make ourselves as comfortable as possible while we wait it out."

Rather than following his advice, Maddy stood and paced about the room, pausing to finger items on the shelves at random. When she reached the door, she rattled the knob. Dropping her hands to her sides, she glared at the door as if she could open it by force of will, alone.

That was his Maddy. "Maddy," he said patting the floor beside him, "come on back and sit down."

She met his gaze warily, worrying at her lower lip with her teeth.

Clay sighed. This would never do. If they were going to be stuck here for a while, he had to do something to put her at ease again. And there was nothing like the direct approach. "Look," he said, "it's obvious you're troubled over what just happened between us. We need to talk about why."

A warm pink flooded her cheeks, but she nodded and crossed back to his side of the room. When she sat, though, she was careful to place a small distance between them.

Clay resisted the urge to put an arm around her shoulders and draw her nearer. Instead, he locked his hands behind his head. He noted with interest that she stared at his bare chest a moment and swallowed hard before looking away.

"Now, tell me what's bothering you." If she was embarrassed about her earlier fervor, he intended to do all he could to convince her she had absolutely no need to feel that way. On the other hand, if there was something else making her shy away from him, he needed to find out what it was.

He couldn't stop the self-deprecating smile that tugged at his lips. "I won't say I regret what just happened, I waited too long and enjoyed it too much to lie." He let the smile fade. "But if I took unwanted liberties, I do apologize for that." Though he would bet his life that she'd wanted it every bit as much as he had.

To his relief, she shook her head. "You have nothing to apologize for." The soft smile on her face caused a strange hitch in his breathing. "It was wonderful."

Some trace of bittersweet regret in her tone robbed the words of their joy.

"But?" His eyes bored into hers, demanding an answer. An answer his heart told him he didn't want to hear.

A bolt of some intense emotion flared in her eyes, then her face shuttered. She didn't lower her gaze, though he could tell it cost her not to. "But," she said firmly, "it can't ever happen again."

Clay sat up straighter. "Never is a long time." She couldn't mean that literally. Never taste her lips again, never hear her sigh with pleasure or feel her melt at his touch again—the idea was unthinkable.

His jaw clenched as his mind tried to make sense of her words. Had he done something to upset her? Had she suddenly remembered his cowardice?

"It's nothing you've done," she said, as if reading his thoughts. "It's me."

Was that supposed to convince him? As if she'd tell him otherwise.

She twisted her hands in her lap. "I . . . I made a promise, to Winston, after he died. I intend to keep that promise."

Clay shifted his perceptions for a third time. A promise to her dead husband? What kind of promise? "Maddy, you can't—"

She raised her hand to stop his protest. "No, I don't want to discuss this."

He noticed that while her chin was set at a determined angle, her hands trembled ever so slightly.

"Please," she added, in a vulnerable tone he couldn't deny.

"Very well," he agreed. "We won't talk about it any more tonight." But that didn't mean the subject was closed. "Now, lay your head here on my shoulder and try to get some sleep. It's likely to be a long wait."

When she hesitated, he gave her a crooked smile. "I said sleep, Maddy. I don't trespass where I'm not welcome." He raised a brow. "You do trust me, don't you?"

"Of course." Scooting closer, Maddy gingerly leaned against his shoulder as he'd instructed.

It took every bit of control he had not to put his arm around her and draw her closer, not to let his hands explore her soft curves. He had to discover more about this secret she guarded so passionately, this vow that erected an invisible, unbreachable wall between them.

Only then could he begin dismantling that barrier, brick by brick if need be, to free the passionate woman inside.

It was quite some time before Maddy relaxed against him and another stretch of time before the soft even sound of her breathing told him she'd finally gone to sleep.

Clay didn't seek sleep himself. For one thing, being so close to Maddy and not being able to do more than lend her his shoulder to lean on was pure torture. The one liberty he allowed himself was the guilty pleasure of stroking her hair while she slept. It was so soft, so sensuously silky. Lifting a strand to his face, he inhaled the intoxicating flowers-and-Maddy scent.

She stirred in her sleep, burrowing more comfortably into his side, and Clay inhaled sharply when her hand stole inside his still-open shirt. He slipped his arm around her waist. Now this felt good, felt right.

What was he going to do about her stubborn obsession with Winston and whatever misguided promise she'd made to his shade? He'd have to get her to talk about it, whether she wanted to or not. He could tell by the easy way she slept, that she hadn't thought their current situation through entirely. Regardless of their feelings for each other, and he wasn't quite ready to examine his feelings for her too closely, circumstances had conspired to take matters out of their hands.

What his mother had not been able to accomplish with all her matchmaking schemes, the storm had taken care of with one gusty breath of wind. Surprisingly, he felt no resentment, no chafing at the inevitable outcome of this night's business.

Would Maddy feel the same?

Chapter Seventeen

Maddy pulled her coverlet up a little higher, refusing to abandon sleep. She'd been having such a lovely dream, one where Clay held her close and promised to always care for her.

"Maddy?"

She could hear the smile in his voice. His finger lightly stroked her cheek. Uhmmm, that felt nice.

"Sorry, sweetheart, but you really need to wake up now."

Sweetheart? He'd called her sweetheart. Maddy opened her eyes to see him smiling down at her, obviously amused by something. Really, he had the nicest smile.

"Good morning," he said, watching her closely as if waiting for a reaction.

"Good morn—"

The realization erased the last vestiges of sleep. The memory of their current predicament flooded back, keeping pace with the heat flooding her cheeks.

Oh merciful heavens, she'd slept in his arms. For how long? Was it really morning? Had she done anything embarrassing?

Had he really called her sweetheart?

Clay leaned over and kissed her forehead. "Don't worry," he said, "it'll be all right."

As he stood, buttoning his shirt, she became aware of the sound of people approaching, something he'd no doubt already heard. By the time she'd scrambled to her feet, clutching the shawl that had served as a makeshift blanket, he was at the door.

"Hello," Clay called. "Is someone out there?"

Maddy heard the muffled sound of a response as she fussed with her clothes, trying to smooth away the wrinkles and brush off the dusty smudges.

"We're trapped in here." He rattled the knob noisily. As if mocking him, this time the door opened easily. From the look on Clay's face, Maddy could tell he was as chagrined as she was.

"Trapped, were you?"

Maddy smothered a groan at the caustically uttered comment. That voice belonged to Mayor Flaherty, which meant Cybil couldn't be far behind.

"You have some explaining to do, sir," the mayor continued. "But step aside so we can make sure our daughter is all right."

Clay had stiffened at the mayor's tone, but his expression reflected confusion. "Your dau—"

Before he could finish his sentence, Cybil had pushed past him. "Sue Ellen, baby are you—" She drew up short at the sight of Maddy. "You! Where's Sue Ellen?"

Reverend Posey joined them. "What's going on here?"

His question was generally ignored as Mayor Flaherty rounded on Clay. "See here, what have you done with my daughter?"

Clay raised his hands. "I'm sorry, sir, but I haven't seen Sue Ellen since I left the schoolhouse last night."

"But that's impossible," Cybil sputtered. "Sue Ellen came here with you to put away the gavel and hymnals." She all but pounced on Maddy, plucking the shawl from her hands. "See, this is hers. She *was* here."

"Sue Ellen hurt her foot," Maddy explained, "so I came with Clay in her place. She loaned me her shawl because of the weather."

Cybil's lips pinched in a tight line. "So *you* spent the night here with Mr. Kincaid?"

Maddy, acutely aware of her disheveled appearance under the scrutiny of the three newcomers, felt her cheeks heat up. Even the sympathetic, we'll-get-through-this look from Clay didn't help.

But her appearance seemed the least of Mayor Flaherty's concerns. "Sue Ellen was hurt? How seriously? Why didn't I know?"

"I don't think it was serious," Maddy hastened to assure him. "She just stepped wrong and twisted her foot."

The mayor raked his hand through his sparse hair. "But if she's not here, where is she?"

"Oh my poor baby," Cybil wailed, seemingly near hysteria.

"I'm sure she's fine." Clay turned from Mrs. Flaherty to the mayor. "I'll help organize a search party, sir, if you'd like."

Maddy couldn't help but admire how Clay automatically assumed responsibility for setting the wheels in motion. His air of authority, even given the current circumstances, was undiminished. He exuded competence and confidence, and those around him responded without conscious thought.

"Yes, of course." The mayor attempted to pull himself together with visible effort. "Reverend, would you ring the church bells to signal an emergency meeting?"

"Of course." The reverend turned to Clay. "After this is over, Mr. Kincaid, I'd like to have a word with you."

Clay nodded. "My thoughts exactly. We need to discuss setting a wedding date for Maddy and me. I'm thinking the sooner the better."

Maddy paused in the act of retrieving her hairpins, jabbing herself in the process. What was this? Marriage? Impossible! She watched Reverend Posey give Clay a relieved, glad-you-see-it-my-way nod as he left the room. Surely the two of them weren't intimating that Clay had in any way compromised her last night? That was ridiculous. "I don't—"

But Clay had already crossed to her side and now took her arm. "I'll escort Maddy back to Barrows House, and spread the word about forming a search party while I'm at it. I should be back before you get fully organized."

Maddy frowned. She no longer liked his take-charge attitude, not when it was her he was taking charge of. She clamped her lips shut with effort, but determined to voice her objections, in no uncertain terms, the moment they were alone.

"And Mayor Flaherty," Clay said as they passed Sue Ellen's father by the door, "the first thing I'd do is see whether anyone knows where Joey Brennon is this morning."

Cybil's drawn out moan followed them from the church.

They stepped outside to find the sun had just barely cleared the eastern horizon. Clay inhaled a deep breath of the rain-washed air with all the gusto of a man who hadn't a care in the world. "Beautiful morning, isn't it?"

Maddy wasn't about to be distracted. She had to make him understand. "What was that exchange between you and Reverend Posey all about?"

"Didn't you hear us? We need to set a wedding date." He raised a questioning brow. "Why so surprised? We were planning to announce our engagement today anyway, weren't we?"

Behind them the church bells pealed, sounding the call to an emergency town meeting, echoing the alarm clanging through her.

"You know as well as I do," Maddy said over the clamor, "that we were not going to take this all the way to a wedding." A treacherous memory of what had happened last night protested that it wouldn't be the worst fate she'd ever suffered.

He shrugged. "So now we adjust the plan."

She couldn't believe he was seriously considering marriage. Hadn't he heard any of her protests? "If you're doing this out of some misguided sense of honor—" She clamped her lips shut as Harvey Thompson stepped out of the Rosethorne Hotel.

"I heard the church bells," he said as Clay and Maddy walked up. "You two got any idea what's going on?"

Maddy could see Lavinia right behind him. And she seemed much more interested in taking inventory of Maddy's appearance than in hearing an answer to her husband's question.

"Sue Ellen Flaherty's missing," Clay answered. "The mayor is forming a search party to help find her."

The hotel proprietor nodded and turned to his wife. "Lavinia, you take care of things around here. I'll head over to the church to see if I can help."

As Harvey set off down the sidewalk, Lavinia turned to Maddy. "My, but you're out and about mighty early this morning." She cocked her head at an angle and flashed a falsely innocent smile. "Isn't that the same dress you had on yesterday evening, dear?"

Maddy didn't have the time or the inclination to deal with the busybody this morning. But before she could say anything, Clay tightened his hold on her arm.

"Excuse us ma'am," he said with a polite smile, "but we need to move along so I can help with the search party, as well."

Lavinia gave him an arch smile. "Of course," she all but purred, "I completely understand. Don't let me keep you."

As they moved out of earshot, Clay looked pointedly at Maddy. "You were saying?"

She lifted her chin, refusing to believe this was as serious as he was making it out to be. "I've weathered gossip before."

"Not like this, I'll wager."

They paused to explain the alarm bells to two others hurrying toward the church. All the time Maddy's mind furiously searched for an argument that would convince him she was serious in her refusal.

As soon as they moved on, she resumed her argument. "Be that as it may, that's still no reason for us to rush willy-nilly into marriage." She waved a hand toward yet another man hastening toward the church. "Besides, this brouhaha over Sue Ellen's disappearance is likely to overshadow any concern over where I spent the night." Maddy felt an immediate stab of guilt over her trivialization of Sue Ellen's predicament. She offered up a silent plea for forgiveness and prayer for the girl's safety.

Clay gave her an annoying, you-know-I'm-right look. "You don't really believe that."

"Don't tell me what I believe," she replied sharply.

Several minutes of silence followed before Maddy realized he wasn't going to respond to her outburst. She tried for a calmer, more reasonable tone. "Mr. Kincaid, regardless of what you or anyone else in this town thinks, I refuse to be forced into a marriage I do not want." Not this way, at any rate.

By the tightening of his jaw, it seemed she'd finally made a dent in his controlled demeanor. Clay pushed open her front gate and bowed. "We'll finish this discussion when I get back."

Maddy swept past him. "There's nothing further to discuss."

"Maddy."

She paused but didn't turn around.

"It felt good holding you while you slept last night."

Startled by not only the words but the wistful tone in which they were uttered, Maddy spun around. But he was already headed back the way they had come.

Slowly, she trudged up the walk to the front porch. He wasn't really serious—he couldn't be. A man like Clay would never want to tie himself to a woman like her. He was just trying to do the honorable thing. As soon as she convinced him she didn't really want or need the protection of his name, he'd back down. And he'd be relieved to be able to do so. Oh, but if only things could be different.

Maddy opened the front door as quietly as she could. It was Sunday morning and they'd all had a big day yesterday. Perhaps everyone was still abed.

Not that she had anything to feel embarrassed about. She just didn't want to give a detailed explanation right now.

But she stepped inside to find Miss Olive descending the stairs. "Maddy!" The seamstress was obviously startled to see her. "Good heavens, child, are you just now getting in?"

Maddy put on her most confident smile. "Yes, I'm afraid so. The silliest thing happened last night. Clay and I were putting some things away in the church storeroom and got trapped inside."

Miss Adeline, dressed in a flowing satin robe, appeared at the top of the stairs. "So you two spent the night together," she drawled, sounding more amused than shocked.

"In a manner of speaking," Maddy replied airily. She kept the heat from her cheeks by pure force of will.

"I heard the church bells," Miss Olive interjected, blessedly changing the subject. "Do you know what that's all about?"

"Yes, Sue Ellen's missing. The mayor is getting a search party together to help look for her."

"Oh, that poor child," Miss Fanny bustled in from the direction of the kitchen, just in time to hear the last part of their conversation. "Is there anything we can do to help?"

Maddy stepped closer and patted the distressed woman's arm. "I'm sure the search party will need some refreshments to keep them going. Some of your cinnamon buns and coffee would probably be most welcome."

"Of course." Miss Fanny squared her shoulders. "I'll whip up enough to feed an army."

And she probably would, Maddy thought affectionately. Then, before anyone could ask any more questions, she headed purposefully up the stairs. "I'm going to freshen up and change clothes. Then I plan to spend the morning in my studio."

"Shall I bring you up some breakfast?" Miss Adeline asked as Maddy passed her on the stairs.

"No thank you, I'm not hungry." Which wasn't exactly true, but Maddy knew Miss Adeline would not be easily dismissed if she got her foot in the door. And the last thing she wanted this morning was to fend off her flamboyant friend's unabashed prying questions and innuendos.

Once in her room, Maddy went straight to her wardrobe, searching through it for one of her stark bombazine gowns. She was determined to be properly armored, both physically and mentally, when next she faced Clay.

Unfortunately, it seemed Miss Olive had either altered or done away with every last one of her widow's weeds. The most conservative dress left was a dove gray gown with lavender cuffs and a collar that *almost* reached the hollow of her throat.

Maddy scrubbed her face and body ruthlessly with the cold water left in her basin. But she could still feel the sweet, heated touch of Clay's hands and lips on her.

Once she'd donned the gray dress, she pulled her hair back severely, making sure not a strand escaped to soften her appearance. Setting down her hairbrush, her gaze caught on the picture of Winston, glaring sternly at her from inside the polished wood frame. "Don't look at me that way," she said mutinously, laying it face down, " haven't forgotten my vow."

Whirling around, she headed for the door, feeling as i she were fleeing from her husband's ghost. She climbed the stairs to the attic, still feeling edgy and unsettled.

This was ridiculous! She had to get herself back unde

control before Clay returned. And the best way to do that was to let her runaway emotions flow into her sketches.

An hour later she had sketches littering the table and floor all around her, and still didn't feel any better prepared to face Clay. Which was really too bad, because she could hear Miss Olive admitting him downstairs.

Clay returned Miss Olive's greeting, reining in his impatience to see Maddy again. Surely by now she'd come to see the wisdom, the inevitability, of their need to plan a wedding. It was her reputation, after all. Why, it could even affect her petition to adopt Katie.

"Has Sue Ellen been found?"

Clay pulled his focus back to Miss Olive. "Yes ma'am. It turns out she wasn't lost after all. She was headed back to town this morning on Joey Brennon's arm, wearing a wedding band."

"They eloped." Miss Adeline laughed delightedly. "I'd guessed as much."

Clay nodded.

The irrepressible leading lady gave him a sly look. "I suppose Cybil took the news well?"

Clay's lips twitched. "About as well as you'd guess, given her expectations." He glanced past the ladies toward the stairs.

"Looking for Maddy?" Miss Olive asked.

He nodded, feeling as if he'd been caught with his hand in the cookie jar. How did Miss Olive always manage to make him feel like a scruffy schoolboy? "There's a bit of unfinished business we need to discuss."

"Unfinished business?" Miss Adeline pounced on the words like a cat on a mouse. "Would that have anything to do with—"

"Adeline," Miss Olive interrupted firmly, "would you let Maddy know Mr. Kincaid is here?"

Miss Adeline pouted a moment, then, with an audible huff, turned and stalked up the stairs.

Miss Olive turned back to Clay. "Fanny and Katie are busy in the kitchen. If you'd care to wait for Maddy in the parlor, I can assure you that the two of you will have complete privacy."

Clay executed a slight bow. "Thank you, ma'am."

"And Mr. Kincaid," she said before he could make his escape.

"Yes?"

She looked down the length of her nose at him. "Don't disappoint me."

Clay resisted the urge to tug at his collar. "No ma'am."

A few minutes later, Maddy entered the parlor as if ready to face a dragon. And not just face, but conquer said dragon. So, she *wasn't* ready to accept the inevitable yet.

It was almost humorous, and downright humbling. Who'd have thought that he, Clayton Kincaid, the target of more matchmaking schemes than he'd care to count, would find himself in the position of having to practically beg a woman to marry him.

Only Maddy could bring him to this point.

Given her earlier panic, perhaps it would be better if he eased into the subject. "I suppose Miss Adeline told you about Sue Ellen and Joey?" he said as she shut the door.

She nodded, moving farther into the room. "I'm glad it wasn't anything more serious." She fiddled with a flower arrangement set near the piano, and managed a wry grin. "Although I suppose Cybil considers this a major catastrophe."

"Let's just say she wasn't ready to welcome Joey into the bosom of her family." Clay watched her carefully. "Anymore than you seem ready to welcome me into yours."

She drew herself up. "You're not comparing me to Cybil, I hope."

"Only on this point. And don't try to sidestep the issue."

"I'm not sidestepping anything. I'm out and out refusing." She glared at him. "I hired you to court me, not marry me. Ultimately, you were supposed to find an excuse to leave before the wedding and just never come back. And that's exactly how it's still going to play out."

Like hell. "Look, it was bad enough knowing I was going to seem a weaselly excuse for a man before, but there's no way I'm going to jilt a woman I played a part in compromising. You *will* marry me, if I have to drag you to the altar to see it done."

Her chin thrust out mulishly at that. "That'll be the only way you could get me there. But even if you go to such lengths, I still won't marry you."

Clay raked his hand through his hair. Devil take it, why was she fighting this so hard? Didn't she know what a prize catch most women thought him?

Of course, most women didn't know what *she* knew about him. Was that it? His jaw clenched. It didn't matter. His honor still dictated he marry her.

"Look," he said stiffly, "I'm sorry you find the idea of marriage to me so repugnant. But—"

Maddy made a sharp movement with her hand, halting his words. "I don't find the idea repugnant." She took a deep breath, then gave him a soft smile. "In fact, it's quite the opposite." The longing in her voice and expression was enough to make him harden uncomfortably.

"Then—"

"It has nothing to do with you," she interrupted, "or what I feel for you. It's just that I have no plans to marry anyone. Ever."

That made no sense. She was no ice maiden, or one of those dried-up spinsters who spurned love because they had none themselves to give. He knew for a fact that she had a warm, loving nature, that she had a wealth of passion simmering below her reserved exterior, just waiting for the right man to come along and set it loose.

Why wouldn't she let him be that man? There was only one reason he could think of.

"Stop that!" She actually stomped her foot at him.

"Don't look like that. I told you, this has nothing to do with you."

"Then tell me why you're so opposed to marriage." A sudden thought occurred to him and he crossed the room to take Maddy's arm. "Good heavens, did Winston do something to you? Did he hurt you?"

"No!" Her shocked denial was mirrored in her expression, leaving him with no doubt that she spoke the truth.

She drew in a ragged breath. "He was never anything but a gentleman to me."

"Then what is it?" When her lips again pinched closed in that mutinous line he raised a brow. "Don't you think you owe me some sort of explanation?"

Her fists clenched tightly at her sides. "I made a vow the day we buried Winston to never marry again."

That's what this was all about? He gently took one of her hands. "Maddy, you were seventeen and had just lost your husband. It's understandable that you would be overcome with strong emotions. But no one would expect you to spend the rest of your life living up to such a vow made in the throes of deep grief. You need—"

"It wasn't grief."

"What?"

She pulled her hand out of his grasp and turned her back to him. "I said, it wasn't grief that wrung that vow out of me."

He placed his hands on her shoulders, feeling the tense set of her muscles. Perhaps he was finally going to get the answers he'd been searching for, the secret she kept buried so deeply within her. "Then what was it?"

"Guilt." The word sounded as if it had been wrenched from her. "The deepest, blackest kind of guilt imaginable."

Guilt? "Maddy, I don't—"

She spun back around, facing him with eyes that burned with a hellish torment. "You want to know my secrets—all right, I'll tell you. I felt guilt over Winston's death because I knew his death was no accident, though I let the whole town go on believing it was. And the reason I knew it wasn't an accident was because . . ." She paused, staring defiantly. Then she took a deep breath and jerked away from him.

"Because *I killed him.*"

Chapter Eighteen

Clay stood rooted to the floor for the three heartbeats of time it took Maddy to flee the room.

Then muttering a string of curses under his breath, he shot after her. He should never have let her run off like that, no matter how off guard he'd been caught by her startling confession. What was she thinking, feeling, as she ran off? He'd tear his own heart out before he'd let her believe he no longer respected or wanted her.

He also itched to take her over his knee for dropping such a bombshell and then running before he could catch his breath.

Miss Olive blocked the stairs, looking none too happy with him.

"You can read me a lecture on my lack of character and insensitivity later," he said, forestalling any comments. "Right now I have some explanations to wring from the stubborn Mrs. Potter."

Miss Olive's expression relaxed somewhat and she nodded, stepping aside to let him pass. Surely that wasn't a gleam of approval he saw in her eye?

But he had no time to ponder on the seamstress's feelings, it was Maddy's he needed to untangle. He raced up the stairs, taking them two at a time, headed for her bedroom. But the sound of racing footsteps drew him toward the attic studio.

She rounded on him as soon as his shoulders cleared the landing. "I didn't give you permission to intrude here."

Clay didn't even hesitate before he stepped into the room. "Give it up Maddy. With or without your permission, I'm not leaving until we talk."

She moved to stare out the window across the room. "There's nothing to talk about."

"Maddy," he said crossing the room to stand behind her, "you can't *not* talk to me after making such a patently improbable confession. I refuse to believe you could ever do what you just claimed." He placed his hands on her shoulders. "Now face me and tell me why you would say such a thing."

She turned and glared at him. "Because it's true." She waved a hand. "Oh, I didn't push him in the pond or hold his head under. But I might as well have."

Clay wanted to hug her close, to kiss away the pain he could see in her eyes, caress away the tension in her muscles. But first he had to get to the heart of her misguided guilt. So he settled for moving a lock of hair from her forehead. "Maddy," he said as gently as he could, "talk to me."

She maintained her defiant pose for another heartbeat, then her shoulders slumped and she passed a hand over her face. "It was my fault."

Clay very much doubted that. He drew her toward the window seat, putting his arm around her shoulders as they sat. "Tell me about it."

She stared down at her hands folded in her lap. "Winston didn't have an accident—he committed suicide." She looked up at him, her eyes filled with bitter self-recrimination. "Because of me."

So many things that had puzzled Clay were beginning to make sense now. No wonder Maddy showed such intense emotion whenever something reminded her of her marriage. But he knew, with unshakable faith, that she was wrong about her blame in the matter. He put a finger under her chin, lifting it so that she had to meet his gaze. "I find that hard to believe."

"It's true." Her expression was hard, grim.

He gave her shoulder what he hoped was a comforting squeeze. "Maddy, you were so young, and had been married for such a short time. Isn't it possible you let your grief cloud your reasoning, that you accepted guilt where none existed?"

"You don't understand." She stood and began pacing. "Ours was not a love match—Grandmother arranged it. I guess I should have refused to go through with it. But Grandmother was so ill and was so desperate to see me married, I just couldn't tell her no."

She paced back and forth, as if she were that caged tiger they'd seen at the circus yesterday.

"Winston was very kind throughout everything. After the wedding he moved in here so I could continue to be close to Grandmother. He even understood the need for us to maintain separate rooms so I could be free to look in on Grandmother during the night."

Clay sat up straighter. They hadn't slept together? Surely, sometime during their three-week-long marriage—

Her hands fidgeted with her wedding band. "I knew the arrangement was unfair to him. But we all knew Grandmother wouldn't be with us much longer."

Maddy paused finally, staring at one of the many pictures of her grandmother. "When she realized how we'd arranged things, though, Grandmother insisted I go to Winston that very night and, as she put it, 'act like a wife.'"

Jealously knifed through Clay. He'd known she'd been married before, of course, but he didn't want to hear this, didn't want to think about another man receiving her favors.

"I won't lie to you." She took a deep breath. "I was nervous, yes, but a part of me was eager." Her wry smile had a bitter edge. "I suppose admitting such a thing is unladylike, but there you have it. I was seventeen, something of a romantic, and married to a man I admired greatly."

Listening to this was pure torture. But he held his peace, let her talk it out as she so obviously needed to. "That night," she said, moving to stare at one of the few sketches of Winston pinned to the wall, "after he'd gone to his room, I donned my prettiest nightdress, let my hair down, and knocked on his door. When Winston realized why I was there, a look crossed his face that I can only classify as revulsion."

Startled, Clay sat up straighter. This wasn't at all what he'd expected. But his guilty relief that she'd remained untouched gave way to a fierce urge to erase the hurt from her expression.

"Winston recovered his poise quickly," she continued bitterly. "He turned me away with some story about being indisposed. But it was too late, I knew how he truly felt about me. And what was worse, he *knew* I knew."

Fool! Clay had to bite his tongue to keep from saying the word aloud. How could the bastard have treated the precious gift she'd offered him with anything but pleasure and tender acceptance?

Maddy turned her back to the picture and moved to stare out a window. "We avoided each other as much as possible after that." Her voice now sounded flat and emotionless. "Whenever we did chance to be in the same room together, we were excruciatingly polite and civilized."

She rubbed her upper arms, as if to ward off a chill. Clay fought the urge to pull her to him and warm her in his own way.

"Then, three nights later, I found myself tossing and turning, unable to sleep. I went down to the study to retrieve a book I'd been reading, and stumbled on Winston seated at the desk there." Her lips tightened. "It took me a moment to realize he'd been drinking."

What had Winston said to her? Clay's hands fisted, the only way he could keep them from reaching for her. He wanted to call a stop to this, halt her painful reminiscences. But he knew she needed to talk it out, to cleanse this poison from her gut.

"I'd never seen him like that before." She raised a hand then let it drop. "He'd always been so dignified, but that night he was maudlin, almost incoherent. I didn't understand a lot of what he said. I . . . I think he was trying to apologize. Buried amongst the slurred gibberish he was spouting, he said something about having made a terrible mistake in marrying me, that no amount of money was worth selling his soul for. That he would find a way to make it right again."

She thrust her chin out. Standing in profile to him, she looked both brave and shatteringly vulnerable as she faced down her memories. "He said he realized I would never be satisfied with a platonic relationship, but that he could never bring himself to offer me anything more. The very idea of being a true husband to me was repugnant to him. Repugnant!"

Her voice broke then, and for just a moment, Clay wished Winston were still alive so he could connect his fist with the bastard's jaw.

"I didn't stay to hear anything else." She pushed a strand of hair behind her ear with a hand that trembled. "It was the very next morning that he had his 'accident.' Only, I knew it was no accident. It was what he'd meant when he said he would 'make it right.' "

Maddy whirled around to face him. "He killed himself rather than remain married to me."

Clay crossed the room and placed a hand on each of her arms. "You don't know for certain that it was suicide."

She remained poker stiff. "I'll never believe it was an

accident—not after what he said. The worst part of it is, he all but told me what he was planning to do. If I'd paid closer attention instead of wallowing in self-pity, I might have been able to stop him."

Clay tried to rub some of the stiffness from her arms. "Even if you're right about his committing suicide, and I'm not ready to concede that you are, it was in no way your fault."

"Wasn't it?" Her eyes both dared and begged him to contradict her. "I failed him as a wife." She smiled, but her expression held no hint of mirth. "And the ironic thing about it is, I don't even know how."

"Listen to me," he said, resisting the urge to literally shake some sense into her. "You are *not* responsible for Winston's death. You did nothing to precipitate his actions. Any man who could turn you away is either a fool or is incapable of feeling true passion." He brushed a lock of hair off her temple. "You are an extraordinarily loving and lovable woman."

"*Don't*—" She took a shaky breath. "Don't try to make me feel better. Winston is *dead*, because he couldn't face being married to me. Nothing you can say will change that."

Clay felt the effort it took her to remain still. In another second or two she would pull away from him and begin that caged-animal pacing again. "Maddy, listen to me." He struggled to find the right words. "Try to think back on what happened with some objectivity. You say Winston declared he could never be a true husband to you."

She nodded.

"Do you think perhaps there could be another explanation for his feeling that way, other than the ridiculous notion that he was repulsed by you personally?" He saw the protest form in her eyes and placed his fingertips on her beautifully full lips. "Is it possible that Winston's affections were engaged elsewhere, that he couldn't be a husband to you because he was deeply in love with someone else?"

"I don't—"

Clay didn't let her finish, more convinced by the minute that he had stumbled onto the truth. "Winston was a great deal older that you, nearly thirty I believe." Barely waiting for her nod, he plunged on. "Yet he'd never married. An illicit affair perhaps, something he could never admit to openly."

"You're grasping for straws." But there was a flicker of doubt in her eyes now.

"My explanation makes a great deal more sense than yours does."

She threw her head back stubbornly. "There's no way we'll ever know for sure."

He decided to try a different approach. He released her arms and frowned down at her. "I knew you had more than your share of pride, Maddy Potter, but I never dreamed you had such a high degree of conceit to go with it."

At least he'd startled the stubborn expression from her face. Good! He executed a deliberately casual shrug. "So Winston wasn't happy being married to you. You attach a great deal too much importance to your marriage if you honestly think that, alone, would be enough to force a man to kill himself. There were all sorts of options open to the man if that had been the only thing troubling him, including seeking an annulment." He could tell from her expression that he was starting to get through to her now. "Don't you see, it doesn't matter. Regardless of why he did it, Maddy, it was Winston's choice to take his life. You did nothing to force his hand."

He caressed her cheek. "The man must have been made of stone. That is the only reasonable explanation for how he could fail to want you, how he could resist the urge to touch you, to hold you." He pulled her against his chest and stroked her hair. "God knows, I'm not strong enough to resist such a sweet temptation."

* * *

For just a moment, Maddy allowed herself to relax in his embrace, savoring the feelings of being cherished and at home there. Almost, she felt worthy again.

Almost.

Was it possible Clay was right? She'd been deeply shocked by Winston's suicide and so certain of the part she'd played in it. She'd never allowed herself to examine the circumstances of his death too closely, feeling it would be too painful, too self-incriminating for her to do so. Had her seventeen-year-old self over-dramatized her own guilt, her own culpability in the tragedy?

She wanted to believe it, wanted with every fiber of her being for it to be true, but she'd lived with her guilt too long to give it up so easily. Now, though, she could believe she was not the sole cause of Winston's suicide. And for that she had Clay to thank. He was such a stubborn, over-bearing, *honorable* man. How could she face life without him when he left Pepper Cloud?

She pulled back enough to meet his gaze, glad when he kept his arms around her. "Thank you."

He gave her a gruff frown, as if uncomfortable with her misty-eyed gratitude. "For what? All I did was point out the obvious."

Heaven help her, she did love this man. "For believing in me, no matter how many reasons I give you not to. You've eased my soul of a torment that's haunted me for seven years. I don't know how I can ever repay you."

He gave her arms a squeeze. "I do. Marry me."

Maddy's heart gave an exultant leap. Then she remembered his reason for asking. He didn't return her love, didn't long for a happily-ever-after relationship with her. His blasted sense of honor demanded he make the offer.

Well, she wouldn't have it. She wanted all of him, heart and soul, or she wanted none of him. It would be too painful to learn later that he regretted his choice, to discover him pining to be free of her. "Thank you, but no. I've had my fill of arranged marriages."

He frowned. "This is hardly the same thing."

"Isn't it? You wouldn't classify this as a love match, would you?" She forced herself to keep breathing normally, to ignore the racing of her pulse as she waited for his answer.

He hesitated and a small muscle twitched at the corner of his mouth. "A marriage does not have to start as a love match to be successful."

Willing her shoulders not to slump, Maddy turned around so he wouldn't see the disappointment she knew was mirrored in her face. "Perhaps not, but I have Katie to think about."

She felt his hands on her shoulders. "Then think about Katie. Wouldn't she be better off with a father as well as a mother?"

Maddy thought about how close Clay and Katie had become over the past week. She remembered thinking what a good father he would make someday. Was that day now? Did he truly want to take on the role of parent, with all its responsibilities, all its joys?

Could she deny Katie that opportunity if he did?

He turned her around and placed a finger under her chin. "Maddy, look at me. This is not some unpleasant corner I'm being backed in to. Can't you see how much I *want* this?"

She searched his face, looking for the truth. She saw heat there, desire. But was there more? Dare she believe that his heart held feelings for her that transcended mere physical attraction?

He offered her a crooked smile. "Don't make me beg— it wouldn't be a pretty sight and I'm afraid I'd be quite difficult to live with afterwards."

Her heart melted at his words and tone. Should she grab at this chance he was offering her? She could make him happy, she knew she could. Searching his face again, she saw sincerity and a blazing purpose that made him seem endearingly vulnerable. How could she not give him the answer he wanted?

Especially when it was what she wanted, too.

Pushing away the last of her doubts, she touched his cheek with a smile. "Far be it for me to bring the proud Clayton Kincaid to his knees. I accept your proposal."

Triumph and something else she couldn't name flashed across his face. He pulled her into a fierce embrace. "That's my girl. We'll do well together, you'll see."

Not exactly a declaration of love. But she refused to second guess her decision. She *would* content herself to live with his affection and friendship for now. As for what the future might bring, hope was a difficult thing to suppress.

He released her and slipped an arm around her shoulders. "Shall we break the news to the ladies waiting downstairs, before we make our visit to Reverend Posey?"

There was a lightness to his tone and expression that hadn't been there before. It sent a tingle through Maddy to think her acceptance had put that there.

The hope inside her took firmer root.

Someday soon, her heart whispered.

Clay whistled as he strolled along the sidewalk headed for Barrows House. Over the past several years he'd deftly side-stepped his mother's countless matchmaking efforts, avoided gold-digging debutantes by the scores, and turned up his nose at countless proposals made by social-climbing mammas or business-merger-minded pappas. All because he adamantly refused to even consider marriage as an option open to him. His pride had stood in the way before, refusing to let him get that close to another person, close enough for her to learn of his disgraceful secret.

Yet here he was, finally facing his wedding day.

Maddy knew his deepest, blackest secret, had witnessed his shameful lack firsthand, and still she professed to want to spend her life at his side. It was a miracle he still couldn't quite believe.

He couldn't be happier.

Life with Maddy would never be dull. Exasperating and endearing by turns, she was always full of schemes to save the world, or at least the folks in her part of it. Undoubtedly, she would keep him on his toes. He found the prospect invigorating, exhilarating. He was fully prepared to help her fight her battles, to slay whatever dragons she stirred into action.

Was this what love felt like?

This afternoon, just a few short hours from now, he'd stand beside her and, before the preacher, the townsfolk and God, Himself, pledge his troth and his heart to her, vow to love and cherish her for the rest of his life. And, as he was just now coming to realize, he'd mean every word of it.

With a hand in his pocket, he fingered the plain gold band hidden there, the best Pepper Cloud had to offer on such short notice. He'd find her something nicer as soon as possible.

Did Maddy mind having to get married this way, without time to plan or prepare? She deserved so much better, something more extravagant, something stately and elegant. He planned to take her to Virginia to meet his family after the adoption hearing was complete.

His family, naturally, would love Maddy. How could they not? Perhaps he and Maddy could even have a second ceremony while in Virginia. He grinned, thinking how much his mother would enjoy planning such an affair. Lord knows, the dear woman had waited long enough to see him wed. He only hoped she'd forgive him for having this first ceremony without her.

Afterwards, they could return via New Orleans. It would be a fairly simple matter to close up his business office there and move it here. And New Orleans would be the perfect setting for a proper honeymoon.

Grinning broadly in anticipation of all that would entail, Clay pushed open the front gate to Barrows House, and increased the pace of his steps. He was suddenly eager to see Maddy's smile again, to hear the sound of her voice. He would soon be able to show her just how desirable a woman she was, would do his best to erase any lingering doubts Winston's despicable conduct had planted in her.

But a faint whining, coming from somewhere behind the house, caught his attention. It sounded like Skipper was in trouble.

Altering his course, Clay strode quickly to the backyard, shaking his head at the sight that met his eyes when he rounded the corner of the house. The puppy had somehow managed to get his head caught in the wire that formed the sides of his pen.

Skipper stopped his whining and started wagging his tail in a hopeful manner as soon as he spotted Clay.

"Easy, fella." Clay stooped beside the pen and cupped the puppy's chin in one hand. Slipping the wire over Skipper's ears, Clay gently eased the dog's head back inside the pen. "There you go, boy."

Skipper yipped his gratitude, and Clay reached through the wire pen. "You're welcome," he said, scratching the puppy's ears. When Clay pulled his hand back, Skipper watched him with tongue-lolling hope for a few moments. When the puppy accepted that Clay was done, he bounded to the other side of the pen to bark at the back door of the house.

"Sorry boy, Katie probably won't be out to play today. I imagine she's being kept pretty busy getting fitted and rested up for the wedding this afternoon." He grinned. "We men folk are considered pretty useless at a time like this."

Which was probably as it should be. Clay leaned back on his haunches, contemplating the fact that when he married Maddy he would not only gain a wife, but also a daughter in the form of Katie. The idea was both satisfying and sobering.

He'd do his best to be the kind of father the little girl deserved. And before too long, perhaps he and Maddy could provide her with brothers and sisters to play with.

Buoyed by that thought, Clay stood. Before he could move toward the house, though, something else caught his attention. The ladder had been left propped up against the tree. He frowned. Had Maddy been adjusting the rope on Katie's swing again? That was no job for a woman. Of course, knowing what she did, she'd never ask him. But there *were* other options.

Besides, leaving the ladder out was *not* a good idea. What if Katie took a notion to climb it herself?

Liking the feeling of fatherly responsibility, Clay strode to the tree to take care of the matter. He'd set the ladder back behind the hydrangea bushes for now, and find a more suitable place for it later.

As he approached the house, Clay heard Miss Adeline's distinctive throaty chuckle coming from an upstairs window.

"It was a masterful bit of maneuvering," she said. "You missed your calling, Maddy dear. You would have made a fine character actress."

Clay grinned. What little plot were the ladies cooking up now?

"Oh, I wouldn't say that." There was a troubled edge to Maddy's voice. "It was such a tricky line to walk. I never out and out lied, but I came much closer to it than I was comfortable with."

That was his Maddy, a paradox of a woman if he'd ever met one. Scrupulously honest, yet willing to go right to the limits of her moral convictions to accomplish her goals. Thankfully, her goals seemed to be altruistic more often than not.

"But the price you had to pay." Miss Fanny's verbal hand-wringing came through loud and clear. "Maddy, are you sure—"

"I knew what this would cost me before I ever set the wheels in motion," Maddy answered firmly, almost as if she were trying to convince herself. "I'm determined to make the best of it now that I've accomplished my goal."

Clay's grin faded and his brow creased. It sounded as if Maddy were sacrificing her needs for someone else's again. He'd have to talk to her about that. It was high time she understood that he was her partner now, in both the good and the ill. She needn't shoulder her burdens alone anymore.

Miss Olive's tsk drew his attention back to the conversation above him. "Don't worry yourself so much, dear. He appears quite happy with the way it all turned out."

What poor sap were they talking about?

"Happy!" Miss Adeline's tone held the hint of a snort. "Why the man was practically preening. You'd think this was what he wanted the whole time."

Clay felt a prickling along the back of his neck. Surely this didn't have anything to do with *him*?

"I rather believe that was the plan," Miss Olive replied dryly. "I must say, Maddy, you did a fine job of making him think this was all his idea."

The words stiffened Clay's back as they hit uncomfortably close to home. Had Maddy played him for a fool?

"He's not the partner I would have shackled myself with," she said matter-of-factly, "but there wasn't any other way to make this work."

Shackled herself with? Certain now that they were discussing him, Clay felt as if he'd been punched in the gut. Is that how she thought of their upcoming marriage? How could he have so misread her feelings?

"I'm determined, though," she continued, "that he'll be happy with the bargain we've struck."

Clay's lip turned up in sneer at this oh-so-noble sentiment. Nice of her to consider his feelings.

"I know he's got a bit more pride and pomposity than any god-fearing man has a right to. . . ."

Anger and a twinge of stung pride heated Clay's cheeks. Pride and pomposity? How dare she speak of him that way. Is that how she really saw him?

". . . but he's agreed to go through with this, in fact, is now insisting that we do."

The amusement in Maddy's voice only intensified his anger. How could he have been so wrong about her intentions? Thank God he'd never bared his soul to her, never mentioned the word love. How she must be laughing at him now.

"For that, at least, I owe him my gratitude and respect. At heart he's a good man, and I'm sure we can make this work. He is never to know that I think him anything but the most perfect of partners."

"Perfect—hah!" Miss Adeline again. "For all his preening, we all know what an unmanly, cowardly little worm—"

"That's enough!" Maddy's tone brooked no argument. "Since he is to join forces with us, it will do none of us any good to disparage him, even amongst ourselves. From now on . . ."

Clay didn't hang around to hear more—he didn't need to. After years of being ambushed by his mother's and sisters' attempts to strip him of his bachelorhood, he understood the damning words all to clearly. Them, he could forgive—they had at least been motivated by love. Not dear Mrs. Potter.

Jaw set, he contemplated with disbelief the fact that the woman he'd planned to give his heart to had performed the ultimate betrayal—told the rest of her household about his fear of heights. Had they laughed about it, sneered about it?

He'd considered the three ladies his friends.

Maddy, he'd considered so much more.

If she'd set out to deliberately humiliate him she couldn't have done a better job. He knew he would no longer be able to look at her without remembering this betrayal of his confidence, would no longer be able to face the ladies without the contempt he'd just heard in Miss Adeline's voice ringing in his ears.

But he'd be damned if he'd let them know how much it had hurt, how thoroughly he'd been taken in by their act. No, much better to make them believe it was *he* who had been pretending, that his emotions had never truly been engaged.

How much of what had happened was staged, how much truth? Had she gone so far in her scheming as to arrange for their getting locked in the church storeroom?

Regardless, he knew his duty, no matter how hollow it now seemed. He fingered the ring in his pocket again, resisting the urge to fling it away. He would give her the protection of his name—honor demanded he do no less. But that didn't mean he had to stay around to face a life that now seemed intolerable. As soon as the wedding was over he would escape.

Before he did he'd make it perfectly clear, to Maddy at least, that leaving was what he'd planned all along. There would be no hint of the whipped puppy or the broken-hearted suitor in his leave-taking. Much better to see he's-harder-to-hold-than-I-thought chagrin on her face than poor-boy-I-broke-his-heart pity.

Not that it would matter overmuch to Maddy—she would no doubt just be happy to see him go. Then she would no longer feel *shackled* to him.

After all, apparently the only thing she really wanted was his name.

His hand was on the gate when he heard the front door to Barrows House open. To his relief it was only Katie.

"Hello Mr. Kincaid," she said as she stepped outside. "Aren't you gonna come in?"

Clay moved to the foot of the porch steps. "Not today. I don't want to bother the ladies—I'm sure they have their hands full getting ready for the wedding."

Katie nodded. "Uh-huh. I even had to fix my own breakfast this morning." She cocked her head as she studied him. "Are you really gonna marry my aunt Maddy?"

Clay shifted his weight but kept his smile firmly in place.

269

None of this was Katie's fault. "I certainly am."

"Well then," she asked, scuffing her toe on the porch floor in a studiously off-hand manner, "does that mean I can start calling you Uncle Clay?"

An arrow of tenderness pierced Clay's heart at the words and the vulnerable expression that accompanied them. "I would be most truly honored to have you call me Uncle Clay." He reached down to give the girl a bear hug. "And you don't even have to wait until after the wedding to start."

Katie wrapped her arms around his neck in a gesture of unconditional love. A torrent of emotions threatened to drown Clay. Bittersweet yearning for a future that held more of these simple pleasures waged war with howling frustration borne of the knowledge that it was not to be.

When he left town today, he'd not only be walking away from Maddy, but from Katie, as well. How would the little girl react? Would she forget him in time, or worse yet, remember him with anger or contempt?

No, he wouldn't have it!

A deep consuming anger started burning low in his gut. Maddy had done this to him. She'd made him believe he could have the fairy tale, lulled him into thinking in terms of miracles and love everlasting, when all the while she'd been scheming and planning how best to make him dance to her tune.

Well, she'd gotten what she obviously wanted, to maneuver him into marrying her.

But she'd soon learn that the getting wasn't always as pleasant as the plotting.

Chapter Nineteen

"You look absolutely radiant, dear."

"Thank you." Standing in the back vestibule of the church, Maddy smiled at Vera and fanned the skirt of the beautiful lavender gown Miss Olive had miraculously managed to get ready overnight. Surely, she could be forgiven a bit of preening on her wedding day.

Maddy felt like a fairytale princess awakened from a long sleep, ready to place her hand, and her heart, into the keeping of her very own Prince Charming.

"Do I look raid'yent, too?" Katie asked, mimicking Maddy's movements.

"Why, of course you do, Buttercup." Maddy stooped to give the little girl a hug. "I dare say you are the prettiest flower girl this town has seen in many a year."

"Here now, Maddy," Vera tsked, "careful you don't muss your dress."

Maddy straightened and allowed Vera to fuss with her sash. It seemed strange to have Vera here with her instead of Miss Olive or one of the other ladies. But Miss Fanny sat at the organ and Miss Adeline stood beside her, ready to sing "Oh Promise Me" as soon as Maddy started her walk down the aisle. Miss Olive had left only a few short moments ago to take her place in the front pew, holding a place of honor as the bride's "family."

"There we are, right as rain again." Vera gave her arm a pat. She stepped back to study Maddy's appearance with a misty-eyed sigh. "I'm so happy that things worked out for you and Mr. Kincaid, dear. I could see the two of you belonged together from the first time I saw him in your parlor, when he stood up to Cybil on your behalf."

Maddy hid a smile, knowing Vera was embellishing her crystal ball abilities just a bit. She lifted her face as the introductory strains of the organ music sounded through the closed doors and felt a moment of panic. It was time! Heaven help her, was she making a mistake? Did she really deserve to—

"There's your cue." Vera's happy, complacent tone checked Maddy's runaway thoughts, calmed her temporarily jangled nerves.

Maddy took a deep breath and smiled, catching the understanding gleam in Vera's eye. Undoubtedly, all brides went through such last-minute second-guessing. She'd be all right, just as soon as she caught a glimpse of Clay waiting for her at the altar.

She hadn't spoken to him since last night, and she wanted reassurances that he still felt good about this. She could live with the fact that half the town believed this to be a forced wedding. But she couldn't stand the thought of Clay believing that, as well.

It would have helped if he'd asked to speak to her when he came by Barrows House this morning instead of just leaving a message with Katie. She supposed he was only honoring the tradition of the bride and groom not seeing each other on the day of the wedding before the ceremony began. It had done her heart good, though, to see the glow on Katie's face when she'd announced that he'd told her she could call him Uncle Clay now. He would make such a wonderful father.

Would he want a big family? She hoped so, because she certainly did. She loved Katie dearly and always would, but felt a stirring inside her for other children as well—her and Clay's children. Which, of course, led her to thoughts of the wedding night, thoughts that set her heart racing and her cheeks on fire.

Fortunately, Vera had turned to pluck a basket from the vestibule table and so missed Maddy's tell-tale blush.

"Now Katie," Vera said as she handed the basket to the little girl, "when I open the door, you walk down the aisle, just like we practiced this morning. Scatter the rose petals gracefully, and remember, this is not a race."

Waiting until Katie had nodded her understanding, Vera turned back to Maddy. "As soon as you start down the aisle, I'll head over to the schoolhouse to help Blanche put the finishing touches on the reception." She patted Maddy's arm once more. "Don't you worry about a thing, it's all going to be beautiful."

"Thank you, Vera. It was so wonderful of you and Blanche to step in and organize the reception. Under the circumstances—"

"Oh pish-posh on the circumstances. This was meant to be, no matter how it came about." Vera placed a hand at Katie's back and eased her toward the door. "Ready?"

Katie lifted her chin and nodded regally. In the blink of an eye, Maddy watched her irrepressible tomboy suddenly become a graceful princess.

Vera opened the door and Katie glided into the sanctuary, strewing rose petals with a flair Miss Adeline, herself, would envy. After a short pause, Vera turned back to Maddy. "Your turn." She gave Maddy a quick hug, then stepped back and held the door open wider.

Taking a deep breath, Maddy stepped into the church just as the whole congregation stood and turned to face her. Miss Fanny changed from the soft waltz she'd been playing to the introductory chords of "Oh, Promise Me," then Miss Adeline's voice rang out, clear and vibrant.

Ignoring them all, Maddy faced forward, her gaze seeking Clay's. He presented a commanding figure, standing straight and tall at the front of the church, dwarfing the sparely built Reverend Posey. Her soon-to-be-husband's expression was somber, aloof almost, as if he sought to treat this occasion with solemn dignity rather than his usual easygoing charm.

Was it because of the circumstances that had landed them so precipitously in this position? Was he trying to show everyone he had nothing to be embarrassed over or ashamed of?

Raising her chin a little higher, Maddy sought to emulate his air of dignity. Then, feeling as if she were on stage in front of an uncertain crowd, Maddy looked around to try and gauge the mood of her audience. To her relief, while there were a few expressions that seemed to reflect a mean-spirited brand of curiosity or self-righteous censure, most of the townsfolk looked on with approval, if not outright pleasure.

Halfway down the aisle, she met Sue Ellen's gaze. Uncowed and unrepentant over her *own* scandalous actions, the girl glowed with happiness and a new air of maturity. The look she gave Maddy held encouragement and something more, as if she couldn't wait to welcome Maddy into the blissful sisterhood of newlywed brides.

Then Maddy glided past Sue Ellen and her gaze met Miss Olive's. Standing with her hands on Katie's shoulders, the dear maiden-aunt-cum-fairy-godmother of a woman smiled as proudly as if she'd been Maddy's own mother.

Maddy felt her own smile turn a bit misty as she acknowledged the silent message of love and encouragement that flowed from her friend.

Then she reached Clay's side and turned to face him. And felt her smile slowly fade.

Something was wrong.

What she'd first taken as quiet dignity now appeared to be a puzzling aloofness. Oh, he met her gaze readily enough, and offered her one of those bold, dazzling smiles he passed around like candy to clamoring children. But his expression held no softness, his eyes offered no warmth.

Was he having serious second thoughts? Or was he just experiencing some of the same last-minute panic she'd felt earlier? Should she call a halt here and now until she knew for certain?

As if sensing her thoughts, Clay firmly took her hand and turned them both to face Reverend Posey.

Feeling somewhat reassured by his determination, Maddy studied Clay from the corner of her eye. Though he appeared composed, seemed relaxed and at ease, she sensed an underlying tension, a brittleness to his smile that worried her. Trying to convince herself this was due to his discomfort with being on display rather than with the commitment he was about to make, she did her best to focus on Reverend Posey's words.

The ceremony, which seemed both endlessly long and amazingly short, passed in a haze for Maddy. She recited her vows at the appropriate point, trying to convey to Clay with voice and expression how deeply she meant them. Clay recited his own vows glibly, an easy smile on his lips, but she could find no hint that any deep emotion lay below the surface of his words.

Again the feeling that something was terribly wrong gripped her. She had to call a halt to this, had to make sure she found out what was bothering Clay before they went any further.

Then Reverend Posey pronounced them husband and wife, irrevocably binding her and Clay together. Beaming fondly at them both, the reverend spread his hands. "You may now kiss the bride."

Clay's hesitation was so brief, so smoothly covered, Maddy doubted anyone else even noticed it. But she did.

The kiss itself was light, brief, and held no promise of

things to come. It chilled her to the very core of her soul.

What had happened to the passionate lover who'd melted her bones in that storeroom just two nights ago, to the ardent suitor who'd wooed her with won't-take-no-for-an-answer persistence? What had she done to douse his passion, to put this emotional distance between them?

Numbly, she turned with Clay to face the congregation.

"Ladies and gentlemen of Pepper Cloud," said Reverend Posey in an avuncular tone, "I present to you Mr. and Mrs. Clayton Randolph Kincaid."

Amid a smattering of applause, Clay escorted Maddy down the aisle. He tucked her arm securely in the crook of his, but his touch seemed perfunctory, impersonal.

He nodded and smiled pleasantly to those they passed, but didn't pause to speak. From the indulgent glances Maddy intercepted, she imagined they looked like impatient newlyweds, in a hurry to get away to somewhere they could be alone. As Clay led her toward the schoolhouse, she spied the carriage that had carried her here to the church. Cleaned and polished to obsidian perfection, it was gaily bedecked in colorful ribbons and bows.

Feeling a sudden shiver pebble across her skin, Maddy saw the buggy as a reflection of herself—wearing a festive garb for the moment, but when all was said and done, everyone knew it was only a disguise. Tomorrow it would return to its drab, austere, black-clad existence.

In deference to the on-lookers, Maddy kept a smile firmly pasted on her face as they marched across the schoolyard. Making sure to pitch her voice so that only he could hear, she went directly to the point. "What's wrong?"

"Wrong?" Clay raised a brow. "What could be wrong? You certainly couldn't have asked for a better turnout, especially given the short notice. It looks like most of the town showed up to see us tie the knot, all right and proper."

Maddy, feeling another piece of her confidence crumble at his tone, tried to focus on getting answers. "I won't trade jibes with you, especially since I have no idea what set you off. You've obviously changed your mind about wanting to marry me. I want to know why."

"Oh, but you're mistaken," he replied smoothly, without bothering to look at her. "I'm still as convinced as ever about the need for us to get married. If not, we would never have exchanged those vows a few moments ago."

Maddy's steps faltered for just a second. Yesterday he'd talked warmly in terms of desires, today he spoke tersely of needs. He paused, but she recovered quickly and they resumed their march.

Oh yes, something had definitely changed, and not for the better. "Don't keep dancing around the question," she demanded, struggling to keep her voice even. "Tell me what's wrong."

But they had reached the reception area by now. Clay ignored her question as they mounted the steps to the schoolhouse. He stepped aside for Maddy to precede him, his lips turning up sardonically. "Smile, Mrs. Kincaid. You mustn't forget our audience."

Then there was no longer time for private conversation as they were surrounded by arriving guests. Clay stayed beside her as they received well wishes and compliments from dozens of friends and neighbors. To Maddy's surprise, no one seemed to notice anything amiss. Like a replay of her nightmarish past, everything appeared perfectly normal and civilized on the surface.

She wanted to scream at the mockery of it all, wanted to fling down her flowers and drag Clay off to somewhere private so that she could get to the bottom of his troubling behavior once and for all. Instead, she smilingly accepted compliments on her "radiant looks" and "glowing smile," and looked on while Clay shook countless hands and received hearty congratulations on his good fortune.

Only Miss Olive seemed to sense that things were not as they should be. As she came up to offer well wishes to the "happy couple," her brow furrowed. "Is something the matter, dear?"

Maddy tucked a wisp of hair behind her ear. "I seem to have developed a touch of a headache. Nothing too terrible, though," she hastened to assure her friend. "I'm sure I'll be better in a little bit."

Miss Olive patted her hand. "Of course you will. It's no doubt all due to the day's excitement." Still, Maddy could tell Miss Olive wasn't entirely convinced.

Lavinia and Harvey Thompson stepped up to offer their felicitations. Harvey handed Clay an envelope as he shook his hand. "This arrived for you at the hotel just after you left for the church," he explained. "Thought I'd bring it along in case it was something important."

Clay opened the letter, glanced it over quickly, then folded it up and slipped it inside his coat. "Thanks, Harvey, I've been expecting this."

When Maddy saw the disappointed look on Lavinia's face she felt her first genuine urge to smile since she'd stood beside Clay at the front of the church. No doubt the woman had hoped to get a glimpse of whatever gossip-worthy news the missive might have contained.

After they'd finally greeted all the guests, Clay escorted her to the refreshment tables. Vera and Blanche had done a wonderful job of preparing the reception fare and setting it all up. The food and drinks were plentiful and everything was beautifully arrayed. But as Maddy nibbled on the slice of cake someone handed to her, she realized she might as well be eating sawdust. Her emotions were in too much turmoil, her stomach churned too miserably for her to taste what she ate.

Finally she'd had enough. Grabbing hold of Clay's arm, she interrupted his conversation with Harvey Thompson and Reverend Posey. "Excuse me," she said firmly, "but I'm feeling a bit faint. Do you mind if we step outside for a moment to get a breath of fresh air?"

She held his gaze, daring him to refuse her. She would
ot be put off any longer.

At last he nodded. "Of course." He turned back to the
wo men with a must-humor-the-little-lady manner. "If
ou'll pardon us, gentlemen."

The masculinely indulgent smiles he received in return
et Maddy's teeth on edge. But she held her peace until
hey had stepped outside. Steering him firmly toward an
rea in plain sight of the reception but safely out of hearing
istance, she wasted no time in going on the offensive once
more. "Tell me what is wrong. Why are you acting as if
his were no more than a Sunday morning church service
nd you and I were nothing more than passing friends?"

He looked down at her with that condescending, raised-
row expression that she was coming to detest. "Sorry if
y acting skills no longer meet your high standards. I'd
hought it all right to relax the engrossed-in-each-other
overs' charade now that we've achieved your goal."

"What was he saying? Had yesterday been all an act?
But—"

"Of course, if you want to continue to put on a show,
m willing to accommodate you." He leaned closer to her.
Shall I give you a passionate lover's kiss right here in front
f our guests?" His eyes glittered with some hard emotion
at frightened her. "It's probably the sort of thing one
ould expect from a pair of newlyweds—especially a cou-
e already viewed as being slightly on the scandalous side."

"No!" She recoiled as if he'd slapped her. How could he
e so hard, so unfeeling? The question kept coming back
 her—what had happened since last night?

"No?" He leaned back, his expression shuttered again,
ut his smile still held a brittle edge. "I suppose you're
ght, we must be circumspect if we want the adoption to
 through without opposition."

She refused to cry. Somehow, she had to make him tell
er. She couldn't go through another hellish nightmare of
ot knowing what she'd done to turn a man away. "What

have I done or not done to make you so angry?"

"Angry? My dear wife, I'm not angry. To be angry, I have to first have cared deeply. Now," he pulled the lett he'd received earlier out of his coat. "I suppose this wou be a good time to mention that I plan to leave town tod on the evening southbound train."

Still reeling from the previous exchange, Maddy tried absorb this latest revelation. "Leaving?" she repeated dull "But where are you going and for how long?"

He looked down at her as if she were slow-witte "Surely you knew I wouldn't be hanging around here fc ever." He looked away as he brushed an insect from h lapel. "It's not as if either of us considered this a *real* ma riage."

His words were a sword that sliced through her chest prick at her heart. If he didn't care, why had he pressed hard when she'd refused his suit?

"I have business dealings back in New Orleans," he co tinued, "and I've been away too long as it is. Now that y have my name, which is all you really needed anyw there's no point in delaying my departure."

His name? Is that all he thought she needed? Wh about his warmth, his companionship, his love?

"Don't worry," he said, obviously misreading the reas for her distress, "you can tell everyone I received word an emergency back home that requires my immediate tention."

She indicated the letter he still held. "Is that what y have there, word from home about an emergency?"

"No, but you can let them assume it is. After all, you a true believer in doing whatever it takes, are you not?"

Why was he being so callous? It was so unlike the m she'd come to know these past few weeks. Or had she rea known him at all?

He handed her the letter. "This is a report from an i vestigator I hired to track down any relatives Katie mig have. He located a second cousin of her mother's."

Maddy felt her heart lurch in her chest. Surely he wouldn't take Katie away from her, too.

"This cousin, a Mr. Woodrow, has five children of his own. He's willing to do his duty by Katie if necessary, but won't contest your petition to adopt if you still want to."

"Of course I still want to!" How could he think there would be any question?

Clay nodded. "Very well, I'll ask Peterson to let Mr. Woodrow know he's off the hook." He waved a hand toward the letter. "Keep that for Katie. She may want to contact her relatives some day."

Using every ounce of control she had, Maddy willed her voice to remain steady. "What do I tell Katie? About your leaving, I mean?"

For the first time this afternoon she saw a hint of some deep emotion cross his face. Regret? Need?

"You won't have to do my explaining for me—I'll speak to her before I go." He stared hard at her, as if daring her to challenge his next words. "I aim to keep in touch with Katie. I may even be back through here from time to time to see her."

But not to see *her*. The sentiment hung in the air between them as if he'd said the words aloud.

Maddy's chest and throat tightened with bottled up heartache. "The door will always be open to you," she managed to say softly.

His jaw worked, and for just a moment she thought he would relent, would smile and tell her it had all been a monumental mistake. Then he straightened and turned them back toward the schoolhouse. "Well then, now that we both know how things stand, let's return to our guests, shall we? It's time to break the news of my imminent departure."

Maddy nodded mutely and fell into step beside him. There was nothing left to say.

Winnie Griggs

Without conscious effort or even awareness of how she'd once again managed to repulse a good man, destroy her marriage.

Why was she so unlovable?

Chapter Twenty

"Don't you think you should call it a night, dear?"

Maddy glanced up from her work to smile at Miss Olive. "In a bit. I just decided to rearrange a few things in here."

The worried crease in Miss Olive's brow deepened. "You've hardly slept at all this past week. You're going to make yourself sick if you keep this up."

Had it only been a week since Clay left? It felt like a lifetime. Maddy tucked a stray hair behind her ear, feeling the weight of her friend's concern press down on her. "I just don't seem to need as much sleep these days as I used to."

Much better to keep busy, to occupy her mind with trivial tasks and her body with hard work. That way, when she *did* finally go to bed, she fell into an exhausted slumber. She didn't want time to think, time to remember, otherwise she'd surely find herself drowning in her own tears.

"Maddy," Miss Olive said gently, "I don't know what set Clay off, but it wasn't your fault."

Perhaps not, but that thought brought precious little comfort.

When Maddy didn't answer, Miss Olive sighed. "Is there anything I can get for you before I go to bed?"

Maddy shook her head. "No, I'm fine. Don't worry, I'm just about finished in here."

With a last troubled glance, the seamstress turned and padded down the hall to her room.

Maddy gave the trunk she'd been moving another shove to position it under the window, then straightened to observe the effect. Deciding it was centered perfectly, she stepped back and surveyed the room as a whole. No longer the dingy, cluttered, storeroom of a few short weeks ago, it was now an inviting child's play room.

She'd spent the first day and a half after Clay's precipitous departure finishing the job they'd started of sorting through Winston's papers. Once that was done, and she'd managed to get a few hours sleep, she decided to transform the room into a rainy-day haven for Katie. She'd discarded all the mismatched pieces of furniture, scrubbed and painted the walls, and cajoled Miss Olive into providing bright, cheery curtains and cushions. The addition of bookshelves and a few pieces of child-sized furniture had completed the furnishings. The center of the room was left uncluttered to provide an inviting play space.

She'd just finished preparing it this morning, but already Katie had put her stamp on the room. Her books and toys filled the shelves. A brightly colored rag she and Skipper played tug-of-war with lay on the seat of a chair. And a collection of odd-shaped rocks littered one end of her table.

Taking a last look around, Maddy picked up the lamp and left, shutting the door behind her. But she turned toward the attic rather than her bedroom. Trudging up the stairs, she wondered what she would find to fill her day tomorrow. Perhaps she would spend some time in the garden.

She set her lamp down on the worktable and glanced at the pictures of Winston pinned to the far wall. There were no lingering feelings of shame and guilt when she thought of him now, only pity. One of the unexpected benefits of her frenzied clean-up efforts had been that she'd discovered Winston's journal in one of the last boxes she'd tackled.

It lay here, next to her sketch pad, and she traced a finger over the worn linen binding. Last night, her need for answers had overcome her reservations over prying, and she'd read through some of the later entries.

It turned out Clay had guessed correctly—Winston *had* had a secret lover. It wasn't clear in the entries she read why Winston and his lover had been unable to wed, but his despair that their relationship could never be made public had come through loud and clear. A thread of shame weaved its way through the entries, as well.

Had this illicit lover, who Winston had only referred to as Chris, been married? Maddy didn't think Chris had been anyone local. Christina Lowell was her grandmother's age and Crystal Summers had only been twelve at the time of Winston's death. Other than those two, the only other Chris in the area was Christopher Jenners, a woodcarver who lived on the east side of town and kept pretty much to himself.

It was a relief to find she didn't know this person, wouldn't have to face the possibility of running into her socially somewhere.

Maddy had shaken off her guilt with regards to Winston's suicide, had even forgiven him for what he'd put her through. He'd suffered enough for what he'd done. Tomorrow, she'd burn the journal, signaling an end to that part of her life, to her guilt.

But Clay's leaving, his biting anger when he last spoke to her, was another matter altogether.

Pushing the journal aside, she picked up her sketchbook and began scratching lines across the page.

She didn't feel guilt, exactly. She'd learned her lesson when she'd read Winston's journal and realized she'd wasted seven years of her life needlessly mired in that emotion. Whatever had happened to push Clay away, she had not knowingly done anything to precipitate it. And if she'd done something unawares, well, it was just unconscionable for him to hold that against her.

Whatever else she might be guilty of, she'd always dealt honestly with Clay. In fact, she'd been more open with him than with anyone else in her adult life.

Except in one area. She'd never told him she loved him.

Would that have made a difference?

It was *that* doubt that ate at her, tormented her whenever she dropped her guard. That and the bone-deep heartache that had become a part of her since he'd left, like a wound that wouldn't heal.

Whether he knew it or not, he'd sliced off a piece of her heart and taken it with him when he walked away from her.

Maddy doubted she'd ever feel whole again.

Clay did his best to ignore the speculative glances aimed his way as he strolled up Pepper Cloud's Main Street. What had Maddy's neighbors guessed or been told about his reasons for leaving?

He exchanged greetings with those he knew, but didn't stop to chat. He wasn't looking forward to this next encounter with Maddy, but it would be best to get it over and done with. The only reason he'd come back at all was because tomorrow was the day Maddy made her appearance before the adoption judge. He wanted to be there at her side to lend his support. He owed her and Katie that much at least.

His steps sped up slightly as he turned off Main Street and the fancifully decorated gables of Barrows House came into view. Funny how it almost felt like coming home. Only there would be no warm welcome for this homecoming. He'd be lucky if the door weren't slammed in his face.

Not that he'd blame them.

It wasn't that he felt any guilt for leaving—he'd had no

choice under the circumstances. But he *was* sorry for the way he'd handled his departure.

He may not have forgiven Maddy, but the truth was, despite all she'd done, he missed her. Missed her with an intensity that almost crippled him. He'd spent the first night, and the better part of the second getting roaring drunk, trying to erase the vision of her staring up at him with that shattered, why-are-you-doing-this look in her eyes. But it hadn't worked. By the time he sobered up he had begun to feel a deep abiding shame for the deliberately hurtful words he'd flung at her, the harsh tone he'd used with her.

For that, at least, she deserved his apology.

No matter that she'd manipulated him into that sham of a marriage. She'd no doubt done it for Katie's sake. He couldn't say he hadn't been forewarned—she'd told him from the outset that she'd do whatever it took to make sure the adoption went through.

If only she hadn't betrayed him, hadn't shared his confidences with the others. No doubt she'd taken it no further than the ladies of Barrows House, but it stung nonetheless.

"Mr. Kincaid!"

Clay looked up at the greeting to see Blanche kneeling in one of her flower beds. "Hello, Miss Crawford. I see your lilies have finally come into bloom."

Blanche smiled proudly. "Yes, they're lovely, aren't they!" Then she cocked her head, giving him a probing look. "Maddy'll be glad to have you back home. She's been moping a bit since your unexpected departure."

"I've missed her, as well." A spark of pleasure flared in his chest at the thought that Maddy might have truly missed him, but he squelched it as he remembered her comment about being "shackled" to him. No doubt her "moping" was just an extension of her act.

A few seconds later he pushed open the gate to Barrows House and marched up the walk to the front porch. Taking a deep breath, he pounded on the knocker. Would Maddy open the door herself? If so, would she slam it in his face

But it was Miss Olive's countenance he saw when the door opened. She betrayed not the slightest flicker of surprise, but neither did she offer a word of welcome.

Her expression was more severe than normal and he worried for a moment that she might actually turn him away. But she stepped aside to allow him entrance.

"Would you let Maddy know I'm here to see her, please?" he requested, trying hard to ignore her reproving glare and remember he was a grown man who had every right to be here.

She crossed her arms. "I don't think so."

Clay drew himself up. "Now, see here." No one, no matter how well-intentioned, would keep him from visiting Maddy.

Except maybe Maddy herself.

"Don't take that tone with me, young man." Miss Olive looked down her nose at him. "Before I let you anywhere near Maddy, you and I are going to have a little chat."

Clay groaned inwardly. A stinging lecture from Miss Olive was just what he *didn't* need right now. He raised a brow. "Perhaps after I've spoken to Maddy—"

She didn't appear at all impressed with his haughty manner. "I don't know what passed between the two of you after the wedding, but you hurt her deeply, and I don't intend to stand around and watch you do it again."

His own feelings of guilt lent added weight to her words. "I give you my word," he said solemnly, "it's not my intention to hurt her." He set his jaw. "But I believe what have to say is best kept between me and Maddy. I am, after all, her husband."

She studied him with pursed lips, not moving from her position blocking the stairs.

He sighed. "I don't mean to be disrespectful, ma'am, but if you don't fetch Maddy for me, I'll go find her myself."

Miss Olive's lips thinned. "Maddy is busy with her sketching right now. She doesn't want to be disturbed."

Clay nodded. "I won't stay any longer than she's willing to let me," he promised. Stepping around her, he started up the stairs, saying a quick prayer that Maddy would give him a chance to apologize. He'd be leaving again after the adoption hearing, and he didn't want his callous behavior on his conscience when he did.

He climbed the stairs to the attic, steeling himself against the interview to come. How would she greet him? Would she be brusquely businesslike, or would she refuse to see him altogether? Would she be grateful for his decision to stand by her at the adoption hearing, or would her pride assert itself in a repudiation of his support?

Despite his determination to maintain an air of detached reserve, his pulse beat a bit faster and his steps increased pace as he drew closer. It would be good to see her again, if only to prove to himself she no longer had any special effect on him.

When he stepped into the studio, though, he saw no sign of Maddy. He moved farther into the room and stood looking around, as if she could be hiding in one of the corners. After the heightened anticipation of the last few minutes, this felt profoundly anticlimatic. He raked a hand through his hair, not quite sure what to do now. Had he misunderstood Miss Olive or had she deliberately misdirected him?

A nearby easel caught his attention. From this angle he couldn't quite make out the subject of her work in progress, but something about it called to him, drew him closer.

Unlike the oil portrait he'd seen on his prior visit, this was a charcoal sketch, rendered in stark shades of black and gray. At first blush it seemed to be a depiction of the angel casting Eve from the Garden of Eden.

The angel stood cloaked in righteous resolve as his finger inexorably pointed the transgressor away from paradise. The woman, her back to the viewer, stood with shoulders bowed under the weight of her despair, her right hand outstretched in supplication.

289

As before, Maddy had managed to use subtle nuances o
shading and pose to evoke a wealth of emotion. The ob
server could feel Eve's confusion, sorrow, pain. There wa
no question but that her outstretched hand pleaded for :
chance to make it right again.

On closer study, though, it became apparent this was no
intended to be a biblically faithful portrayal. Adam wa
nowhere in sight—Eve faced the angel of judgment alone
Her left hand pointed to a nearby tree, where an apple stil
hung, untouched. Even the blurred image of Eden in the
background was not as it had, at first, seemed. The shadow
images, when one looked closely, were not those of a lush
jungle garden but rather of people—couples locked in lov
ing embraces, mothers cradling infants, parents with chil
dren playing at their sides.

Clay felt a bittersweet ache at this insight to Maddy'
view of paradise.

The figure of the angel drew his attention again. It dom
inated the center of the canvas. Drawn in meticulous de
tail, the heavenly messenger appeared both magnificen
and terrible in his purpose. Supremely assured of the right
eousness of his mission, he stood unmoved by Eve's en
treaty. Ignoring her hand pointing to the tree, to her claim
of innocence, his expression made it plain he was here t
carry out a judgment, not to hear pleas for mercy. Hi
handsome face, aloof and unrelenting, had more of hel
than heaven in it.

And it looked exactly like Clay, himself.

Clay slowly descended the stairs. He wasn't sure how lon
he'd stood looking at that picture, how long he'd castigate
himself with the truth he'd read there. Miss Olive said he'
hurt Maddy—now he knew just how much.

She'd been innocent of betraying him, he knew tha
now. No matter what he'd overheard, how damning th
words had sounded, some other explanation existed.

He'd done it again. Somehow, as with the poker game

he'd misinterpreted a situation he'd intruded on, had jumped to disastrously erroneous conclusions, and condemned her out of hand. He'd flung those cruel, hateful words at a woman who'd made herself vulnerable to him, a woman who'd trusted him with her secrets and her heart.

Miss Olive waited for him at the foot of the stairs. "Did you find what you were looking for?"

"You've seen the picture?"

The seamstress shook her head. "No. I don't go up there unless I'm invited. But Maddy has always poured out her emotions in her drawings. I had a feeling you'd find something of interest in her studio."

He raked a hand through his hair, feeling the need to explain himself. "The day of the wedding," he confessed, "I overheard the four of you talking about some kind of deal Maddy had made, one that shackled her to a pompous, cowardly worm of a man." He gave a wry smile. "Naturally, I thought you were discussing me."

"Ah, so that was it." Miss Olive shook her head with a gentle tsk. "Didn't your mother teach you not to listen at keyholes?"

He shrugged. "My mother would tell you that some lessons come hard to me."

"Clayton, we weren't discussing you."

This was the first time she'd ever called him by his given name. Did this mean she'd forgiven him? But it wasn't *her* forgiveness he needed. "I know," he said, forcing the words through the constriction in his throat. He prayed the knowledge hadn't come too late.

"It was Mayor Flaherty," Miss Olive elaborated. "Maddy plans to set up a theater here in Pepper Cloud and to do it she needs use of a building he owns."

"Let me guess, Miss Adeline is going to run this theater."

He didn't need Miss Olive's nod of assent to confirm he was right. Maddy's schemes always involved helping someone else achieve a goal.

"Where is she?" he demanded.

291

Miss Olive gave him a half smile. "As I told you before, she's sketching."

Clay's nerves were already stretched tight, he had no patience for any more games. But Miss Olive's raised hand halted his protest.

"I didn't say you'd find her in her studio. She took her sketch pad out to Dragon's Teeth."

Clay's heart lurched and he swallowed several choice oaths. It served him right, he supposed. It was fitting penance that he had to face his nightmares and Maddy at the same time.

Miss Olive looked at him with a puzzled expression, obviously perplexed by his reaction. Further proof, if he needed it, that Maddy had never betrayed his secret. "Do you know where it is?" she asked.

He smiled and nodded. "Yes ma'am. If you'll excuse me, I have some groveling to do."

Chapter Twenty-one

Maddy looked up from her sketch pad, rolling her neck to ease the stiffness from her muscles. Coming up here had been a good idea. Not only was it a beautiful day, but just being in this place healed her spirit, exhilarated her soul. This lip of land that jutted out into space made her feel both anchored to the earth and close to heaven.

She lifted her face, savoring the warmth of the sun along with the light breeze that offset the heat and ruffled her hair. Greedy for more, Maddy set her pad and pencil down and lay back on the blanket she'd spread earlier, opening her senses to the serenity of her surroundings.

She stared up at the sky, admiring the perfect shade of blue, the gauzy puffs of clouds, the sight of a lone bird circling high overhead. She took a deep breath, inhaling the scent of the grass beneath her and the wildflowers that dotted the clearing. If she held still, she could hear the drowsy buzz of bees intent on harvesting nectar from those same blossoms, the faint call of that lone bird, the rustle of the wind through the underbrush.

Rolling over on her stomach, Maddy plucked a stemmy bit of grass and stuck it between her teeth. Watching a beetle lumber across a corner of her blanket, she studiously ignored her sketchbook.

It contained another picture of Clay, of course. That was all she seemed able to draw these days.

Well, no more.

It was time she moved on. Tomorrow would ring in a new chapter in her life. She would travel to St. Louis and finalize her adoption of Katie. It was a time for rejoicing, not pining, a time to look forward to what was to come, not back to what might have been. She owed that to Katie as much as to herself.

When she left this place today she would leave behind her long face and her yearnings for something that she now accepted would never be. The emptiness in her heart might not ever heal, would surely ache dully for a long time to come, but it would not be put on public display ever again.

"Hello, Maddy."

Startled, she sat up and stared across the clearing at the man she'd just vowed to put from her mind. Clay watched her with an uncertain, hopeful smile.

"What are you doing here?" From his wince she gathered the words had come out a bit more harshly than she'd intended.

He flashed her the dimpled-chin, eyes-just-for-you smile that always made her heart flutter. She drank in the sight of him, felt the familiar tingle of awareness race through her veins.

His smile warmed as he took in her reaction. "I've come to apologize."

Apologize? For the past nine days she prayed for just this moment, longed to hear him say it had all been a mistake, yearned with all her being for a chance to make things right between them again. Yet, now that it was happening, she felt a spurt of anger rather than relief. All the hurtful things he'd said to her before walking away played back in her mind. He'd put her through a hellish nightmare of heartache and grief, and now he expected her to just up and forgive him as if nothing had happened? Well, it wasn't going to be quite that easy.

The attraction that sizzled across the clearing between them might still be as strong as ever, but that didn't mean she had to give in to it, or even acknowledge its presence.

She tossed her head. "Well then, let's hear it."

His forehead creased. "What?"

"Your apology. Let's hear it."

He made no move to approach her and she remembered his fear of heights. This jutting promontory with its unfettered view and sheer height must be his worst nightmare. How much of the tenseness she sensed in him came from where he stood and how much from his anxiety over her reaction?

Did he truly understand what she'd gone through?

He rubbed the back of his neck, then nodded in acceptance. "I acted like an idiot. I overheard something that made me think you'd betrayed me, played me for a fool. I judged and condemned you out of hand, when what you deserved was my trust and faith in your integrity. I treated you horribly and for that I am most truly and humbly sorry." His countenance sobered in self-remonstrance. "I don't know how I can ever make it up to you."

She'd never heard him sound so humble, so apologetic. Still, she wasn't satisfied. Setting her jaw, she stared at him without blinking. "Neither do I."

Clay stood there, staring at her across the distance. He looked so much like a little boy who'd lost his best friend that Maddy almost relented. But then he seemed to make a decision. Straightening, he lifted his chin and let his gaze bore into hers. "Then I suppose I'll have to come over there and convince you of my remorse." With that he took a determined step forward.

Was he serious? She wasn't seated on the edge, but close enough to experience the exhilaration of the heady view.

There was no way he could come near her without feeling as if he stood on a mountaintop.

He took another step and she saw his hands fist at his sides, tight enough to turn his knuckles white.

By the time he took his third step it was his face that was white. He stood out in the open now. There were no walls or balustrades here to provide a sense of enclosure of protection. The top of the promontory spread out around him, flat and open on three sides. His forehead glistened with the hint of sweat, and still he took a fourth step toward her.

All the time he kept his jaw set and his gaze glued to her face. As if to torment him, the breeze kicked up just then. He swayed and his face grew whiter still.

Enough was enough. She believed in his sincerity now, believed he truly repented and wanted back in her good graces. She stood, ready to go to him, ready to do anything to end this self-flagellation that was as painful for her to watch as it must be for him to endure.

But he held up a hand in a jerky movement. "No!" He took a ragged breath and then offered her a crooked smile. "You once told me you would do whatever it took to claim Katie as your own. Well, I love you, Maddy Potter Kincaid, and I aim to prove your love is worth that and more to me. I *will* come to you."

Love? Maddy's heart jumped and goose bumps skittered across her skin. Had he just said he loved her? She stood there, watching his tortuous advances, silently cheering his progress, accepting each step he took as an offering of his love.

When he stood within a few yards of her he stopped, as if he'd reached the end of some invisible tether. She could almost feel the battle rage inside him as he willed his no longer-obedient legs to move. A bead of sweat trickled down his face and his hands clenched and unclenched.

She forced herself to stay where she was, ruthlessly denied the urge that pounded through her to wrap her arms around him and lead him away from this place. She would not strip him of the chance to prove himself, would not give up on his attempt until he gave up on it himself.

Maddy tried to pour all the love she felt for him into her expression, tried to lend him a measure of her own confidence in his efforts. After standing with gazes locked for what seemed hours, Clay lowered his head and slowly dropped to his knees.

Maddy's shoulders sagged, her heart splintering in empathy for the defeat she knew he must feel. But before she could move toward him, he looked up again, a teeth-gritted determination reflected in his expression. Very deliberately he placed his hands on the ground and moved forward.

With tears of love and pride streaming down her face, Maddy watched this proud, arrogant, wonderful man crawl the last few feet to her.

It was the bravest, most noble sight she'd ever witnessed.

Dropping to her own knees, she opened her arms and threw them around him as soon as he reached hugging distance.

"Oh Maddy," he murmured, burying his face in her neck, "I am *so* sorry for the things I said, for the pain I put you through. Please tell me that someday you'll be able to forgive me."

Maddy stroked his hair, reveling in his closeness, in the knowledge of his love. "How could I stay angry with a man of such courage and determination?" She snuggled her cheek against his bent head. "A man whom I love with all my heart and soul."

With a strangled growl, his head shot up and he captured her lips with his own, kissing her with a desire and intensity that set her senses reeling and her heart hammering in response.

When he finally lifted his head, she felt tingly and bemused and hungry for more.

Tenderly, he cupped her face between his palms. "Ah, Maddy my love, I don't deserve you." He wiped her tears away with his thumbs. "But I swear by all I hold dear that I will never knowingly hurt you again. I will do whatever it takes, as often as it takes, to prove my love for you."

Maddy felt as if she would burst from the happiness filling her. "Just promise you'll never leave me like that again."

He grinned, a bit of his cockiness returning. "Just try and get rid of me. Like it or not, Maddy, I'm your husband and you're stuck with me, now and forever."

She traced a finger along his jaw. "I think I can live with that." Then she straightened and dropped her hand to her lap. "Give me a minute to collect my things and we can leave." She tossed her head saucily. "Find some place more comfortable." It was a shame to break the mood, but after what he'd just gone through, she didn't want to force him to be the one to suggest they leave. Much easier on his pride for her to do it. Besides, there would be time to pick up where they'd left off later. Hadn't he just promised her forever?

He leaned forward to nibble on her ear as he slid his hands down to massage her shoulders. "What's your hurry?" he asked huskily. "I just got here."

Maddy's skin prickled at the feel of his warm breath on her neck, the nip of his lips on her flesh. "But, don't you . . . I mean, the view . . ." His hands slid lower, making it hard to think coherently.

His lips moved to her throat. "Right now, all I can see is you, and there's nothing wrong with that view." Gently he laid her back on the blanket and pulled the pins from her hair. "And right now, there's the matter of a long overdue wedding night to take care of."

She felt her breath catch at the look in his eyes, at the touch of his hand spreading her hair reverently around her. But surely he didn't seriously mean to. . . . "Out here, in the open, in the middle of the day?"

He flashed that crooked grin again. "We have more privacy here than we will at Barrows House." He kissed her, then lifted his head just enough to meet her gaze. "I want you Maddy, in every sense of that word. I want to set free the passion that lurks inside you, to feast my eyes on the beauty that you've kept hidden from the world. I want to feel your flesh against mine, I want to watch desire darken your eyes and build inside you until it sets you on fire. I want to hear you scream out my name as you find your release."

He stroked the hair from her face. "There have been times, like right now, when I thought the wanting and not having would drive me mad." He took her hand and kissed her fingertips. "But what I want more than anything else, is for you to want it, too. If you have any doubts, would rather we wait for whatever reason, then we'll wait. It'll be one of the hardest things I've ever done, but we won't do anything until you say you're ready."

Maddy saw the hot hunger in his expression, saw the love and barely leashed desire burning in his eyes. But she also saw the tight rein he had on his passion, the determination to wait on her decision. Clayton I-have-to-be-in-charge Kincaid voluntarily put the control in her hands.

And as easy as that, her momentary bout of panic faded.

Clay watched the play of emotions cross her face, held his breath while he waited for her answer. When he saw her expression soften, saw the anticipatory smile tug at her lips, a wave of relief and triumph washed over him, rendering him momentarily lightheaded.

"Oh yes, husband," she said, her voice low and seductive. "It's what I want, more than anything."

He reached for her, but she held him off with an upraised hand and a cheeky grin. "But impatient as I am to have you live up to the poetic promises you just made to me, I have no desire to go plunging off the cliff while we are so pleasantly distracted."

She was right, of course. But he wasn't eager to repeat

his earlier down-on-all-fours method of crossing the clearing.

There *was* another way, however.

He pulled her snug against him, taking satisfaction in the way she fit so perfectly to his side. The feel of her in his arms was heady, arousing, perfect. Silently vowing to make more intimate contact soon—very, very soon—he used his free hand to grab the edge of the blanket. "Your wish is my command." With that he set them rolling across the clearing, taking care not to put undue weight on her body.

When they had traveled a safe distance, he halted and untangled them from the blanket. To his relief, she was laughing.

"I never realized just how resourceful a man you are. I'm going to have to keep my eye on you."

He raised a brow. "That's the general idea." He grinned, plucking a blade of grass from her hair. "Now, where were we?"

She lifted her arms to pull him toward her, the very place he most wanted to be. Her sultry smile, full of womanly promise and blossoming desire, set the blood pounding through his veins at breakneck speed.

"Where were we?" she repeated with a come-hither look. "Why, you were just about to make me burn."

Epilogue

Pepper Cloud, Missouri
January 1895

"Don't fidget, dear."

Maddy blew a stray lock of hair from her forehead and stood straighter on the low platform table. "Sorry."

The rich burgundy-colored dress Miss Olive was fitting her for today was intended for Maddy herself, not Ruby Jane or one of the other girls from the Silver Buckle. Maddy hadn't been able to enjoy the naughty pleasure she took from playing "dress-up" for quite some time. Not that she minded terribly, given the reason. Perhaps, in another three months or so, after the baby arrived—"Oh!"

Miss Olive looked up, her forehead wrinkled in distracted concern. "Something wrong, dear?"

Maddy grinned apologetically. "The baby kicked again." She rubbed her tummy proudly. Soon she would actually hold her child, cuddle this new life that had flowed out of her and Clay's love. She could hardly wait.

301

The seamstress smiled and added another pin to the hem. "No doubt the child will be as energetic as his parents."

Maddy raised a brow at that. "His?"

"Mark my words, it'll be a boy," Miss Olive predicted without bothering to look up.

Maddy secretly hoped her friend was right. She'd love to have a little boy to raise, one with all of Clay's roguish manners and head-turning charm. Of course, those qualities would make for an interesting daughter, as well.

"Is that the gown you'll be wearing to the theater opening tomorrow?" Miss Adeline, decadently attired in an embroidered dressing gown and matching turban, stood in the doorway.

"Yes, it is." Maddy spread the skirt. "Don't you like it?"

Miss Adeline patted her turban absently. "The color is lovely on you, dear. But the neckline is *much* too high." She turned a disapproving eye toward Maddy's companion. "For goodness sake, Olive, Maddy is with child, not entering a nunnery. I've seen more revealing gowns on a preacher's wife."

Miss Olive shrugged as she draped the measuring tape over her shoulders. "Tell that to Clayton, not to me. He's made his wishes known on this subject more than once."

Miss Adeline gestured dramatically. "Husbands! The wedded state turns the most delicious scoundrels into jealous bores."

Maddy grinned as Clay sauntered up behind the irritated leading lady.

"My dear Miss Adeline." He slipped an arm around her waist. "I'd take offense, except you can't possibly be talking about me. We both know what an unreformed rake I am." He planted a lusty kiss on her cheek, then released her with a wink.

Miss Adeline pinkened in pleasure, but sent him a reproving look. "If you weren't so handy to have around when there's heavy lifting to be done, sir, I'd have sent you packing months ago."

"Ahem." Maddy placed a hand on Clay's shoulder as he greeted her with her own kiss and an affectionate pat on her abdomen. "I might have something to say about that."

Miss Adeline sighed loudly. "There *is* that, I suppose."

"Oh, by the way," Clay said nonchalantly, "Mr. Hannah sent over some notes on costume changes for tomorrow night's performance. I left them for you in the study."

Miss Adeline, theater manager extraordinaire, drew herself up. "Costume changes? Without consulting me? We'll just see about this." With that, she swept dramatically down the hall.

She'd barely left when Skipper shot into the room, closely followed by Katie. The little girl grabbed hold of the dog before he could do more than earn a frown from Miss Olive.

"I'm sorry," Katie apologized to the room in general. "Miss Fanny and I were about to give Skipper a bath when he ran off." Then she gave Maddy a broad smile. "You look real pretty in that dress, Momma."

It still warmed Maddy's heart to hear the familiar address slide so easily off Katie's tongue. After the adoption, they had let the little girl choose for herself what she would call them. Katie had used "Momma" and "Poppa" shyly at first. Now, though, it came to her as naturally as breathing.

"Thanks, Buttercup." She raised an inquiring brow toward Miss Olive. "I think we're finished with my fitting." At Miss Olive's nod, she lifted her skirt to step down from the platform.

But Clay grasped her under the arms and swung her down lightly. He was slow to let her go, and Maddy felt her heart skip a beat at the message in his eyes. Even as thick-waisted and awkward as she knew she must appear these days, Clay could still make her feel cherished and beautiful with just a look.

303

Clay cleared his throat. "Little Bit, don't you owe that mutt a bath?"

"Yes, sir." Hefting the uncooperative dog, Katie moved to the door.

"Watch your step on the stairs with that handful you're carrying," he called to her retreating back.

Maddy touched his shoulder lightly, just for the pleasure of the contact. He was such a good father.

Clay placed his arm around her as he turned to Miss Olive. "I was at the mercantile this morning. Mr. Welborne has a new shipment of fabric in that you might want to investigate."

The seamstress gave him a contemplative, finger-to-her-chin look. "Is that so?"

"Yes, ma'am."

Did he think that choir-boy innocent expression of his fooled anyone? Maddy struggled to keep a straight face as he surreptitiously caressed her backside.

"Well then," Miss Olive declared dryly, "I suppose I should go have a look before the best bolts are snapped up by someone else." Her lips twitched slightly as she eyed the two of them. "I'm sure I can trust you, Clayton, to see Maddy doesn't get scratched by those pins when she changes out of this dress."

Clay hooked his arm through Maddy's. "It's a duty I won't take lightly, I assure you." With that, he quickly made his exit and headed down the hall, Maddy in tow.

As soon as he closed their bedroom door behind them, he flashed Maddy a roguish grin. "We should have the up-stairs to ourselves for at least half an hour."

Maddy shook her head. "You, sir, are incorrigible."

He smiled, his eyes bright with purpose. "Am I?"

She stood her ground. "Most assuredly." Not that she would change him, even in the slightest.

He patted her arms, indicating she was to raise them. "Come on, we're supposed to be getting you out of this thing."

304

Maddy grinned at the impatience in his voice. "I hope the performance goes well tomorrow," she mused as he eased the dress over her head. "Miss Adeline has worked so hard on this."

"Uhmm," Clay replied noncommittally, laying her gown over the back of a chair, the same chair that held the garment she'd planned to change into.

"You covered up my dress."

"So I did." He eyed her rounded, chemise-clad form in a way that set the heat pooling in her stomach, had her nipples pebbling in response.

Maddy moistened her lips as she watched him cross the space between them. As soon as he was close enough, he began nibbling on her bare shoulder, sending the gooseflesh rippling across her skin.

"Mmmm, that feels nice," she murmured.

Without further encouragement, he lifted her in his arms, kissed the part of her that cradled their child, and carried her to the bed. "It gets better," he promised as he eased down beside her.

As if to prove he meant it, he treated her to a sweet, languid, thoroughly arousing kiss, then pulled back and nuzzled her throat.

Maddy rubbed his back, savoring his attentions and his closeness. This was the life she'd always yearned for, dreamed of—all her favorite people around her, a wonderful man to cherish and be cherished by, children to fill her home and her heart.

Yes, indeed, this was her idea of paradise.

"This is nice," she said, snuggling more comfortably against him. "I'm glad luck conspired to give us some time to cuddle."

Clay raised up on one elbow to toy with the lace on her chemise. "Luck had nothing to do with this," he said, looking slightly aggrieved. "I'll have you know it took quite a bit of orchestrating and a masterful sense of timing to pull off."

She cast him a mock-severe glance. "You know how I feel about schemers," she said as she moved his hand down to her tummy, "but I think our child is signaling his approval."

As the baby delivered another healthy kick, Clay's gaze flew to hers in a delighted grin. "As well he should."

Maddy's heart melted yet again at the look of pride and awe on his face. He was as eager to welcome this new addition to their family as she was.

"As for my being a schemer," he said, bending over her with eyes that promised more toe-curling kisses to come, "remember what I said that day at the cliff. When it comes to loving you, Maddy, my sweet, I'll do *whatever it takes*."

And with that he swooped down on her, delivering the promised kisses and stealing her ability to speak or think for some time to come.

But not her heart.

That he already had.

Winnie Griggs
What Matters Most

Reed Wilder journeys to Far Enough, Texas, in search of a fallen woman. He finds an angel. Barely reaching five feet two inches, the petite brunette helps to defend him against two ruffians and then treats his wounds with a gentleness that makes him long to uncover all her secrets. But she only has to reveal her name and he knows his lovely rescuer is not an innocent woman, but the deceitful opportunist who preyed on his brother. Reed prides himself on his logic and control, but both desert him when he gazes into Lucy's warm brown eyes. He has only one option: to discover the truth behind those enticing lips he longs to sample.

_4829-9 $4.99 US/$5.99 CAN

Dorchester Publishing Co., Inc.
P.O. Box 6640
Wayne, PA 19087-8640

Please add $2.50 for shipping and handling for the first book and $.75 for each book thereafter. NY and PA residents, please add appropriate sales tax. No cash, stamps, or C.O.D.s. All orders shipped within 6 weeks via postal service book rate. Canadian orders require $2.00 extra postage and must be paid in U.S. dollars through a U.S. banking facility.

Name_____
Address_____
City_____ State_____ Zip_____
I have enclosed $_____in payment for the checked book(s).
Payment <u>must</u> accompany all orders. ☐ Please send a free catalog.
              CHECK OUT OUR WEBSITE! www.dorchesterpub.com

COMING IN JULY 2002!

CALLIE'S
CONVICT
HEIDI BETTS

Wade Mason has been to Hell—and escaped. Shackled in iron manacles, the fleeing inmate arrives at Callie Quinn's house to claim his newborn son. But the beautiful angel who guards his child strips him defenseless by plopping the crying bundle of joy straight into his unsuspecting arms. And Wade knows he's found Heaven in Callie's embrace.

When the intimidating outlaw shows up on her doorstep, Callie vows she will fight to protect the infant entrusted to her. After all, what does a hardened felon know about babies? But one heated kiss tells Callie that Wade understands all about tender care. And soon she realizes he might be the convict, but she is prisoner to his touch, to his desires . . . to his love.

Dorchester Publishing Co., Inc.
P.O. Box 6640   _5030-7
Wayne, PA 19087-8640 $5.99 US/$7.99 CAN

Please add $2.50 for shipping and handling for the first book and $.75 for each additional book. NY and PA residents, add appropriate sales tax. No cash, stamps, or CODs. Canadian orders require $5.00 for shipping and handling and must be paid in U.S. dollars. Prices and availability subject to change. **Payment must accompany all orders.**

Name: _____

Address: _____

City: _____ State: _____ Zip: _____

E-mail: _____

I have enclosed $_____ in payment for the checked book(s).

For more information on these books, check out our website at www.dorchesterpub.com.
_____ *Please send me a free catalog.*

KNIGHT ON THE TEXAS PLAINS
LINDA BRODAY

Duel McClain is no knight in shining armor — he is a drifter who prides himself on having no responsibilities. But a poker game thrusts him into the role of father to an abandoned baby, and then a condemned woman stumbles up to his campfire. The fugitive beauty aims to keep him at shotgun's length, but obvious maternal instincts belie her fierce demeanor. And she and the baby are clearly made for each other. Worse, the innocent infant and the alleged murderess open Duel's heart, make him long for the love of a real family. And the only way to have that will be to slay the demons of the past.

Dorchester Publishing Co., Inc.
P.O. Box 6640
Wayne, PA 19087-8640

_____5120-6
$5.99 US/$7.99 CAN

Please add $2.50 for shipping and handling for the first book and $.75 for each additional book. NY and PA residents, add appropriate sales tax. No cash, stamps, or CODs. Canadian orders require $5.00 for shipping and handling and must be paid in U.S. dollars. Prices and availability subject to change. **Payment must accompany all orders.**

Name: _____

Address: _____

City: _____ State:_____ Zip:_____

E-mail: _____

I have enclosed $_____ in payment for the checked book(s).

For more information on these books, check out our website at www.dorchesterpub.com.
_____ *Please send me a free catalog.*

ATTENTION
BOOK LOVERS!

Can't get enough of your favorite **ROMANCE**?

Call **1-800-481-9191** to:

✳ order books,

✳ receive a **FREE** catalog,

✳ join our book clubs to **SAVE 20%!**

Open Mon.-Fri. 10 AM-9 PM EST

Visit **www.dorchesterpub.com**
for special offers and inside
information on the authors you love.

We accept Visa, MasterCard or Discover®.

LEISURE BOOKS ♥ LOVE SPELL